TALKING TO
STRANGERS

ALSO BY FIONA BARTON

FIONA BARTON

TALKING TO STRANGERS

BERKLEY
NEW YORK

BERKLEY
An imprint of Penguin Random House LLC
penguinrandomhouse.com

Copyright © 2024 by figbarton productions ltd.
Penguin Random House supports copyright. Copyright fuels creativity,
encourages diverse voices, promotes free speech, and creates a vibrant culture.
Thank you for buying an authorized edition of this book and for complying
with copyright laws by not reproducing, scanning, or distributing any part of
it in any form without permission. You are supporting writers and allowing
Penguin Random House to continue to publish books for every reader.

BERKLEY and the BERKLEY & B colophon are
registered trademarks of Penguin Random House LLC.

Library of Congress Cataloging-in-Publication Data

Names: Barton, Fiona, author.
Title: Talking to strangers / Fiona Barton.
Description: New York : Berkley, 2024.
Identifiers: LCCN 2023051048 (print) | LCCN 2023051049 (ebook) |
  ISBN 9781984803078 (hardcover) | ISBN 9781984803085 (ebook)
Subjects: LCGFT: Detective and mystery fiction. | Novels.
Classification: LCC PR6102.A7839 T35 2024 (print) |
  LCC PR6102.A7839 (ebook) | DDC 823/.92--dc23/eng/20231031
LC record available at https://lccn.loc.gov/2023051048
LC ebook record available at https://lccn.loc.gov/2023051049

Printed in the United States of America
1st Printing

Book design by Katy Riegel

For Carol

Whoever you are—I have always depended on the kindness of strangers.

—TENNESSEE WILLIAMS
(*A Streetcar Named Desire*)

TALKING TO STRANGERS

PROLOGUE

Friday, February 14, 2020

THERE WERE NO takers at the pub despite Karen's new dress—red and sparkly. Fun, like her. She and Mina carried on laughing loudly at their table, but when Karen looked round, the dead eyes of people's wives stared over, disapproval coming in waves. But she didn't care.

Doll Harman, the landlady of the Neptune, came over to clear glasses and have a quiet word.

"All right, ladies? You sound like you're enjoying yourselves."

"We are, thanks. You've done a great job with the cocktails and all the decorations," Mina said, raising a lurid-looking Love Potion in tribute.

"Yeah," Karen added. "Not many blokes on their own, though."

Doll pursed her lips. "No. Well, it's for couples, isn't it? Valentine's Day?" she muttered.

Not you went unsaid.

"We're going on to a club in Brighton, anyway," Karen shot back.

"What are you talking about?" Mina hissed as soon as Doll was safely behind the bar. "I've got to get back for the babysitter."

"Don't worry—I'm happy to go solo."

"It's late, Karen."

"That's when clubs really get going."

"And you can't drive after what you've had."

"Oh, what are you, my mother? I can get a taxi." Karen swallowed the last of her Pink Lady and slammed her glass down. "Right, I'm off."

But Mina had to steady her when she got up.

"What a shit evening," Karen murmured when they reached the pavement outside and gusts of rain drenched them. Her thin jacket would be ruined, and she could feel her straightened hair frizzing.

"Well, I enjoyed it," Mina said sourly, turning on her heel and marching off without another word.

Karen sheltered in the doorway of the newsagent's until the shower eased to mizzle. The windows were full of hearts and fat cartoon cupids, and she suddenly wanted to smash the glass. And scream at Doll with her pursed lips and the wives club judging her. Who the hell were they to tell her how to act? She was allowed to have a good time. She was forty-five, not eighty. Instead, Karen rested her forehead against the window and closed her eyes. The maraschino cherry from her last drink was repeating on her, and she knew she needed to slow down. She needed to regroup.

Sorry, didn't mean to get arsy, she texted Mina. Thanks for being such a brilliant friend—I don't deserve you. Off home for an early night.

She was already in bed when she heard her phone ping. She looked to see who it was and smiled, pulled her red dress back on, and spritzed herself with Joy perfume.

She'd regroup tomorrow.

SATURDAY:
DAY 1

ONE

KIKI

Saturday, February 15, 2020

"WE'VE GOT A body!" Miles shouts, bouncing on his chair as if he's won the lottery. I stand up from behind my computer screen and try not to hate him. My news editor is twenty-four and skinny, and his crazy hair makes his head appear too big for his body.

"He looks like a lollipop that's been left in someone's pocket," I told a friend during one of my regular venting sessions. But I keep the peace at work. Miles thinks someone taking a dump in a changing room is newsworthy, but he's still my boss. And I need the job.

"Where's the body?" I ask, going to stand beside him.

"Some wood down the coast. Ebbing, according to this tweet. Hey, you were there the other day for your *Desperate Housewives* thing, weren't you?"

Desperate Housewives? I scream in my head. My boss clearly hasn't done the company's diversity and inclusion course. But then, nor has anyone else. One of the suits in advertising had decreed we needed to "reach out" to older people with disposable income, to bring adverts for river cruises to the Sussex Today website. He—it must have been a bloke—thought an investigation into middle-aged women looking for love would be a draw.

"Like *Love Island* for the perimenopausal" was how Miles tried to sell it to me two weeks ago. I put on my barely-tolerating-the-situation smile and saved my roar of disbelief for later in the staff toilet.

"Don't let him get to you," I fumed into the mirror. "You can't afford to lose this job. And he probably doesn't even know what perimenopause is."

My hair was a mess, and I dampened my hands to press my fringe flat. And sighed. *What's the point? The only person who's going to see me is Miles. And he won't notice.*

"Shut up and get on with it!" I issued the order. "Let's go and clock up some mileage expenses."

Actually, it was fun in the end. I ended up meeting some great women with some brilliant tales. That's why I'm here on one of my precious Saturday mornings instead of having waffles with my daughter. I should crack on and get finished so I can take Pip blading, as promised.

But the body in the woods is a real story. I can't walk away from it. My heartbeat thrums against my bra wire as I try to read the screen over Miles's shoulder.

"Don't crowd me!" he snaps, his fingers flying over the keyboard. "Okay, it's a woman, found in a place called Knapton Wood. No identity. Come on, we need to be all over social media. You take Facebook—you are on that, aren't you? I'll do the rest."

"You're joking," I snort, one arm already in my coat sleeve. "I'm on my way over there. You can hoover up the rumors and TikTok theories while I talk to people who actually know something. The police, for a start. They'll be at the scene, and I need to speak to them face-to-face. It's basic journalism, Miles."

But he's stopped listening and has disappeared into his screen like my thirteen-year-old does. Blank eyes, slack mouth.

"I'll call you," I say.

"Yeah," the bot mutters.

As I walk, I text my mum to let her know I'll be late picking up Pip and stumble on the stairs as I scroll down to a saved number. No answer. I leave a message and try another.

Mina Ryan picks up immediately.

"Mina, it's Kiki Nunn. The reporter from the other night. I interviewed you for my dating feature."

"Kiki? Oh, right, yes." Mina's voice is hoarse, like she's been crying.

"Are you okay?" I say. "Sorry if I've caught you at a bad time." An apology never hurts to get people onside.

"You've heard, then?" Mina says. "About what's happened?"

"Well, only that a woman's body has been found in a wood. Do you know any more?"

"I think it's Karen." Mina gulps for air. And so do I.

"Oh, Mina, I'm so sorry," I murmur, trying to keep my voice even, but my hands are trembling, making my phone jump against my ear. Karen Simmons, a sparky hairdresser from Ebbing, was my first unanswered call. I know the victim—I met her last Monday with some of the members of her singles group, the Free Spirits.

"Her mobile is off and she's not opened the salon," Mina says, weeping. "Look, I've got to get off the phone—the police are on their way round to talk to me. I was with her last night."

There's a beat of silence, and I wait for Mina to say it. The regretful friend's refrain.

"I should never have let her go home on her own, should I?" Mina sobs.

"It's not your fault," I say softly. "Can I call you later?" But she's gone.

Poor woman. I almost did the same last week. Karen had wanted me to stay for one last drink after Mina and the others drifted off.

I wasn't sure—her eyeliner was slipping sideways, and there was more of her red lipstick on the empty glasses in front of her than on her mouth.

I sipped my soda water—"I'm driving . . ."—and watched enviously as Karen finished her glass of Chardonnay.

"I wish I had your energy," I said, laughing. "And your social life." I couldn't remember the last big night out I'd had since Pip.

"I'm having the time of my life," Karen said loudly. "I just wish I hadn't waited until now."

A young bloke at the bar glanced over. "Look at the state of her," he jeered to his mates.

If Karen heard, she didn't react. It was time to go—before the atmosphere in the pub soured any further. I ushered Karen out and got her into my car.

I'd counted on being home and in bed by ten thirty, but Karen's wine buzz was fading fast and she had a little weep in the car. I couldn't just leave her at the door. So I ended up staying for a coffee while she slipped off her heels and told me why I was a fool not to do online dating.

She'd hit the jackpot in week one, apparently. "We danced on the beach," she said, with a watery smile. "A bit of a cliché, I know, but nothing beats kissing for the first time under the stars, does it?"

I nodded. "Nothing wrong with a good snog," I muttered, wondering if I would ever have one again. I looked at my watch—I needed to leave. I'd have to pay an extra hour to the babysitter as it was. But Karen was in full flow.

"He was wonderful. A little older than me, separated, and ready to try again. Mina thought it was all going a bit fast—she didn't want me to get hurt. But I really thought this was it. God, I even started reading articles about fertility in your forties." And she fell silent.

"What happened?" I prompted gently.

"His wife," she murmured. "She came back. And he said he had to give it another chance. Just my luck, really. Still, I haven't given up. There is someone out there for me. Whenever I feel a bit down, I go online and read all the amazing love stories that have resulted from people meeting on apps, and look at photos of their beautiful weddings. It'll be my turn one day. And I've met some nice men along the way."

"And some horrors, I bet?" I tried to lighten the mood.

She laughed and moved on to the man in the world's worst toupee—"Why do they even make them in ginger?"—and the one who'd brought his mum on the date. "He said she didn't get out much. She drank us under the table and went home with a darts player."

My coffee had gone cold and Karen had stopped smiling by the time she got on to the date with a goatee and gray teeth.

It was off the record at the time—of course it was—but what about now? Karen's dead. Almost certainly murdered. Does it still count? Can I use it? The private stuff? God, I could write a brilliant piece. Take the reader right under the victim's skin. Show them what it's like to be a woman, alone and loveless in her forties. *Like you* rings in my ear, but I bat it away.

Maybe I don't have a relationship, but I don't have time to be lonely—every minute of my day is accounted for. But the idea trips me up. And I see myself piloting my sad little boat alone. *Don't be so dramatic,* I tell myself. *You've got Pip.* And I wonder if she's a lonely girl, too.

This is all getting too depressing, and I make myself stop. Instead, I let my mind slide to the possibility that this story could get me noticed again by the big boys in the national media.

Something to think about . . .

TWO

ELISE

Saturday, February 15, 2020

THE BODY HAD been found by walkers. *It's always walkers,* Detective Inspector Elise King told herself, struggling to zip her forensic suit over too many layers. *Running is far safer. Move fast and you don't risk being drawn into random horror.*

She nodded to the constable manning the freshly stretched blue-and-white police tape, ducked under, and headed into the gloom. Shreds of mist clung to her legs and aching cold seeped through the soles of her boots as she walked through the trees toward the flash of a camera.

Detective Sergeant Caro Brennan was already there, holding the flap of the pop-up tent open for her.

The scenes of crime officer inside put down his camera and stood to one side so Elise could take it all in. The victim was sitting against the trunk of a tree under arc lights. Thin, bare legs sticking out like one of the Barbie dolls Elise's niece loved undressing. Flesh waxy with death. Red strappy dress. Not out for a walk, then. Hair glittering with frost under the lights. Two false nails torn off, lying on the ground like exotic beetles. Head angled down to the right. Elise half knelt to look into her face. Dirt blackened the nostrils and the corners of her mouth. The hairs on Elise's arms suddenly rose.

"Oh, Christ," she said, voice muffled by her mask. She leaned forward to be sure. "It's Karen Simmons."

"Who?" Caro asked.

"She's a hairdresser here in town. Her salon is a few streets from my place."

"Is there a partner?" Caro inquired. "I'll get someone round there."

"No, Karen lived alone," Elise said, standing too quickly and having to steady herself on her sergeant. "She started a singles group in town recently. Walking, pub evenings—that sort of thing. The Free Spirits, she called it."

"Did you sign up, then?"

Elise gave Caro a warning look as the scenes of crime officer sniggered into his mask.

"No, Sergeant. Well, I went on a walk she organized, once. For the exercise."

"Right." Caro grinned, making her own mask slide down. She hitched it back up and straightened her face. "Were there men in the group? Maybe she found someone? Not Mr. Right, obviously."

"Some," Elise muttered, groping for the faces who had been on that freezing hike along Ebbing beach in late December, just a couple of months ago. But her memory was still warming up. The legacy of chemo brain lingered six months on. She squeezed her eyes shut. It helped sometimes. She'd hardly known anyone—most had been like her, curious first-timers—and they'd all been lagged into anonymity by huge coats, hats, scarves—eyes the only distinguishable features. But when Karen and some of the other women had taken off their outer layers in the pub at the end, they'd been dressed up to the nines with a thumb-smear of glitter in their cleavage and lippie in their pockets. This was what they'd come for. Elise felt completely wrong-footed. *It's a singles group, you idiot,* Elise had berated herself for judging them. For a second, she'd wished she had their confidence but had shrunk farther inside her coat to escape interested eyes. She wasn't ready to be on display yet and had left after the first drink.

"Any names?" Caro prompted.

"Er . . ." Elise floundered, each face slipping back into the fog in her head. "I'll have a think, okay? Anyway, I can't see a bag," she said, changing the subject. "Let's start searching the immediate area."

"There are other things missing, though. Look," her DS said, shining her penlight up the mottled legs. "No knickers. I wonder if she was wearing any when she arrived?"

"You'd have taken my name if I'd said that," the SOCO muttered from behind his camera.

"I wasn't judging her," Caro snapped. "I was just looking at the evidence."

"Yes, let's get on with that," Elise muttered. "It looks like she's been posed against that tree, doesn't it?"

Elise went to squat again but stopped mid-bend. She couldn't face another undignified judder back to standing. "But she's been face down on the ground at some point, to get that amount of muck in her nostrils and mouth. The rest of her face has been wiped clean, though—look at the streaks of mud near her hairline."

"Someone's tidied her up," Caro said. "Have you got that?" she snarled at the SOCO.

"Yep," he said sullenly and carried on placing a red marker next to the false nails.

"The pathologist is on her way," Elise pushed on. "She reckons another thirty minutes or so. Thank God it's Aoife Mortimer on duty this weekend—she'll whistle through everything without any nonsense." She sighed. The intense cold was draining her energy too fast. She used to be able to stand in freezing woods all day long. But she had to pace herself now. "Keep going," she whispered to herself under her breath.

"Sorry, what was that?" Caro muttered, giving Elise a concerned frown.

"Nothing. Okay, let's talk to the couple who found the body. Who are they?"

"Noel and Evelyn Clayton. They own a local DIY shop," Caro said as they made their way back through the trees.

"Right. Clayton's. It's tucked away behind the library. I've never been in—I don't really do hammers and nails," Elise murmured. "How are they doing?"

"He's making a fuss about getting home to open his shop, and she's hardly said a word."

The couple was sitting in the back seat of a parked police car, shivering despite their matching puffer coats. "Turn up the heating, for God's sake," Elise told the constable in the driving seat. She slid into the passenger seat and twisted round to face the couple. She'd seen him in the street before, but not her.

"How are you doing?"

"Evelyn is in shock," Noel Clayton growled. "When can I take her home? I was supposed to be open at eight thirty—half an hour ago. Saturday's my busiest day. And I've told your colleagues everything we know."

"And I'm very grateful for your patience. But I'd like to hear for myself. Do you mind?"

Mr. Clayton obviously did. His face darkened, but he compressed his lips and shook his head.

"Do you walk in Knapton Wood regularly?"

"Sometimes." *He isn't going to make it easy for me, then.*

"Right. But it must have still been dark when you got here? I understand that was at seven fifteen?"

"Yes, but we like to take photos of the sunrise, don't we, Evelyn?"

Mrs. Clayton nodded slowly, her eyes darting to her husband's face.

"And we get the place to ourselves that early," he added.

"Okay. When you arrived this morning, was there anything out of the ordinary?"

"No. As I've already told the first officer, we didn't see or hear anyone. We just set off on our usual route, on the footpath to the top of the hill beyond the trees."

"In the dark?"

"Head torches." He pulled his out of his pocket and dangled it slightly too close to Elise's face.

"And then we saw her," his wife whispered.

There was a beat of silence, and Evelyn Clayton's teeth started chattering like Morse code tapping out the terrible news. She closed her eyes as if to blot out the vision in the wood.

"Did you recognize the victim?" Elise asked her, looking at the inch of gray that parted the woman's dyed chestnut hair. She clearly hadn't been to Karen's salon lately.

"No." She blinked at Elise. "I can't even remember seeing her face. I couldn't take it in. What I was looking at. Do you know what I mean?"

Elise nodded. She noticed Mrs. Clayton's bare knees sticking out from under her coat. She wasn't wearing trousers or leggings—no wonder she was cold.

"But we didn't stand there staring." Noel Clayton barged back into the conversation. "We didn't know if the bloke who did this was still around. I told my wife to run, and when we got back to the car, we locked ourselves in and I rang nine-nine-nine."

"At seven thirty, ma'am," the constable added.

"Okay," Elise said. "And you didn't touch the victim? To see if she was still alive?"

"No," Mr. Clayton muttered.

"Could she have been?" Mrs. Clayton's chin quivered. "Should we have done something to help her?"

THREE

KIKI

Saturday, February 15, 2020

A LOCAL TELEVISION crew is already at Knapton Wood when I drive into the car park, setting up among the potholes. I know the TV reporter—she's a bit of a diva and is brushing her hair and mouthing the script to herself while her cameraman gets his clichéd shots of a lone constable on duty, the police tape flapping and close-ups of menacing trees. I consider stopping and seeing what they've heard, but a movement on the tree line makes me carry straight on. I've spotted my quarry: a tall figure standing by an open car boot. It's DI Elise King from the Major Crime Team—*halle-bloody-lujah!* An officer I've dealt with before. She'll speak to me, I'm sure of it. I'm on a roll today. I brake, throw open my door, and scramble out before she can disappear back into the wood.

"DI King," I call, and she turns.

"Oh, hello, Kiki," she mutters. She doesn't sound thrilled, but I bounce over regardless.

"So, how are you doing?" she sighs.

"Good, thanks. How about you? It's been a while."

Three months, in fact. The last time was on the pavement outside Lewes Crown Court after justice was dispensed in the Charlie Perry case. Elise had looked exhausted as she read a statement to the waiting press. Of course she had. It was her first major case after returning to work from breast cancer. And the toxic side effects of treatment had still been dragging her down.

She looks different now. Not back to full power, but her chemo curls are growing out like wild brambles, and the black circles under her eyes are now a pale, dirty gray.

"All well?" I prompt, reaching for the vanilla words that allow people to talk about cancer without actually mentioning it.

"Yes, thanks." Elise nods sharply. "I must get back. Just changing my boots."

"Of course." But I'm not about to let her go yet—this will probably be my only chance to get her on her own today. "It must be really muddy in there after all the rain we've been having. When was the body discovered? Has it been there long?"

Elise smiles wearily. "Look, it's way too early for me to be saying anything."

"But it's Karen Simmons, isn't it?" I say quickly as she slams the car boot shut. "Her friends can't find her and she's not answering her phone."

Elise's expression doesn't even flicker, and I have to give her points for keeping a straight face. "We can't confirm the identity of the victim yet," she says. "Come on, you know the drill."

I do, but that doesn't mean I can't give it a try. "But people already know," I say. "Her friends are telling everyone. And the thing is, I met Karen last week—I'm writing about her singles group."

"Are you?" Elise hesitates, and her poker face wavers for a second. I cross my fingers in my pocket. She finally makes her decision and moves round to open the car door. "Let's sit in here for a minute."

She clears a fancy water bottle from the passenger seat, and I slide in and close the door.

"I saw her on Monday at the Neptune in town," I say as she turns to face me. "It was the group's monthly social night. I talked to some of them, and then Karen and I stayed on to have another drink and I drove her home. She talked quite openly."

"Openly about what?"

"Her love life. That's what the feature's about. She was out there."

"Out where?"

"Online—on the mainstream dating sites, mainly, but I think she was dabbling in the apps. She said she'd decided to leave no stone unturned in her search for love. She said she was having a brilliant time. But it didn't all sound brilliant, to be honest. There had been some real creeps."

Elise's eyes narrow. "Had there? When? Did she mention any names?"

I take a breath. I need to decide how much I'm telling her. Do I have to tell the police everything? Or anything? They'll have access to Karen's dating history through the official channels. And I've got a story to protect.

"No—well, the creeps wouldn't have used real names, anyway, would they?" I say.

"Right." Elise pauses, and I force myself to maintain eye contact. "Okay. Off the record, the victim is Karen Simmons," she says. "You can use the name. The parents have been informed, but I haven't seen them yet, so I'm asking you to hold off publishing your interview with Karen. I need to warn them—and there could be information in it that might jeopardize our investigation."

"Well, I'll have to talk to my news editor," I mutter, feeling my exclusive slipping away from me.

"So will I," Elise says sharply. "And I'll need you to make a formal statement. We've set up an incident room at Southfold police station. Can you come in later this morning?"

I nod slowly, realizing that this could turn out okay after all. They'll be asking questions—but so will I.

FOUR

ANNIE

Saturday, February 15, 2020

SHE WAS SORTING through some patient records after the early rush when she heard. Nigel, the other receptionist, was reading out the day's headlines from his phone. He did it a lot, mansplaining the news to Annie, and she tried to treat it as background noise. But the words "Knapton" and "dead body" were like an electric shock, making her shoot to her feet.

"Wait, what?" Annie said too loudly, and a couple of patients whirled round on their chairs in the waiting room to look at her.

"All right, Annie," Nigel said. "No need to shout." And she wanted to scream in his smug face that she had every reason to shout. Every reason. But Nigel didn't know anything about her private grief. And she was not about to share it with anyone here. This was her safe space: the tatty old Park Medical Center with its graffiti and unweeded front garden. Where she was just Annie Curtis, mum of two, former nurse, part-time receptionist. Not the mother of a dead boy.

"Sorry," she said. "I just remembered something I forgot to do."

"Did you leave the iron on?" Juley, the nurse practitioner, laughed. "I do it all the time."

"No, you're all right. I haven't burned the house down," Annie replied.

She was back on autopilot. Smiley Annie. But in her head, she was a madwoman. Shrieking like a banshee—like she had that day—as images and memories uncoiled and vomited their poison.

"Just going to the loo," Annie said and went to sit in the cubicle with the broken sanitary bin. She breathed it out, counting slowly, like the therapist had taught her. When she was ready, she got her phone out of her cardigan pocket and looked it up.

She skimmed the words so she didn't have to see everything at once. But it didn't make sense. And she realized it wasn't about her boy. Of course it wasn't. They'd found his body years ago. This body was a woman's.

"Annie? Are you all right? You looked very pale," Juley called through the door. And Annie put the phone away.

"I'm fine, thanks. Bit of a headache, that's all. Just coming."

At lunchtime, she cried off the team's treat of tea and cake in the park café and went and sat on the seafront. She needed open skies and fresh air. "To blow the badness out." It was what she used to say to the boys when they moaned about Sunday afternoon walks. But then, she always went for simple solutions.

Annie pulled up the news story again and read new details. Slowly this time, mouthing the words to herself. The victim had been named on a number of websites as Karen Simmons. She knew that name. But couldn't remember why. Then, suddenly, she did. It was chatty little Karen. Who used to do their hair when they lived in Ebbing. She was trying to concentrate on Karen, but other phrases lit up in her brain. *Found under a tree. Being treated as murder. The people of Ebbing are horrified.*

It was like last time.

And she wondered if the police would knock on their door.

FIVE

ELISE

Saturday, February 15, 2020

"KIKI NUNN—THE reporter on Sussex Today—and the rest of Ebbing have got the name," Elise told Caro as they went to talk to the officers searching the undergrowth. "How are Karen's parents?"

"Okay—still at home in Worthing with the family liaison officer. She's bringing them over later this afternoon to formally identify Karen."

"I wonder how much they know about their daughter's life."

Caro raised an eyebrow. "Why?"

"Because Karen gave Kiki Nunn a pretty frank interview about her online dating," Elise said. "She wasn't leaving any stone unturned, apparently."

"For God's sake!" Caro hissed. "She's not publishing that?"

"I've just given her news editor a hard word, but we can't stop them. We'll have to tell the parents what's coming."

"God, why do people talk to reporters?" Caro almost spat the word.

Elise sighed. She really didn't want to get into yet another round of "why the media are wankers" with her sergeant. "Still," she went on quickly, "Kiki may have some useful info. Get one of the team looking for Karen's dating profile online. Sorry, have I already asked you? Have we found Karen's phone yet?"

Caro gave her a sympathetic look. "No, boss. We're still looking. And no sign of a handbag. We're applying for her call records, and the van's on its way to collect the body. And the coroner has asked for the postmortem to be conducted first thing tomorrow morning. Everything's under control."

Elise took a deep breath. The plates were spinning—a moment she used to get such a kick from. Before the cancer and the brutal chemicals to kill it. Before the scrumples of yellow Post-it notes in her pockets replaced her synapses. Before her DS became her safety net.

"Is there anyone we should be looking at locally?" Elise asked, pulling her hat down over her ears. "Anyone with a history of violence against women?"

There'd be someone. There always was. Small seaside towns absorbed all sorts with their shifting populations of weekenders and out-of-season cash rentals.

"There are three in Ebbing on the sex offenders' register and a dozen in Southfold and the surrounding villages," Caro said, "but no one's popping. They're low-level perverts—flashing and hands up skirts, that sort of thing—plus a couple of online offenders. Downloading images of women being sexually assaulted."

Elise swallowed hard, the memory of the shocked eyes of a weeping teenager silencing her. Unknown Victim 639. It was the first sexual abuse victim image Elise had seen as a young officer. There'd been hundreds since, but that face had burned its way through all her professional defenses into her core. She'd hated the fact that the girl had been just a number.

"Perhaps one of them has dipped his toe into the real world to try his luck?" Elise muttered, blinking to blot 639 out. "Send me their details and let's get the team together at Southfold police station and see where we are."

"On it," Caro said. "God, I'm starving. I didn't have time for breakfast at silly o'clock this morning."

"I made a sandwich—you can have that if you like." Elise rummaged about in the depths of her coat pocket. "Shit. I've left it on the worktop."

"Never mind. There's a lot going on. We could pick up a cheeky Big Mac en route?"

Elise's stomach turned at the thought.

"No, thanks. You go and poison your system," she said, fishing in her bag again for her car key. "I'll swing by mine and rescue my lunch. See you at the station."

"Is IT HER?" Elise's neighbor Ronnie poked her head around Elise's door, making her jump. "Everyone's saying it's Karen."

"Ronnie! I've just dived back to pick up a sandwich. I haven't got time to hold a briefing for casual callers."

Her neighbor followed her into the kitchen, as Elise had known she would. Ronnie wasn't about to stop her probing—and Elise had no one to blame but herself. She had created a monster when she'd done some extracurricular detective work during her convalescence from cancer surgery and Ronnie, a retired librarian with an unhealthy interest in other people's lives, had inserted herself as her number two. In her head, she was still Watson to Elise's Sherlock.

"Go on, then, what else are they saying in the Co-op?" Elise asked, looking for a semi-decent apple in the fruit bowl.

"That she was probably killed by someone she picked up," Ronnie said, perching a buttock on the high stool she'd made her own in Elise's kitchen. "A stranger. You know that Karen was on the hunt for a man, right? Well, everyone in Ebbing knew. Last time I had my hair done, she was joking about shaving eight years off her age. Everyone does it, apparently. We were laughing about it, but it's like getting a tin without a label out of the cupboard for your dinner. You think you're getting peaches, but it turns out to be dog food. I imagine it can make people turn nasty. If they think they're being conned."

SIX

KIKI

Saturday, February 15, 2020

I BLOODY LOVE police stations—the institutional, disinfected-lino smell of them, the edgy tension, the terrible chipped green-and-cream paint-work you only ever see in public buildings, the alkies hanging around the entrance. It brings back happier times. When I was a real reporter covering crime, not some online avatar copying and pasting schlock from the internet.

Back then my byline was my actual name, Erica Nunn. "Kiki" was invented by a paunchy male features executive when I ended up writing about women wearing the wrong size bras. "It sounds younger—more relatable, don't you think?" he said, and to be honest, I was happy to hide behind a new identity. I didn't want my peers to know this was what I'd been reduced to.

It was mortifying stepping back from the front line, but having a baby meant being on the road was no longer an option. Not with Danny, my other half, being a photographer for another paper. We couldn't both be sent off at a moment's notice with no idea when we'd be back. One of us had to be the still point in our chaotic lives. And it was never going to be Danny. So, features. I told myself it would be great—in-depth interviews and big reads. And it was for a bit, but a change on

the desk brought in women journalists panting to write about themselves in increasingly humiliating situations. And I was shuffled off to
the tampon beat and Kiki-dom.

I stuck it out for a few years, as the money was too good to walk
away—"the mink-lined coffin," we used to joke. But Danny didn't last
the course. "We never see each other," I explained to our journo friends
when he moved out. And they shrugged. Like they'd always known that a
reporter and a photographer working for rival publications was no basis for
a long-term relationship. Danny found a bachelor pad in Notting Hill,
and Pip and I moved to Brighton to be near my mum and free childcare.

I freelanced from my kitchen while Pip went through the terrible
twos, easier threes, fours, fives . . . all the way up to the currently tricky
early teens, but it was a precarious existence. Danny kept disappearing,
off on jobs when it was his weekend to have his daughter. And making
a living is often down to who answers the phone on the features desk on
the day—and whether they've had sex, a row, or their first coffee of the
morning. Like Roman emperors at the Colosseum: thumbs-up/thumbs-
down. I might bad-mouth it, but the job at Sussex Today was a lifeline.
The owner, a start-up entrepreneur, had told me to call him Ali as he
skimmed my CV and smiled patronizingly over Zoom. "We're going to
need at least one proper journalist on board," he said. "When can you
start?"

But I feel a jolt of excitement at the thought that this story might be
the way back. I'm going to make Miles use my real name on this one.

I take it all in as I'm led to an interview room, glancing through half-
open doors, listening to snatches of conversations. Stashing material.

"The boss will just be a minute," my uniformed guide says reveren-
tially. *Newbie.*

I hear a woman's voice saying: "She's in here." And in they sweep. DS
Caro Brennan leads the way.

Which is a shame. I know from our last encounter that DS Brennan
has no time for the media. But Elise King does. And she's in charge.
And they need me onside. So Caro Brennan can sod off.

"Can we get you a cup of tea?" Elise asks. Good Cop.

"Lovely. Milk, no sugar, please."

The newbie officer is tasked with the drinks-machine run, and Elise, Caro, and I sit looking at one another for a moment.

"As you know, we are investigating the death of Karen Simmons," Elise plunges in finally. "How did you know her?"

"As I said, I spent an evening with her last week and we had a couple of phone calls before that," I reply. "I contacted her because I'm writing about the dating scene for women in their forties and fifties."

"I see," Elise says.

I find myself wondering if she's on the scene. I try not to smile.

"And Karen was very helpful," I go on. "I found her singles group on Facebook, and I met a few of them at the Neptune last Monday."

"Were you invited?" DS Brennan mutters.

"Oh, yes," I say smoothly, refusing to rise to the bait. "Karen was very keen—she thought the publicity would bring in new people."

"So who was there?" Elise asks.

"Karen's friend Mina Ryan came—single mum in her late thirties. Nice woman. And there was Barry Sherman—he's the temporary manager at the Lobster Shack gastropub on the harbor. Loud. Ordering cocktails in the Neptune—the landlady was a bit short with him when he asked for a Slow Screw on the Beach. You know the sort. And Ash Woodward—quiet guy. He didn't want to be interviewed, but Karen said he's a handyman at the caravan park on the edge of town. Look, you can see them—I did a short video to go with my piece."

I turn up the sound on my phone and pass it to Elise. DS Brennan leans into her shoulder to watch. I've caught the group still getting their expressions ready before posing and raising their glasses to the camera, shouting, "Cheers!" and laughing.

"Was Karen seeing either of these men?" Caro Brennan says, reaching to pause the clip and enlarging their faces on the screen.

"She said not. Said she was casting her net wider."

"Where was she looking?" Elise asks as the constable comes in balancing three plastic cups.

"Various dating sites—I've written them down." I push across the list. "These are the ones where everyone is checked out. Karen didn't say, but I bet she was also using the hookup apps where you can be anyone you want."

"Did Karen use her real name?" Elise says, stirring her tea.

"You have to on most of the sites. But on hookup apps, well . . . It can be pretty anonymous, that scene, isn't it? People can call themselves all sorts of things. Fantasy stuff. It's all part of the game. Although research shows that Hannah is the most swiped name."

"Right. You seem to know a lot about it . . ." DS Brennan says.

"I'm writing about it," I say, shutting her down. "I make sure I do my research."

"Did Karen say how many men she'd met?" Elise steers us all back to calmer waters.

"No. It wasn't about numbers. She was definitely looking seriously for Mr. Right—she was talking about wedding dresses and starting a family."

"Right. Had Karen ever been to Knapton Wood to meet a date?" Elise asks.

"Not that I know of," I say firmly. "I looked through my notes right away, but she didn't mention it. Maybe she was abducted and taken there?"

"Shall we leave the police work to us?" DS Brennan snaps. "Can you email a copy of your notes and photos? We need to check for any dates and places mentioned."

"Have you got a cause of death?" I ask, deliberately ignoring the request. I'm not sharing my notes with anyone—especially when she's being so rude.

"The investigation is ongoing," Elise responds quickly. "This is really useful info, Kiki. Thanks for coming in. Look, I've got to get ready for the press briefing. Are you sticking around for that?"

I SIT IN the waiting area afterward and get out my laptop. If the police are going to be difficult when I've been super helpful, I'll just have to do my own thing. Why should I do the cops any favors?

I have a quick look through Karen's emails to me after the interview. She'd sent links to success stories—Tash and Kent raising flutes of champagne in a marquee, somebody else's fifth-anniversary story—for the feature. She'd also sent me her online profile photo. I click on it to enlarge it, and a caption comes up, too.

"Hi there! I love nights out, slow dancing on the beach, and walks in the woods. Do you want to join me?"

I breathe out slowly. Did Karen's killer see this playful invitation and use it to lure her to some horrific encounter? I wonder if snarky Caro Brennan has seen this. She will when she reads my exclusive interview.

My intro is already writing itself, but last-minute doubts about the ethics of my decision crowd in, making my fingers fumble the keys. But when I look up, the opposition has started to gather for the press conference. The rest of the reporters will be all over the story, combing out the locals about Karen's hunt for men.

I start typing again.

SEVEN

ELISE

Saturday, February 15, 2020

ELISE FLEXED HER shoulders and tried to stop her mind meandering. But the press briefing had gone on too long. The reporters were circling back to the questions she'd already declined to answer.

"Okay," the district commander at her side said loudly. "That's all we have for you at the moment. We've released a photograph of Karen Simmons that was taken at the start of the evening—please get that out there. We want to hear from anyone who saw her last night. Where was she during the hours between leaving the Neptune pub and her body being discovered? How did she get to Knapton Wood?"

"DI King," someone called from her left-hand side, "is Karen's online dating history the focus of your investigation?"

"As I've said, we are following several lines of inquiry at this stage," Elise said and stood up. "Thank you for coming."

"Bloody hell! That didn't take long to get out, did it?" Caro hissed when they reached the other side of the swing doors. "Who asked the last question? Bet it was Kiki Nunn—I thought we'd warned her off?"

"I did, but it wasn't her—it was the woman from *South Coast News*. In fact, I'm not sure Kiki was even there. Did you see her?"

"Don't think so. She must have had more important things to do," Caro growled.

"Or she's avoiding us," Elise said, and the two women stared at each other.

"Shit," Elise spat. She quickly punched "Sussex Today" into her phone and found herself staring straight into Karen Simmons's eyes. It wasn't the image the police had released—a carefully cropped full-length photo taken by her friend Mina as they left home for their night out. This was a selfie with Kiki Nunn, taken close up and, by the look of it, several drinks into a night out. Karen's dark eyes were shining and she was laughing wildly. She'd been so full of life. It stopped Elise in her tracks. She was so busy dealing with Karen's death that she'd forgotten the living human being. Elise stroked the face with a finger as she tried to reconcile this Karen with the gray, frozen face she'd seen in the woods. Her gesture made the image disappear off the screen, and Caro tutted loudly. "Give me that," she said, and pulled Karen back.

Elise let her gaze slip to the headline beneath and gaped. "Caro!" she yelped. "Look at this . . ." She read on. "Karen's dating profile mentions walks in the woods! Why didn't we know about that? Get the bloody reporter on the phone."

AN HOUR LATER, Elise felt like a limp rag. She'd spent too much time and energy bollocking Kiki's idiot news editor about the use of potentially crucial details, warning the family liaison officer sitting with Karen's parents, and briefing her boss, Detective Chief Inspector McBride, about the situation. And not enough getting into the victim's head.

Elise stood at her desk, thinking about Karen—the woman Ronnie had known, joking about online dating tips above the roar of the hair dryer. And the woman who'd confided in Kiki about the weddings and babies she was planning. She just needed to find the right man. But Elise knew that hope could blind you to all sorts of things. She should have known her ex-partner was straying—she was a detective, for

Christ's sake—but she had ignored any flickers of unease in pursuit of happiness. Had Karen's unshakable optimism blinded her to online predators? Or had her attacker been closer to home?

She pulled up the Free Spirits video Kiki had shared. Elise recognized some of the members. Mina worked for the estate agency that had sold Elise her house in Ebbing back in 2018; Barry was from the Lobster on the seafront; and she'd seen Ash's face around the town. She watched the short clip several times, focusing on the two men. Ash Woodward, fair-haired, with sad eyes, was saying something into Karen's ear, but Elise couldn't make it out above the noise of the pub. She watched Karen put her hand on Ash's shoulder. He smiled, but his face went blank when she turned to put an arm around Barry. Barry himself didn't seem to notice—he was too busy smoldering straight at the reporter's camera, giving it his all and showing off some expensive-looking dental work.

Karen had told Kiki Nunn she wasn't seeing either of the men, but she'd also said she was leaving no stone unturned . . .

Elise's gaze drifted beyond the Free Spirits and into the Neptune. It'd been a busy night for a Monday. The tables were full, and she could see the backs of people lining the bar. She wondered if someone had been watching Karen then. And making their plan.

EIGHT

KIKI

Saturday, February 15, 2020

"Dɪᴅ ʏᴏᴜ ᴋɴᴏᴡ she was going to ring me?" Miles splutters, rounding on me. "Why didn't you warn me?"

"Look, don't worry about it," I say. "A hard word from the cops is all part of the job. It means we've got something right."

"What are you even talking about?" he barks. "I could be locked up or something for what you wrote."

"That's bullshit!" I snap back. What a baby. And then I remember he's never worked in a real newsroom, where bollockings are the sound-track of your day. Miles is one of the new generation of media hires. Where being master of social media trumps news sense—and being young means they don't have to pay him much.

"No one's going to put you in a cell," I say firmly. "The police have got far more important things to do. And so have I. I'm going to try to talk to the victim's parents."

The prospect doesn't exactly fill me with joy. I've never liked death knocks. That lurch of nerves as you approach the house, questions bunching in your head. But I've found over the years that most bereaved people welcome the chance to talk about their loved ones. Reporters are like the stranger on a train you can open up to about personal feelings because they are not involved. They won't cry or wail. They just listen and let you talk.

"Will the police be okay with that?" he mutters.

"Oh, for goodness' sake, Miles," I call over my shoulder. "We have a free press in this country. Haven't you heard?"

He puts his head down, and I hear him ringing his mum as I shut the door.

THE SIMMONSES' HOUSE is a smart detached villa on one of the big roads down to Worthing seafront. I have to squeeze past a lethal holly bush to get to the front door and manage to snag my new tights. I'm still swearing when the door opens. Mary Simmons stands in front of me, swaying slightly, so pale her features are almost invisible.

"Hello, Mrs. Simmons," I say gently, hoping she hasn't heard me effing and jeffing. "I am so sorry to hear about Karen. You must be devastated. My name's Kiki Nunn and I'm a reporter. I just wondered if I could talk to you about your daughter."

"She was a lovely girl. Everyone loved Karen," she says, and her mouth trembles. "Why would anyone kill her?"

"I know," I say. "It's so shocking. She was such a nice woman."

Mrs. Simmons blinks. "Did you know Karen?"

"A bit—I met her last week, and we spent an evening together at a pub in Ebbing. Look, I don't want to keep you on the doorstep in the cold. Is it okay if I come in for a minute?"

She blinks again and nods.

There are no lights on in the house when Mary Simmons leads me through to the sitting room, and my eyes take a moment to adjust to the gloom. When they do, I can see Karen's dad is dozing, head back, on the sofa.

"I've given him one of my sleeping pills—he was so upset," Mary whispers and slumps down beside him, while I perch on the nearest chair.

"How did you say you knew Karen?" she says. "Did she do your hair?"

My hand goes automatically to my unruly fringe. "No, as I said, it was more of a social thing," I remind her.

"That's right," Mary says, and reaches for a photo album on the coffee table. "She was so much fun, wasn't she? I was just looking at these. This was taken in Tenerife ten years ago," she croaks, grief fighting to close her throat. Karen looks fabulous—laughing up from a sun lounger, hair in a messy bun, and wearing film-star sunglasses. "And this was my nephew's wedding. Karen did all the little girls' hair. All those ringlets and updos. She didn't have time to do her own in the end. But she just wanted everyone else to be happy."

I sit quietly, taking it all in, as Mary carries on narrating her dead daughter's life. When she gets to the last page of the album, her head drops. "This is all we've got left," she says. "I can't stop looking at the pictures since they told us. It's like she's still here when I'm looking at them."

The words light up in my head. It's the quote I'll use to finish my interview with the devastated parents. The kicker, the old subs used to call it. Clickbait, now. I reach over and pat her arm in sympathy, and she looks up at me. "Do you know what happened to Karen?" she pleads, and I can smell the sharp tang of desperation on her breath.

I wish I could tell her something. "Haven't the police told you anything?" I ask.

She shakes her head. "We're meeting the woman detective in charge this afternoon. Our family liaison officer, Jenny, is taking us. She's been so kind—she's just gone to pick up a prescription for me."

I catch myself glancing out the window to check the FLO is not coming up the path. Thank goodness I arrived when she was out. I'll be out on my ear as soon as she gets back.

"But why was Karen in a wood? In the middle of the night?" Mary suddenly asks, her voice shrill. "What did they do to her?"

"I don't know, Mrs. Simmons. I am so sorry. When did you last talk to her?"

"Last week," Mary says, closing her eyes. "Was it someone she knew, do you think?" she whispers, shrinking down in her seat as if she can hide from the horrific reality. "We didn't meet many of her boyfriends—none seemed to last long. I don't know why. Karen was so pretty, and such a kind person. But none stuck. I can't say what she was looking for, but she didn't seem to find it. And lately, she's kept her private life to herself."

I gulp a breath and plunge in. "Well, had Karen told you she'd met some new people?"

"No," she says, and her head jerks up. "Who?"

"I don't know their names, but Karen told me she was using dating websites."

"Oh, God," Mrs. Simmons groans.

Cliff Simmons stirs on the sofa.

"Are you all right, love?" Mary says.

"Who's this?" Cliff says loudly.

"A reporter. She wants to know about Karen."

I watch as she fusses over her husband, straightening his hair and patting his trembling hand. I wonder how they'll cope. The bereaved can cling together on a life raft of denial—or sink into grief in separate rooms.

I feel the sudden urge to have a moment alone to gather my thoughts. "Can I use your loo?" I say and stand up.

"Top of the stairs," Mary mutters. "Opposite Karen's room."

The door to Karen's bedroom is ajar, and I hesitate before pushing it open. *I'm only having a look,* I tell myself. And Karen clearly hasn't slept in this room for years. It's almost bare. The single bed has been stripped down to the mattress, and a lonely cardboard box stands on the dressing table.

It's a different world from her flat above the salon. Karen had twiddled a fader light switch to gradually reveal the sitting room when I took her home from the Neptune last week. "Wow! You could get a coach party on that sofa," I said. On the wall behind it was a neon sign that beamed *Love.* Karen had to move heart-shaped cushions to lie on it, nearly knocking over a lamp draped with silk scarves.

"Do you want another drink?" she said, pointing at a table with a dozen bottles of sticky-looking holiday souvenir liqueurs, but I went and made her a black instant coffee.

The archway to the kitchen was flanked by framed photos of people strolling hand in hand on the sand and dancing in a tight embrace. I had a look as I passed. Neither featured Karen. It was almost like a stage set or something—weirdly impersonal. But her teenage bedroom doesn't offer any clues, either.

I open the flaps of Karen's box of belongings and have a look. There's a hoodie, a hair dryer with no plug, an ancient baby doll with a lazy eye and ballpoint pen tattoos, and two small photo albums. I have a quick flick through—the pictures look like they date from when Karen's salon opened in Ebbing, judging from the blond streaks everyone is rocking.

Mary is waiting for me at the foot of the stairs when I come down with the albums in my hand.

"Sorry, I took the wrong door," I say quickly. "I hope you don't mind—I saw these and there are lovely photos of Karen in them. Is it okay if I use some of the pictures for the article?"

"Er, yes. I suppose so," Mrs. Simmons says. "What are you going to write about her?"

"Just what you've told me—about her life and how everyone loved her. I'm talking to her friends and some of her hairdressing clients as well. About the weeks leading up to her death."

"Not this online dating?" she says.

"The thing is," I say carefully, "Karen told her friends about it. And me. She did an interview about it."

"Oh, God!" Mary cries. "What did she say?"

"That she'd met some very nice men—but not all. She'd had, well, a mixed experience. Like most people who use these websites." There is a silence and I stumble on. "It might help the police find the killer. If she met him online."

As if summoned, Jenny the FLO calls through the door: "Mary, it's me. Can you let me in?"

With a quick hello as she comes in, I slip past her and away. I can hear Mary filling her in as I skirt the holly. I text Miles to expect another call.

NINE

ANNIE

Saturday, February 15, 2020

She started weeping as soon as she got through the door from work. The news about the body had capsized her. Even the house didn't feel safe anymore. The pain at the base of her skull made her slide down onto the floor in her coat and curl in on herself.

Annie clutched at happy memories, desperate to stop herself sinking further. The boys—always her first impulse. But the tense family gathering the night before crowded in and darkened her thoughts. Their firstborn, Xander, clever and remote in his London clothes, with his London girlfriend and unfathomable job in underwriting; Gav, still the baby and drifting through life. Just the two of them, now. She'd been so looking forward to seeing Xander. It was a rare home appearance. A flying visit on his way to some awful Las Vegas–themed stag weekend in Brighton. And bringing Emily, the girlfriend they'd never met, to eat Henry's famous roast. Gav had managed to rouse himself from his room, and they'd made such an effort, Annie and Henry working as a team in the kitchen, peeling, rinsing, salting, simmering, searing, basting, whipping, chopping.

"Wow, something smells amazing," Xander's girl had said as she walked through the door. It was her first time in the bosom of his family, and Annie could see she was putting on her best game.

Henry had kissed her on both cheeks, putting on his best game, too, while Annie had hovered nervously.

"Come through to the living room," Annie had said, giving the girl a quick self-conscious peck. "Are these for me? You shouldn't have."

The roses were hand tied. No garage chrysanths with a perforated price tag half torn off. *It must be serious.*

Henry had fluttered around Emily, putting a glass of prosecco in her hand, making her laugh while Annie watched. He was wearing black jeans and his favorite flowery shirt. The strain of meeting the girlfriend for the first time had made Annie gulp her own drink and choke on it.

"Are you all right, Annie?" Henry had said, trying to pat her on the back as she coughed and her face got redder.

She'd had to mime getting a glass of water and disappeared into the sanctuary of the kitchen. Gav had followed.

"What can I do?" he'd said and put his arm around her shoulders. He was only fourteen but he towered over her—the little woman. "Strain the carrots, please," Annie had said and pointed to a serving dish. It was part of a set they'd been given for their wedding a million years ago. Twenty-six years ago, actually. Anyway, there wasn't much of the set left now—three ham-fisted boys helping with the washing-up and kicking footballs around in the house had seen to that.

Henry had suddenly appeared, grabbing for a tea towel and wrenching open the oven door. "I forgot about it," he muttered. "It'll be ruined."

"It'll be fine," Annie had said quietly, wondering if there was something she could get out of the freezer as a last-minute replacement.

When they'd all sat round the dining room table later, the sound of overcooked beef being chewed into submission filling the silences, Annie had looked at Henry at the other end of the table and smiled. He was still the same man, wasn't he? The groom who'd waited for her at the register office door, the wind whipping his hair and the fern on his carnation.

Same eyes, same lovely slow smile, same, same, same. But not.

Neither of them were those people who'd giggled with nerves as they'd exchanged vows about loving each other until death parted them. It had all sounded so romantic at twenty-two. Undying love. They'd had no idea how dirty and destructive death was.

Annie had carried on looking around the table at their sons. She suddenly wanted to gather them up in her arms and whisper her love to them, like when they were small.

"Mum," Xander had been saying beside her, and Annie had realized he was telling her about the friends he was meeting and the costumes they'd bought on the internet, and tried to focus. But she hadn't known any of the names. They belonged to Xander's new life.

"Sounds like it's going to be fun," she'd said, and he'd turned back to Emily. He didn't need his mother anymore. Any of them, really. In truth, the things that had bound the family together—the games, the holidays, the evenings by the telly—had always seemed to chafe Xander. He'd disappear off as soon as he could.

"Alexander has a wonderful imagination—he creates whole worlds in his head. But he prefers his own company," the teachers had said, and Annie had tried not to hear the note of concern in their voices. She'd wanted to shout: *He's been through a terrible trauma—what do you expect?*

Annie had startled when her eldest suddenly leaned forward and dinged his spoon against an empty glass. Emily had jumped, too, flushed red, and put her hand to her perfect throat.

"Can I have a bit of hush?" Xander had said. "We've got an announcement."

And Annie had wanted to reach for Henry's hand, but he was too far away, so she'd smiled over at him and he'd winked back.

"We're getting married," their son had said, then bent to kiss the girl at his side.

Annie had wanted to say how happy she was for them, but Henry had got in first and said it all. She didn't blame him. He'd got into the habit years ago when grief had taken her words. When she'd retreated into herself and he'd become the family spokesman. He'd said all the right things, of course he had, but they'd been his things. Not hers. Annie had had to wait until later when they'd drunk lots of toasts, each one sillier than the last, and gone into the sitting room to look at old wedding photos.

Annie had sat on the arm of Xander's chair while his bride-to-be, sandwiched between Henry and Gav on the sofa, cooed over Annie's nineteen-nineties wedding dress.

"I'm so happy for you, love," Annie had said and touched Xander's hair, his blond curls long since shaved off. She'd felt the slight flinch but ignored it. She'd worried about him for so long, her quiet boy. But he was going to be fine.

"Thanks, Mum. She's wonderful."

Emily had raised her head and smiled, damp-eyed with happiness.

"She is. You are a lucky boy. Your whole life is in front of you. No looking back."

"Mum . . ." And his eyes had gone blank.

Emily's devoted ear had heard the ping of tension and she'd called across: "Come and look at this, Xander. You won't believe your dad's shoes."

Annie had watched Emily stroking Xander's face and caressing his arm like she herself used to do to Henry, and listened to her talking about her dream wedding. She wondered what this girl knew about them. What Xander had told her. Had he told her? Or was he planning a marriage held hostage by secrets?

She'd wanted to talk to Henry about it, but she'd been asleep by the time he'd dropped Xander and Emily off at the station. Annie had only seen Henry fleetingly this morning—he'd been up well before her and was spooning the last of his cereal into his mouth when she got downstairs.

"I slept in Xander's room so I didn't wake you last night," he'd explained. "I didn't, did I?"

Annie had shaken her head.

"Good. I'm off now—I've got to take the car over to the garage to get it checked. I only just got home last night—bit of a nightmare, actually," he'd burbled as he stacked his bowl in the dishwasher. "A warning light came on, and it took an age to work out what it was."

Annie was thinking about warning lights, deep in her head on the hallway floor, still in her coat, when she realized she wasn't on her own in the house. Henry was blowing his nose noisily in another room.

He glanced up quickly when Annie came into the kitchen, but he didn't speak. He carried on typing, face computer-blank.

"Henry," Annie said as she sat down and reached to still his dancing hands. "Someone else has died in Knapton Wood. The girl who used to cut our hair."

He looked at her for a moment as if she was a stranger. "Sorry, yes, I heard it on the local news," he muttered. "Look, do you mind if I finish this bit of work? Anyway, it's nothing to do with us."

"But the police might want to talk to us," she said quietly.

"The police?" Henry's head shot up. "Why would they be interested in us? For God's sake, Annie, our horror show is over. Has been for fifteen years."

"Nearly sixteen," she whispered to herself as she turned away. She knew it could never be over.

They'd kept the peace for years, complicit in their silence to ensure a fresh start was possible for their family. For years, they'd let sleeping dogs lie. But this new killing had stirred them. Would make them howl.

TEN

ELISE

Saturday, February 15, 2020

WHEN SHE FINALLY got home, Ronnie knocked just minutes later.

"Yes!" Elise barked at her and stood back to let her in. "Seriously, Ronnie, have you got cameras trained on my front door?"

"That's an idea," Ronnie laughed as she squeezed past into the front room. "Are they expensive? How was your day? Mine was rubbish. Ted's been under my feet, fussing about his model railway tracks. He needs a left-hand bend. He's driving me round the bloody left-hand bend."

"Tea?"

"Well, if you haven't got any gin."

Elise laughed and put the kettle on.

"How's it going? What's the sitrep?"

"Sitrep? For God's sake, Ronnie. This is not *Line of Duty.*"

"Well, I bet it was cold up at Knapton Wood," Ronnie said, taking up her position on the high stool.

"Bitter. I can't believe people walk there at dawn—the couple who found the body went in the dark."

"The Claytons, wasn't it?" Ronnie said. "Well, they're a funny couple."

Elise sighed. Ronnie had made it her business to have personal insights into almost every one of the town's ten thousand inhabitants.

"Go on, then. I know you're dying to tell me. Funny how?"

"Well, not hilarious. He doesn't let that poor woman out of his sight."

Elise nodded, unsurprised. She could still see the frozen look behind Mrs. Clayton's eyes.

"Have they lived in Ebbing long?"

"He has. His dad started the hardware shop round the back of the library, and when he died of a heart attack at fifty, Noel got lumbered with it. The only son, you see. It wasn't what Noel had planned, by all accounts, but you can't always get what you want, can you? Evelyn was sort of part of the package—she used to work in the shop, so he didn't have to look far for a wife. My Ted doesn't go in there. He says Noel's got a dirty mouth on him."

"Has he? I noticed Mrs. Clayton doesn't say much."

"No. She doesn't really mix. A bit like you, really."

"I mix!"

"Barely. So"—Ronnie's voice suddenly dropped—"have you seen the new man next door in number seven yet? He moved in weeks ago, but I haven't managed to speak to him."

"You must be slipping! And why are you whispering?" Elise said but found herself doing the same.

"Because he's probably just the other side of that wall," her neighbor hissed. "I've told you before, these party walls are like paper. I can practically hear you unbuttoning your coat when you get home—if I turn down the radio."

"Seriously," Elise muttered, and gave her a look. She liked Ronnie a lot. She'd been there for her—"in charge of morale"—when Elise had been dealing with the terrors of breast cancer and recovery, but sometimes, just sometimes, she wished she still lived in an anonymous block of serviced executive flats where no one wanted to know your business. A terraced house on Ebbing High Street meant she couldn't avoid being watched and overheard. Still, she could hardly complain. She'd done her own share of scrutinizing her neighbors since moving into 5 Mariner's Cottages.

"Mina Ryan's office is letting it," Ronnie was telling her. "So she'll be all genned up on him. He looks right up your alley."

He did, but Elise was admitting nothing to the matchmaker in her kitchen. She'd clocked the new tenant straightaway. Of course she had. The house had been in darkness since well before Christmas, and she'd been a copper too long not to notice a light in the window when she'd come home from work a month ago. She'd listened for movement at the wall and carefully peered over her fence into the kitchen. There were big cardboard boxes on the worktop, but no one was unpacking.

Elise had gone with an apple to sit and wait in her window that looked onto the High Street. There was nothing on Netflix, anyway.

She'd spotted her new neighbor slowing and fumbling with unfamiliar keys under the streetlight, and had taken it all in: six foot plus, clean-shaven, athletic stride, forties? Or a fit fifty? He'd been carrying a small takeaway bag from the Golden Gate Indian restaurant. A meal for one. And he hadn't called out "Hello" as he'd let himself in. No one else in the house, then.

But Elise wasn't letting on to Ronnie. The woman didn't need any encouragement in her mission to fix Elise up.

"You should pop round with a bottle of wine or a cake to welcome him," her friend urged.

"Shut up! He might be a recovering alcoholic or gluten intolerant," Elise said, trying not to smile. "Look, haven't you got a home to go to? I need to read my notes."

"I could help. I know Knapton Wood, for a start. My daughter, Meggie, used to play there with her friends and ran there when she was a teenager."

"Did she?" Elise took a sip of tea and pulled a face. "Shit, I forgot to put the milk in. Where is my head?"

"Don't fuss—you've got a lot on," Ronnie soothed, getting the carton out of the fridge. "God, are you still using oat milk? Makes tea taste like porridge."

"Shut up—it's good for me. Anyway, I'm not sure I would have run there. This morning was the first time I'd been there. It's a bit spooky, isn't it? Those huge dead trees . . . I prefer open spaces—or the treadmills at the gym."

"Seriously? And they're not dead—they're yews, and hundreds of years old. They're known as the Ancient Watchers," Ronnie said.

Elise snorted. "I thought that was you."

"Rude," Ronnie said. "Anyway, Meggie stopped going up there. Well, everyone did after the Curtis boys were attacked."

Elise turned. "In Knapton Wood? When was this?"

"Oh, ages ago. Meggie was about twenty—so must be fifteen or sixteen years, I suppose," Ronnie said. "Little Archie Curtis was killed. Don't you remember? You were a police officer back then, weren't you?"

"Not round here, I wasn't." She'd been on Traffic at the other end of the force area. But she would have known. Of course she would. The killing of a child would have invaded every corner of every police station in the country, let alone her own. It was what every officer dreaded. Children were not supposed to die. But groping around in the wisps of chemical fog that lingered in the corners of her brain, she couldn't locate Archie Curtis.

"Come on, Ronnie, you know how forgetful I can still be." She'd got good at covering up the occasional terrifying gaps in her memory at work, but she didn't need to pretend with her friend. "Remind me."

"He was eight. He and his brother were building a tree house . . ."

And the fog cleared. The tree house. An intricate collection of twigs and leaves in the lower boughs of a tree. The newspaper photos had made it look much more sophisticated than the giant bird's nests Elise and her brother, Leo, used to attempt when they were kids. And the blond boy with the wide smile. There he was. Little Archie Curtis.

"Got him," Elise said. "God—how had I forgotten it was Ebbing? They caught the killer the same day, didn't they? Wasn't he a registered sex offender?"

"Yep," Ronnie said. "Not a local. We were all so shocked when we found out we had a pedophile living among us. No one knew. No one had told us. And he didn't look like one. Just an ordinary young bloke. All neat and smiley and living alone in one of the holiday lets down by the harbor. Nicky something, he was called. The family moved away and never came back. Anyway, nobody wanted to play or walk in Knapton Wood after that."

"I bet," Elise said. "But people forget, don't they?"

SUNDAY:
DAY 2

ELEVEN

KIKI

Sunday, February 16, 2020

I'M MEANT TO be catching up on my accounts while Pip's with her dad for the day. Half term is always a nightmare—a war-gamed campaign of babysitters, playdates, and sleepovers is plotted out on the kitchen wipe board so I can continue to work. But I can't concentrate. Can barely sit still. Because my interview with Karen has been picked up by the nationals. A first since joining Sussex Today. A couple of old mates from the major news sites rang yesterday to ask me if they could run it in full, and I made Miles agree. "Make sure it links to our website and we are fully credited," he said, not making eye contact with me. No "well done" or "great job." But what do I care? The piece has unleashed a torrent of messages and emails: from women wanting to tell me online dating has been a revelation and how they've met "The One" after years of searching, to what feels like an equal number of those with horror stories to spill.

I haven't finished going through them all, but once I've cleared out the hate comments from trolls and incels, there'll be some fantastic material. I clench my fists so hard my nails make marks on my palms and punch the air. *This is it,* I tell myself. *I am not going back to press releases and internet sensations now.*

I FaceTime Miles while I'm still pumped.

"Have you seen how many comments I've got on the online dating murder?" I blurt as soon as he appears on my screen, half-asleep. "One hundred and forty-three. That's more than anything else on the site. Even the bloody rock-and-roll parakeet."

Miles yawns but he nods, making his big hair wave around his head.

"So, I've decided I'm going to do a column, anonymously. I'm calling it 'The Secret Dater.' It's a play on words—you know, dater/data . . ." Miles yawns again. "Anyway, I can take a deep dive into the scene, go on dates, and talk about a different one each week. I'd disguise the blokes, obviously, but there are great stories out there—some horrors, some big romances, and some real laughs."

I'm babbling now and he nods again—probably to make me stop— and puts a thumb up. And that is good enough for me.

I close the spreadsheet on my laptop and sign up as my ex, Danny, on some of the big dating sites to look at how women are operating— just to give myself a head start. *He won't mind,* I tell myself as I upload an old photo of him in shades, hair slicked back, and create a fake email address. His listing starts racking up Views and Likes immediately: thirty-two in the first ten minutes. And I feel the scorch of acid burn in the pit of my stomach. An echo of our last months together. Nights I sat waiting. Him not answering his phone. The ghost of someone else's scent on him. I close my eyes against it. *That is history now,* I tell myself. *No looking back.*

"You wouldn't want to date him if you knew the truth," I mutter to the women queuing for the privilege. "That he cuts his toenails on the sofa."

I wince as I scroll through their faces. It's like a Farrow & Ball paint color chart of human hope—from the palely shy to the dark hinterland of aggressively erotic. I doubt I will ever unsee Lynda X spilling out of a cheap basque in an untidy kitchen, a frying pan sticking out of the sink and desperation beading her upper lip.

"Come on, Lynda," I murmur. "You don't need to do this."

But maybe she does. Maybe loneliness has driven this woman to strip off for strangers instead of finishing the washing-up. And she is certainly not alone. Hundreds of Lynda Xs are laying out their stalls online.

In my search, I stumble across Karen—dead in the morgue but still very much alive online, her voice crackling with nervous energy as she coos to her webcam: "Do you want to join me?"

Well, someone did. I just need to find out who. And I know this is really why I'm doing "The Secret Dater." There's a chance I'll find Karen's killer while the police are still cataloging exhibits. *And be all over the media as the person who caught him,* a voice in my head whispers. *Okay, and be all over the media,* I whisper back. *So what?*

I put my fingers back on the keyboard and take a deep, calming breath. I'll have to get my hands dirty. I'll have to sign up as myself to do the job properly. *Go live.* Friends have been nagging me for ages to do it, anyway. "People don't meet partners in real life anymore," one said. "It's a separate activity. People have Bumble or Tinder apps sitting on their phones with Deliveroo and eBay. You need to get on with it if you want to find someone."

But the thought of putting myself out there like a takeaway meal or pre-loved shoes was too depressing.

Okay, but this is different, isn't it? It's not about me. It's for research. And I tap in the necessary information, altering some things slightly and creating a new email. But I do use a genuine photo of myself and carefully write my profile. I need to attract the same men as Karen did, so I nick a couple of her lines: "Hi, I'd love to meet new people and kick-start my social life. I like walks on the beach and nights out." And wait. And wait. I check my Wi-Fi connection twice, but the realization that no one fancies me is curdling in the pit of my stomach.

What's wrong with me? I want to scream. And am pathetically grateful when I finally get my first real bite. Not that he's Brad Pitt. Eamonn from Hove has a comfortable face, is forty-nine, no kids, dog lover, and wearing a baseball cap in every photo. So, probably hat-fishing. I feel a bit sick when I start the chat, sure he will see through my pretense, but he keeps everything friendly and low-key. And within an hour I agree to an IRL meeting at lunchtime.

While I wait for the appointed time, I keep leaping up to pee, my bladder signaling strongly that I should stay at home. But when it's time to leave, I take a good, hard look at the anxious face in the mirror.

"Get your big-girl pants on, Kiki. You need to get in the game."

TWELVE

ANNIE

Sunday, February 16, 2020

ANNIE WOKE AND reached for Henry. Her dream of running through Ebbing, banging on the windows of empty shops for help, wouldn't clear. She could still taste the dry panic in her throat, and her legs felt weak and trembly. She hadn't had the dream for a long time. Years. But this fresh horror in Knapton Wood had summoned it up.

Karen's death had been like a rock thrown into their domestic waters. Bringing things back to the surface—buried hurts and grievances from the time of Archie's death. She and Henry had ended up hissing like alley cats in bed last night.

Her fluttering hand found only cold space in their bed. *What time is it?* She flailed around, knocking over hand cream and a tiny elephant with a missing tusk on the bedside table before finding her phone. Eight thirty. She lay back, immediately exhausted by the thought of the day ahead.

She could hear Henry now, moving around the kitchen below her: turning on the radio for the news, clattering plates together as he emptied the dishwasher, scraping chair legs on the tiles.

He'd bring her a cup of tea in a minute. And maybe they could put last night's row to rest. Normally, if they'd argued, Henry would make the first move and come and put his arms around her, and she would say sorry and kiss him. It was marital muscle memory. And they'd be thankful to make their peace and move on. But after last night's spat, they'd slept with their backs to each other, and their resentment had lingered, like a Victorian illness.

They hadn't rowed like that for a while, and Annie struggled to remember what the last fight had been about as she rolled onto her side. But things had been building since Friday's engagement dinner. It'd been stressful, playing happy families for three hours. By the end of the evening, Annie had sat mute, guiltily longing for the happy couple to leave so she could talk to Henry about what he thought about it all. But she hadn't had a chance. It'd all ended in a mad rush when Henry had realized the time and hustled Emily and Xander into the car to drive them to the station. Emily had needed to get back to London, and Xander was off to Brighton to meet his mates. Annie had stood in the doorway with her hand still raised in a last wave after the car had disappeared up the road, and then she'd trudged upstairs to bed. She hadn't even had the energy to pick up her book.

She smiled warmly when Henry stumbled in, balancing two cups and a plate of toast. "Oh, how lovely," she cooed, sitting up with her arms out to hug him, but Henry perched out of reach on the end of the bed.

"I'm sorry about last night, love," Annie murmured. "I hate it when we row."

"So do I," Henry muttered. "I don't know what's got into you lately. Bringing up all this old stuff and rehashing ancient arguments. You even brought up the bloody ceiling I didn't paint properly—what? Twenty years ago?"

Annie dug her fingernails into her palms under the covers to stop the row reactivating. "I've said I'm sorry, love. But it's been so horrible, hasn't it? With this new death."

"Annie," Henry growled softly. "You've got to stop talking about that—it's nothing to do with us. We should be focusing on the good things happening in our life. Our son is getting married to a lovely girl."

"I know," Annie murmured, trying hard to picture Emily and Xander's happy day but failing. "Xander hasn't told her, has he? About Archie?" she blurted.

Henry closed his eyes. "For God's sake, you don't know that. She would hardly have brought it up at an engagement dinner, would she?"

"No, you're probably right," Annie said quietly. "Everything's making me anxious at the moment."

"I know. Look, have the morning in bed if you like. I'm going to sort out the shelves in Gav's room."

He pecked her on the cheek as he left. And Annie told herself it was all forgotten. She'd do his favorite chicken cacciatore for lunch. She needed some tinned tomatoes—and a bottle of Chianti. And she almost felt normal for a moment. Annie on a typical Sunday. A day of rest and domestic chatter about the week ahead. But she suddenly felt like a stranger in that world. She was all about death and loss again.

THIRTEEN

ELISE

Sunday, February 16, 2020

ELISE PICKED UP the pace as she jogged along the path above the beach, gazing out at the curve of the horizon, getting in her steps. She took off her hat as she ran, loving the sensation of her hair being blown about by the wind.

She knew that winter by the seaside was an acquired taste. Gray layered on gray and sea blackened by lowering clouds wasn't for everyone. But she loved its unsentimental starkness after the postcard sparkling seas, ice creams, and little cafés with bunting and scones in the summer.

There'd been a sharp frost every morning for a week, and the pebbles on the beach had become lethal icy marbles underfoot. Elise had noticed that most of the Bluetits—the women she saw plunging in daily for a dawn swim—had put their swimsuits away for the moths to devour. Only the hardiest kite surfers were out there, skimming the waves, then standing with their wet suits stripped to the waist in the car park, swapping triumphs behind their rusty camper vans.

The weekenders had locked up and left by Halloween. They wouldn't be back until spring, and Ebbing had hunkered down, grumbling to itself. Elise had flipped through the online neighborhood forums when she'd first arrived two years ago and discovered a master class in barely contained fury. In among the ads for secondhand sofas and window re-placement were people festering about the things they saw and resented every day—dumping rubbish illegally, dog mess, blocked views, bad parking. And, of course, the wealthy blow-ins who priced locals out of the housing market.

She wondered how long she'd have to live here before she stopped being an outsider. Or if she even wanted that. She could end up like Ronnie.

As she reached the homestretch, she tried to unpack her plans for the day. The media were all about Karen's online dating, but Elise wanted to focus on Karen's immediate circle. The statistics showed that most victims knew their killer. Despite what the papers said, the streets were far safer for women than their front rooms. Their attackers were over-whelmingly jealous boyfriends, violent husbands, angry exes, or, occa-sionally, controlling fathers. Not strangers.

Elise had sat across from these men in interview rooms over the years, listening to their self-serving excuses. "She knew she was winding me up. She wanted to provoke me," one fifteen-stone laborer had said after stabbing his seventeen-year-old former girlfriend to death with a kitchen knife. He'd got a life sentence. But then, so had his victim.

The team was looking at all of Karen's known connections, but the waters were muddied by the online strangers in her life. This could end up an electronic needle-in-a-haystack job. She crammed her hat back down over her mad hair. She'd better get on with it, then.

She was on her way home to change when she remembered she'd meant to pick up milk and popped into the supermarket.

The assistant at the till was talking about the case, her face creased with concern. "I'm not walking home from work on my own after dark. My eldest comes and gets me."

Her customer, a tired-looking woman in a dirty anorak and old leg-gings, stopped packing her shopping and settled on one hip to consider the matter. "I know. He could still be out there, watching us."

"Don't," the assistant breathed. "Mind you, she was asking for trou-ble, wasn't she? Doing that online stuff. Everyone knows it's just for sex."

Elise sighed loudly and picked up a Snickers that was winking at her from the display. She looked at her watch. She was due at the hospital morgue for the postmortem in an hour, and she couldn't turn up in her sweaty tracksuit bottoms.

"I know," the customer said. "What the hell was she thinking? At her age?"

Elise gritted her teeth. She wanted to shout that Karen was only forty-five. Not past it by any stretch of the imagination. That middle age was not some sort of cutoff point for desire or falling in love. She hated that kind of knee-jerk victim blaming. Who were these two—or anyone—to judge Karen for dating online? It was the default way to meet anyone now. The new normal.

Not that Elise was in the market herself since her ex Hugh's departure three years ago. No way. She should never have hooked up with another copper in the first place, but he'd seemed so perfect for her— and the only other men she seemed to meet were criminals.

And, for almost ten years, she'd thought she and DI Hugh Ward were a team. She didn't want kids, and he didn't see the need to get married—they were both ambitious and happy to skip a cozy family life for their careers. But at some point, without her noticing, he'd changed his mind and dumped her for a younger woman he'd met jogging in the park.

For weeks, they'd managed to avoid each other at work, until Hugh had been seconded to another force for a project and Elise had stopped having to check rooms before entering. She'd thought she was over it, but six months later she'd learned on the grapevine that Hugh and the jogger had got engaged, and she'd spent a week sleeping and weeping. And then she'd put him away.

She'd really thought she had. But Hugh had sent a "get well" card when he'd heard about her cancer a year ago, and Elise had kept it under her pillow for weeks. They'd bumped into each other during an investigation last year, and it had floored her, but she'd managed to style it out. Better than he had, in fact. She was so over him. At least, that was what she told her mum and Ronnie when they breached all norms of privacy to inquire about her love life.

"I'm perfectly happy on my own. I don't need a man," she snapped. "I've got a career that fulfills me. I haven't got time for all that flirting and nonsense now."

But they weren't fooled. They'd somehow joined forces to find her a new partner. She should never have introduced them when her mum had come for a visit last year. She suspected they now spoke on the phone.

"Everyone needs someone," Ronnie had said. "You haven't even got a goldfish."

"You're hardly an advert for domestic bliss!" Elise had laughed. "The first time we met, you were devising ways to murder your husband."

"I'm still working on it. Anyway, I'm not talking about Ted—you need a real man."

Back in the shop, the woman in the anorak was fishing half-heartedly for her purse, and Elise edged forward, trying to pressure her into action.

"Some women are their own worst enemies," the shop assistant said, folding the long receipt slowly and unnecessarily. "Throwing themselves at men. My friend saw her that night. At the pub. She was making a complete spectacle of herself."

Elise cleared her throat. "I'm sorry, but I'm in a hurry. Can I pay?"

The two women glared at her. "No need to be rude," the customer muttered under her breath.

"I need to get to work," Elise muttered back as she waved her contactless card and grabbed the milk.

When she got outside she realized she'd left the Snickers behind and marched back in.

"She's the one with cancer," she heard the assistant say.

"Well, that can make you go funny, can't it?" the customer said.

"It can," Elise snapped as she whisked up the bar and left them open-mouthed.

———

CARO AND AOIFE Mortimer were waiting when she pushed through the door to the viewing gallery.

Below, Karen's body lay on its back, chest and arms marbled by death.

"Sorry, I got held up," Elise said to Caro and repeated it over the gallery microphone.

"It's okay. Let's get on." Aoife adjusted her visor and turned to begin work.

Elise sat back and tried not to breathe too deeply. The first PM she'd ever attended had made her gag, and she'd never got past it. She'd tried everything—vapor rub under her nose (which only made it worse), a relaxation tape, and herbal remedies—but nothing worked. She had learned not to make a fuss, though; she breathed slowly and evenly through her mouth. The technique had worked well, but chemotherapy had heightened her sense of smell, and every note still hit her like a slap to the face.

Aoife glanced up at the gallery and caught her eye. "Okay?" she mouthed. Elise nodded and looked across at Caro. Her sergeant loved postmortems and leaned forward to watch every move, her nose practically on the glass.

The pathologist's commentary as she explored and exposed the body was brisk and to the point.

"There are superficial abrasions and scratches on the face and nose, possibly from vegetation," she said, carefully removing soil from the nostrils and then opening the mouth. "A laceration of the frenulum." Elise found herself automatically touching her tongue to the ridge of tissue between her teeth and lip. "Abrasions and scratches on the knees. All evidence of a struggle with the victim on her front."

Elise nodded to herself and watched as the pathologist moved down the body. "There's deep bruising to the muscles of the back and sides of the chest. I would say the assailant put their full weight on her."

"You mean they sat on her?" Caro asked.

Aoife looked up and nodded. "Or lay. I'll have to wait for the samples to come back, but it looks very likely she suffocated."

"What about sexual assault?" Elise said.

"Well, I'll send sex swabs to check for recent activity, but I'm not seeing any evidence of an assault. No bruising or tearing of the perineum."

"It could be a sex game that went wrong?" Elise muttered.

"They don't go much wronger than this, do they?" Caro replied.

"But who was she playing it with?" Elise murmured. "Let's clear the ground in Ebbing first. Starting with the men in the Free Spirits. Have you looked at Kiki's video again?"

Caro opened it on her phone.

"See!" Elise jabbed her finger at the screen. "Look at that body language between Ash Woodward and our victim. He looks frozen in front of the camera until she touches him. Then he relaxes and smiles for the first time. And that look on his face when she turns away to Barry Sherman."

"Never mind that," Caro said, and paused the clip. "Watch Karen's hand."

Elise peered closer and saw the hairdresser's hand secretly snake round behind Sherman. "Look at his eyes light up!" she gasped. "She's touching his arse."

"I wouldn't do that to a man I didn't want to sleep with," Caro muttered. "Or wasn't already."

FOURTEEN

KIKI

Sunday, February 16, 2020

WE'RE MEETING IN a pub I know, next to the railway station. I'm not taking any chances in case he's a weirdo. *Or Karen's killer,* my head whispers. It's big and busy with a ladies near the exit and a taxi rank right outside. Just in case I need to make my escape. The nerves are making my heart drum against my ribs, and I feel a bit lightheaded as I scan the room.

"Hello, Kiki, I hope I'm not late." A man who looks like he could be my date's dad is standing a fraction too close to me at the bar. He's never forty-nine.

"Er, Eamonn? Hello. I was just about to get a drink—what would you like?"

"A woman who takes charge." Eamonn grins and lets another customer push him even closer. "But I'll get these."

I ask for a white wine spritzer and grit my teeth. It's going to be a long afternoon.

"So," I say, once we find a table and I've shifted my stool back another foot. "This is all a bit new for me. Have you been dating online long?"

"Awhile. I split up with my wife a couple of years ago, you see. What's your story?"

I'm sensing Eamonn doesn't really do foreplay.

"I moved down from London recently and I'm just finding my feet, really."

"Right, well, you should try the singles nights in town," Eamonn offers. "They're brilliant. No one comes away disappointed."

I look at the man sitting opposite me—the bed-hair rosette on the side of his head, T-shirt with radiator creases across the stomach—and try to imagine his home life. *Microwave meals on the sofa in front of bad porn. I bet he sends dick pics.*

"Not sure about nightclubs, to be honest," I say. "They're not really my scene—it's so hard to talk against that loud music, isn't it?"

"I'm not much of a talker, if you know what I mean?" He leers. "Man of action, me."

My stomach clenches, and I take a restorative gulp of warm spritzer.

"Right," I say. "But it's a bit risky, isn't it? I'm definitely nervous about leaving with someone I know nothing about, late at night."

He shrugs. "But that's part of the fun. I love a lucky-dip date. A bad experience can still be worth it."

"Right, but look what happened to that poor woman in Ebbing. What was her name?" I say, pretending to struggle. "Was it Karen something?"

"Karen Simmons," Eamonn mumbles, and then takes a long slurp of his beer and belches quietly. I try not to hold my breath. Did he know her? I shudder despite myself.

"Are you warm enough?" he asks. "We could move to a table away from the door?"

I shake my head.

"Anyway, you don't need to worry about ending up like her," he carries on. "She liked a drink a bit too much, by all accounts. She was the sort who always said yes to a date. Asking for it, really."

"What? Being murdered?" I say a bit too loudly. It's an outrageous comment, but that's not what's raising the hairs on my arms. How the hell does he know if Karen liked a drink or not? I look at that doughy face, searching for something that reveals his hidden nature. But there's nothing.

Eamonn loses the leer.

"Sorry, didn't mean to offend," he says, then smiles apologetically, picks up his empty glass, and waggles it in front of my face. "Another?"

My stomach is churning and I desperately want to say no but I nod. There's no way I'm leaving now.

When he sits back down, I'm ready. "You seem to know quite a lot about Karen," I say and lean in. "How did you meet her?"

He shakes his head. "I didn't. But other people did. They've been talking about her online."

"Who's talking about her?" I push.

"Oh, just some blokes I chat to sometimes. We share an interest—in meeting women and such. And swap info. You know, if someone is a bunny boiler or doesn't wash."

I realize my mouth is hanging open and clamp it shut.

"I'm sure the girls do it, too," he adds quickly.

"Really?" I mutter. "As I say, I'm a bit too new to all this to have plugged into that sort of circle. Sounds useful, though." I coax him onward. "How did you find them?"

"I spend a lot of time online, in dating chat rooms and forums. I got talking to X-Man—he's another Brighton football club supporter. And he introduced me to some of the others—Lenny, Deadpool, the Captain, and Bear and the rest. They're a good bunch of blokes. It's funny, we talk most days but we've never actually met."

"So X-Man talked about Karen?"

"Yeah, turned out he'd had a date with her once. He gave it a three out of five."

"When?" I blurt, and Eamonn looks startled. I feel the rush of adrenaline turn on the heat in my chest and curse my treacherous hormones. I wonder if I can possibly be as red as I feel and put a hand to my cheek. Eamonn doesn't seem to notice that I'm on fire, so I stumble on. "Sorry,

I mean, it must have been a terrible shock for him when she died," I mumble.

Eamonn nods slowly. "Him and the others," he murmurs. "Some of them had a go, too. She was a popular girl, it turned out."

I gulp down my wine as fast as I can so I can begin my search for this vile brotherhood. I reach behind me for my coat. "Look, it has been nice to meet you," I say, "but I really need to get going now. Good luck with everything.".

"Go?" he splutters. "But I've bought you two drinks."

Outside, I walk fast to the taxi rank and check behind me before getting into a cab.

I sit scrolling through possible fake superheroes on my phone. There are loads, and I need to make a proper list and plan. I rest my head on the window and replay the conversation.

Three out of five. And I find myself wondering what X-Man deducted points for. What I would score. I shudder. I'm truly in Karen's world now.

FIFTEEN

ELISE

Sunday, February 16, 2020

THE LOBSTER SHACK car park was only half-full when Elise and Caro drew up. The Sunday lunch crowd had dribbled away, and inside, Barry Sherman was sitting on a stool on the customers' side of the bar. Elise took in the heavily muscled shoulders, the carefully curated stubble, the luminous veneers, and the tattooed dragon tail creeping out of his rolled-up shirtsleeve. And wondered how often he looked in a mirror . . .

"Life can be funny, can't it?" he was musing, legs wide, hands on thighs, holding forth loudly to a couple of wide-eyed girls. "It was meant to be a three-week gig here, minding the pub while the owners went on holiday. But"—he shrugged and allowed himself a small smirk—"things went a bit tits up— Oops, sorry, ladies. Got complicated, I mean."

Elise risked a glance at Caro. "Ladies!" her sergeant mouthed. "What is this—1950?"

"Mr. Sherman," Elise cut in, "can we have a word? We're investigating Karen Simmons's death, and I understand you were part of her singles group."

One of the girls gasped and nudged her friend, and Barry quickly hopped off his stool to take the officers farther down the bar.

"No need to tell everyone," he hissed.

"Sorry, I didn't realize it was a secret," Elise said crisply.

"Well, it isn't, but I just dabble. I've met some nice girls, actually."

Girls, not women, then, Elise noted.

"Was Karen Simmons one of those girls?" she asked, and Sherman's charmer mask slipped a couple of inches.

"No," he muttered. "Course not. I just went to a few things Karen put on—pub nights and bowling, that kind of thing. I thought it would be a good way to meet new people. It can be tricky to have a social life when you work in the hospitality game."

"So, was it always in a group?" Elise pushed on. "Or did the two of you meet on your own? You looked very friendly at the last Free Spirits do at the Neptune."

"Were you there?" Sherman mumbled. "I didn't see you."

"No, but a reporter with a camera was. I can show you the video if you like."

Sherman glared. "Karen had had a drink," he said. "Look, I don't want to speak ill of the dead, but she could be a bit handsy when she was pissed. So, like I said, no. I've never been on a date—or on my own with her. Karen wasn't my type. I don't really go for the older woman."

Elise's hackles rose. "How old are you, Mr. Sherman?"

"Er, thirty-nine."

"So she was only six years older," she countered.

"Well, yeah, but, as I say, not my type."

Elise looked down the bar at the twentysomething blondes he would doubtless revisit as soon as she and Caro left.

"It was a good night, though," Sherman added. "I went on somewhere with someone I met in the pub."

"I see. Did Karen ever talk to you about who she was seeing?"

Sherman shrugged. "No, but I heard she was online. You'll have to ask Mina Ryan. They were thick as thieves. Look, it's busy in here. I need to get back behind the bar."

Elise looked around. There were only three people waiting to be served.

"Okay," she said. "Just one more thing. I thought it was a bit odd there weren't more members of the Free Spirits. I thought it was a bigger group."

"Oh, it can be—depends on the event."

"Are there other men? Or is it just you and Ash Woodward?"

"Ha! Good old Ash." Sherman grimaced. "He came to everything. Anything to be near Karen. Didn't do anything about it, of course. He's the strong, silent type," he muttered. "Him and his binoculars."

"Binoculars?" Elise said sharply.

Sherman smirked and crossed his arms. "Look, all I'm saying is he's not just looking at seagulls. You should talk to him."

"We will, thanks. I heard it was rammed at the Neptune on Friday—don't suppose you dropped in?"

"Hardly. It was rammed here, too. Valentine's is one of the biggest nights of the year."

"You didn't fancy kicking back after closing time?"

He looked at Elise sideways. "No, I was clearing up."

"On your own?"

"Yes," he sighed heavily. "I let the waiting staff go home or I have to pay overtime."

"And you didn't see or speak to Karen that evening?"

He reddened. "No," he hissed, and his arms tightened across his chest, making his voice breathy.

I hope you don't play poker. Elise allowed herself a moment of triumph for finally rattling him.

SIXTEEN

KIKI

Sunday, February 16, 2020

I SIT BESIDE Pip at the kitchen table, in sympathy for her struggle with her holiday math homework. I feel her pain as I think back to the hours I spent staring at numbers, willing them to make sense. But what I really want to do is hunt down Eamonn's toxic gang. I can't resist sneaking a quick look. The banter is pretty graphic in some of the chat rooms, and I get so lost in it that I don't notice Pip looking over my shoulder. "Mum, what's an obtuse angle again? Wow! Who's that?"

"No one," I say and snap the laptop shut. "Come on—show me the question and let's google it. You've still got your history project to finish before next week. And you need to wash your hair before bed."

Pip groans. "But I just don't get it, Mum," she whimpers, and I put my arm around her.

"We can do it!" I chant, and Pip looks up at me with teary eyes. "We can, lovely girl. And I've bought that stupidly expensive conditioner you like."

She's still hunched over her worksheets when I slip back into the world of men in gray underpants playing at being superhero studs. But I instantly flounder. I look over at Pip. She'd know how to navigate this—and I could do her history project in return. I love a bit of

mindful coloring in. I snort at the thought, and she looks up all wide-
eyed. Okay, not Pip. Someone who will be less scarred by the experience.

"Miles, I need your help," I say when I've retreated to my bedroom
and he picks up his phone. He sighs theatrically, and I sit on my bed and
grit my teeth against his indifference.

"This is the second call on my day off, Kiki," he mumbles. "Couldn't
it wait until the morning?"

"I'm sorry, Miles. But it's urgent. I'm trying to find a group of blokes
in a chat room for men on dating apps. They're sharing information
about women."

"Urgent? Seriously?" And I can hear the scowl on his face. "Is this
how you spend your Sundays? Anyway, there'll be thousands of them,"
he says. "It's a no-hoper."

"But I've got nicknames for some of the men." Miles groans. "They
call themselves X-Man, Captain, Bear, er, Lenny, and Deadpool."

"You are kidding," he mutters. "Why are you looking for them, anyway?" He's finally got there. It would have been the first question I
asked.

"They've been posting about Karen Simmons. One of them met her
online and wrote some horrible, intimate things about her. Will you
help me?"

There's a beat while he absorbs the information, and then he blurts,
"Wow! This could be like one of those true crime podcasts. Okay, send
me everything you know and I'll have a look."

I wish I was in the room with him, urging him on, feeding in ideas,
but I've got my other child downstairs to worry about.

I start making cheese on toast for us both to cheer Pip up even
though my head is everywhere but my kitchen. I'm texting Miles another suggestion when my daughter shouts that something is burning. I
chuck the toast in the bin and start again—there are only crusts left
now, and Pip will bitch about it, but what can you do?

I can't sit still while the minutes tick by, so I eat mine standing up.
I'd expected instant results. *Stupid,* I tell myself, but he's so fast nor-

mally. And mocks me for taking more than a nanosecond to find something online. When Pip goes upstairs to have her shower, I noodle on my computer and see that Miles has used a boring shot of Knapton Wood from the car park to go with my story—so lazy. I want something deep in the trees. Something sinister and atmospheric. I'm searching through the thumbnails of twisted branches when a little boy with curly hair appears.

"Archie Curtis, aged eight," the caption reads.

Random, I think. I click on the child's face, and his tragically short life opens in front of me. And I remember. Archie Curtis. Killed in 2004, when I was still a real reporter. Before Pip. I hadn't felt the terrifying vulnerability of being a mother when I'd written sidebars on other murdered children the day his body was found. I read on and stop. I had forgotten he was killed in Knapton Wood.

I jump straight down the rabbit hole, and within ten minutes I've reminded myself that the killer was Nicky Donovan, a twenty-four-year-old sex offender, arrested at his mum's house in Portsmouth.

But it hadn't come to trial. Donovan had killed himself while in custody.

That must have been torture for the Curtis family, I think. *Not seeing his reckoning in court.*

"Mum," Pip calls. "Where did you put the conditioner?"

And, with a resigned sigh, I force myself back into the here and now.

SEVENTEEN

ELISE

Sunday, February 16, 2020

"You'll find Ash down at the ice-cream kiosk," the boy at the Sunny Sands Caravan Park reception mumbled without looking up from his phone.

"Bit cold for ice lollies," Elise said.

"He's painting it," he snapped back.

"Well, he's not going to win employee of the month," Caro said loudly as they left, and the boy finally lifted his head and gave them a death stare.

They were buffeted by the wind, their coats flapping violently as they walked the cement path through the static caravans, the windows like dozens of eyes watching them. Rusting ornamental windmills whirred among pots of blackened stems and dead inflatable toys.

"Bloody hell," Caro muttered. "Where are the zombies? In the amusement arcade? Trading Standards should do them—Sunny? No. Sands? No. God, Baz is booking a holiday in a caravan at Easter."

"You are kidding. They're the seventh circle of hell." Elise laughed grimly. "We used to go every year on the Norfolk coast when I was a kid. Sharing a chemical toilet with four other people, every pee overheard. It gave me a horror of public loos for years."

"Right. Well, thanks for sharing. Is that him?"

A kneeling figure was just visible behind a sign advertising Magnum ice cream.

"Mr. Woodward?" Caro shouted over the weather, and the figure sat back on his heels, paintbrush in hand.

"Yes," he said and struggled to his feet, not meeting their eyes.

He was taller than Elise had expected—in the video, he hadn't towered over Karen—but Ash Woodward stooped as soon as he was upright, as if ducking down. Or hiding. Elise had been like that as a teenager—disguising her height so she didn't stand out. It hadn't worked. The mean girls had spotted her anyway.

"Hello. I'm DI King from the Major Crime Team, and this is my colleague DS Brennan," she said. "We're investigating the death of Karen Simmons, and we understand you were a friend of hers."

Ash Woodward pulled down his scarf to speak. "Well, yes."

"Can we go somewhere a bit warmer?" Elise shouted over the roar of the wind. "Do you live in one of the mobile homes on-site?"

Ash nodded but pointed at the door of the kiosk, and they all crammed into the space between two ancient chest freezers.

"That's better," Elise said. "Now, let's start again. You were at a Free Spirits do with Karen last Monday, weren't you? Was that the last time you saw her?"

His eyes flickered. "Yeah, why?" he mumbled.

"We're trying to establish her movements, Mr. Woodward. And find the man who killed her."

Ash's head went down. "Sorry. I'm just a bit upset."

"Of course." Elise pushed on. "So, tell me about Karen. What was she like?"

"She was lovely," he said, ramming his fists into his coat pockets. "Everyone liked her."

"And you were friends? Just friends? Or did you have a relationship?"

He shook his head.

Caro picked up a pair of binoculars on top of a stool so she could sit down, and Ash quickly reached for them.

"Sorry, are these yours?" Caro said.

"Yes, I use them all the time. To watch my birds. Especially at dusk when the owls are out hunting for voles."

"Right," Caro said. "My old man is a bit of a twitcher." Elise had to fake a cough to stop herself laughing. What was her sergeant up to? Baz, Caro's other half, would rather put pins in his eyes than go bird-watching. He didn't do outside unless it was a pub garden.

Ash looked up. "Is he?" he said, his voice animated for the first time. "I'm looking after a starling with a broken wing at the moment. People bring me injured wildlife to nurse. Where does your husband go birding?"

"All over," Caro said vaguely. "How about you? What have you been watching recently?"

"We've got barn owls in Ebbing—you can hear them screeching to one another."

"Anything else? Any*one* else?"

Ash Woodward's mouth closed in a hard line. "What do you mean?" he said quietly.

"You said Karen was lovely," Elise said, her voice deliberately light. "Were you keeping your eye on her?"

"Course not. Not like you mean, anyway."

"How, then?" Elise pressed.

He swiveled his head slowly. "I just looked out for her. She called me her guardian angel."

Just the once, I bet. A throwaway remark—like "Bless!" or "You're a star"—but poor Ash Woodward hadn't realized. He'd taken it as a job description.

"Did you want more?"

He shuffled his feet. "It didn't matter what I wanted; it wasn't going to happen. I find it hard to ask women out."

Elise could see that might be the case.

"But if she'd been with me," Ash went on, "she wouldn't have been wandering about in the wood. Wouldn't have got herself murdered."

"She was the victim," Elise said firmly, "not the perpetrator." And Ash looked mortified.

"I didn't mean that," he muttered.

"Were you in the Neptune on Friday evening?"

"Er, no. I was here."

"Did anyone see you?"

"Like who? There's no one here in the winter. It's like a morgue . . ." He broke off, blushing. "Sorry."

"HE CERTAINLY HAD a thing for Karen," Elise said as they marched back to the car. "And he's definitely nervous." She glanced back to where he was standing like a statue beside the kiosk, watching them leave. "Let's start digging into his movements."

Caro nodded. "I'll get someone onto it."

"Can you drop me on your way home?" Elise asked, and grinned.

"What? What's funny?" Caro shot back.

"Nothing, but you don't want to be getting back too late tonight." Elise laughed. "Baz will want to get out looking for his feathered friends."

"Shut up!"

IT WAS GONE eleven and pitch-black when Elise took her rubbish out to the bins in her yard. She was trying to find the torch on her mobile phone when she heard number seven's back door open, and light flooded out of the house and through the slats of the fence. The door was pulled to, and Elise listened for activity, but there was nothing except the crunch of waves on the stones below the houses. She tried to finish up silently, but the lid of her recycling bin crashed down and sent an empty tuna tin rattling across the patio. She flinched and held her breath.

"Hello!" a man's voice called from the gloom. "Everything okay?"

"Yes!" she called back. "Sorry, just putting my rubbish out."

His head appeared above the fence, his face in shadow.

"Hi, I'm Mal," he said. His voice sounded as if he was smiling. "I was just breathing in this lovely sea air—well, having a ciggie and a break from all the faff of unpacking, if I'm being honest. I hate it, don't you?"

"Er, yes. Sorry, I'm Elise." Why did she keep apologizing? He must think she was an idiot. At least it was dark. She wrapped her arms around herself.

"I shouldn't keep you out here talking in the freezing cold. But look, I meant to come and introduce myself to the neighbors at some point— do you mind if I knock on your door?"

"No, of course not. But I'm at work a lot."

"Okay. I'll catch you when I can. Good night, then."

"Yes, good night."

Back in the house, she released her arms, shaking the aching tension from them. And smiled.

MONDAY: DAY 3

EIGHTEEN

ANNIE

Monday, February 17, 2020

SHE DIDN'T USUALLY work on Mondays if she'd done a Saturday, but the surgery had someone off sick, and Annie needed distraction from the thoughts whirring constantly in her head.

Henry didn't comment when she said she was going in. He lifted his eyes from his iPad for a second and then burrowed back in. When Annie walked past him, she glanced at the screen. It was a bank statement, but she couldn't read the figures without her glasses.

"Everything okay?" she murmured. "We need to pay the car insurance this month."

Henry closed the window. "Absolutely," he said, his voice overbright. "Where's the reminder?"

Annie rushed round finding the paperwork but decided she'd check their accounts as soon as she was on her own. She hadn't done that for years. She thought all that had been put away after she'd discovered the debts Henry had been running up. Annie had been pregnant with Archie when she'd finally found the letters from the bank he'd been hiding. She could still see his face, the color draining from it, when she'd confronted him. It had been a work colleague who'd egged him on to play the stocks and shares, he'd said in this strange flat voice. "He gave me tips that paid out, and I had almost enough to take us on holiday. I knew you needed a break before the baby came. But then there were some losses and . . . well, I thought the markets would come back up."

It had been hard, but they'd sorted it without anyone else knowing, and Henry had sworn he wouldn't do it again. Ever.

And they'd moved on. Henry had still been the life and soul with their friends, joking with the husbands and flirting with the wives. But when it was just them, he'd been quieter. Less himself. It had been his own fault, but he'd tried to lay it at Annie's door. In his world, she knew he saw her as the cause of his humiliation.

Gavin was getting ready for the first day of half-term rugby training, stuffing cereal into his mouth and his kit into a bag and looking for his phone. "I need money for lunch," he muttered. "Have you seen my gum shield? Oh, and Xander says he had a great time at the stag do. He's WhatsApped photos of them all dressed up as Elvis and doing karaoke. Look! Hope everyone had earplugs."

Annie half laughed as she went upstairs and brushed her teeth again. She put on work clothes and flat shoes and looked in the mirror to apply a pale pink lipstick. Making an effort. She wondered when the skin on her throat had started collapsing into her neckline. Wasn't that supposed to happen later? She scrabbled in her drawers for a scarf and knotted it loosely. Better. But who was it for? Henry didn't seem to notice these days.

Gav was waiting for a lift to the sports center from his dad when she got downstairs, but Henry was still fussing around with emails.

"I'll take Gav," Annie said, forcing herself back into her mum role. "I can go that way round."

In the car, her lovely son sang along with the radio, making her join in and laugh.

When he got out, he kissed her cheek. He didn't do it very often now. Too big for all that. But he seemed to know when she really needed it.

My little hero. Poor boy doesn't know he was supposed to save us.

Annie had thought her family was complete after Xander and Archie.

But when Archie was . . . when he died, that whole time had been like living underwater, everything moving in slow motion around her, eyes straining to focus, voices distorted. And when she'd found she was pregnant again in the weeks after Archie's death, Henry had said a new baby would help them recover.

"Nothing can replace Archie," he'd whispered, holding her so close she could hardly breathe. "But we need to find a reason to keep going."

Gavin had been born before the first anniversary. Annie had wept for hours—her grief for her lost son still so raw she couldn't bear to be touched. Or to touch her new, unnamed baby. The nurses had had to feed him bottles when he woke and only brought him back to the cot beside Annie's bed when he went to sleep. And she'd lain with her back to him. But on the fourth day, he'd murmured and there'd been no nurses when Annie had called. She'd rolled over and looked at him. Seen that face she felt she'd always known. Breathed in his beautiful sweet, milky smell. Finally, she'd reached for him.

But, of course, poor Gavin hadn't made everything better. Nothing could.

DURING THE FIRST lull of the morning, Annie volunteered to walk up to the post office with the appointment letters. She told herself it was for some fresh air, but she knew it was so she could check on the current account. There was nothing out of place that she could see and guiltily clicked out of the app. And onto the local news site. She'd told Henry she wouldn't, but she couldn't help scrolling quickly through the updates about the killing. Annie was halted by a photograph of Karen laughing wildly at the camera. It had been taken by a reporter called Kiki Nunn, who'd apparently interviewed Karen just days before she died. It was all about her love life. Exposing her loneliness and search for a partner. Annie pored over the tiny, tragic details and felt herself being pulled further into Karen's story.

There was no harm in it, she told herself as she set up an alert for Karen's name. And Henry didn't need to know.

NINETEEN

KIKI

Monday, February 17, 2020

"WHAT?" MILES BARKS as I try to hover discreetly.

"Morning," I say, ignoring the tantrum warning. "Where are we with the toxic crew?"

"Who?" He feigns bewilderment and I count to ten in my head. "Oh, is that what you're calling these jokers?" he mutters. "Look, I'm under pressure from the top boss. There's been a dip in online traffic." I know I'm being dismissed, but I don't move. He's not getting away from me. "Okay, I'll work the information when I have time. And you need to find some stories to boost the audience. Can you have a look at TikTok?"

"If we find these men, we'll have a brilliant story," I growl. "I'm going back to Ebbing. There's a police briefing this morning." And I make my exit.

I'm early, so I make a detour and cruise past Karen's salon to see if the police are still there. Might be a helpful SOCO I can talk to. The lights are on—someone's in there—but the door's locked when I try it. I knock on the window, and a weeping teen drifts out of the back room, pale and skinny in a cropped T-shirt and leggings.

"Are you the police? They told me to bring the keys and wait for them." The girl sniffs. "I don't know if I'm allowed to let anyone else in."

"I'm a reporter covering Karen's death," I say. "I'd love to talk to you about her? You must have known her better than most."

The girl stops crying and pulls the door open. "I did," she says. "I'm Destinee. I only started just before Christmas, but Karen let me lock up and everything." Her teeth chatter.

"Are you cold?" I say. "It's freezing in here."

Destinee wraps her arms around herself and shakes her head. "I can't believe this is happening to me," she whispers.

Well, it happened to Karen, really, didn't it? I want to say, but instead go with "It must be such a shock for you."

She nods.

"But perhaps you can help find the person who attacked Karen?"

Destinee's eyes widen, and I catch her glancing at herself in the mirror. Star of her own true crime drama.

"Who was she seeing? Did she mention any names? People use nicknames on some of the dating apps, don't they? Did she talk about someone called X-Man or Captain? Or Lenny?"

Destinee mouths each name silently and shakes her head. "No, I don't think so. But you should ask Mina. They were best buds."

"Okay. Maybe she put something in the diary? On the computer?" I push us forward. Karen's dates could be sitting there on the screen.

Destinee types in a password, and I crane forward to scan the entries.

"There were lots of appointments on Friday," I say as I scribble down the names.

"Yeah, well, it was Valentine's, wasn't it?"

"Course. I didn't get any cards—I bet you did," I say, keeping it light.

She gives me a watery smile. "Three," she says, unable to hide her triumph.

"Lucky you," I say, scrolling back and forth. "Did Karen?"

Destinee shakes her head sorrowfully.

I flick back through the diary, and the initials AW reappear more than any other name. "Who is Karen's three o'clock on Tuesdays?" I ask.

"That's Ash Woodward," Destinee says. "He comes in every week for a trim."

It's the shy man who was standing next to Karen at the Free Spirits do.

"His hair must grow fast," I say.

"Oh, I don't think he came for the haircut," Destinee says, all serious. "He just loved chatting to Karen. Well, she did the chatting, to be fair. He lives on his own in a caravan. I dunno, he gives me the creeps, but Karen liked him."

"Right," I say and underline his name in my notebook.

Destinee sniffles noisily, and I pull a tissue out of a box on the counter and hand it to her.

"Are you on Karen's social media?" I ask.

"Twitter and Instagram. We post pictures of wedding hair and stuff."

"What about other platforms? Not the work ones."

Destinee shook her head. "Nah, it'd be like following my mum. Don't want to see that."

I can practically hear Pip saying exactly the same thing to her mates about me.

"Are you going to be okay?" I ask, and Destinee sniffs again.

"I'll have to get another job, won't I?" she says, Karen seemingly forgotten.

I get back in my car and wonder how long it will be before everyone else forgets about her, too. But not me. Karen Simmons could be my ticket out of mind-numbing local news. I'm not about to let her fade away.

TWENTY

ELISE

Monday, February 17, 2020

ONE OF THE young detectives was peering sulkily at his screen in the incident room. Elise hovered by the door, fumbling for his name. She remembered that he was new to the team. He'd been assigned because he was from the area, originally. And HQ thought she could use someone with local knowledge. DC . . . ? Did it begin with P?

"Andy," someone called across the room, and the sulker looked up.

Thank you. Elise walked over.

"How are you doing, Andy?" she asked, hoping his full name would come to her. "Are you working Ash Woodward?"

The young detective straightened his face to full attention. "Yes, ma'am," he said.

"I prefer 'boss,'" Elise said. "'Ma'am' makes me sound like the Queen Mother." *DC Andy Thomson* suddenly pinged into her brain, and she acknowledged it with a nod of relief. "Have you found any bird clubs Ash belongs to yet?" she went on.

"I'm just having a look, boss," he said. "They're all nutters, aren't they? Sitting in bushes in their waterproofs, waiting for some crow or something to fly past. Where's the enjoyment in that?"

"Well, be sure to ask when you speak to them."

Elise retreated to her office to look at the sex offenders who lived among the unsuspecting people of Ebbing. They were everywhere—more than sixty thousand nationwide, hidden in communities like this one. Flashers, voyeurs, and pedophiles. Quietly joining in, being good neighbors, picking up milk and bread for the pensioner next door. Until they weren't. Like Nicky Donovan.

Caro had already combed through the names, and a couple of the DCs were out knocking on doors.

She wondered when Mal next door would knock on hers. She'd have to get some beers for the fridge in case he didn't drink wine. And buy some new lipstick.

Elise was still doing her shopping list when Andy Thomson tapped and came in, his face flushed and already talking.

"One of the old birders says Ash Woodward was in trouble when he was a teenager," he blurted.

Elise frowned. "There's nothing on him on the Police National Computer. What sort of trouble?"

"It was something about stealing women's underwear. It must have been hushed up."

It was just a crumb, but he'd been nervous when they spoke to him and had clearly been besotted with Karen. Elise stood, her pulse quickening.

"Okay," she said. "Let's chase it down. Ash is—what?" She looked at her notes. "Thirty-nine? So in his teens in the mid-nineties. Is there anyone still around from this station who might remember?"

"The nineties? That's thirty years ago. They're probably all dead." Thomson grinned.

"Hardly," Elise bristled, trying not to take it personally. The young DC blushed. "Sorry, boss," he muttered as she dialed the duty inspector.

"You want Bill," he said when he'd picked up and she'd told him what she needed to know. "He's a legend here—retired but still living in Southfold. Actually, I think it's the old-timers' lunch at the station today. I'll find his address, but he might be in the canteen. Oh, and can you tell whoever has parked in the chief super's space to move sharpish? He'll go apeshit if that vehicle is still there when he gets in."

"Absolutely," Elise said. Relations with the local force always needed careful handling when the Major Crime Team arrived to run an inquiry. They didn't want to be seen stomping all over Southfold's turf—she'd have to have a word with the team.

BILL WAS SITTING at a table of old boys at the back of the canteen, pushing a plant-based fry-up around his plate.

"Be a love and take this horrible slop away," he said to a passing female officer.

"DC Thomson can do that," Elise said, adding, "can't you, Andy?" when the young detective constable hesitated.

"Right, well, now then," Bill muttered, starting to roll a cigarette for outside. "What can I do you for?"

"We're interested in a local called Ash Woodward," Elise said.

"Ash? Up at the caravan park? He's Gus Woodward's grandson. Gus was desk sergeant here back in the day. He died yonks ago. Had a great send-off. Anyway, why are you asking?"

"He knew our murder victim, Karen Simmons," Elise replied. "He was part of her singles group."

"Was he? Well, I wouldn't figure him for hurting anyone. Ash is soft as lights—he saves birds with broken wings."

"Yes, he said when I spoke to him yesterday. But we've heard something about Ash stealing women's underwear when he was young," Elise said.

Bill licked the gum on the Rizla cigarette paper thoughtfully. "It was nothing," he said. "Stealing underwear off washing lines—a knicker nicker, we called them. You don't get it now, do you? Not now everyone's got a tumble dryer. Anyway, he was caught in the act. Clothes pegs in his mouth."

"And on his nipples, I bet," another old copper at the table snorted. Elise rolled her eyes.

"No, Ash was just a lad—fourteen or fifteen," Bill said. "And every-one liked his granddad, so it was made to disappear." He fluttered his hands like a magician and grinned, but Elise didn't smile back.

"Come on," the old copper said. "He never did it again."

"That we know of," Elise muttered.

TWENTY-ONE

ELISE

Monday, February 17, 2020

"RIGHT. COME ON, DC Thomson, we'll go and talk to the lad at reception first," Elise said to her new sidekick as they arrived at Sunny Sands. She marched into the hut at the gate, and the sullen boy remained scowling at his phone. But he brightened a bit when he caught sight of Thomson and nodded a greeting.

"All right, Andy?" he said.

"Yep. How about you, Luke?" the DC replied, all matey. "How's your rugby training going?"

"Good."

"Is Ash Woodward about?"

"No, he cycled off this morning and I haven't seen him since."

"Hasn't he got a car?" Andy Thomson said, leaning on the counter.

"Nope. He hates them."

"Eco-warrior, is he?"

"Dunno. He's a bit of a pain in the arse, though—him and his birds. He feeds the gulls, you know? They're like rats with wings. And then they crap all over the statics and I have to scrape it off. It sets like concrete, you know."

Elise cleared her throat to break up the lad fest. "Any idea where he went?" she growled.

Luke shrugged without bothering to look at her. "Hey," Elise snapped, exasperated. "I'm talking to you. Ring us when he comes back. This is the number. Okay?" The lad nodded.

"Friend of yours, DC Thomson?" Elise muttered when they got outside.

"Nah, he's just a kid," Andy said. "I used to help with the junior rugby coaching. He's not a bad lad, really."

"Right," she murmured.

She didn't speak when they got back in the car, but as they drove through Ebbing town center, she suddenly instructed DC Thomson to park up. Ash Woodward might return quickly, and Elise didn't want to be driving back and forth all day.

"Okay," Andy chirped. "I'm starving—how about you, boss?"

Andy disappeared into the bakery on the High Street and Elise waited, eyes straying to Mal's house, willing him to come out.

Lines of inquiry were forming a tangled mess in her head. She was trying to unpick and prioritize while fighting off random thoughts of her new neighbor and a fizz of anticipation. *Stop!* she commanded herself and hoped she hadn't said it out loud. She wished she had brought Caro with her instead of Andy Thomson. He was all right, but she couldn't talk to him like her real oppo. But Caro was busy directing the house-to-house. Andy would have to do. She looked around for him.

"Come on, Andy," she said as he emerged from the bakery with a sausage roll. "We're walking Karen's route from the Neptune to her flat. You can eat as we go."

Karen had turned right out of the pub—the newsagent's had CCTV of her leaning her head against their window—and then she must have walked past the fish-and-chips shop, then right, up Shore Drive, where the new houses had been built, and finally left into Creek End. A fifteen-minute walk. *Maybe twenty if you were a bit pissed,* thought Elise. It was all residential—many of the front windows were only feet from the pavement, and there were plenty of streetlights. Karen must have stood out in her red disco dress. But only two witnesses had come forward so far. Both were dog walkers, dragging their pets out in the drizzle for a last pee. They had placed Karen halfway home, on her own, and looking "a bit worse for wear," according to the owner of the golden retriever. "Pebbles was getting wet," the dachshund's mummy had explained, "so we didn't stop."

But had someone else? Had someone offered her a lift? Someone she knew? Would Karen have got into a stranger's car? To get out of the rain? Or because she'd been lonely? She'd had a lot of cocktails, and when you're drunk everyone can look like a friend—or a prospect.

"What do you think happened to Karen?" Elise asked DC Thomson when they stood in front of the salon, looking up at the drawn curtains of the flat.

He swallowed hard, trying to clear a wodge of flaky pastry and pink meat. "My money's on her reaching home safely and picking up her car to drive to Brighton. Because it's disappeared, hasn't it?"

"True. But we haven't picked it up on any of the cameras on the main roads. And where the hell is it now? And if she went to Brighton, why did she end up back in a wood in Ebbing?"

Thomson nodded thoughtfully and stuffed the last inch of his snack into his mouth.

"Maybe she got a lift back with the killer," he mumbled.

TWENTY-TWO

KIKI

Monday, February 17, 2020

I SLAM MY car door shut, my frustration mounting. The so-called briefing was a complete waste of time. The press officer wasn't making eye contact with anyone as she reeled off a series of "no news on this at the moment" to our questions.

"Why have you called this press conference if you haven't got anything new to say?" I complained finally, and she glared at me.

"Because the media wanted one," she snapped. "And we are making a fresh appeal for sightings of the victim's car."

I stomped off afterward. I didn't even bother with the invitation from a couple of reporters to go for a quick drink at the pub. Everything felt like it was being held at the gate: my investigation and the police's. I can hear the rasping growl of my first news editor—a sixty-a-day man with nicotine-stained eyebrows—imparting his wisdom: "When in doubt, go back to the beginning." *Might as well,* I think gloomily. *And then pick up speed. Isn't the scene of the crime where killers return? Maybe he's been back?* I've heard of murderers laying flowers, to revisit the moment. My energy is back full bore, and I roar off like I'm in bloody *Happy Valley* or something. The tires on my ancient VW Golf squeal to the evident alarm of my compadres. "Shit! Where's she going?" I hear the diva from the telly shout to her cameraman.

I laugh as I turn up Taylor Swift on the radio.

THERE IS AN eerie silence when I get to Knapton Wood and turn off my engine. The only sound is the buzz of ideas in my head. I'm the only car, and I give a silent cheer that I've got the place to myself. I head for the first police cordon, daring myself to slip under it and follow the team's trail to the spot where Karen died.

I feel a guilty twinge of relief when a young police community support officer suddenly emerges from the trees and I know I don't have to do it. I'm not as brave as I used to be, when I had a news desk snapping at my heels. Miles would have a conniption if he knew I'd even considered doing it.

The officer is stamping his feet and rubbing his hands together to keep the circulation going.

"You can't come in here, I'm afraid," he calls across in an officious tone. "It's a crime scene."

"Okay, I quite understand," I call back and keep walking toward him. "You look cold," I say. "Did you draw the short straw?"

He half smiles. "Yep, it was my turn to freeze to death," he mutters and blows his nose loudly. "And I left my gloves at the station."

"Have you had many people up here, wanting to have a look?" I step closer and mirror his attempts to stay warm. *We're in this together,* my flapping arms and toe rises are saying, I hope.

"A few," the officer says, waving his tissue at a bedraggled cluster of bouquets and candles on the grass verge.

"Well, the florists are doing well out of it." I grin.

"They always do." He grins back. "People have been leaving stuff since Saturday. Local women, mainly, but the misery tourists always turn up, don't they? I think some of them just want to get on the telly. You see them hang back until the TV crews start filming."

"I bet. So just women?"

"Well, a few blokes. Why?"

"I'm writing about the murder," I murmur, and see his mouth harden. "Just a color piece," I add hastily, "about Karen and how the locals are coping with this happening in their town."

"It is just horrible," he says bluntly. "My family's in Ebbing, and my sister was in tears on the phone about noises in the garden last night."

"Poor thing," I say gently. His face softens.

"What about the men?" I go on. "How are they doing? It must be awful having people look at them as potential predators."

The CSO nods. "Yeah, I've just had Ash Woodward from Sunny Sands up here all upset." I feel an anticipatory tingle in my fingers. Ash of the haircuts. Had he come back to the scene?

"He's a nice bloke," the officer continues. "A bit quiet for some people—but he's no trouble. Very upset about this, though."

"Were he and Karen very close?"

The officer shrugs. "Dunno, to be honest, but someone will if you ask around. Ebbing's a small town. Everyone knows everyone round here. And their business."

"Sounds cozy," I say and struggle not to pull a face. It actually sounds bloody claustrophobic to me. It's why I've always lived in cities—the sort of neighborhoods where you can say hello to the same shopkeepers every day but lie dead for months without anyone noticing. That wouldn't happen in Ebbing. They'd miss you the first morning. But with that kind of daily scrutiny, I imagine people must have to bury their secrets very deep.

"Did Ash say anything to you when he turned up?" I push him on.

"Um, just was it okay to put his flowers down."

"He brought flowers?" I squeak, resisting the urge to hug him.

"Didn't I say? Yeah, red roses from the Co-op." I try not to run—I don't want the officer knowing how eager I am, but I walk straight over to the floral tributes and search through the sodden mass of leaves and packaging. Where there are flowers, there are messages.

Ash's are right at the back, despite being the most recently laid, like he's hidden them on purpose. There's nothing stuck to the packaging. I swear under my breath and am about to shove them back. But then I spot it. A scrap of paper poked down in the leaves. I almost tear it in my hurry to see what it says. There are just five words. "Sorry. I loved you. Ash."

Sorry for what? I think as I straighten up. *That she's dead? Or for something he did to her?*

TWENTY-THREE

ELISE

Monday, February 17, 2020

WHEN ELISE FINALLY got home that night, it was too late to eat, so she made a cup of herbal tea and sat in the window, looking out at the High Street. She might have seen the victim if she'd looked out of her front window on Friday. The pub was directly opposite the fisherman's cottage on Ebbing High Street that Elise had bought two years ago. There'd been a time, just after her mastectomy, when she'd spent hours at the window, eyes on the street, rediscovering the addictive buzz of surveillance.

But she was back at her real job now, and some days the curtains never got opened. The night Karen had died, Elise had spent her Valentine's evening catching up on paperwork, transcribing reminders onto the clutch of neon-colored Post-its in her pockets.

She was in the kitchen when someone knocked on the door. She glanced up at the clock. Who the hell was knocking at nine thirty? Work would have rung, not turned up at her house. Ronnie? She really wasn't in the mood, but she crept back to her window to look, just in case. And there he was, standing with a bottle of wine in one hand. Elise saw him spot the twitch of the curtain and smile. She smiled back and went to let him in. She hadn't bought the lippie or beer, but at least she wasn't in her pajamas.

"Hi. Hope I'm not too late, but I saw your lights on. I'll only stay for five minutes," Mal said when she opened the door. He stood back. Not pushing his way in.

"No, no, come in. I've got some work to finish, but I can do that in a bit," Elise said, automatically introducing her escape strategy.

He ducked his head as he entered and seemed to fill the tiny front room while she cleared her laptop and files off the sofa. He was a bit older than she'd thought, but he was Elise's physical type: taller than her, which was always a bonus, strong, and athletic. His sandy-colored hair was a bit thin, but then, so was hers.

"Come and sit," she said. "Can I get you a drink?"

"I, er, I brought a bottle with me." He handed it over and she picked up the slight stammer. Was he as nervous as her? Her stomach un-clenched a notch. "But I'm happy with anything that's open," he added.

"This looks great—I'll get the glasses." She went and stood in the kitchen and took deep breaths. This was a casual drink. Nothing heavy. But he made her feel . . . oh, God, he made her feel like she used to. When she was still a woman. Not a diagnosis. Not a struggling boss. Just her. And it felt bloody wonderful. She pinched her cheeks to get a bit of color going. Flashed a smile at herself in the window. And strode back in.

He was looking at the handful of books on her shelf. "I've read this one," he said, pulling out a thriller. Elise hadn't. Ronnie had pressed it on her and she'd shoved it on the shelf.

"I don't get much time for reading," Elise murmured.

"You certainly work long hours," Mal said and went a bit pink. "Sorry, I'm not watching you or anything. It's just that you usually park under my bedroom window."

Elise laughed. "Don't worry. It's hard not to notice, living side by side like this. Have you met Ronnie yet?"

Mal grinned and his eyes lit up. They were blue. Elise wondered when she'd last noticed the color of a man's eyes outside of a witness description. "Oh, yes!" he said. "She finally caught me today and gave me the third degree. The estate agent warned me she's a bit of a sticky beak."

Elise felt herself bristle. Even if Ronnie was a terminal busybody, she was still her friend.

"Perhaps. But she's been wonderful since my cancer was diagnosed," she said, and wanted to bite her tongue off. Why had she mentioned her cancer? It would be all he could think of now. All he'd remember about her when he left.

"Poor you. My mum had it, too," he said, suddenly serious. "The treatment is awful, isn't it? But you look great. Right, well, cheers." He clinked their glasses lightly and moved the conversation on. "I think I'm going to like it here."

"Where were you before?" Elise said gratefully.

"All over the place, really. In the military for a bit and then working for a digital marketing company. How about you?"

"I work for the police. So what brought you to Ebbing?" *Stop interviewing him,* she silently screamed at herself. *He's not a suspect!*

"The sea. I love swimming and surfing. I'd prefer warmer water, but I can't afford Hawaii. Do you go in?"

"You must be joking—I'm defrosting my car some mornings. Sounds like cruel and unusual punishment to me."

"It certainly gets the blood racing," he laughed. "So, police? Where are you based?"

Here we go.

"Sussex HQ. Major Crime Team."

"Oh," he said and took a mouthful of wine.

She hated this moment. Judgment. Morbid fascination. Being a detective could provoke extreme reactions. She wondered what he'd ask next. Would it be *Have you ever met a serial killer?* Or would he make his excuses and scuttle off—and leave her wondering if he was hiding something?

"I applied to join the police when I left school," he said. "But they turned me down. Don't know why—I certainly met the height requirements." Elise laughed with him. "But I probably wasn't bright enough," he added.

"I'm sure that's not true," she said, touched by his honesty. "Can I top you up?" She could feel the gravitational tug of attraction in her chest and stomach and immediately blushed. Mal offered up his glass and steadied the bottle as she poured too quickly. Brushing her fingers. He had beautiful hands.

He finally left at gone eleven—"Sorry to keep you up on a school night"—and Elise sat for a few minutes to steady herself.

Well, that was nice, she told herself. *More than nice.*

Mal had made her laugh a lot and even persuaded her to consider sea swimming. She'd found herself wondering where she'd put that halter-neck swimsuit Hugh used to love. She could wear her prosthetic insert she still hadn't got used to. And there was no Mrs. Mal. He'd said moving around with the army had meant he'd missed the boat when it came to marriage. He'd stood close to her as he said good-bye and she'd inhaled his scent. Clean. Slightly salty.

In the kitchen, rinsing the wineglasses, Elise found herself imagining kissing him and caught sight of her reflection in the window. Grinning like a monkey. *Oh, get over yourself,* she thought suddenly. *Why would he be interested in you?* Her damp hand went to the shiny scar that snaked across her chest into her armpit. She couldn't let anyone see her naked now. She'd moved the full-length mirror out of her bedroom after the mastectomy, preferring to see herself exclusively from the shoulders up, like a portrait in a gallery.

She looked back at her reflection in the window and found that she was no longer smiling.

TUESDAY:
DAY 4

TWENTY-FOUR

ANNIE

Tuesday, February 18, 2020

ANNIE KNEW SHE should have been getting ready for work, but her mind kept sliding over the latest row, snagging on the details. She tried to drink the cup of tea that Gavin had put in front of her half an hour ago, but her hand was trembling too much to hold it straight.

"Come home," her youngest was saying quietly in the hall, and Annie's stomach lurched. Was he ringing Henry? *I need to talk to him first.* But it wasn't his dad. "Xander, there was another big row last night and Dad's gone off," he whispered. "I don't know—they were shouting about Archie and other stuff... No, no one called the police. But, Xander, can you come home? Please."

When Gavin came back in, he sat opposite her. White-faced and stricken. "Xander's coming," he said.

"But he's working. And he's only just been down. Ring him back and say he doesn't need to," Annie said. "I've told you everything's fine."

But they both knew that was a lie.

"And you need to go to your rugby training," Annie said.

"I can go in later," her son said, his lips trembling. "Where do you think Dad is?"

"I'm not sure, love, but he'll be back soon," Annie said, trying to sound confident, but she felt sick. Henry had turned off his phone after he'd walked out. She'd lain awake, frantic with worry, most of the night. Now she waited until Gavin had gone upstairs, then called Henry's number and almost shouted with relief when it started ringing.

"Annie," he said when he picked up, voice cracking. "Oh, Annie, I'm so sorry. I was about to ring you. Are you okay? I just don't know what is happening to us."

"I know. I'm all right. But where are you? I've been so worried."

"I slept in my car. Look, I'm on my way home. I want to make this right. I should be back in twenty minutes. Is that okay? Is Gavin at training? Did he hear us?"

"He's upset, but let's talk when you get home. Drive carefully." She ended the call and sat in the window to watch for his car.

He looked terrible when he walked up the path. His face was gray and gaunt, his shirt untucked on one side, and Annie wanted to put her arms around him.

"Oh, love," he called softly as he opened the door and saw her standing there. But before Annie could speak, Gavin appeared at the top of the stairs.

"Dad?" he said, and stood looking at them. Annie felt like they were characters in a soap opera, face-acting through another horrible plot twist.

"Come into the kitchen, Henry," Annie said. "Can you give us a moment, Gav?" He nodded uncertainly, but she heard him tiptoe down the stairs as they went through. She knew he wanted to be on hand in case things escalated again, and Annie blew him a kiss in her head.

Henry took her face in his hands, and she could see the fear and distress in his eyes.

"Darling, I didn't mean it to blow up like that," he said. "I was so upset after what you said. About me trying to forget Archie. You know I'm not. How could I? I loved the bones of him. Why did you say those awful things? I just wanted you to stop." *My fault, then,* rang in her head.

Annie was suddenly too exhausted to speak. So she simply nodded and Henry put his arms around her and held her close. And it was over. It would all get put away again. Like it always did. Buried with everything else.

XANDER ARRIVED AN hour later, rushing up the path from the taxi and into the kitchen, where they were still sitting. In all the emotion, Annie had forgotten he was coming, and Henry looked shocked.

"Xander? What are you doing back here?" he said as their eldest came through the door.

"Never mind that. What the hell has been going on?" Xander said too loudly, and Annie looked up at him.

"Mum? Are you okay?" he blurted.

Henry got up and stood behind Annie's chair.

"Your mum and I had a silly row last night," he said. Speaking for both of them again. "But we've sorted it out. It's good of you to come, Xander, but there really was no need."

Xander didn't even look at him. He couldn't take his eyes off his mother's face. And she had to look away.

TWENTY-FIVE

ELISE

Tuesday, February 18, 2020

RONNIE WAS WAVING over the fence when Elise looked up from her toast. She lifted her hand without enthusiasm. It was a bit early for heart-to-hearts. But her neighbor clearly didn't think so, bursting through the back gate and door and flicking on the kettle.

"Well?" she said.

"Well what?" Elise said, playing for time.

"You had a visitor last night? I knew he would call. He said he was going to."

"Who?"

"Who! Mr. Gorgeous from next door, as you well know."

Elise tried not to grin, but it got away from her.

"Ha! He did." Ronnie sniggered triumphantly. "Go on, then—how did it go? Was there snogging?"

"Back off, Ronnie. It was just a glass of wine and a chat."

Ronnie smiled broadly. "Right," she said. "That's for next time, then. What did you find out? Did he tell you he used to be in the military?"

"Yes, yes. He said you'd got to him first."

"Yup. Finally cornered him in the Co-op. Got him to reach me a bag of pasta from the top shelf—I don't know why they put it up there. Anyway, he was very charming. And lovely hands."

"I didn't notice," Elise said primly, but then ruined it by grinning again. "Anyway, how come you were at your listening post last night? I thought it was book club at the library."

"No. It was canceled," Ronnie said. "No one wants to come out after dark. Not at the moment."

Elise sighed. "People just need to be sensible," she said.

"Women, you mean," Ronnie said. "And why should we? Men need to stop attacking us."

"Yes," Elise said wearily. "But while they still are, women need to look after themselves."

"Funny you should say that," Ronnie chirped.

"Oh, God. What are you up to now?"

"I'm starting a WhatsApp group for me and my friends to stay in touch and report any new suspicious characters in the town. And I'm recruiting men to walk us home when it's dark. We're having a meeting tonight in the Neptune—you should come."

"Wouldn't it be better to get your community officer to attend?" Elise said, idly sweeping crumbs off the table into her hand.

"I don't mean as a copper," Ronnie snorted. "As a woman. As a local. You do live here."

Elise stood to shove her plate in the dishwasher. She'd still be a copper, though, wouldn't she?

"And Mal and his lovely hands might come," Ronnie added.

"Too busy," Elise muttered. "I'm absolutely up against it at work." But she was already thinking about what she'd wear as she picked up her work bag.

"WE'VE GOT KAREN'S car," Caro said, head round Elise's office door as soon as her boss got in.

"Excellent." She jumped to her feet. "Where is it?"

"Brighton. Looks like Karen did go nightclubbing after all. Andy

Thomson has phoned it in—it's in a multistory in Brighton. Top floor, where the security guard couldn't be arsed to check. Do you want to go over there now?"

"Good on Andy," Elise said. "Let's make sure to name-check him in the team meeting."

THE FIAT 500 was poked into a dank corner on the eighth floor, out of range of cameras.

"Well done, Andy," Elise said, breathless after the climb. The young officer beamed as he strode over. "God, it stinks up here," Elise wheezed.

"The nearest public toilets are padlocked at six o'clock," he replied. "Needs must, I suppose."

"Is the car locked?"

"No. The key was in the driver's footwell."

"Careless," Elise said, "but we don't know what state she was in when she arrived."

Elise and Caro pulled on gloves and opened the doors. Both knelt on the concrete floor to look under the seats, but there was no sign of Karen's handbag or phone. Or anything else.

"This looks like it's just left the showroom," Elise said. "Let's give it to forensics and go and talk to the security guard."

He was waiting for them in his office, already tucking into his lunch.

"This place isn't automated," he said, his mouth full of tuna sandwich and crisps. Elise glimpsed a shred of lettuce caught in his teeth and fixed her gaze on his bank of camera shots instead. "You park and buy a ticket from the machine and put it in your car. Old-school. We go round and check them every hour."

"Were you on duty last Friday night? Valentine's Day?"

"Yeah. It was busy."

"And did you see this Fiat 500 on the top floor?" Elise showed him the car on her phone.

He took another bite of his disgusting sandwich, wiping a gobbet of mayonnaise off some paperwork, while he considered his answer.

"No," he said. "My last trip up to the top was at oh-one-hundred, according to my log. I had to use the stairwell because the bloody lift was acting up again and I didn't want to get stuck in it all night. I didn't bother again—everyone's gone home by that time in the morning, anyway."

"But not this car."

"No, well."

"And since then? Why did no one spot it?"

"You'd have to ask the others. But the lift still isn't fixed."

"Yes, I noticed." Elise put a protective hand to her heart. "But surely the car is on one of your security cameras?"

He fiddled with the images on a screen. "There's only a few working—the people who own this place won't invest in new ones," he said. "They're only interested in the money coming in."

"Hold on, is that it?" Elise cried, jabbing a finger at the rear of a vehicle disappearing up a ramp. "Go back, go back!" The guard pushed the wrong button and the film whizzed forward.

"Sorry." He grinned, and Elise clenched her hands into fists. Pinpointing the arrival of the car was crucial for their timeline. If they could identify the driver as Karen, they could refocus their investigation.

The images ran backward and then stopped on the car. She could make out most of the number plate. It was Karen's.

"What time was that?" she snapped.

"Oh-one-sixteen," the guard said sulkily. "I was probably walking down the stairs at that point."

"Let's hope the digital team can clean up the images to get the driver," Caro said when they got outside.

"So, Brighton's only a forty-five-minute drive from Ebbing," Elise said. "But the car didn't get here for nearly three hours after Karen's last text to Mina Ryan. Where was she in between? Have we got the data on her mobile phone yet?"

"No, but wherever it was, she didn't take major roads—there are no sightings of her car on the number plate recognition cameras," Caro said.

"And . . ." Elise started and stopped. She felt her thread of thoughts snap, leaving her flailing. "And" now stood like a monolith in her head. Blocking her way forward.

"What?" Caro said.

"And . . . Oh, shit, I can't remember what I was saying."

"It'll come back to you," Caro said.

"Will it?" Elise muttered. "Oh, wait. Yes, I wouldn't have parked my car on the deserted top floor of a run-down multistory at one o'clock in the morning. You'd have to get into a lift with God knows who or take that scary stairwell. I'd have parked near the guard. Or on the street."

"True," Caro said.

"And where would she have gone from here at that time of night? Where was still open? How are we doing with the bars and nightclubs? Did I ask DC Thomson earlier?"

"Er, no," Caro said. "Slow down, boss. I'll chase him up."

Elise wanted to say she was perfectly capable of doing her own chasing, but she didn't have to pretend with Caro. Just everyone else.

She rang the digital team for an update on Karen's phone while Caro drove.

"The phone stopped transmitting at twenty-three forty on the night of the fourteenth. Last location was in Creek End—the victim's home and business address," the techie told her.

"Thanks," Elise said. She hung up and sat staring out at the traffic. "Did she turn it off at home?" she asked Caro. "Or did someone else?"

TWENTY-SIX

KIKI

Tuesday, February 18, 2020

"GOT HIM," MILES says, throwing himself down in the chair at the next desk over and crashing it into mine.

"Whoa!" I snap. "What?"

"X-Man," Miles crows, and I yelp, all irritation with him evaporating in an instant. "You star bot," I yell, and we laugh together—a warm, fuzzy bonding moment of sorts.

"So," he says, his voice high with excitement. "Luckily, X-Man has been pretty careless with his security and identities. He's called Simon Allman in real life. And he's from Portslade. You should see some of his posts on the BOBs forum—stands for Band of Brothers. Anyway, he's a total tosser. But what are you going to do with this info?"

"I'm going to get him to tell me how he knew Karen. And, hopefully, the IDs of the rest of the group who were trolling her online. Look, I think a man called Ash Woodward could be associated with them. Can you plug his name into your search?"

"Right." He notes it down. "You do your thing and I'll do mine."

I beam my appreciation and click on the link Miles has sent. I'm looking at Simon's dating app profile. He's no Hugh Jackman but is less creepy than some of the others who've Liked me. "Looking for love," his pitch reads, and I swipe him. Within half an hour, I'm choosing a wine bar in the city center for our date tonight. I avoid the station pub in case Eamonn comes looking to make good his investment.

My mother tuts when I ask her to babysit for a second evening in three days.

"You never go out, usually. I have got a life, too," she complains.

"It's for work, Ma. I wouldn't ask you, but I'm hoping to be paid extra to do this—and I need the money if Pip is going on the school ski trip."

"Are you sure she wants to go? She doesn't do any sport—apart from Olympic-class TikTok."

"I don't know—she seems dead set on it."

"Are boys going?"

"Yup. And lots of teachers. So, don't fret."

But I know she will. Pip is thirteen. A dangerous age, as Ma and I both know. I was a mare at thirteen—bunking off school to shoplift mascara in Boots and hang out with the excluded kids. It didn't last that long—one nightmare year, tops, until Dad got a new job and we moved away from the problem. But mothers never forget.

I spray perfume behind my ears, keen to look and smell the part.

"Wow, that's horrible," Pip says, appearing behind my reflection in the mirror. She's wearing too much eyeliner, but I bite my tongue.

"I've got some samples from my magazines you can use if you like." She offers me her wrist to smell.

"Hmm, lovely, but I'll stick with mine. Be good for Grandma, and bed by nine."

"Nine? Seriously, Mum? No one goes to bed that early. And it's half term!"

"Start getting up in the morning without moaning and maybe you can stay up later. Night night, gorgeous girl." I kiss her head and sling my handbag across my body.

X-MAN HAS ARRIVED first and is fidgeting with his trendy glasses and watching the door when I walk in. At least he looks like his photo.

"Hi," I say. "You must be Simon."

The man at the table nods, struggles to his feet, and, when he tries to speak, looks like he's about to burst into tears.

"Oh, Christ, are you okay?" I say, completely wrong-footed. People at adjoining tables are trying not to stare, and I start to panic. "Why don't we sit down," I mutter. Bloody hell! It can't be something I've said. Not yet, anyway.

"I am so sorry," Simon whimpers from behind a tissue. "It's just it's my first time since my wife, Rosie, passed. She died just before Christmas."

Seriously? Well, this is going well.

Simon smiles bravely through damp lashes. "I'll be all right in a minute. Maybe we could just have a drink?"

"Sure—shall I go and get them?"

"Thanks—that's so kind of you. Can I have a brandy? I still feel a bit wobbly," he says. "Take my credit card. I'm really sorry. God knows what you must think of me. I wouldn't blame you if you made your excuses."

"No, no," I murmur. "Back in a mo." I'm grateful for the thinking time. Could this weepy bloke really be a predator? Bloody Eamonn must have given me a bum steer. The disappointment leaches all my energy, and I have to force myself to burrow into the scrum at the bar. I'll get him his brandy, then make tracks.

I check on him in the mirror behind the optics. He's sitting with his head bowed, and I feel a stab of shame that I've raised a lonely man's hopes by swiping him under false pretenses. But when he looks up, Simon isn't crying anymore. He looks down again, but I can see he's typing on his phone. And, bloody hell, he's grinning. I wrestle my phone out and pull up the forum that Miles dug out, and there my date is. "Game on!" X-Man posted thirty seconds ago. "Hot widower gambit aces it."

Gotcha! God, he almost had me with his disgusting pantomime. Is this what he did with Karen? Cry her into bed? Then abuse her with his mates? Rage is making my hands tremble, and I have to breathe deeply to bring it under control. I'm in charge of this situation, now. He'd better buckle up.

"Feeling better?" I appear at the table out of left field so he doesn't have time to get the tissue back to his eyes.

"Er, yes, thanks," he says, flipping his phone over and taking a mouthful of the brandy. "It's a terrible thing to lose someone."

"Yes," I say quietly and pull my own sad face. "Actually, a woman I know died last week. Lovely girl. She was only forty-five."

He shoots me a worried glance. This clearly isn't the way the conversation is supposed to be going. "Oh, I'm sorry to hear that," he says, his concern so fake I want to slap him. "Er, what happened? Was she in an accident?"

"No." I pause, pretending to choke on my words, milking the drama. "Someone killed her," I croak.

"Really?" Simon rocks back in his seat.

"Yes, it was in the papers." I watch his face slowly brighten as it dawns on him.

"Not Karen Simmons?" he breathes.

I nod miserably.

"I knew her, too," Simon says, all excited. His "dead wife" act apparently forgotten. "I went on a couple of dates with her."

"No! Did you?" I say, pretending to hang on his every word. "When was that?"

"Er, last month. Yeah, I couldn't believe it when I saw it on the local news. She called herself LaDiva when we hooked up, but I recognized her from her photo straightaway. She was nice, but she drank so much the last time she threw up in the back of my car." *And that's why you deducted two points.* "I told my mates it was worth the cleaning bill."

"Your mates?" I say sharply.

A bead of perspiration forms on his hairline, and he brushes it away with a finger. "Just blokes I chat with online. We share intel sometimes."

"Intel about Karen?"

"Well, just that she was a bit of a drinker—some blokes don't like that in a woman."

"Right. I hear you also told your mates that she always said yes."

Sweat is now making his forehead glisten, and a single drop runs down the side of his face before he can get his tissue back out of his pocket.

"Who told you that?" he grunts. "How did you know her, anyway?"

"I met her when I was writing a feature on online dating."

He freezes mid-mop. "Fuck! You're a reporter!"

"Yep," I say and move my stool closer to him. "So, who did you tell about Karen?"

"Er, just blokes on chat rooms. I don't know them."

"So you told a bunch of strangers humiliating and explicit details about Karen Simmons? Just weeks before she was killed?"

His eyes are practically popping out of his head. "No, well, er, yes. Look, I don't have to answer your questions." He stumbles to a stand-still. "This is a con."

"Ha!" I laugh. "That's rich coming from you. And, just so you know, I'll be sharing my intel on your MO online."

The length of the hesitation is a confession in itself.

"What MO?" he finally blusters.

"The hot widower gambit. Oh, and quick tip: You really need to check your script. According to your dating profile, your fox terrier is called Rosie."

Simon drains his glass and mutters, "I'll get my coat, then."

I throw his credit card in the bin outside the pub and catch the bus home, fuming about his betrayal of Karen and trying to envisage a scenario in which I would invent a dead spouse in order to have sex with someone. *Not happening.*

I write my first column when I get home, while I'm still angry, my fingers punishing the keyboard.

TWENTY-SEVEN

ELISE

Tuesday, February 18, 2020

THE PATHOLOGIST TOOK an age to answer her mobile, and Elise drummed her fingers on her temples to ease the building tension.

"Elise," Dr. Aoife Mortimer finally barked accusingly down the phone. "I was in the middle of something. Is this urgent?"

"Well . . ."

"Look, I'm still waiting for bloods and fluids to come back from the lab to complete my report, but I can give you a couple of headlines," Aoife said, voice softening slightly. "Particles of debris from the victim's nostrils, mouth cavity, and throat are consistent with soil and leaf mold samples from the spot where she was found."

"Her attacker must have held her down as if he was drowning her," Elise said, scribbling notes.

"Her blood alcohol was high," the pathologist went on, refusing to take part in Elise's hypothesizing. "She was legally intoxicated and likely to have had impaired decision-making function and been unsteady on her feet."

"That's what three Pink Ladies and a couple of glasses of wine will do," Elise said.

"Quite. She put up a struggle—you saw the fake nails that came off—but she would probably have lost consciousness within two to three minutes."

"God, that must have felt like a lifetime," Elise said, running through the hideous stages of suffocation in her mind: air hunger; blind, thrashing panic; and the clawing struggle against death. Then oblivion.

Karen had fought for her life. Elise needed to fight for the truth.

She was so knackered when she got home that night that she simply pulled on a sweatshirt over her work clothes and flicked some mascara around her lashes before heading over to the pub for the launch of Ronnie's vigilantes.

Her neighbor was holding court at the bar, surrounded by Postie Val, Mina Ryan, Destinee Amos and her mum, plus three or four others Elise didn't recognize. A handful of men were sitting around a table near the window, trying to make themselves heard over Tom Jones's greatest hits.

"What are you drinking, Elise?" Ronnie said as she reached the bar.

"Er, Diet Coke, please. I'm still working."

"That's good," Doll Harman said as she poured. "But are you getting anywhere? Are you any closer to catching this man?"

"She's been to see Barry Sherman," Mrs. Amos added. "But he's still strutting around the Lobster. And trying it on with all and sundry."

"Barry is just a bit of a show-off," Mina said.

"Who has he been trying it on with?" Elise asked.

"A couple of the young ones round here," Doll said. "His waitresses, I've heard. But someone's mum had a word and he backed off. Perhaps they've had a lucky escape."

"Stop it, Doll!" Mina blurted. "You can't think he had anything to do with Karen's death."

"Not death—murder," Mrs. Amos chipped back in. "And how do you know? Just because he's in your Free Spirits circle? It could be anyone. I know I'm checking the back door is locked every five minutes."

"And I'm not sleeping," Destinee murmured. "I keep hearing noises and think someone is breaking in."

Gloves off straightaway. I should never have come.

"Look, I know how worrying this must be and how upset you all are," Elise said carefully, "but I really can't discuss the case. All I can say is that the police investigation is ongoing."

The women's mouths hardened.

"Well, I'm looking out for unfamiliar faces on my rounds—it won't be anyone local," Postie Val said as if Elise hadn't spoken. "Silly woman was meeting strangers."

"For Christ's sake, Val!" Mina snapped. "Have some respect. Anyway, why shouldn't Karen have had an active love life? She was just having fun. She wasn't the predator."

"Well, you say that." Doll pursed her lips. "But she was eyeing up the men so openly at the Valentine's do, I had to come over and say something."

As if on cue, "Sex Bomb" echoed round the bar.

"Don't exaggerate. She was just having a laugh," Mina said, close to tears. "Blokes do it all the time, but they don't get labeled slags."

Elise flashed Ronnie a warning look.

"Right, well, why don't we get this meeting started?" her neighbor said and moved off. "Ted, make some room," she barked at her husband, "and pull that other table over, can you?"

Elise hovered at the back of the group, wondering if she could quietly peel off without anyone noticing, when Mal suddenly stood to help rearrange the furniture.

"Hello," he said over the heads. "I didn't know you'd be here. Thanks for the drink last night—I really enjoyed it."

"So did I," she murmured, stomach fluttering. She was acutely conscious of the twitching of lips as the other women absorbed the exchange and stashed it for later examination.

Elise took a deep breath, sat down beside Ted, and sipped her drink.

Half an hour later, names had been drawn out of a beer glass for the Safe Ebbing buddy system, numbers had been typed into phones, and a new round of drinks had been ordered. Faces were flushed, and voices rose to talk over one another.

Elise shifted in her seat, preparing to get out of there while the going was good. And caught Mal's eye.

"Walk you home?" he mouthed. And she smiled her acceptance back and swallowed hard.

The group raised their glasses in mock salute as they left, and a buzz of conversation rose behind them as Elise closed the door.

"Well, that's given them something else to think about," she said, and Mal laughed.

"Do you fancy dinner this week?" he said at her front door.

Out of the corner of her eye, Elise could see Ronnie's face practically pressed against the pub window opposite. "I, er, I . . . well, yes. But I might have to cancel last minute—it's a tricky time with work."

"Course. Understood, but let's talk Thursday and see how you're fixed for the weekend?"

"Okay. Good plan."

"See you by the bins." He grinned. "Sleep tight."

INSIDE, ELISE SAT making notes for the morning and wondering how long she'd got. Ronnie didn't disappoint. Twenty minutes later, she was installed on the sofa, combing out Mal's offer of dinner. "Did he say where? You can't go to the Lobster, can you? Awks. What about that fancy fish place in Wittering?"

"Go home, Ronnie," Elise laughed. "Ted will be waiting for his cocoa."

"He's your problem now. Ted's your buddy—don't you remember? Well, you were distracted, weren't you . . . You drew the short straw and got my husband as your emergency escort. Think you'll be protecting him—Ted couldn't fight his way out of a wet paper bag."

Poor Ted. But I don't suppose I'll have to put him to the test.

"Who got Mal?" she murmured. Just asking.

"Ha! Mina won the raffle, but you snaffled him before she could get him to walk her home. She stormed off on her own after you left. It's not like her, to be honest. She's a bit of a mouse since her divorce—she relied on Karen for her social life. But Mina was really upset by the remarks about Karen. The meeting broke up pretty quickly after that. I don't know. It was supposed to bring the community together, but you just can't help some people."

WEDNESDAY:
DAY 5

TWENTY-EIGHT

ELISE

Wednesday, February 19, 2020

ELISE KNEW NOTHING about the candlelit vigil until Ronnie button-holed her first thing in the newsagent's.

"A vigil? Er, okay," Elise said, rummaging through the evening's conversations in her head but coming up with nothing. "I don't remember anyone mentioning it last night. Did they?"

Ronnie squeezed her arm warmly. "No, don't worry—and anyway, it's just a few friends," she chirped. "Mina emailed me this morning and said she decided on her way home—she was so furious about what people were saying. Blaming Karen and such. She just wants us to remember Karen as she was: a lovely, funny woman who'd do anything for anyone."

A care assistant in a pink nylon tunic tutted loudly beside them and squeezed past, her face stiff with righteous indignation.

"And the women are the worst," Ronnie added loudly enough to turn heads in the queue at the counter. "Not much sisterly solidarity in Ebbing."

"It makes people feel safer," Elise murmured, trying to reach past an indecisive pensioner for some mints. "If they can point at reasons why it won't happen to them."

"Hmm!" Ronnie grumbled.

"A vigil could make people think about her differently, I suppose," Elise said carefully as she paid and edged toward the door. "I hope they're telling the local police."

RONNIE CAUGHT UP with Elise across the street and grinned. "Well, I've put her right—how can she call herself a carer, for God's sake? Her ears must be buzzing now. Anyway, are you going to come tonight?"

"Absolutely," Elise said. She'd have Karen's circle of friends and acquaintances in one place, sharing stories about her. Someone might know more about her love life than Mina Ryan was saying. "How many are going?"

"Mina says she's hoping for about twenty or thirty. We're gathering in the car park at seven o'clock. Mina's going to say a few words, and we'll have a two-minute silence. And if the witches of Ebbing don't like it, tough."

When Elise rolled up at Southfold police station, she passed on the details to the duty inspector and they discussed a discreet police presence in case there was any trouble. "I don't think anyone will bother traipsing up to Knapton Wood to denounce poor Karen Simmons, but if it's a quiet night on the telly . . ." she said.

"Have you seen this vigil stuff?" Caro called over to her as soon as she walked into the incident room.

"Yep, it's just a few of Karen's customers," Elise said, shrugging off her coat. "A local car's going to drive by to keep an eye on it, and I'm going."

"I hope it's just a few customers, but there's some traffic on social media—women tweeting about Karen, saying she should have been safe walking home."

"We don't even know if she was taken off the street." Elise growled her frustration. "Bloody hell, it's tense enough in the town—people sniping about Karen and at one another. I get that they're frightened, but this could really stoke things up."

TWENTY-NINE

KIKI

Wednesday, February 19, 2020

KAREN IS STARING out of practically every shopwindow in the High Street. Eyes flashing accusingly at me and the people of Ebbing, scrutinizing our every move. And I wonder if the killer is among us. One of the anonymous BOBs? Or someone closer to home? Feeling himself being watched by his victim. I shiver and glance around quickly, but there are only two old ducks trudging along, arm in arm.

I slip into the doorway of an empty shop and check the number of comments on my column. They're going up, but I'm furious with the company high-ups for taking out Simon's name. They didn't even ask me before they did it. The word came down via Miles, who had the grace to look a bit sheepish. "It could cost us money if he sues. Invasion of privacy or something," he parroted.

I go back to flicking through the forums, my fingers stiff with cold, looking for X-Man back on the prowl. The thought that I should call Elise King and tell her about him nags at me, but I just need Miles to pull his finger out and identify the rest of the brotherhood first. I want to be a couple of steps ahead. This is my story. My work. And anyway, I've written about it, so it's in the public domain. And the police can call me for more details when they see it. I tell myself I'll give Elise a call in a couple of days. Then all thoughts of right and wrong are swept away as I see the new post.

Here he is! Good old Simon has posted about me on a BOBs thread—I'm "REPORTER BITCH" in shouty capitals, not named, just identified as a snaky female who tricked him. I start to type a blast of invective in response but delete it. *Don't show out, you idiot. They'll disappear back under their stones. Change their names. And you'll lose them.* I switch to Danny's identity and fake email I created for the dating app and post: "The media is scum." And keep a silent watch on them. I just hope they reveal themselves quickly.

But in the meantime, I've got to find something to push the story on—online news is like a great white shark: It dies if it stops moving forward, and all I'm getting is the drip, drip, drip of pointless police briefings. There was nothing about the murder in the national papers this morning, and even Miles is bored with it. "Nothing's happening," he sighed at his desk. "It's just 'police are investigating' every day. Blah, blah, blah."

"That's how murder inquiries work," I told him. "It's not a video game where you run around town bashing down doors."

"No, well, take a look at the crash on the A3 last night, can you? There's a spectacular video clip—you can see it about to happen and then, *pow*, the lorry hits three cars. Pity there isn't sound."

I ground my teeth and stretched what should have been a two-hundred-word story into one of those interminable online articles, each paragraph repeating the same sparse facts with a dozen photos and clips. Then I put my coat on and was out the door before Miles could wrest his eyes off the screen in front of him.

I'm reduced to videoing Ebbing High Street, lingering on the frontage of the Neptune with a couple of leftover hearts stuck to its windows while I wait for inspiration to strike. But it's too bloody chilly.

In the end I give up and seek sanctuary in the Ebb and Flo café. I'm hit by a wave of warm, damp air when I swing the door open. The clientele looks up as one. They all seem to be making their toasted tea cakes last while watching condensation run down inside the panes of glass. The eponymous Flo calls over to me: "What can I get you, love?"

"Tea, please. And a piece of lemon drizzle."

"Good choice. I made it this morning. Lovely and sticky."

"Thanks, I need a treat." I smile at her. "I'm covering the murder case. It's a bit heavy going."

Flo leans in immediately. "You're a reporter?"

"Yes," I say, hoping I'm not going to get an earful about the media and the many reasons to hate it. I try not to let it affect me—and it doesn't most days—but Simon's nasty rant has rattled me more than it should.

"It's a shocker, isn't it?" Flo smiles back. "Karen came in here on a Sunday morning sometimes. She used to treat Mina and Mina's little boy to brunch. He loved it—always ordered a whole stack of pancakes and syrup . . ." She stutters to a standstill. "Sorry, but I just can't believe something like this could happen. I heard that the killer got hold of her and suffocated her—snuffed her out. Who would do such a wicked thing? Here. In our little town. I mean, everyone knows everyone."

"Maybe we don't," a woman in "look at me" earrings speaks from the table closest to the counter. "Know people, I mean. You can never really *know* someone completely, can you? I hear the police are focusing on Karen's online activities, but I'm looking a bit closer at the local men I pass in the street."

"Yes," her younger companion adds. "It could be anyone—a stranger in our midst. Someone living next door, even. Couldn't it, Mum?"

"Next door? Who do you mean?" Flo snaps, then flushes. "You shouldn't talk like that."

"Well, it's a possibility," the older woman mutters, and one of her earrings catches and pulls a thread in her jumper. "Not everyone in Ebbing can be Mr. Wonderful. That Noel Clayton always looks like he's on the edge. That angry face—like a smacked arse. I pity his poor wife. I don't know how she puts up with him."

"And his carry-on," Flo mutters. And my ears prick up.

"Clayton? He's the one who found the body, isn't he?" I ask, beginning to thaw as I stir my tea at the counter. "What carry-on?"

"Oh, he fancies himself as a bit of a photographer, apparently," Flo says, wiping the counter with a cloth.

"Oh?" I say, my hackles rising on Danny's behalf—only I am allowed to criticize my feckless ex's profession. "Actually, I was married to one once."

"Hmm, just saying," Flo replies.

"What does he photograph?" I say, making a note of his name on a napkin.

"I wouldn't know," she says, and won't meet my eye. *What's that about?* "Are you coming to the vigil tonight?" she hurries on.

"Vigil?"

"Yep, Mina is getting some of Karen's friends together in the car park by the wood. Just to remember her. You know, everyone does it now, don't they? First it's flowers and tea lights, then a vigil and everyone sings sad songs."

"Definitely." And I thank the god of slow news days and brush the crumbs out of my scarf. "Delish," I say. "And thanks for the info." I go back into the cold and huddle inside my coat while I ring Mina to get all the details and quotes. The trouble is, it's all a bit low-key and hippie-dippie, really. There's a bit of chatter about it online, but I need to give it a kick up the bum to get a good showing on the news site. I google Reclaim the Night groups in the area and begin ringing round.

AFTER I FILE a holding story from my car, I ring to nag Miles about finding the other forum users, but he brushes me off. "Busy," he mutters. "Later."

I try to do it myself for five minutes, but I know I just haven't got the skills. Legwork is my thing. I'll go and pay a visit to Noel Clayton. Have a look at him and his carry-on. It'll keep me busy until the vigil, anyway.

As soon as I get through the door at the Claytons' shop, the smell of wet wood with a hint of paint thinner hits the back of my throat. The *bing-bong* of the door sensor echoes round the store, and a woman somewhere deep in the shelving squeaks: "Noel, there's someone at the counter." Silence. "Noel! Sorry, my husband must be outside."

"Don't worry," I call out. "There's no rush."

The woman emerges from the shadows. "Sorry," she says, pushing dyed chestnut hair off her face. "What is it you're after?"

"Ah, actually, I'm a reporter, Mrs. Clayton," I say quickly. "And I wondered if I could talk to you and your husband about finding Karen Simmons's body."

Mrs. Clayton's eyes widen. "W-We're not talking to the press," she stutters. "Noel said we shouldn't. And, anyway, there's nothing to say. We found her and phoned the police."

"That must have been terrifying," I say gently. Evelyn droops and nods. "How are you doing?"

"I haven't been sleeping, actually," she murmurs. "I keep seeing her sitting there."

"Sitting?" I say. *Sitting? Not lying on the ground?* "Goodness—had she been tied up, then?"

"No, I don't think so. It was so strange. It looked like she was at a picnic or something. But she was all glittery when Noel's head torch shone on her. Her dress and the frost in her hair. Poor woman."

"Oh, God!" I say. *This is great copy* pings into my brain unbidden, and my heart pumps harder in response. I try to shove the thought aside and focus on what Evelyn Clayton is saying, but I can't stop myself. It's a hardwired reaction to a developing news story. Ask any reporter. *Not heartless*, I tell myself. *Professional and objective.* But it sounds hollow, even to me.

"What did you do?" I push myself out of my queasy navel-gazing.

"We stood there. Neither of us spoke. I couldn't move. I wanted to, but my body just went rigid."

"That will have been the shock," I murmur, and Evelyn nods, eyes closed against the memory. "Did you recognize her right away?"

"No, I couldn't see her face—her head was hanging down—so I

didn't know it was Karen. She hardly looked human, really. More like a shop dummy. I'd never seen a dead person before."

"God, how awful," I say, but these are the quotes that will bring the reader right into the murder scene. Allow them to feel what Evelyn Clayton felt. And see Karen, not just an anonymous victim.

"And then Noel shouted to run and I did," Evelyn goes on, grasping the counter so hard her knuckles shine bone white. "But I had stupid shoes on and I fell over." She pauses, then mutters to herself, "I knew I should have worn my trainers, but Noel wanted the red high heels."

"Red high heels?" I ask.

"Evelyn!" a voice rumbles from the back. "Who are you talking to?" Real fear flickers across Evelyn's face and, for a second, panics me into wee-or-flee mode. My legs tense in readiness for a fast exit.

"A customer," she says, her voice too high. "Don't say you're a reporter," she hisses urgently. "He'll go mad."

I nod, somehow complicit in her domestic nightmare. "I'll have two packs of picture hooks, please," I say loudly, like I'm in a play.

Noel Clayton appears, glowering when he sees me. He's a bulldog of a man, compact, running to jowls, with close-cropped hair and hard eyes. He stands guard in the shadows as his wife rings up the hooks on the till with trembling fingers.

When Evelyn hands me the receipt, I slip my business card into her hand. "In case you want to contact me," I whisper.

THIRTY

ANNIE

Wednesday, February 19, 2020

XANDER WAS IN his old room—he was insisting on staying. Annie kept saying it was all sorted, but her son claimed his boss at the insurance company was happy for him to work remotely for the rest of the week.

And if she was honest, Annie was happy, too. It was lovely having him there. It'd been too long since they'd had some proper time together. Xander worked so hard he didn't really have time to come home. Annie understood that, of course. Well, she tried to. And she tried to imagine how he felt when he walked through the door, back onto Planet Curtis. Where the bad stuff still lived. Where Archie still lived. He'd never had a room in this house so there was no shrine or anything. Henry had vetoed that when they'd bought the place—"It won't help any of us; think of Xander"—but Annie had made sure there were photos of him among the family ones on the stairs. Archie, tongue poking out while he drew her a picture; him running down the beach; and her favorite, him laughing straight into the camera. Straight into her eyes sometimes, when she wasn't ready. Her little ghost. Whenever that happened, she'd have to sit down on a step to catch her breath. She wondered if it was the same for Xander.

Annie took him up a coffee, tapping on his bedroom door before she went in. Perhaps, if she was lucky, he'd be up for a chat.

"Thought you might want a break," she said.

"Thanks, Mum," he muttered from his boyhood desk. "Sorry, I've got to finish this. The deadline is today. Are you okay?"

"I'm fine. I'll leave you to it."

"Has Dad gone to work?" he said as she was halfway through the door.

"Yes. Why?"

"No reason. I'll come down in a bit."

He and Henry were circling each other like wary dogs. Nothing new, really. They'd never been particularly close. Annie thought the problem was that Xander had never been sporty like Henry. He hated being cold on wintry football pitches and the salt and sand that got into his wet suit when he was taken surfing. Henry said he didn't try—but then, neither did her husband when it came to hiding his disappointment. She got that he'd been looking forward to having a son he could cheer on from the touchline, but Xander hadn't needed that for the games he played, building his own intricate worlds. Annie had sat at the edges, handing him Lego and superhero weapons until Archie had been old enough to take over and bring Xander out of himself—and fulfill Henry's dreams of a team player.

But after . . . after his brother died, Xander had burrowed back into his imagination, feeding it with fantasy books and tiny model armies of orcs and elves. And, guiltily, Annie had felt relief. Their new baby, Gavin, had filled every waking moment—which was every moment. She hadn't been able to cope with anything else.

Gavin had grown tall and strong, made for rugby. So everyone was happy. At least, she let herself believe that.

Xander and his dad hadn't talked about what she and Henry were calling "their domestic," but Henry had hardly been there. He'd gone off to work when the dust had settled yesterday and come back late. Bringing her flowers.

"You deserve them," he'd said.

"Thank you," Annie had said and kissed him hard on the lips.

SHE WAS DEFROSTING a casserole for supper hours later, watching the dish revolve in the microwave, when her phone beeped. The alert for news about Karen was telling her they were holding a vigil for her tonight at Knapton Wood. Annie knew immediately she was going to go.

Henry came home as she was getting ready. Annie could see him trying his hardest not to lose it when she told him, but his lips trembled when he spoke. "Why on earth would you want to go back there? Nothing good can come of it, love. We talked about this yesterday, and the effect it has on you." He reached for her hand, and she tried not to pull back. "This isn't about Archie. I thought we had agreed to put this away," he said softly.

I can never put our child away, she wanted to yell at him. *Like a piece of clothing that doesn't fit anymore. And nor can you.* But she didn't. Couldn't reignite the row. "I just want to pay my respects to Karen," she said slowly so she wouldn't trip on the lie. "We knew her, after all."

"But it means going to Knapton Wood, love." Henry sounded desperate. "It will be too much for you. Please don't go."

"I'm sorry, but I am, Henry," Annie said and went to find her coat, leaving him wringing his hands in the kitchen.

"I'll come with you," Gavin called down the stairs, earwigging again. "Xander can drive us."

Her eldest appeared behind his brother but didn't say anything.

"You don't need to," Annie said quickly. She couldn't put him through it. Xander hadn't been back to Knapton Wood since it had happened. They hadn't gone home from the hospital—the police had collected their things and the three of them had been taken to stay with Annie's parents. Annie had had to go back to the garden to show the police where they'd all been that day, but she hadn't been able to bear being in the house with Archie's things, looking out at those trees.

The family had moved into a rented place afterward. Annie and Henry had only gone back to sell the house. They'd let the removal people jumble up their old life in cardboard boxes with no labels. Some of them had never been unpacked.

"I'm perfectly capable of going on my own," Annie said, but her boys ignored her, and she was quietly grateful. Henry didn't come out of the kitchen while they were finding boots and hats. Annie saw him at the window watching them get into the car. He looked so lonely standing there.

As they drove the twenty miles to Ebbing, Gavin read out tweets about the vigil and women's safety. "It's going to be a big thing," he said. Xander turned up the radio for a traffic announcement about congestion around the town and sighed.

"I really appreciate this, Xander," Annie said. "You don't have to get out of the car."

"Course I do," he growled, looking at her in the rearview mirror. "I don't want you walking about in the dark on your own."

But when they got to the wood, Annie realized there was no question of anyone being on their own. The crowd filling the space was so huge Annie could hardly see the trees around them. But she could feel them. Pressing at their backs. She wondered if Xander could, too.

She reached out and squeezed his shoulder. "Are you okay, love?" He nodded, and she wanted to hold him like she had that day. When he was ten and Archie died.

THIRTY-ONE

KIKI

Wednesday, February 19, 2020

GETTING TO THE vigil is a nightmare. It's raining, and cars and vans have already started pouring through the town when I start away from the Claytons' shop, clogging up the High Street and side roads. I sit in the jam, drumming my fingers on the steering wheel. I'm going to miss it if we don't get a move on. I hear whistling and cheering and crane round to see that some early drinkers in the Neptune have come out on the pavement to have a look.

I crawl along in the drizzling rain, wipers smearing my windscreen, wishing for the umpteenth time that I'd started out earlier. In the end, I pull off the road well before the site and leave my poor old car jammed so tight against a hedge that I have to clamber out of the passenger door, bum first.

Others are doing the same, and I'm carried along by the crowd. There's a bobbing stream of lanterns, candles, and torches all around me, and the quiet, emotional thrum of the conversations pulls me in. Karen would have been overwhelmed by this response. Even I am. Especially when I hear the faint strains of a song and some of the women close to me join in with "Over the Rainbow."

I tell myself to pull it together—I'm here to work, not sing—and look around for good interviewees. Destinee, Karen's teenaged assistant at the salon, is standing a few feet away. She's in a thin jacket and what look like fluffy slippers, clutching the arm of an older girl.

"Hello," I say, sliding alongside them. Destinee startles and clings harder to her companion.

"Sorry, didn't mean to make you jump," I say. "This is a brilliant turnout for Karen," I add quickly. "What a wonderful tribute to her."

Destinee tries to smile, but it goes all watery and the tears start to fall. "Come on," the other girl says. "Let's find a place to stand."

They're turning away when Elise King appears out of the gloom. "Hello, Lucy," she says, and Destinee's companion straightens her shoulders and walks over. She's a copper. Should have known. I'm good at spotting them usually, but the blokes are easier than the women, for some reason. I stay back, blending into the crowd, and listen, hoping for a new line on the investigation.

"I thought you were visiting nightclubs in Brighton with Andy Thomson," DI King says.

"I was, boss, but Destinee Amos from Karen's salon asked me to come. I interviewed her at the salon on Monday and gave her my number. She didn't want to be on her own, and DS Brennan thought it might be useful for me to be here. I think Andy is, too."

"I'm really grateful," Destinee says tearfully. "Mum refused to turn out. She said it was too scary up here—and she wasn't going to help turn Karen into some sort of saint. But I had to come."

DI King just nods and tells Lucy: "Okay, but keep your head down. Leave it to the local coppers to manage things. The police make easy targets when people are frightened and angry. Now, let's get down there."

There's a huge circle forming in the darkness when we arrive, people huddling together, well away from the shifting shadows inside the tree line.

The rain stops as Mina Ryan steps forward and a forest of mobile phones rises above the crowd, lighting her up with their screens.

Everyone falls silent as she starts speaking, and I turn my phone to record.

"Karen made me laugh more than anyone else. She was the first person I'd call if I was having a bad day—she always said the right thing to cheer me up. She was funny and kind and was her best self when she was with a crowd of friends, singing the wrong words to Abba songs and dancing. I wish she was here to see you all."

The circle begins clapping, the sound, like a flock of birds taking off, echoing off the trees. Mina carries on, half talking, half sobbing as she remembers her friend, and the women around her seem to sway in time with her words.

I look around the half-lit faces, noting the handful of men who have shown up. Barry Sherman, who is looking uncharacteristically grave. Noel Clayton, without his wife. And there are others I don't recognize— some quite young, probably dragged along by their girlfriends. One of them suddenly links arms with an older woman who is weeping.

I shove my phone in my coat pocket when the two-minute silence starts and heads are being bowed, but my phone suddenly pings, and the woman next to me gives me an appalled look. I'm mortified and struggle to get it out of my pocket to mute it. Then I catch sight of the screen. And everything stops. There is a rushing noise in my ears, and I let go of my phone. I hear someone scream. And realize it is me. The women around me scream, too, their fear on a hair trigger. Lucy the copper whirls round on the spot, looking for an unseen attacker, and dips to pick up my phone.

"Quiet! Show some respect," someone at the front shouts, and heads turn to see who has shattered the moment.

Elise pulls me, Destinee, and Lucy back into the darkness. "What the hell is the matter?" she hisses between clenched teeth. But I can't speak. Can't form the words to explain what I've just seen. Can't unsee. Am choking on.

"Take deep breaths, Kiki," Elise commands in a strained voice and pushes my head down.

There's snot running out of my nose when I straighten up, and Elise hands me a tissue.

"Better?" she mutters.

"She was there," I stammer. "On my phone."

"Who was?"

"Karen."

"Karen?" Destinee shrieks.

Everyone is openly shushing us now and glaring.

"Take Destinee home," Elise whispers to Lucy. "This has obviously been too much for her. DC Chevening will drive you home, Destinee."

But Lucy Chevening isn't moving.

"What happened, Kiki?" Elise turns back to me.

"Something horrible," I whisper.

"Go!" Elise says and herds us back to the road.

When we're out of earshot of the crowd, Elise stops and takes my arm. "Right! Tell me!"

"It was Karen's photo on my phone," I say.

"I'm not sure I'm getting this." Elise holds my eye. "You've probably got dozens of her on your phone. You used them on your website."

I shake my head. "Karen was dead."

Destinee starts wailing and rocking on her feet.

"Stop that noise, Destinee," Elise says sharply, trying to wrestle back some sort of control. The teenager wraps her arms around herself and cries softly. "What are you talking about, Kiki?"

"The photo. I think it was taken when she was dead," I stutter.

"Show me!" Elise says, her voice increasingly urgent. "Where is this photo?"

"It's gone," I say, stabbing my finger at the screen, which is now just showing a photo of my daughter—my screen saver. "But it was there. It must have been sent by someone—they must have cyberflashed me. But when I saw it, I was so shocked I just threw it down. And it's disappeared. You can look—it's not here."

Elise flicks through the recent photos on the phone, but they are all shots of the vigil crowd.

"Are you sure?" she asks, kindly. Like I'm an old woman with a shaky grip on reality. And I suddenly think, *Am I? Have I imagined it? In all the emotion of the evening?*

"I saw it, too," Lucy suddenly adds, her voice wobbly. "I saw it when I picked up her phone."

"You saw it?" Elise barks, and the young officer nods.

"Karen was sitting against a tree in the dark. In her red dress," I say, teeth chattering. "With her legs stuck out. And her eyes . . ."

But I don't need to say any more. Elise is nodding. She knows what I have seen. She must have seen it, too, when she stood in front of Karen on Saturday morning.

My thoughts are scattering. Was it one of the police photos from the scene? Or did someone else take a picture of Karen after killing her?

"But who sent it? Who?" Elise hisses at me. "Where's the number?"

"I don't know," I groan.

"Seriously?"

"You don't always know, boss," Lucy says haltingly. "Women get sent porn anonymously on their phones all the time. By strangers. Anyone can do it within a ten-meter radius of you if you've got AirDrop switched to 'all users.' Most people don't know they're vulnerable. It happens on buses and trains or in queues. They send a preview of some gross photo so you see it whether you want to or not. You have to press 'accept' to download it. If you press 'reject,' it disappears. I must have rejected it when I picked the phone up. I'm really sorry."

"So, hold on—someone within ten meters of Kiki sent her the photo?" Elise whirls round, and we both run back toward the vigil. Lucy and Destinee come racing after us.

"Where were you in the crowd?" Elise mutters to me. "We need to see who was near enough to do this."

But the circle is breaking up, softly singing "Dancing Queen" as they drift away in the dark. Some are already getting into their cars.

"Shit," Elise says. "Who was standing near you?"

I try to reconstruct the scene, turning slowly on the spot to try to resee the faces. But the image of Karen has blurred everything else. She is all I can see.

THIRTY-TWO

ELISE

Wednesday, February 19, 2020

KIKI HAD RUNG the *South Coast News* cameraman covering the vigil from the car.

"He's sending me everything he's got," she'd told Elise by phone as they drove in separate cars to Southfold police station. "And I've got photos and videos of the crowd," she'd added.

Elise looked through them quickly in the interview room before sending them on to the digital team for analysis.

Then she tapped her pen on the table between them to bring matters to order.

She could see that Kiki was still shivering despite the heating being on full blast.

"Sorry, I just can't stop seeing Karen's face." Kiki gulped. "What did they do to her?"

"That is still being determined. Look, I know this goes without saying, but you absolutely cannot write about what happened tonight."

Kiki opened her mouth to say something, but Elise carried on. "It could be key to the investigation—to finding out who killed Karen. You do understand how important it is to keep it confidential?"

"Yes," the reporter said. "But where did they get that photo?"

Elise sighed. "I wish I knew. Your mobile will be examined by the digital team in the morning, but it's unlikely to give us much. It's you and Chevening who hold the information. Look, I'll try not to take too long, but we need to go through what you saw again. Okay?"

"Yes, course," Kiki said, moving forward onto the edge of her chair, leaning into the memory. "I heard a ping and remembered I hadn't muted my phone," she said. "And I was looking right at the screen when the photo flashed up. I probably only saw it for a second, but I knew who it was because of the red dress."

"Good. Describe the image. Every detail."

The reporter rubbed her eyes, then closed them to concentrate, and Elise could see that flakes of mascara had gathered in the corners of her lids.

Elise sat completely still as Kiki recounted the scene.

"That's very good," she said when the reporter began to falter. "Now I'd like you to look at these photos."

Elise pulled up the scenes of crime images of Karen on the computer, teeth clenched and praying hard it wasn't one of them. That was the worst-case scenario—a leak by one of her trusted squad. She'd heard whispers on the conference circuit about a horrifying new trend: posed trophy photos of crime victims being taken and shared by a handful of sick officers. Elise knew there'd always been dark humor in the job—joking about the horrors they faced gave them power over the situation. If they could laugh at it, it couldn't hurt them, was the rationale. But of course it did. Dealing with violent crime was a steady erosion of sensitivity. But when had edgy banter tipped over into swapping images of dead bodies?

If it had been one of hers? She flew through the roster in her head, looking for a deviant in their midst. This could blow up the team. She'd have to rebuild from scratch. Elise's mind was racing out of control down the catastrophe route, and she made herself haul on the brakes. With a heavy heart, she turned the screen so Kiki could see.

The reporter swallowed hard. "That's it." Kiki pointed at the first picture. "Well, that's how she looked. Except she wasn't in a tent," she murmured almost to herself, and stopped.

"Thank you, God," Elise muttered under her breath. No tent must mean before her detectives got there. Mustn't it?

"Sorry?" Kiki said.

"Sorry," Elise murmured. "Thinking aloud."

"Okay," Kiki said. And gulped hard. "And there's no hand," she whispered.

"Hand? What hand?" Elise jumped out of her chair and hurried round to stand beside her.

"In the photo I saw. It was right at the edge of the frame. A blue glove. Against Karen's left shoulder. Like it was pushing her upright."

"Show me," Elise said, and sat down on the floor to re-create the pose, her head sagging like Karen's had. Kiki crouched down over her and put her left hand hard against Elise's shoulder to sit her up while she took a photo with her phone.

Elise braced herself against a chair to get to her feet, and they looked at the image together.

"That's how it was," Kiki said. "But a bit farther away. Maybe the person who did it was taller? Had longer arms?" There was a sickening beat while her brain raced ahead. "It was the killer, wasn't it?" Kiki whispered. "He was there tonight. Standing less than ten meters from me. Sending me his sick photos. Oh, God, did he target me deliberately, Elise? Does he know who I am?"

"That is yet to be determined," Elise muttered and avoided the reporter's eye. It was a strong possibility, but she didn't want to spook her any further.

She dialed the forensic team leader.

"You need to focus on the left shoulder."

THURSDAY:
DAY 6

THIRTY-THREE

KIKI

Thursday, February 20, 2020

IT'S SIX THIRTY a.m. and still dark outside, but I'm sitting at the kitchen table, scanning the faces in the television footage over and over again. Searching for answers to the questions that kept me awake most of the night.

The question of why Karen's killer would send her photo to me is drumming on the inside of my skull. Elise said it could be because of my byline on the articles about Karen. Some sort of gross grandstanding to the media. But the thing is, she doesn't know about the BOBs. I still haven't told her about X-Man or his cronies. Or that they're aware I'm on their trail. Only I know this could have been a sick warning to watch my back. Or a direct threat. The image of Karen, frozen in death under the trees, sits behind my lids when I close my eyes. I wrap my arms around myself and rock gently while I talk myself down.

My head is ringing with tiredness, and I know I should go back to bed for an hour, but I can't leave him out there in the darkness. I draw a ragged circle in my notepad and plot in the faces I recognize. But my mate, the cameraman, has only zoomed in on women. Typical! The close-ups are all of weeping girls. Still, he managed to get me in one of the clips he sent, so I can move outward from my position. It was so crowded; there must have been at least fifty people within the ten-meter range of my phone. I stare and stare at the images, willing someone to jump out of the sea of faces. DI Elise King must be doing the same thing with her digital team—and they'll do a much more accurate job, piecing together the images to make a complete 360-degree panorama—but I can't wait for her. I need to know now.

My eye snags on the faces I already know: Barry Sherman, two rows behind me, holding his phone torch up high, and Noel Clayton, standing four or five people off to the side. I enlarge him, studying his blank expression. Clayton was definitely alone at the crime scene before the police arrived. His wife said he'd sent her ahead, to run for safety in her high heels. So he'd been on his own with Karen's body. But if he'd killed her a few hours earlier, why would he go back to "discover" the body with his wife? What sort of monster would you have to be? I shudder as I try not to imagine.

Where's Ash? I can't spot him in the clips. He could still have been close enough, though. I add him to my very short list and try enlarging one of the unidentified male faces—a pale oval in the darkness wearing glasses—but as I pull him closer, he dissolves under my fingers.

I can hear Pip moving about upstairs and realize another hour has passed while I've sat here.

"Cereal or a boiled egg for breakfast?" I shout up through the ceiling.

"Oooooh, dippy yolk and soldiers, please!" my girl shouts back—her favorite since she was a baby. I hug the heartwarming image of her in her high chair to my shivering skin.

My phone rings while I'm watching the eggs bob about in the simmering water. It's a withheld number, but I take it anyway. It could be one of the national news desks—maybe they've seen my exclusive interview with Evelyn Clayton about finding the body.

"Hi," I chirp down the phone, trying not to sound half-dead.

"Never mind 'Hi,'" Mrs. Clayton hisses. "Why did you quote me? Noel is furious."

Bugger.

"Oh, hello, Evelyn. You've seen the story, then? I thought it was a very moving account of your ordeal. And so did the audience. Have you seen the comments under the story?"

"Er, no . . ." The fight starts to leak out of her voice. "What do they say?"

"That you were incredibly brave and public-spirited," I say, crossing my fingers and taking the pan off the heat. I'll post that comment anonymously as soon as I get off the phone.

"Oh," she says. "I'll tell Noel. I think he'll be okay about it."

Job done.

I'm stupidly pleased with myself for a moment. I've swerved the dressing-down like a pro, and Pip arrives in front of me, dressed, hair brushed, bag packed for an overnight at the home of her best friend, Zoe. My headache ratchets down, and I sit across from my daughter, stealing dips of her eggs and trying to pretend this is a normal day.

But as soon as I've dropped her off, the dread creeps back in and I sit in the car, staring at the traffic crawling past. Ordinary people going about their lives. Not worried that a killer is out there watching them. And for a second, that's all I want. To be what I've always railed against. Ordinary. *It's simple,* the Mrs. Sensible lurking inside me says. *Stop your investigation and just let the police deal with this. You're a single mother with a child to think about. Not a twentysomething with a name to make. Keep your head down.*

But I can't. Karen was murdered by this man. She was shut up by him—but I won't be. *"Screw you!"* I shout at my windscreen, and a bloke in a car idling at the traffic lights beside me sees and gives me a smirky thumbs-up. I take that as a sign and start the engine. I'll be careful, but I'm going to track down all the BOBs and present them to Elise. And, yes, get my scoop. I rev my engine and pull out.

My first thought when I get to the office is to check the comments on my first "Secret Dater" column. I'm hoping it will bring me other women who've had contact with Simon and his mates.

"Morning," I call to Miles on my way to my desk. "Have you got any of the other names yet?"

He shakes his head slowly. "No—and I've heard from the boss. Ali doesn't like your 'Secret Dater' thing. He thinks it's a bit safe."

"Right," I snap, and breathe out through my nose. *Do not lose it.*

"He wants you to up the ante and get on the hookup apps for next week—become a Tinderella and get the full experience of swiping right."

"A Tinderella?" I squeak.

Miles flushes beetroot red and his Adam's apple dances in his throat. "It's not my idea," he mutters.

I go and buy chocolate and walk my anger out on the pavement. *You need this job* is my mantra, reinforced by the knowledge that my credit card bill will empty my account in six days. *And it's only until you get back to proper journalism. Suck it up!*

It takes two minutes to sign up to a couple of hookup apps, and I open my Twix and start looking at the prospects in a fifteen-mile radius of Ebbing. It's quite a range.

Eamonn is there. Bloody hell, he's like *Where's Wally?*

I keep scrolling, the taste of defeat souring my mouth until I suddenly get swiped. I sigh. I bet he's sixty, claiming to be thirty, and wearing a fake Prada T-shirt.

But he isn't. Rob says he is forty-nine and likes the outdoors. He also has gorgeous eyes and is only minutes away. It's the first good thing that's happened to me since last night.

I swipe back and carry on looking at the app while I wait. But I can feel my heart picking up pace like I'm a teenager about to be asked to dance. I check myself, but who am I kidding? This is no longer research. But, hell, I deserve something better than sweets on a shit day like today.

Rob doesn't take long. His first message pops up: Hi, **great photo!** You've got a lovely smile.

I spend the next five minutes composing my reply: typing, editing, deleting a dozen times.

Hi! Thanks. This is my first time! Hardly Hemingway.

But Rob doesn't seem put off.

I'll be gentle with you. ☺ Do you fancy a coffee?

That would be lovely. ☺ What the hell am I doing? I hate emojis.

There's a place on the front in Hove. The blue café. Can be there at eleven if that's good for you?

Will be there.

I sit, catching my breath for a moment. This is why Karen did it, I realize. This rush.

THIRTY-FOUR

ANNIE

Thursday, February 20, 2020

HENRY BROUGHT HER tea when she woke and climbed back into bed with her. He never did that on a weekday. And Annie felt her fingers tighten on the duvet as she wondered what was coming.

"I want you to ring your therapist," he told the wardrobe. Annie knew—and couldn't help resenting the fact—that he found it hard to have eye contact when discussing personal things. *Or when he's lying,* a voice in her head whispered. "I think this new thing is dragging you down again," he said and pried her hand off the cover to squeeze it.

New thing. He meant Karen's killing, but they never really called anything by its real name. Since Archie. They never said the word "murder" at home. Other people did—the police, the press, her therapist. But not here. They couldn't have that in the house.

"I'm okay," Annie said. "It was just difficult being at Knapton Wood. And people were so upset. One woman right behind us screamed. It really shook me."

It had. Much more than she'd been prepared for. The scream had come out of the silence. Like hers, that day. Sixteen years ago. When she'd carried her boy out of the wood. Someone had taken the screaming woman off last night, and that had made Annie cry again and Gavin had wanted to leave. But Annie wouldn't go before the end. She'd gone and waited for her chance to speak to the organizer, a woman called Mina. There'd been so many people milling around her, but a tall man with sad eyes had made a space for her. "Hello, Mrs. Curtis," he'd said, and she couldn't remember his face. And then Mina had taken her hand, and Annie had turned away and told her she'd known Karen back in the day, and they'd hugged each other.

"It was just so sad," Annie said to her husband, and burst into tears. She didn't mean to—she thought she'd got it out of her system at the vigil. But all those feelings that quietly blipped in her chest, like a malignant sourdough starter, had clearly just been waiting for another chance to erupt.

"Come on, love," Henry sighed. "Don't cry. I did tell you. I knew it would end like this. Why don't I run you a bath?"

Annie mumbled that she'd make an appointment and watched as Henry got dressed, noting he was putting on a new shirt.

"Where are you today?" she asked.

"Er, over Southampton way," he told the window. "There are a couple of customers I haven't visited for a while. One's got a chain of pharmacies, and I need to nudge the boss to up his order. I'll probably be late. I might have to take him out for a drink after work."

"Okay," Annie said automatically. "Ring when you're on your way home."

She finished her cold tea and moved herself on to the day ahead. She needed to change the beds. And get the washing on. And the fridge was empty. But she knew none of it would get done.

She was going back to Knapton Wood.

ANNIE PARKED UP by their old address. It took her a moment to recognize it after all that time. Someone had painted the front door black. Like a plague house. This was where they had lived for ten years as newlyweds and young parents. But Annie couldn't see them there now.

There were no cars in the drive, and she hoped the new people were at work. It'd been a young, hard-faced couple who'd bought it—they'd whispered together in the kitchen while she and Henry had stood watching from the garden and then beaten the price down mercilessly. They'd known the Curtises were desperate. So desperate to leave they'd let them have it for almost nothing. Annie had hated them for it. She wondered if they were still there.

There was a deflated football in the front garden and Spider-Man stickers in the window of Archie's old bedroom. A new child in the house. Annie's heart twitched in her chest.

The entrance to the alleyway at the end of the houses was overgrown with brambles, and the path was studded with ancient dog turds. She got herself caught on thorns as she walked through to the wood and scratched her hands when she released herself. When she emerged back into the thin sunlight, she stood for a while at the spot where their rickety old back gate used to be. The new owners had replaced it with a big sturdy one—and locked it with a padlock. *Keeping the bad out. It's what we should have done.*

Annie suddenly wondered if anyone was watching her and glanced up at the windows. There was no one there.

She'd come to walk back into the trees, as the detectives had made her do over and over again during the investigation, but she couldn't do it. She just stood there weeping. She'd sobbed the first time—had to be held up by officers—but Annie had stopped crying by the end. She had made herself not feel anything. Because even the tiniest thing could destroy her. A discarded sock under a bed. The biscuits Archie loved. A baby on the television.

Today, there was rain in the air, misting her glasses. It had been so hot that day. Shorts and T-shirts weather. Annie pulled her coat closed and zipped it up. And stood. And stood.

It was only when she heard a back door open and someone shout for a dog that she bolted clumsily for the tree line and ducked under a branch.

It was so dark. Annie heard herself call, "Archie!" and wondered if she was losing her mind like Henry said. *Your little boy isn't here,* she told herself. They'd had Archie cremated because they couldn't bear the thought of his little body cold in the ground, and had scattered his ashes into the sea on a gray day like this one.

The trees had been in full leaf back then—a great green canopy over her—but they were bare-boughed now. Like fleshless arms. Dead. Annie leaned against a trunk and gathered herself. She walked on and suddenly realized she was there. Standing where Archie and Xander had made their last camp.

It'd taken her three minutes at most to reach the place. Three minutes. People interviewed in the newspapers had said they would never have let their kids out of their sight, never mind "deep" in the wood. *Like you did.* The neighbors had wanted to be sympathetic, but there had always been an edge to their words. *Your fault* seemed to hover at their lips.

And they'd been right. She should never have let them be alone here—or anywhere. But Annie hadn't seen the danger. Only the freedom. It was one of the reasons she and Henry had bought the place— the gate onto the footpath and the trees just beyond. When they had kids, they'd wanted them to have the sort of childhood that wasn't ruled by screens and video games. The boys were in and out of the wood all day long that summer—it was a brilliant place to play, and Annie had let them eat their sandwiches in the various dens they'd built. They'd known not to go farther than the big yew with the broken branch so they would be within earshot when she called them in. It'd been family law.

Her worries had been that they'd hurt themselves climbing trees. Not that something horrible lurked, waiting for them. That a Nicky Donovan lurked.

Annie had been shocked when she'd seen his photograph in the paper. Nicky Donovan had been so young—twenty-four—with curly hair like Archie's, smiling for the camera with an ice cream in his hand. Someone's son. And she remembered thinking: *They've made a mistake. Why would this smiling boy hurt my children?*

Henry had been furious when she'd said it out loud. But he'd been angry about everything then. He hadn't cried. He'd shouted to vent his feelings. Blaming everyone for failing to protect his boy. So she hadn't said it again. And the police had been so sure they'd got the right man. But no one could tell Annie why. Why the smiling boy had killed Archie. She'd told herself she'd have to wait for the police and a jury to get to the truth. But Nicky Donovan hadn't let her. He'd hanged himself in his cell at the station while the shifts changed and no one was watching, they said. So she would never know.

Annie realized she'd been there for ages, sitting in the damp dirt. And she was no further forward. Her boy was still dead. But the questions had resumed their insistent drumbeat in her head.

When she emerged, Annie sensed rather than saw the man at her elbow and turned sharply.

"Mrs. Curtis?" the man said in a soft voice. "I don't know if you remember me."

It was the man from the vigil. Annie still had no idea who he was and looked around nervously for passersby. But they were alone.

"My name's Ash Woodward," the man said, standing an inch too close.

"What do you want?" Annie replied, her voice shrill.

"Just to say how sorry I am for your loss," he said. "I wanted to say it last night, but I didn't get the chance. I understand how you must feel. My mother died last year—and now Karen."

Annie could feel her chest tightening, shortening her breath. "Thank you," she managed to say. To end the bizarre moment. "But I have to go."

As she turned, her foot went over and the stranger caught her before she clattered to the ground. "Careful," he murmured, and his kindness tipped her into tears. "Where's your car?" And she let him take her arm and guide her back to the street where she had parked.

"Do you live in Ebbing?" Annie said to break the silence. She thought she sounded like a royal. *Have you come far?*

"All my life," Ash said. "But you moved away, didn't you? After your little boy was killed."

Annie stared at him, shocked at his directness. He clearly had no filter. "Yes, that's right."

"It was an awful time, wasn't it?" he was saying. "And now Karen's death has made it all come back."

He sounded close to tears, and Annie just wanted him to let go of her arm and escape, but pity won out.

As they reached the end of the street, a police car drove slowly past, and Ash Woodward watched until it disappeared. "The police were everywhere back then as well, weren't they?" he mumbled to himself. "They came to the house."

"Your house? Why?" Annie said and struggled to remember his name again.

"Oh, I had nesting boxes in the wood. They wanted to know if I'd been up there that day."

"They talked to a lot of people, I think."

Ash looked away.

"Mum told them I was shelling peas with her at home," he murmured. "She said I shouldn't put myself in the picture. It never went well when I did. I always said something wrong. She said I talked myself into trouble."

Annie's head jerked up to look him in the face. What was he telling her?

"But you weren't with her?" she heard herself say.

"No. I was watching birds in Knapton Wood," Ash whispered, and Annie grabbed his arm so hard he yelped and wrenched it away.

"You were there?" she cried. "Did you see my boys?"

Ash's mouth opened but no sound came out.

"And why are you here today?" Annie was shouting now. "How did you know where to find me? Have you been following me?"

A sudden roar of "Oi! You!" from behind them made them jump apart. "Is that your car?" a white-haired man with a red face was yelling through his open window. "My wife can't get out of our garage."

"Sorry," Annie mouthed and fumbled for her keys.

"I need to go," Ash muttered. "Take care of yourself."

"No, wait," Annie called after him. But Ash kept walking.

THIRTY-FIVE

ELISE

Thursday, February 20, 2020

THE FOOTAGE FROM the camera outside the Indian restaurant on the corner of Creek End had been downloaded, and Elise dragged Caro away from her spreadsheet to have a look.

They watched as Mina and Karen walked past, arm in arm on their girls' night out. "Not great quality, is it?" Caro said. "The owners of the Golden Gate must have gone for the lowest frame rate."

"Higher spec would eat up too much storage space, I suppose—and it's not an Amazon warehouse. Whizz it on."

The evening in Creek End unfolded like a badly made flick book.

"Business doesn't look great, does it?" Elise muttered as virtual tumbleweed blew down the cul-de-sac. "Oh," she said, and hit pause. A figure had jerked onto the screen and stepped toward the door. And her heartbeat picked up.

"Who's that?" Caro said, peering closer.

"Um," Elise squeaked, and had to clear her throat. "That's Mal Coles, the man who's moved in next door to my place. He's renting. Did I mention him?" She knew she hadn't. Didn't want to discuss him with anyone yet.

Caro raised an eyebrow.

"No, you've kept him quiet. He's nice-looking, though. Why's he going to a restaurant on his own?"

Elise felt a flush rising up past her collar. "He's single and it's where he gets his takeaways."

"Okay," Caro said. "Is he on your list?"

"No," she snapped.

"I meant to call in case he saw someone or something that night." Caro grinned. "What's this other list?"

"Shall we get on?" Elise tried to barrel past the awkward moment, but her finger still hesitated before pressing the play button. He was ringing tonight about going out for dinner. She felt her stomach flip and told herself she didn't have to go. For God's sake, she had a murder investigation as an excuse if she changed her mind.

She and Caro sat in silence, watching Mal reappear with his meal, and then sped up acres of nothing. "Shit, we've gone past the time Karen texted Mina Ryan," Elise said, shaking her head to clear it.

"Well, I didn't see her, did you?" Caro muttered as she rewound to check.

"We're both tired," Elise murmured, rubbing her eyes. They were still gritty after another night of jolting awake every hour.

"We didn't miss her. She's not there, is she?" Caro said. "Could she have come back another way? Without passing the restaurant camera? Her road's a dead end, isn't it?"

"Yeah, but there's a footpath at the end—the locals call them twittens," Elise said.

"How very twee." Caro laughed. "I don't know how you stand all this picture-postcard nonsense. We call them dog shit alleys where we live."

"Hark at you, living in the urban badlands of Horsham." Elise grinned. "Anyway, there are loads of them linking the harbor and High Street with some of the residential roads. They go round the back or down the sides of gardens. There are lights at some of the entrances and exits, but I wouldn't use them on my own after dark."

"No, but Karen had been drinking." Caro sighed. "She may just have taken the shortest route and that's why no one saw her."

Christ, they hadn't even got her returning to the flat. Elise cast about for alternative explanations and wanted to scream with frustration. There used to be tabulated, cross-referenced files in her head—she was the go-to when colleagues couldn't remember a name or make of car in an old case—but it was now just a ragbag of ideas.

"We've got to nail her movements that night," Elise said wearily. "Where are the witnesses? What about staging a reconstruction tomorrow? I know it's short notice, but it'll be a week on. Get someone dressed as Karen to sit in the Neptune and walk the walk home. Get the media involved. We need new energy, don't we?"

"Yep," Caro said, stifling a yawn and sitting up straighter. "I'll get on with the arrangements."

"Good," Elise muttered and glanced back at the images still flickering on the screen.

"Okay, stop!" she barked, catching the blur of a vehicle passing the now darkened windows of the Golden Gate. "Is that her car?" Caro replayed the segment, and they both saw the blur of a small vehicle. "Looks the right shape for a Fiat Cinquecento," Caro said, noting the time for the technicians to have a closer look.

"And what's that?" Elise jabbed at the screen. There was a dark shape in the restaurant doorway as the car passed. But only for one frame. It was gone by the time the film flickered on.

"Was she being watched?" she asked, her synapses finally awake and whirring through the possibilities. Her hand reached for the phone to flag what they'd spotted to the digital crew.

"Yep, got the Fiat," the techie said. "At eleven forty-one."

"On her way to Brighton?" Caro wondered aloud. "But what made her change her mind?"

"Or who?" Elise murmured.

THIRTY-SIX

KIKI

Thursday, February 20, 2020

"Are you all right?" Miles says as he walks past my desk. "You've gone all red in the face."

"Bit hot in here, actually," I snap and close my screen. He's caught me googling beautiful matchy-matchy underwear—a different universe from my own jumble of old and older.

"Perhaps we could save the planet and turn the heating down?" I tell his retreating back.

I look down at my outfit. Black trousers and pink jumper. Mum clothes. I've got an hour. I grab my coat and bag and run down the stairs to the shops.

I'm rattling through the racks at H&M when my phone goes.

Kiki? It's Zoe's mum. Nothing to alarm you,
but Pip's a bit upset. Could you come and
take her home?

But I'm at work, I say, pulling a silky blouse off a hanger. Have she and Zoe had a row? They'll be over it in half an hour.

Well, her first period has started, actually. I've
sorted her out with pads but I think she needs you.

The terrible mother puts the blouse back.
"I'm on my way," I mutter.
I stand outside the store and message Rob.

Very sorry, family thing has come up. Can we
rearrange?

Sure. Family first. How about a
drink tonight? There's a lovely little
bar just up from the café.

I'm still smiling when I get to Zoe's house.
"Hello, gorgeous girl," I say, and Pip bursts into tears.
"I've got tummy ache," she weeps, "and everyone knows. Zoe's
brother kept looking at me."
I pull her close. "Come on, let's go home and talk about it. We can
find your old panda hot-water bottle. And watch *Frozen*."

SHE'S MOUTHING "LET IT GO" and I'm waiting beside her on the sofa for
my mum to arrive when I open the BOBs forum to do a quick check on
X-Man and crew.
There's a new thread: "Vigil."
Eamonn has posted: "Nice to finally meet you. Froze my nuts off up
at the wood, though."
Where the hell was he hiding that night? I definitely didn't see him.
I stand up and scroll down frantically to see who has replied. And when
I spot the thumbs-up emojis, I sit down again heavily.
It's Lenny and the Captain.
So they were there. In the darkness.
I pull up the vigil footage and stare and stare again for their faces.

THIRTY-SEVEN

ELISE

Thursday, February 20, 2020

ASH WOODWARD WAS in the interview room. He'd turned up at the front desk and asked to see DI King. "He says he's got some information, ma'am," the officer on duty said. "Shall I bring him up?"

Elise shot up in her chair so fast her vertebrae clicked. Andy Thomson had been back to Sunny Sands twice since Monday, but there'd been no sign of Ash. Now he'd come to them. Had he heard they were digging into his past? What had he come to tell them?

She rubbed her eyes as she strode the corridor, feeling the papery skin under them pull and crease. She'd have to put concealer on for her date with Mal at the weekend or she'd look like her mother. If he ever called . . .

Woodward was shuffling in his seat, and she noticed him touching a silvery ladder of scars on his left forearm.

"Mr. Woodward, we've been trying to talk to you for days," Elise said crisply as she took her seat. "Did you not get my messages?"

Ash shook his head.

"I see. So why have you come?"

"You should be talking to Barry Sherman about Karen's killing," Ash gasped as if he had been holding his breath too long.

"Why is that, Mr. Woodward?"

He took a breath, and Elise could see the strain making his lips twitch. "He was seeing Karen," he replied, looking her in the eye for the first time. "I wasn't supposed to know. No one was. Sneaking around. But he's been going to her flat."

"How do you know? Were you watching Karen's home?" Elise asked quietly, her senses now on full alert. What was this man really telling her? Was he the shadow in the doorway the night Karen died?

"No, no," Ash insisted, dropping his gaze. He clearly knew he'd said too much. "I'm out and about round there at night, that's all. I've been keeping a record of a pair of barn owls nesting in an old shed on the allotments round the back of Creek End. So I was up and down the road. On my bike."

Too many excuses and so much detail. Almost as if he'd practiced it before sitting down . . .

"Right." Elise stretched the word as she made notes, and his hands began rubbing his knees under the table. "So why didn't you tell us about Barry before? When we asked you about Karen's relationships."

"I was worried he might hear it was me who'd said something. And I thought he'd tell you himself. But he hasn't, has he?"

He hadn't. In fact, Sherman had outright denied being anything more than a friend when she and Caro had interviewed him at the weekend.

Elise leaned forward to force Ash to look at her. "Why don't you tell me everything you saw, Mr. Woodward?"

"Everything I saw?" Ash yipped, eyes wide.

"Yes," Elise pressed. "You said Barry Sherman was at Karen's flat."

"Oh, yes," he said, and his face relaxed slightly. What did he think she'd been asking about? What else had he seen? But before she could ask, Ash launched into his story.

"Right. Well, on the Thursday, the night before Karen was killed," he mumbled, "I saw him ringing the bell to her flat, late and all secretive, and being let in. And saw him leave again. It didn't take long—twenty minutes. He was only there for sex. It's what he's like. He uses women, but Karen wouldn't listen."

Elise's ears pricked.

"You talked to Karen about it? When was that?"

Ash looked away again. "After I joined the Free Spirits," he murmured. "I just warned her to be careful with men like him, but she said I didn't need to worry."

"But you did, didn't you? You were watching her. Watching her visitors."

Ash shook his head, but he couldn't meet her eye now.

"I told you. I just passed by on my bike sometimes," he insisted. "I wasn't *stalking* her or anything."

The word seemed to echo round the walls.

THIRTY-EIGHT

ELISE

Thursday, February 20, 2020

THE SMELL OF overheated oil caught in Elise's throat when she and Caro walked into the Lobster Shack.

A heavily made-up woman behind the bar smiled a weary welcome.

"What can I get you?" she asked, wiping her hands on her "Cracking Claws" polo shirt.

"Mr. Sherman, please."

"Oh, he's out the back, wrestling the accounts into submission. Who shall I say?"

"DI King and DS Brennan."

"Right-ho." She went out and quickly reappeared. "Just go through. It's the last door on the left."

The pub manager was sitting with his back to them. Screwed-up pieces of paper formed a ripple of frustration around him.

"Er, hello again," Sherman sighed, raking his hair with both hands. "How can I help you today?"

"We're piecing together Karen Simmons's last days," Caro said, "and we're told that you visited her flat the night before she was killed."

Sherman sat bolt upright in his chair.

"Who told you that?"

"Well, it wasn't you, was it?" Caro said. "You said you'd never been on your own with her when we spoke the other day."

He hesitated, and Elise wondered if he was really going to try to carry on the pretense.

"Er, yeah, sorry, I forgot," he said, trying to shrug his shoulders as if it was nothing. "I was just dropping off a scarf she'd left at the Free Spirits thing in the Neptune."

"What kind of scarf? What color was it?" Elise was trying to visualize the video clip of the group. Karen hadn't been wearing anything round her neck.

"Er, was it blue?" Sherman stuttered, the lie drying his mouth. "I can't remember. Does it matter?"

"We'll have a look for it in the flat. Anyway, it was late for just dropping by. How long were you with Karen that night?"

"Umm, I don't know. A couple of minutes, I suppose. Just the time it took to hand it over and for her to thank me."

"You were there for almost twenty minutes, according to our witness," Elise explained. "What else have you not told us, Mr. Sherman?"

"What witness? Oh, don't tell me! Ash Woodward. Creeping around, peering in windows. You should be looking at him, not listening to his lies. Look, he hated it that Karen flirted with me occasionally. Just flirted. But he used to stare like he wished I was dead. He's trying to drop me in it."

"Let's continue this at the station, shall we?" Elise said. "It appears we have things to discuss."

THIRTY-NINE

ANNIE

Thursday, February 20, 2020

"Have you ever heard the name Ash Woodward?" Annie asked Xander when she got home.

"Who?" he said, not bothering to stop typing.

"He was there at the end of the vigil," she said. "And I met him again today."

"Okay," Xander murmured.

"He said he was in Knapton Wood the day Archie died," Annie said quietly, and Xander stood, color leaching from his cheeks.

"Oh, darling, I'm sorry. I didn't mean to make you sad," Annie said, reaching up to stroke his face.

"No, I'm just upset for you, Mum," Xander said softly. "He sounds like one of those attention seekers. You know, people who try to insert themselves in a drama. I mean, why would he say that now? All these years later? Forget it, Mum."

"I can't," Annie whispered.

"Have you told anyone else?" Xander said softly.

Annie shook her head, and her son put his arms around her. "Please don't," Xander whispered above her. "It will only encourage him—and other weirdos."

She nodded. Annie didn't want to put her boy through any more. She went and sat on her bed and tried to quieten her thoughts. But her unnerving encounter with Woodward had only increased her determination to dig deeper. She stood and opened her wardrobe door, then stretched her arm up to the top shelf where the secret things lived and pulled a shoebox from the deepest recesses.

The box contained pictures and notes that Archie had scribbled and made. And a letter. Only she knew it was there. Annie felt torn between triumph and despair when she fished it out and brushed off stray glitter and flakes of dried poster paint. She saw she'd even got as far as putting a stamp on it.

But she hadn't posted it to the other mother.

The letter should have been read by Mrs. Donovan sixteen years ago. But she hadn't sent it. She couldn't. Henry had said he'd never forgive Annie if she contacted "that monster's" family. And everything had been too fragile to push back. She and Henry had had to cling together, braced against a common enemy who lived with them, sitting at the breakfast table, lying down with them at the end of the day. Even after he'd hanged himself.

The man in charge of the investigation had come the morning after Nicky Donovan died. Face grave, a cigarette burn on his polyester tie. Annie hadn't been able to focus on what he was saying, but he'd taken her hand and sat her down.

"Annie," he'd said, "we are not looking for anyone else in connection with this. Donovan wrote a note telling us what we already knew. That he was responsible."

"But why? Why did he kill Archie? What did he say?" she'd said, dry-eyed.

The detective had cleared his throat. "He didn't tell us why, just that he was sorry for what he did. That he couldn't help the way he was. And to tell his mum that he loved her."

It was that that had undone Annie. The mention of the other mother. And she'd wanted to reach out to her. If anyone could understand Annie's grief, it would be her. But Henry hadn't seen that. The message had just redoubled his fury.

"He was a coward who killed himself rather than face what he'd done," he'd said, his voice so tight it sounded as if it might shatter like glass. "How can you even think about writing to his mother? It was probably her who made him the disgusting, violent pedophile he was. You are betraying our child."

But Annie had written the letter anyway, sitting on a bench on one of her solitary walks. It hadn't taken long—she'd only wanted to say one thing: "I am sorry for your loss. I know what it is to lose a son."

During the bottomless nights that followed, Annie had lain staring at the spot on the ceiling that Henry's paintbrush had missed. Unable to close her eyes in case their child's dead face was waiting there. And thinking. Pawing frantically at the scraps of things she'd heard.

Donovan's sister had been on the television, telling everyone who would listen that her brother was innocent. Wouldn't have hurt anyone. Cried at soppy films. Was a lovely man.

But how could he have been that sweet boy? And the monster? Was it possible to be both?

"He confessed. In his suicide note," Henry had screamed at the telly, and Annie had sat in silence.

Now, SHE TURNED the envelope over in her hands and looked at the address. She'd overheard two reporters outside her parents' house the day after Nicky Donovan was arrested and had written it down.

"Can you get over there to doorstep Donovan's family?" one of the journalists had said, reeling off the address. "I've already knocked, but the mother wouldn't talk to me. She wouldn't open the door."

Annie wondered if she would today.

She didn't even know if Mrs. Donovan would still be there—she might have been forced to move to escape. Like they had. But the address was only twenty minutes from where the Curtises lived now. Annie got her things, called good-bye to Xander as if she was popping to the shops, and climbed into the car.

The other mother's house was in a scruffy town-center terrace next to a bus stop. The tiny front garden had empty crisp packets and fried-chicken boxes stuffed in the hedge. There was a sign on the door warning against cold callers and junk mail.

Annie's hand was shaking so badly she couldn't keep her finger on the bell, and it rang in shouty blasts.

"Who is it?" a woman called from inside.

"Annie . . . Annie Curtis . . ." she squeaked. The door cracked open. A sliver of face appeared. One eye took her in, and a tear formed.

"Mrs. Donovan," Annie started, but she was crying, too.

"You'd better come in," the older woman said, leading the way.

They sat in the front room clutching tissues—Annie still in her coat and Sylvie Donovan in her pink slippers—and looked at each other. She wasn't what Annie had imagined. But people rarely were, were they? She was bigger, somehow. In Annie's head, she'd always been tiny—withered by what had happened. A tragic, lonely figure frozen in time. A Miss Havisham. But the photographs of babies and wedding couples on the mantelpiece showed that Mrs. Donovan's life hadn't stopped in 2004.

"Why have you come?" she spoke into the silence. And Annie pulled out the letter. It had got creased in her pocket, but Mrs. Donovan smoothed it on her soft lap and waited a moment before she carefully opened the envelope and pulled out the single sheet of paper. She sat staring at the handful of words without saying anything.

"I wrote it a long time ago," Annie said, unable to bear the growing tension. "Just after your son . . . Well, afterward. But my husband said he wouldn't talk to me again if I sent it. He was too upset. Too angry with everyone."

"Of course he was," Mrs. Donovan said quietly, and looked Annie in the eye. "Thank you for writing this. It's funny, isn't it? That no one else understood. Just you. You know, I thought about you every day. Dreamed about you. And still do, sometimes. You and little Archie."

Her son's name being spoken by Mrs. Donovan made Annie cry again and she couldn't speak. Nicky's mum just nodded and patted her arm.

"But why have you brought your letter today, Annie?" she asked.

"Someone else has been killed in Knapton Wood."

Mrs. Donovan nodded again and got up. "I know. Shall I make us some tea?"

TENTATIVELY, THEY TOLD each other about their boys while the ancient gas fire popped and the tea went cold in the pot.

"Nicky struggled with who he was," Sylvie Donovan said. "I knew from very early on that he was gay—it didn't make any difference to me. He was my child and I loved him. But his dad wouldn't have it. There were terrible fights, and Nicky left home as soon as he could. He went off to London to stay with his big sister. And got himself into trouble. I visited him in prison without my husband knowing, and Nicky came back to live near me after his dad died. It said emphysema on the death certificate, but he never got over Nicky being put in jail."

She twisted the thin wedding ring on her finger. "I still miss him," she whispered. "Both of them."

"Why did Nicky kill my son, Mrs. Donovan?" Annie suddenly asked, and the other woman closed her eyes.

"He didn't," she said. "I know it isn't what you want to hear, but Nicky told me he didn't. He wouldn't have lied to me."

Annie sat like a statue, her legs aching with tension. "But," she tried to say, but her mouth was so dry she gulped the word. Mrs. Donovan passed Annie her cup, and she took a sip. "But he committed suicide," Annie said. "And said he was sorry for what he did to Archie. In his note."

"Archie?" Mrs. Donovan said quietly. "No. That's not right." She looked away, struggling with a mixture of emotions that Annie couldn't read, then stood on shaking legs. "I won't be a minute," she said. "You need to see."

When she returned, she pushed a sheet of paper into Annie's hands.

Annie unfolded it. It was a photocopy of the short note Nicky Donovan had written before he hanged himself. It was just three lines: "I'm sorry for what I did to the boy. I can't help the way I am. Mum knows. Please tell her I love her."

"He said he was sorry, that's right." Mrs. Donovan spoke slowly, as if explaining to a child. "Sorry for what happened with the boy—see." And she pointed to the line. "But he's not talking about Archie."

"How do you know?" Annie whispered. *A mother always knows* echoed in her head.

"He told me on my last visit. He was very, very low and frightened. He said the police just kept hammering at him, telling him he must have murdered Archie. But Nicky said he hadn't. He confessed to me what he'd done to your other son, Xander. How he tried to touch him in the wood. He said there was something inside him that made him do these things. I tried to tell the police, but they weren't interested. I'll never forgive them. My son killed himself because they wouldn't listen. I think he just couldn't see any other way out."

Annie sat, stunned, and reread the words with fresh eyes. Had the police made a mistake? She felt her world tilt, and she clung on to the edge of her seat with one hand.

She took a deep breath. "But then, who did kill Archie?" she blurted. Her whole body ached to know.

"I'm so sorry, dear," Sylvie Donovan said. "I don't have an answer to that. Nicky didn't know. He said he ran back to his motorbike after your eldest son pushed him off, and he rode here. He didn't know any-thing had happened to Archie until later. Neither of us did. Nicky looked a bit pale and sweaty when he got home, but it was a hot day. I sent him up for a shower, and I'd just made him a ham salad for his tea when the police knocked and took him away and . . ." She trailed off.

Annie hugged her close when she got up to leave. She wanted to feel that the other mother was real. That Nicky Donovan had been real. "Can I ring you if I need to?" Annie asked, and Mrs. Donovan nodded.

Annie sat in the car after Mrs. Donovan had closed the front door. What would she tell Henry when she got home? The truth? Or nothing? Would she keep it a secret—a splinter to go septic in the flesh of their marriage?

FORTY

ELISE

Thursday, February 20, 2020

AFTER FIVE DAYS of intensive work and not nearly enough sleep, Elise was flagging, but there was so much to do. Caro hadn't got any further with the manager of the Lobster and his hastily arranged solicitor. "Sherman says he and Karen were just talking at her flat—and there are no photos of Karen on his phone. He's being swabbed at the moment. Reluctantly."

"Okay," Elise said, bracing her shoulders as she called the team together. "We're being told that Barry Sherman was in a sexual relationship with the victim," she said. "Our witness is Ash Woodward. A man who admits he was devoted to Karen. He says he saw Sherman visit the flat the night before her death and that Sherman was a regular visitor. Mr. Woodward claims he wasn't watching Karen. It was a coincidence."

"But he lives miles from her place," DC Lucy Chevening pointed out.

"Yes," Elise said. "So we are looking at both men. Where was Woodward all evening? He says he was on his bike. Let's see if he's on any of the town's cameras. And send Sherman's vehicle registration to the ANPR bods. He's got no alibi after his last member of staff left at eleven."

"I'll do that," Lucy chirped and started making notes for the task.

"And then . . ." *Blank.* Elise froze and groped blindly for her next thought.

"We also need to identify all the men at the vigil last night," Caro said, deftly taking up the baton, and Elise gave her a grateful smile.

"We know some of them already, but who are these two for a start? This one looks very young. How did he know Karen? Have we heard from the website Karen was using?" Elise asked.

"Fishing for Freaks?" Andy Thomson grinned. "Well, that's what people call it, and there's definitely pond life—you should see some of the photos. Anyway, they've agreed to cooperate with the police investigation. There was an email this afternoon."

"Why are we hearing this for the first time now?" Caro said, frowning.

The grin disappeared. "Er, everyone was busy."

"Apart from you, it seems."

"Okay." Elise cut short the bickering before it could turn into something—it was getting late and everyone was tired and irritable. She sat at a computer and downloaded the file containing Karen's account details and password. Caro pulled up a chair beside her, and Andy Thomson drifted across to look over her shoulder.

"Let's see who was looking at you," Elise muttered, clicking on the first contact.

HALF AN HOUR later, Elise was still clicking through them. She knew she needed to leave it to someone else, but she couldn't stop looking for a face she recognized from the vigil.

At her side, DC Thomson was making a list of the names. Elise wondered how many would cooperate.

"Shall I check the free apps as well?" Thomson said when they took a break. "They're more . . . well, free."

"Better for predators," Elise muttered. "Well, that's who we're looking for. Where do we sign up?"

"I've got an account," Thomson said. "Everyone does it now. All my friends. For a laugh," he added quickly.

"Okay, if she's on these apps, we'll need a female, won't we?" Caro said. "To look for the creeps. You'll have to sign up as a woman, Andy."

Thomson's face fell. "Why doesn't Lucy do it, then?"

"Because you've just offered," Elise said impatiently. "And DC Chevening is busy with other lines of inquiry. Okay?"

"Yes, ma'am. What shall I call myself?"

Elise felt her personal phone vibrate in her pocket.

"I'll leave that to you," she said, hurrying out into the corridor. "Er, hi," she said, trying to lose the professional clip to her voice. "Mal?"

"It's Mum, love. Are you still at work? Sorry, I thought you'd be home by now."

Disappointment flooded through Elise as the adrenaline drained away. Not him. Why hadn't he rung?

"Is something wrong, Mum?" Elise murmured, steeling herself for her mother's minor domestic dramas.

"No, it's just I haven't heard from you for a week and I know your checkup is coming up."

She knew, of course she did, but it still jolted her to have someone say it out loud. Her checkup meant she couldn't pretend the cancer was history. "Sorry, Mum." She gulped. "I should have called. The appointment's next week, and I promise I'll ring and let you know how I get on. Are you and Dad okay?"

When the call ended, she stood for a moment and took a breath. He'd call. Wouldn't he?

FORTY-ONE

KIKI

Thursday, February 20, 2020

MY MUM LETS herself in bang on six o'clock and shouts a cheery hello up the stairs. I let out a breath and smile. I'd expected Ma to still be huffy after Tuesday's outburst, but turns out there's something she wants to see on my Disney Plus.

"You look nice," she says as she pulls Pip to her on the sofa. I do. I've blow-dried all my hair, not just the front, put on a dress and heels, and feel like a woman with a date instead of just me.

"Thanks." I do a twirl. "Right. Are you okay for snacks? Cheesy films?"

"Go on—we're fine, aren't we, Pip?"

"I won't be late," I say, dropping a kiss on my daughter's head when I hear the taxi outside.

Sitting in the back, I redo my lipstick and try to stop thinking about the BOBs, telling myself I need a few hours off. And that I've probably overreacted to the events at the vigil. The BOBs are saddos, not dangerous predators. "We're talking about Eammon, for God's sake," I say out loud, and the driver raises an eyebrow in his rearview mirror.

My phone rings to save my blushes. It's Elise King, and my pep talk dies on my lips. I go to say, "Do you know who sent me the photo?" but she gets in first.

"I see you've lobbed another grenade into our investigation," she snaps, and for a second I have no idea what she's on about.

"Are we talking about the cyberflashing?" I say.

"We are not." She clips every syllable. "We are talking about your exclusive interview with Evelyn Clayton. I've just caught up with my news alerts."

Shit! I thought I'd got away with that.

"Are you deliberately trying to sabotage this inquiry?" Elise barks down the phone.

"I don't know what you mean." I try wounded innocence, but I know it won't wash—she's got too many miles on the clock.

"Telling the public that Karen was posed," she snaps. "We were keeping that back for operational reasons."

"Okay, I'm sorry. I didn't know." I could tell her about Evelyn's red shoes and Noel's hobby, but I'm fed up with being told off. She can wait.

When she hangs up, I sit back in my seat and try to recapture my mood.

Rob is waiting outside the bar, looking out for me. He's exactly like his picture, and I want to cheer.

"Hi—I didn't want you to have to walk in on your own," he says when I reach him. "You look lovely. Shall we?"

It's nicely noisy inside, so I don't need to fill any awkward silences in the conversation. We keep smiling at each other as we weave through the crowd to a table, and I try to relax while he gets me a glass of wine.

He's tall enough to reach over people's heads at the bar to take the drinks and is back within minutes.

"Cheers," he says and clinks my glass. "Thank you so much for coming—I have a good feeling about this evening."

So do I. He starts asking me about myself, and I've already decided to skirt round the whole reporter issue. It can derail things. People start saying, "I'll have to be careful what I say, won't I?" or give me grief about phone hacking. So I'm a writer tonight. Short stories. Well, it's sort of true. And we move swiftly on to the hilarious pitfalls of adult dating.

Rob makes me laugh more than anyone has done for years. And when he looks deep into my eyes, something inside me does a backflip. Warmth floods through my body and I love this feeling. Of being desired again. He moves closer, so our thighs are almost touching. And I tell him things I haven't told anyone for a long time as he strokes my fingers.

When we leave, I happily get into his car—there are no red flags here—and when he glances across and says, "Are you really ready to go home yet? I'd love to carry on talking," I say yes without hesitation.

"Do you want to go to another bar?" I murmur.

"It'll be so noisy. We could park up and chat. Just the two of us?"

He drives past my road and out of town to a quiet lane near the sea. I can hear the waves when we get out. It's freezing and I pull my coat tighter. "Are you cold?" Rob whispers, and puts his arms around me to warm me up. "Is that better?"

I nod against his chest. I can smell his musky aftershave and feel the strength in his arms, and I have a tiny flutter of nerves. But it's as if he senses it. He lets me go and takes my hand.

"Can I?" he says softly. And I nod.

And the power of that first kiss catches me completely off guard. It's been such a long time since I've experienced any sort of heat and passion. I just don't want it to stop.

And I don't resist when he pushes me against his car and opens his coat.

It's so cold, the sex is quick and urgent before Rob rushes me back into the car and kisses me again. He puts the heating up high and turns the radio on, humming along, occasionally stroking my hand while I look out the window, still in a sort of trance. Struggling with how I feel now.

"You can drop me off at the end of this road," I say when we get close.

"No, no, I'll take you to the door—there are all sorts of strange people out there," he says. "You must have heard about the murder down the coast." And the reminder of Karen makes me go all shivery. I had judged her for doing exactly what I've just done. I can't get out of the car fast enough.

"Oh, God, you've had sex with a man you only met tonight," I whisper to myself once I've waved off my mum and stood in front of the bathroom mirror. Angry-looking blotches bloom on my neck and face. The stigmata of shame. I scrub at my cheeks with a flannel.

"Stop it!" I tell my reflection, and put down the flannel. "You had a great time. And he won't be a stranger next time you see him." Next time. I smile at the memory of that first kiss. It was lovely. He could be a keeper.

FRIDAY:
DAY 7

FORTY-TWO

KIKI

Friday, February 21, 2020

I CAN'T GET going this morning. I sit on the loo seat after my shower and slowly dry my feet as I remember last night. His smile, those eyes, and the instant attraction between us. It was like being pulled into one of those Meg Ryan and Tom Hanks romances I used to happy-cry over as a teenager.

Pip starts banging on the door, demanding her turn, and I stumble up and wrap myself in a towel, telling myself I'll text him later.

"MILES!" I SAY for the third time, and his head finally jerks up. He hasn't spoken to me since I got in, and I've kept myself busy interviewing a sea swimmer about sewage—"We call it going through the motions," the swimmer said obligingly—but I can't get past the intro.

"What?" Miles barks back.

"The BOBs!"

"What? Oh, yeah, yeah, yeah. On it."

I give it five minutes, then go and stand at his side, upping the pressure in case he decides to disappear down some other virtual wormhole.

"Sadly, they're not all as stupid as the numpty from Portslade," he mutters. "A couple of them know what they're doing. They're using VPNs so I can't get to their IPs and locate where they're based."

I nod as if I know what he's talking about.

"Luckily, Lenny and the Captain are less savvy." He smiles in triumph. "Their IPs show them in the Ebbing area, but that's as far as I can get."

"Ebbing? But that's bloody brilliant," I cry, and he almost jumps out of his chair.

"Chill!" he mumbles. "I haven't got their names and addresses. You'll have to track them to other chat rooms and forums where they might share different pieces of info you can piece together to ID them. Course, they'll likely go under different names."

"So how the hell will I know it's them?"

"By looking at the language they use—people repeat words and phrases all the time—and matching bits of personal information from the first chat room." Miles grinned. "Treat it as a sort of psychological Tetris."

"What do you mean, 'you'll have to'?" I scowl down at him. "I thought we were doing this together."

"Busy," he says, and pulls down the shutters.

I groan and go to buy coffees from the shop downstairs.

In the queue I look at my phone. There's a text from a withheld number, and I almost drop my phone in my haste to read it.

Hi, the sex was great last night. Let's do it
again tonight. Maybe somewhere warmer?
😬 Rx

It's like a slap in the face. Nothing about the laughter in the bar. The slow burn. The connection between us. *You silly cow!* I shout silently at myself. *What were you thinking? This was only a big romantic moment in your head. It was just a hookup for him.*

I tap out my reply, my disappointed fingers fumbling the keys:

Sorry—need to put my social life on hold for a bit—up to my ears with work and family. Good luck online!

I just want to close the whole episode down.

But it doesn't work. Rob texts back immediately with reasons why I should go out with him again. He clearly isn't taking no for an answer, and I can't block calls and texts from his withheld number. He told me last night it was a work security thing. And I nodded along while giving him my mobile number, like an idiot.

Ignore him. He'll get bored in the end. Find Lenny and the Captain.

An hour later, my head hurts from the tedious toss that people talk in chat rooms. Why do they bother? It's mainly just pile-ons—let's all hate *insert as applicable*—or pretending to have inside knowledge on international conspiracies despite being a shelf stacker in West Bromwich.

The Captain's old posts could be the work of a fourteen-year-old—sniggering about tits and scoring dates like a judge on *Britain's Got Talent.*

Lenny clearly spends more time online, spreading his misspelled wisdom on gay men, femminists *(sic)*, and working mothers. But he's not sharing today. Scared off by Simon, no doubt. I'm about to give up when I stumble upon a random thread with him giving advice on tiling a bathroom. Apparently, you need to add 10 percent to your calculations or something. Maybe this is the way into his sad little world. Posting as Danny, I try a dingbat question first, building Lenny up as the tiling guru: Good to find someone who knows what they're talking about. What color grout for metallic tiles?

Gray, Lenny responds five minutes later. What surface area?

I pick a number and pretend I'm having second thoughts on silver.

Mettallic tile's are a bugger to clean, he posts back. Mite have to get your old lady on the job.

Bloody hell, he doesn't hang around, does he?

I reply with a winky emoji, and he sends me a link with the message Have a look.

When I click on it, the back view of a woman cleaning a bathroom wearing only yellow rubber gloves appears on my screen. *Bleach-scented porn? Bit niche.*

I'm about to click back to the chat room to pick up the banter with Lenny when the naked cleaner turns her head to say something and her expressionless face is caught in the mirror over the sink.

"Bingo," I say, and pick up my car keys.

THE CLAYTONS' SHOP is closed when I get there. There's a piece of paper stuck to the door announcing "Stock Take." When I walk round to the outbuildings to see if I can see anyone, it's deserted. But I can hear a dog barking frantically somewhere behind the back fence. I stand on tiptoe to look over and see a shabby-looking bungalow. Evelyn Clayton is at the window. She's got her clothes on now.

Her husband suddenly comes out with a big dog, which is pulling and biting at its lead.

"Back in an hour," he calls. "I'll have that ham for my lunch."

I wait until he's loaded the hound into his car and driven off.

"Come on, Kiki," I tell myself, slipping through the gate and walking up to the house. "You might be able to get her to talk about her husband and his revolting hobbies. And if he took pictures of Karen."

The curtains have been closed by the time I get to the door, but I press the bell hard. Evelyn opens the door on a chain, a towel around her shoulders.

"Hello again," I say, and she frowns, clearly trying to place me.

"Oh, God," Evelyn says, panic making her voice shrill when she remembers. "Did he see you? You can't come in."

"I've seen the video of you cleaning the bathroom," I say gently.

Evelyn blinks and whispers: "It's just a hobby—a bit of fun."

"Is it?" I say.

"He's always taking pictures. Of trees and things."

"And you—in the wood with your red shoes on."

Evelyn Clayton closes her eyes. "Just a bit of fun," she repeats, the mantra she's been taught.

"For who?" I ask. "Look, can I come in? Just for a minute?"

Hair dye paraphernalia is all over the kitchen table, and the smell of ammonia makes my eyes water.

"I'm doing my roots," Evelyn explains unnecessarily. "He said I looked a mess. Look, he can't know I've talked to you again. He went mad about that article you wrote." She touches her left shoulder unconsciously.

"What did he do?" I ask, queasy at the thought that my questions may have provoked him.

She just looks away and shakes her head.

"Did he take photos of Karen, Evelyn?" I ask softly.

"Karen?" She gasps. "No, she wasn't interested, he said."

"No, I mean after you found her body?"

Evelyn sits in silence, playing with a comb for a moment, then looks up, face a blank. "I don't know what you are talking about. I'd like you to go now."

She walks behind me as I file out, and when I turn to say good-bye, I stub my toe hard on the hall table and a basket of scarves and wooly hats goes flying. "Oh, God, I'm sorry," I say and bend to scoop everything up.

"Don't worry, I'll do it," Evelyn twitters, clearly anxious to get me out of the house, so I hand her the black beanie I've just picked up and two gloves fall out. Blue gloves.

FORTY-THREE

ELISE

Friday, February 21, 2020

MAL HADN'T CALLED Elise like he'd said he would, and she'd told herself it was probably for the best as she'd tossed and turned last night. But she buttered her burned toast so violently it shattered beneath the knife, sending shards under the table.

She was reaching to pick them up when she heard his back door open and close. She half stood and then forced herself back onto her chair. *He's changed his mind. End of.*

Mal's face suddenly appeared over the fence, and she was in plain view through the kitchen window. "Hi," he called, smiling like he meant it. "Can I pop round?"

Elise scrambled to her feet as soon as he disappeared, stripping off her old dressing gown and throwing a jumper over her pajamas. She listened for his footfall outside.

He knocked lightly, and she opened the front door so quickly he stepped back, laughing.

"Hello! How are you doing?"

"Good, thanks. You?" *Play it cool, Elise. He may be here to make his excuses.*

"Fine. I decided I'd talk to you face-to-face instead of ringing—bit of a nonsense when we live next door, isn't it?"

He hasn't changed his mind, she thought, and felt the blush rising up her neck.

"So, have we got a date tonight?" He smiled. "I thought we could drive into the South Downs and find a cozy pub. What do you think?"

"Er, I'd love to, but I've got a reconstruction."

"Reconstruction?" Mal's face fell.

Oh, God, he's thinking about my lost breast.

"It's a week since the murder," she babbled. "We're reconstructing Karen's known movements on the night she disappeared, hoping to jog memories. We're hoping to find new witnesses who might have seen or spoken to her."

"Oh, right, of course, I see," he babbled back.

"But what about tomorrow?"

"Done," he said, his face glowing. "I'll pick you up at eight. Hope it goes well tonight."

Elise sank onto the sofa after he left. She needed a moment to catch her breath. And enjoy the butterflies fluttering flirtatiously in her stomach. This was good, wasn't it? A proper date after three years of solitary. What the hell would they talk about? The butterflies became a swarm of flies, buzzing with anxiety.

For God's sake, she told herself. *It's dinner, not a proposal. And it's not for another thirty-six hours. I'm going to be too busy to even think about it until then.*

When she finally arrived, the incident room was crammed with bodies—the district commander had given them dozens of uniforms to swell the ranks, and Caro was briefing the troops to flood Ebbing later.

"We need to be everywhere Karen was a week ago," she said. "Jogging memories, asking questions. Mina Ryan has agreed to walk the route from Karen's flat to the Neptune and back. DC Lucy Chevening will be with her, dressed like Karen. Any questions?"

There were, and it wasn't until an hour later that Elise was able to extricate herself and look at the day's task list.

Andy Thomson was deep in the dark world of Tinder prowlers when Elise went to find him.

"Hello, boss," he muttered.

"Go on—who are you today?" Elise asked.

"Er, Angie. I'm using an ex-girlfriend's picture. She's about Karen's age."

"Is she?" Elise said, raising an eyebrow. "Did she give permission?"

"She won't mind," he mumbled.

"Get her to sign a consent form, Andy—okay? Has anyone contacted you yet?"

"Yeah. I've kept it local—radius of twenty miles from Ebbing—and so far Stud and Sailor have swiped right. They're really keen to message me privately—classic technique. Get the women off the app so there's no safety net. I'll carry on messaging with them—and there'll be others. It'll probably get more interesting later. After closing time."

"How romantic," Caro said, appearing with a cup of tea. "What are Stud and Sailor offering?"

"Er, a good time."

"Go on, then, Angie. Get them talking." Caro grinned. "Find out where they want to have this good time."

Thomson typed his reply, and Elise noticed there was a slight tremor in his fingers.

"Everything okay?" she asked quietly. DC Thomson was young and relatively inexperienced. Maybe she should give the job to one of the older guys?

"Yeah, course." Andy Thomson tried to laugh, but it turned into a nervous cough. "But can I just ask: How far will I have to go? Am I going to actually meet these blokes?"

"Not sure you'd get far as Angie with that stubble." Elise laughed but stopped when Andy reddened at his gaffe. "Look, let's not get ahead of ourselves," she went on. "Your job is to identify the sharks—the men who pressure you to meet in dodgy places like Knapton Wood."

Thomson nodded uncertainly.

"I thought you'd used these apps already?"

"I have, but I was batting for the other side. I was the one offering the good time. This just feels a bit weird."

"Well, that should give you a big advantage in spotting the fakes and creeps, won't it? This man is still out there. We need to find him before he targets anyone else."

Elise's phone rang and she groaned. *Bloody Kiki Nunn again.*

"Hello," she said sharply.

"Hi," the reporter said, apparently completely unaffected by their last exchange. "I've just been to the Claytons' bungalow. Noel likes taking pictures of women. Thought you'd want to know. And he wears blue gloves."

FORTY-FOUR

KIKI

Friday, February 21, 2020

"Okay, where are you?" I ask the smudged faces in the video clips when I've parked up on the harbor, waiting for the reconstruction. My car windows have steamed up, and I wipe them with my sleeve to get a bit more light on the subject. I think I've found Eamonn, hat pulled down to his eyebrows, and I've got Lenny, aka Noel Clayton, but there's no one with either of them. I search outward with my fingertips, zooming in and out, but with everyone bundled up against the cold in big coats, I can't even tell if they are male or female. But the Captain was definitely there. I grit my teeth in frustration. And then realize I'm only looking for middle-aged men like Eamonn. The Captain could be any age.

I look with fresh eyes. There are two younger blokes in the middle of the crowd—Elise King pointed them out when we looked at the footage together that night. I zoom in on them.

They're standing with a woman in a red hat. One either side. Like her guards. They've got their heads down. It must be the two minutes' silence.

But that red hat is like a flare, pinpointing the trio in several of the clips as I fast-forward and freeze frames, trying to catch a glimpse of their faces.

It is only when the crowd begins to fragment that they move. The woman heads off on her own, and the two men follow a little way behind. *Where are you going?* I ask the figure battling against the flow of people leaving.

I find her again with her arms wrapped around another woman. When she pulls back, I can see it's Mina Ryan. And there's Ash Woodward. He was there. Standing right beside her.

I dial Mina's number immediately.

"I hugged hundreds of people that night," Mina says when I ask about the woman. "It was a real scrum."

"But this happened at the end, when everyone was leaving. She was wearing a red beanie. And had two lads with her."

"Oh! Hang on," Mina says. "I think I remember her. She said Karen used to do her hair years ago, when she'd been a young mum in Ebbing. I don't know if she said her name—she probably did, but there were just so many people there that night, I can't remember. I couldn't believe how many came. Some traveled from the other side of Brighton. Karen would have been made up."

"Did you talk to the young lads with her?"

"No, just her. But, actually, I think one of them called her Mum."

"What about Ash Woodward? He was there, wasn't he?"

"Well, he adored Karen—trailed after her like a puppy. It was a shame, but she just didn't fancy him. Don't get me wrong, Karen was sweet with him. She said we needed to look after him like he did with his birds. Did you know he nursed his mother until she died last year? He told Karen all about it when she was cutting his hair. Every week. Karen didn't want to charge him anything, but he insisted. And he's rung me several times since she was found, to make sure I'm okay. He's got a kind soul."

"Ash left some flowers up at the wood," I say, moving on carefully.

"I'm not surprised," Mina replies.

"And a note saying he was sorry."

"Sorry? Really?" Mina squeaks. "Why would he say that?"

"That's what I'm wondering. He didn't look happy at the Free Spirits thing I went to, did he? Did they argue?"

"No, he adored Karen." But she doesn't sound as sure now.

I PARK POOR lovelorn Ash while I search for the woman who used to be a customer of Karen's. She must have had hundreds of customers over the years. Where will I even begin?

Ebbing High Street is quiet. It's too cold for the Ebbers to hang around gossiping. I put my head into the supermarket, but the aisles are empty. Destinee Amos is standing behind the till at the checkout, peeling off her gels.

"Oh, hello," I say. "Are you working here now?"

"It's only temporary," she mutters, her face a picture of misery. "I'm not staying. Not if I have to wear this horrible uniform."

"Poor you," I say, stopping myself from adding: *You're lucky to have a job.* "Anyway, where is everyone?" I ask. "It's like a ghost town out there."

Destinee shrugs. "There were a few people in earlier. But nothing's normal at the moment, is it?"

"No, I suppose not."

Destinee is too young and uninterested to recognize the woman at the vigil, but she directs me across the street to the town's oracle.

Ronnie Durrant is a small bird of a woman with a sharp nose and bright eyes. She strips off her rubber gloves at the door. "I'm cleaning the kitchen cupboards as therapy. I'm about to run up and down the High Street naked, I'm so bored. Are you a reporter? Come in."

I love her instantly.

"I saw Karen the evening she died, you know," she carries on as we walk through to her kitchen. "She waved when she walked past my window on her way to the Neptune. I still can't believe it's happened."

"People must be very jittery about her death," I say, pulling out a chair while she puts on the kettle.

"Women, you mean? We are. I've started a Safe Ebbing group so we can spread the word if we see anyone odd."

"Oh." I note it down. "And have there been any sightings?"

"Not yet," Ronnie says. "It's early days. But we've got people joining the WhatsApp group—including local men volunteering to walk us women home after dark."

God, I hope she hasn't asked Noel Clayton.

"That's a good idea as long as you are checking everyone out," I say.

"Course," she chirps as she plonks a cup of tea in front of me. "I know most people anyway."

"Well, I've come to the right house, then," I say, and she beams back at me. "I need help identifying someone from the vigil footage, and Destinee at the Co-op says you know everything about everyone. Because you and your husband have lived here forever."

"Well, don't ask Ted anything!" Ronnie snorted. "He wouldn't notice if my head fell off. Let's have a look, then?"

Ronnie pores over the frames of Mina and the woman, tutting quietly to herself.

"I didn't see her at the vigil, but I definitely know the face," she murmurs. "When do you say she lived here?"

"Not sure," I say, "but she told Mina Ryan she was a young mum in Ebbing, and one of the boys who's with her looks in his twenties. The other mid-teens, perhaps. So, early noughties, maybe?"

Ronnie closes her eyes and starts humming tunelessly.

Oh, dear . . . red flag alert.

"You're not communing with the spirit world, are you, Ronnie?" I give a loud fake laugh.

"Sorry!" Ronnie grins, eyes still shut. "I'm flicking through my filing system. So, my Meggie must have started at the bank and I was full-time at the library. The hairdresser's where Karen first worked was still above the paper shop in the High Street, so . . ." Her eyelids suddenly spring open. "Oh, bloody hell, I know who it is."

"Who?"

"She's the mother of Archie Curtis."

"The boy who was murdered in Knapton Wood?" I cry out. I can't believe it. The boy in the tree house.

"Yes. It's Annie Curtis." Ronnie smiles, well pleased with herself, then frowns. "And she came for the vigil? That's strange, isn't it?"

Good strange, though, I think. Another day, another story. I start looking for an address for her as soon as I get outside.

FORTY-FIVE

ELISE

Friday, February 21, 2020

ELISE WHISTLED SOFTLY to herself when she opened the email and the image filled her screen. It was the last person she had expected to find when the techies ran the vigil footage through facial-recognition software.

But Annie Curtis had been in the crowd. She'd come back to the scene of her child's murder. Elise rocked gently in her chair while she tried to imagine why the grieving mother had returned. Not for Karen, she thought. This wasn't nostalgia for haircuts or highlights. The killing must have reawakened all sorts of terrible memories. And drawn her back to the place they were created.

"What made you come?" she murmured to the face creased by grief, hair lank and as lifeless as the eyes.

Elise pulled up a photo of Annie Curtis from the days following the murder of her son. She'd only been thirty-three, according to the newspaper reports, but she looked twice that.

Caro put her head around the office door. "Can you put one of your special rockets up the lab? We need to know what we've got from Karen's shoulder. Fibers from the glove might help us find the make and nail the wearer."

"Yep," Elise said, only half listening. Then she sat bolt upright. Oh, God, had she told Caro about Kiki's call? About the blue gloves at Noel Clayton's? She scrambled back through every exchange they'd had since lunch. But there were gaping holes she could no longer fill. She'd forgotten if she'd forgotten. Elise slumped down in her seat, exhausted by the effort required to stay in the saddle.

"Noel Clayton has got blue gloves," she murmured, as if she could sneak the information under the wire and into Caro's consciousness.

"Yes, you said," Caro retorted, peering over her shoulder, and Elise felt a burst of relief in her chest. "What are you looking at?" Caro asked.

"The mother of a child murdered in Knapton Wood sixteen years ago. Do you remember little Archie Curtis? And his tree house?"

Caro nodded. "God, was it Knapton Wood?" she muttered.

"Yep. And we've identified Annie Curtis as one of the women who showed up at the vigil. This was her at the time of the killing."

"Really? Let's see. God, she looks destroyed. I suppose she was. How did you ID her?"

"Digital magic upstairs. My neighbor Ronnie told me the family moved away immediately afterward. They used to live in the road at the back of the wood—Yew Tree Lane. It must have been unbearable to see the scene of the crime every day. No one heard from them after they went. But Annie Curtis came back this week."

"So sad," Caro said, and Elise could hear the "anyway . . ." coming.

"Anyway," her sergeant said, "they caught the bloke, didn't they? And we've got a lot on our plate already . . ."

Me—she means me. That I can't cope with more than one thing at a time. Elise forced her hunched shoulders down, away from her ears.

"Doing it," she chanted and lifted her phone. But as soon as Caro left, she put it down and woke up her screen again.

She'd already located the Archie Curtis case file and gave herself fifteen minutes to speed-read the important bits: They'd found DNA evidence of the encounter on Xander's T-shirt and skin and Donovan's jeans—and, crucially, a couple of strands of Nicky's blond hair had been found on Archie's clothing. Given the chaotic, unplanned nature of the attack, she might have expected more on the second victim. *But it's never entirely predictable,* she told herself as she flicked through the scene-of-crime photos. Of course, the victim wasn't there. Archie Curtis had been found a matter of minutes after his death, if the timeline was accurate, but his body had been scooped up by his mother. They only had her witness statement—and the ten-year-old brother's account—to rely on.

After Donovan's suicide, inquests and two funerals were held. And the case had been closed. All nice and tidy.

But at the back of the file, she found Nicky's criminal record. It was a bit of a surprise, if she was honest—he'd been convicted at the age of twenty-three of paying two lads aged sixteen and fifteen to give him hand jobs in a park. No threats or violence used, as far as Elise could see. And no under-thirteens. Not then, anyway. Maybe a year in prison with other sex offenders had changed that.

Elise wrote down the names of the original detectives. She knew she should be focused on the current case, but there were loose ends tickling her. She'd just have a quick chat.

She found DS Larry Agnew on a forum for retired coppers. He was now running a pub in Portsmouth old town.

"Hello," he said when Elise rang and told him who she was. "Caught up with me at last . . ."

Odd reaction, Elise thought, but maybe it qualified as banter in his book.

"Ha!" She gave a fake laugh. "Sorry to bother you, but I just wanted a quick chat about the Archie Curtis murder."

"Right. Is it about the woman in Knapton Wood? I'm not sure what I can help you with, Elise." *No rank given,* she noted. *Is he being matey or making some sort of point?*

"Of course, we got our man straightaway," he continued, firmly. *So, not matey.*

"Right. Nicky Donovan."

"Yep. A sex offender they dumped on Ebbing. No one knew who he was. Who they'd got living in their little town. Until he killed one of their kids."

"Yeah, I've been having a look at the case—and his record. His previous was with older lads, wasn't it? A fifteen-year-old was the only underage victim, not children of Xander and Archie Curtis's age. And he'd never used violence before, had he?" Elise asked.

DS Agnew exhaled noisily—the "here we go" sigh she knew so well. The "you might be senior to me, girlie, but I've been around the block more times than you've had hot dinners" sigh. *Bet he gets my name wrong. Just to show me he couldn't care less,* Elise thought.

Look, Elsie," he said, and she gritted her teeth. "This was different. You have to realize that Donovan must have been terrified when Xander Curtis ran off—he knew he'd be straight back in prison. And he must have panicked when he chased after him and came across Archie Curtis. We think the younger boy shouted and he was trying to shut him up and used more force than he meant, and the boy suffocated."

"Okay. You picked him up very quickly after the attack."

"If you've read the case file, you'll know Xander Curtis gave us the name. Xander said a man called Nicky had touched him and the boy banged his head against a tree when he tried to run off. Xander said he hid for a bit and when he got back to his little brother, he couldn't wake him. Listen, I looked Donovan in the eye. He was guilty as sin. And he confessed before he hanged himself."

"Did he?" Elise asked slowly. "There's no statement under caution to that effect, is there? Unless I've missed it?" She knew she hadn't, and her unease about the speed at which the case had been handled was building.

Larry Agnew breathed heavily. "He left a note. Look," he growled. "I've got a bar to bottle up."

"Oh, well, there are a couple of other matters," she added, but the phone had gone down. "I'll be in touch, Harry," she told the dead air.

FORTY-SIX

KIKI

Friday, February 21, 2020

I LOOK AT my watch for the umpteenth time, as if it might be playing tricks on me, but no, it hasn't suddenly gained an hour. I groan. The day has got away from me, and there isn't time to drive to Southsea to see Annie Curtis now. The reconstruction of Karen's last walk through Ebbing is taking place in an hour or so. I ring in to tell Miles to expect my holding piece—five hundred words on a town held hostage by fear.

"It'll make a nice color piece," I say.

"Haven't they caught the bloke yet?" Miles grunts.

"No. Have you found the rest of the brotherhood?"

"Got some new ideas, actually. Get lots of visuals."

MINA RYAN IS in tears before she even sets out. "Are you okay?" I hear Elise King ask her as they stand on the pavement outside Karen's salon. She sounds tetchy—I wonder if she's got her own big-night nerves. All eyes are on her. The cops, reporters, cameras, locals. I don't envy her—it must be like running a three-ring circus with a hangover.

"We're so grateful you are doing this," Elise adds as Mina wilts beside her. "Just remember that Lucy will be with you and we'll be right behind you the whole time."

I lead the peloton of journalists that forms ahead of them in the dark street. Some of the photographers walk backward to video Mina and Chevening's unsteady progress, bumping into each other and stumbling over their own feet. I keep clear of the melee and capture Mina's distraught face on my phone.

Around us, police officers are handing out pictures of Karen in her red dress to passersby, and Elise is watching for reactions and faces appearing at lit windows and on doorsteps. When we finally reach the Neptune, I see DI King suddenly raise a hand to wave at someone, but I can't see who.

Minutes later, we're in the fug of the Neptune. The atmosphere is edgy and conversation sounds forced as Mina and Lucy Chevening walk in. Then silence, apart from the scraping of chair legs as the two women take a seat.

DC Chevening goes to get Mina a much-needed brandy, and I peer around at the watchful drinkers. All locals. I tick off some names. I stop when I get to Evelyn Clayton, drooping on a stool at the end of the bar. Is she here alone? No: Noel Clayton is coming out of the gents, shaking water from his hands. At least, I hope it's water.

"Hello," I say. "How are you both doing?"

He looks at me, cold fisheyes taking me in. "You're that reporter, aren't you?" he growls. "What are you doing here?"

"I'm here for the police reconstruction—helping them find the man who killed Karen Simmons," I say, and some of the blokes at the bar murmur their approval. "How about you? Have you come to help? Or are you a regular?"

Clayton picks up his pint. "I didn't know it was happening, but we thought we'd stay to see what was going on," he says, sounding defensive. "The Neptune's all right, but I prefer the Lobster."

"Really? I wouldn't have thought it was your kind of thing." I try to imagine Noel Clayton propping up the bar in the over-pimped gastropub.

"It's handy for my place," he mutters.

"Isn't here closer?" I point out, and he scowls. "Were you here last Friday?"

"Er, not sure," he mumbles, and Evelyn squirms on her stool.

"Yes, I think you came in later, Noel," Doll, the landlady, chimes in. His scowl deepens.

"Oh, right. I dropped in for one drink," Clayton growls. His wife drains her glass. She hasn't spoken.

"We went out for a curry, didn't we, Evelyn?" She nods but doesn't look at me. "Evelyn went home after, but I fancied a nightcap."

"Yes, that's right," Evelyn says, her eyes flicking to her husband.

"So you must have seen Karen Simmons."

"No," Clayton says, a fraction too quickly.

"Are you sure?" I press him. "Other people are saying she really stood out. She was being very loud and laughing a lot."

"No," Clayton repeats. "I didn't see her."

Until you did. In the wood. With your blue gloves on.

"Right. Maybe you knew her from other occasions? She joined in lots of things in Ebbing."

"I don't do community stuff," Noel says.

"What about your photography?" I say evenly. "I hear you're quite the cameraman. You were taking pictures the morning you found Karen's body, weren't you?"

Clayton's eyes bulge, and a vein in his forehead begins to pulse. Evelyn's handbag falls to the floor, and as he stoops to pick it up she finds my eyes. *Don't tell* is written all over her face.

"No," he barks when he stands up. "And it's none of your business what I do in my spare time."

Elise King appears behind him. "Hello, Mr. Clayton. Mrs. Clayton," she says. And Noel's vein throbs harder.

"Hi," I chip in. "How's the response to the reconstruction? We were just discussing Mr. Clayton's hobby. He's a keen photographer," I say, and Elise's lips twitch.

"Oh, that's right," Elise says. "You were at Knapton Wood for the sunrise, weren't you? I don't suppose you took any photos of the crime scene?"

"Of course I didn't," Noel explodes, and the other drinkers edge farther down the bar. "Why would I do something like that?"

"No need to get excited," Elise says firmly. "I simply thought you might have taken some to show the police."

"Oh, right," Noel mutters. "I don't remember."

"Okay. Well, perhaps I could have a look at the photos you took last week on your phone?"

"What for? Look, this is an outrageous invasion of my privacy. I'm going to talk to my solicitor about this."

He's got a solicitor, then.

"Of course, if you feel you need to," Elise says calmly. "You can bring him when you come in to see me at Southfold station tomorrow morning."

I love the way she's handling him—like a starchy headmistress. I expect some men might get off on it, but Noel Clayton clearly doesn't.

"I'll do no such thing. This is harassment."

"Not at all, Mr. Clayton. You are an important witness. Ten o'clock tomorrow morning, please. Or should I send a car?"

The implication takes a moment to register, and when it does, his face darkens further. "Noel . . ." his wife murmurs, eyes fixed on him.

"Shut up, Evelyn," he snaps. "I'll go."

MINA LEADS THE way out of the Neptune at ten thirty, holding Lucy Chevening's arm as they stumble through the tables of drinkers and reporters. She lets go outside the newsagent's and stands beside Elise as Lucy makes her way alone up the High Street in front of the curious locals. Elise and Mina follow slowly, and when they reach Karen's flat, Mina looks round sharply.

"Ash! I didn't see you there," she squeaks.

The shy bird rescuer slips out of the shadows and goes to stand beside her as they both gaze up at the darkened windows.

SATURDAY:
DAY 8

FORTY-SEVEN

ELISE

Saturday, February 22, 2020

ELISE HAD WOKEN in a knot of sheets and duvet that morning, and her head was still untangling her thoughts from the previous night. It'd been a late one when Caro had dropped her off at the Ebbing town sign. The debrief back at Southfold after the reconstruction had taken longer than Elise had anticipated. But it had produced some results.

Noel Clayton had been there that night, for a start. He'd failed to mention that before, and he'd made a big thing of denying seeing Karen enjoying herself. He'd have to have been wearing ear defenders and a blindfold, if the other witnesses were to be believed.

Elise had left the team to finish up the last bits of paperwork at eleven thirty when Caro offered her a lift. They'd talked about next steps in the car, but Elise had asked to get out early, telling her sergeant she needed a walk to finish processing the evening. Ebbing had been deserted, and she'd heard the clatter of her boots echoing off the shop fronts. Elise had pictured Karen stumbling in her heels along the same pavement. Who had been watching her? Was anyone watching Elise? She'd glanced round and told herself to get a grip. But she'd walked faster. She'd wanted to get home quickly for another reason. Mal had waved when she'd spotted him standing in his doorway earlier. And

she'd waved back. Not very professional in the middle of a police oper-
ation, but she hadn't been able to stop herself.

It had been just after midnight when she'd stood in front of his
house. But there'd been a light on downstairs. He was only a door knock
away. Elise had shivered and felt the delicious tingle of goose bumps on
her arms. She'd run into her house and pulled a bottle of wine out of the
fridge. But as she closed her front door, Mal's light had gone off. And
she'd stood listening at his door like a stalker.

Elise had gone home, shoved the wine back, and taken off her coat.
And lain in bed catastrophizing: Had he avoided her? Seen her coming?
Heard her door close? Changed his mind?

*Don't be ridiculous! It's the middle of the night. You just missed him,
that's all.*

But it was the first thing she thought of when she woke. And she knew
she was looking forward to tonight more than she should. It was beginning to frighten her—it was becoming too much of a thing too quickly,
distracting her, making her giddy. *You need to calm down,* she told herself
as she smeared foundation over her sleep-deprived skin. *And find the killer.*

KAREN'S CAR HAD produced dozens of prints—mostly her own—but
there were none on the steering wheel, gear stick, hand brake, or driver's
door handle. "They've been wiped," the crime scene coordinator, Lionel
Brewer, phoned to tell Elise. "He's been very thorough."

"Karen wasn't the last person to drive the Fiat," Elise said, all business, when she walked into the incident room. "Someone carefully
cleaned the things they touched."

"Like Karen's face," Lucy Chevening said.

"Exactly. We need to know who was in the car. Has the car park
video been analyzed yet?"

Before anyone could answer, Elise marched straight upstairs to look
for herself.

A world-weary sergeant was stretching in front of his screen, flexing
the backrest of his office chair to the breaking point.

"Hello, ma'am." He grinned. "How can I help?"

"Hi. Have you got to the Brighton multistory footage?"

"No, I was prioritizing the Ebbing town center stuff. Give me a few minutes to pull it up."

Elise stood fidgeting with her phone until the sergeant sighed pointedly. She stepped back to give him space to work.

"It's not great quality," the older man said. "Cheap cameras, and our vehicle is moving fast and away from us."

"Can we see how many people were in it?"

The sergeant enlarged the image, instantly blurring the definition. "Looks like one individual to me," he said. "We've only got the back view, but the driver's head is a good few inches above the headrest."

"It would have been set for Karen," Elise said, trying to remember the victim's height. "She was five four. So this is a six-footer."

"Give or take. I'll get the techies on it."

She watched the footage back and forth, frame by frame, willing herself to see through the blurred graininess like those Magic Eye pictures that hold hidden secrets. But however hard she squinted, the details refused to be seen.

"My feeling is that Karen was dead in the wood by the time her Fiat was parked in Brighton," Elise said, back in the incident room, as Caro updated the timeline on the whiteboard. "The killer took the car and drove away. It looks likely he knew the area. He didn't take main roads and chose an out-of-the-way car park to dump it. But where did he go from there?"

"Home?" Caro said. "Why else would he drive to Brighton?"

"To hide the car?" DC Chevening suggested.

"Bad plan if he's from Ebbing," Caro replied. "The trains would have stopped by then, and there are no night buses back this way. It'd have to be a taxi—or phone a friend. I'll get someone on the cab firms."

"We can only see the back of the suspect's head in the images, but we believe he's around six foot. Ash is tall—let's see if Karen's guardian angel has any Brighton connections. And put Barry Sherman on that list, too. And Noel Clayton. He troubles me. Him and his terrified wife."

FORTY-EIGHT

ANNIE

Saturday, February 22, 2020

ANNIE HADN'T BEEN able to stop thinking about the suicide note since getting back from Mrs. Donovan's, the words playing in her head—the police's version, Sylvie's version, the nuances, the possibilities—while she'd been doing the washing-up last night or pretending to watch the television with Henry. Him sitting beside her, complaining that the weather forecasters had got it wrong again or tapping on his computer on his lap. In his own world. And that was good. He couldn't be in hers just now.

He'd been getting something he'd left in the car when the late local news had shown bits of the police reconstruction. Annie had turned it down in case Henry heard it from the hallway and told her to turn it off. She'd watched, quietly gripped, while Xander texted Emily from the sofa. He'd been so absorbed he hadn't even looked up when the woman in a red dress started walking up the High Street. Annie had been sitting forward on the edge of her chair, looking for someone she might recognize, when she'd yelped and made her son jerk his head up.

"That's him," she'd said, breathless and pointing. "The man who said he'd been in Knapton Wood."

"Oh, God, Mum," Xander had croaked, and stood in front of the television to block her view. "Please let this go."

"What's going on in there?" Henry had called through.

"Nothing," Xander had snapped, and then sat back down with his message to Emily.

This morning, Annie had suggested that Henry take the boys to the driving range—a bonding exercise that no one looked keen on as they left. But it meant Annie had a couple of hours to herself. Well, just her and Nicky Donovan.

The internet took her straight back to August 9, 2004, the day Nicky Donovan had slipped into their lives. Annie couldn't remember seeing any of the front pages at the time. They'd probably been kept out of sight by Henry or the police officer looking after them. Not that it would have mattered. Annie hadn't been capable of putting one foot in front of the other, let alone reading.

Every article seemed to have Archie's face laughing out of it. It was the photo Annie saw every day on the stairs. Henry must have given it to the police. She stroked the face on the screen and stopped herself. *I need to keep moving. Or I'll sink.*

The day after Archie died, the papers had announced, "A twenty-four-year-old man has been arrested in connection . . ." but Nicky Donovan's name hadn't appeared until later. Until he'd been charged and appeared at the magistrate's. And the reporters had got hold of the ice-cream picture.

Annie read everything, making notes in a small exercise book. Times, dates, movements, distances. She used to love puzzles as a child—piecing jigsaws together with her dad on the green baize card table. Not speaking, just trying things out in their heads until they got the whole picture.

She got an old road atlas out of the hall cupboard, shelved when the GPS tyrants had arrived in their cars, and plotted it all out on the most well-thumbed pages. The pages where they used to live. And Archie died.

The police must have done similar things. But, of course, they'd had their man the same day.

The first time Annie had heard Nicky Donovan's name, they'd still been in a state of ignorance. In the small room without windows at the hospital where she, Henry, and Xander had huddled together on one small sofa. They'd had to leave Archie. His little body was under a fresh white sheet, and Annie had wanted to tuck him in one last time, but Henry had taken her hand and led her away, and she'd been too dazed to resist. Xander, his head bandaged, had fallen asleep in Annie's arms, like he used to as a toddler. Before he'd grown too big for cuddles and baby names.

"Can you tell me what happened this afternoon?" Annie could remember a police officer saying to her and how she'd tried to focus on his face but all she could see were the black hairs coming out of his nose.

"I don't know," she'd said, shredding a tissue in her lap. "The boys were playing in the trees. Climbing and making camps. This summer was the first time we'd let them go on their own. We thought they were old enough, didn't we, Henry?"

Her husband hadn't said anything.

"I could hear them from the garden," Annie had gone on, pleading her innocence.

"Could you?" Henry had said under his breath.

"But you couldn't see them?" the policeman had carried on.

"No." She hadn't looked up. Couldn't bear seeing the judgment in the officer's eyes. *The Terrible Mother.*

"And where were you, Mr. Curtis?" He'd turned to Henry, and Annie had held her breath.

"I'd gone to the office in Portsmouth to catch up on paperwork," he'd said, and she could hear the dry squeak of the lie in his voice, like a telltale floorboard. But she'd kept quiet, telling herself that now wasn't the time.

"I see. And what did you hear, Mrs. Curtis?"

"I don't know—the boys shouting to each other. I don't know."

Annie hadn't told him that she'd been on her knees, trying to still her head and pretending to pull out weeds between the paving slabs after Henry had stormed off over a pointless row about his absences. She'd had no way of really knowing where her husband was every day in his job. As a medical rep, *on the road* covered so many sins. But his phone had started running out of battery, and his appointments with customers overran every other day. She'd tortured herself with the thought he might be seeing someone else. There'd been a couple of secretaries on his sales patch who'd sent him jokey, sexy messages the year before. He'd laughed it off when Annie saw them on his phone. "Just silly girls bored at work." He'd dismissed the subject. And she'd managed to laugh with him.

But that day, it had felt different. He hadn't laughed. He'd been defensive when she'd asked too many questions about where he'd been. And Annie hadn't been able to stop thinking about it. The truth was, she'd stopped listening for her boys.

"I didn't hear the accident," she'd told the detective. "I didn't know anything had happened until Xander came running out with his head bleeding."

"What did Xander say?"

Annie had noticed her son's eyelids flutter and still themselves and wondered if he was really asleep.

"That Archie had fallen down. I thought they must have been climbing the big tree and slipped."

"And Xander didn't say anything else?"

Annie had reached down to stroke his scratched, bare leg.

"No, he was in shock and injured. I just ran to find Archie. And he was there, under the tree."

"Can you describe exactly what you saw, Mrs. Curtis?"

"He was sort of half lying, half sitting where he'd landed. With his head down. I couldn't see his face," she'd said, silent tears dripping off her chin onto her son's head.

The officer had hesitated and then leaned forward to be closer to her. "The thing is, Mrs. Curtis, his injuries do not suggest that Archie fell. We'll have to wait for the full report, but early indications are that he asphyxiated. Sorry, suffocated."

Annie and Henry had looked at each other, wild-eyed, but neither of them had been able to speak. Annie had automatically hugged Xander closer, and their boy had opened his eyes.

"Darling," she'd said, turning him to face her. "What happened to Archie?"

"There was a man," he'd whispered. "In the wood."

And he'd buried his head in Annie's neck and sobbed. Terrified all over again. He'd been too frightened to say before. The man had touched him, rubbed his bottom through his trousers and whispered things. And chased him when Xander had run away. He'd hit his head on a tree and hidden. And Archie had been lying there when he'd got back to the camp.

"Who was the man?" the detective had asked gently. "Did you know him?"

"He said his name was Nicky," Xander had said.

The police had picked him up within hours. He was a known sex offender living ten minutes from their home. From their boys.

It had all been so clear. So horrifyingly clear for a moment.

But not afterward. The picture had quickly gone out of shape.

Annie thought she heard the gate close and scrambled to hide her notes and the atlas. And put on her mum face. But there was no key in the lock. Someone was knocking on her door.

FORTY-NINE

KIKI

Saturday, February 22, 2020

Annie Curtis appears at the window when I knock, and I pull my "sorry to disturb" face.

She cracks it open and I say: "Hello." Not too brightly. This is a death knock, even sixteen years on. "Apologies for calling on a Saturday, but I wondered if you had a moment for a chat. I'm a reporter for Sussex Today."

"Oh!" Annie Curtis says. "You were in the crowd on Wednesday, weren't you? Asking people about Karen Simmons and women's safety."

"Yes, that was me," I say, pleased she recognizes me. "I heard you were there, too. That must have been so difficult for you, given your family's history with Knapton Wood."

I try not to hold my breath. This is the knock-back moment. When the punter decides whether to let me in or not. Sometimes it's obvious I'm not getting through the door. But today, I think it's fifty-fifty.

"I've never spoken to a reporter," Mrs. Curtis says quietly. "It was terrible when the press came after Archie died. My dad had to go out to ask them to leave."

But she doesn't close the window, and I keep going.

"Karen's death must have made you relive all that," I push on. "And suffer all over again. You poor thing."

The face at the window softens. It starts to rain, and I do a dance in my head. Annie Curtis doesn't look the kind of woman to leave someone out in this weather.

"Oh, you'd better come in," Annie announces, disappearing and opening the front door. "Come through. We can sit in here."

I sit opposite her at the kitchen table and put my phone to record.

"Do you want a hot drink?" Annie says. "You look frozen."

"That's very kind, I am." I rub my hands together to warm them.

"Anyway, I'm not sure what I can tell you," Annie murmurs half to herself as she switches on the kettle. "You must have looked it up on the internet already. It was in the papers for weeks at the time."

"But that was when it happened. I'm interested in how you are now—and what you feel about this latest death. How it has affected you," I say, and nod her on.

"Well, obviously, it was a terrible shock to hear about Karen," Annie says, still standing at the counter. I can see the tension building in her shoulders and get up to stand beside her.

"You sit down," I tell her. "I'll make the drinks."

"Thank you. It's just so hard to think about. Even after all this time."

"Of course it is."

"People tell you time is a great healer, but it can still feel like it happened yesterday. As if Archie is about to run in all breathless and tell me he's off to play in the wood with his brother. And then I remember. And it crushes me."

"How do you even start to deal with that?" I ask, putting our mugs down on the table. "I've got a daughter of thirteen, and I am completely terrified about the years ahead. About letting go."

The bereaved mother looks at me. "You have no idea," she whispers. "I'd give anything to be in your shoes. Anything. I should never have let them go and play in Knapton Wood. I should have kept them closer."

"But we can't, can we?" I reply, thinking about my prickly girl. One minute it's all eyeliner and attitude; the next, wanting me and *Frozen*. "We can't smother them," I add without thinking.

And the word clangs between us.

Annie closes her eyes. "No," she whispers. "Someone else did that."

"Oh, God! I'm sorry." I curse myself, mortified. "I didn't mean to . . ."

There's silence in the room. Annie stands on trembling legs to fetch a piece of kitchen towel.

"I can't imagine how you coped," I say softly, scrambling to save the interview.

"I didn't," Annie murmurs, sagging down in her chair as a tear escapes. "We didn't. Xander—well, he disappeared inside himself, playing on his own, you know, building tiny models, creating little armies with his figures. That was how he coped."

She sniffs and looks across at me. "He had a wonderful imagination, you know? His form teacher said he was gifted. He once told her that he was adopted as a baby, like Superman," she adds. "She told us at a parents' evening because she thought it was so sweet."

"Right," I say, impatient to shift us away from tiger mother tales. "But you moved away from Ebbing?"

"We had to. To get away from it."

"Of course. So, how did you know Karen? Were you very close to her when you lived in Ebbing?"

"No, not really," Annie remembers. "She was nice, but I only knew her as a hairdresser, really. She wasn't a friend or anything. We had different lives—I had the kids, and she was younger, free, and single."

"So why did you come back last Wednesday?" It's the question I've been waiting to ask since I came in.

Annie hesitates and I lean in.

"I suppose I felt it was time," she says.

"Time for what?"

"Time to go back. To face it. Face what happened that day. The day my son died. There wasn't time then for the questions I wanted to ask. A man was arrested straightaway."

"Nicky Donovan," I say, and she squeezes her eyes shut.

"Yes. But everything moved so fast, and then Donovan killed himself and took all the answers with him. I needed to know why. Why had he killed my little boy? But I didn't get the chance."

"That must have been fresh trauma for you and your husband."

"Henry didn't have any questions," Annie whispers. "He didn't want to know anything else. It was just me. And Nicky Donovan's family," she went on.

"Yes. He had a sister, didn't he?"

"And a mother. I've met her."

"Nicky Donovan's mother? When?" I think back over my research, but I'm certain I haven't seen that in the cuttings.

"The day before yesterday," Annie says. "After the vigil, I just wanted to talk to her."

Bloody hell! There might actually be a story here, not just a sidebar. "Why?"

"You sound like my husband. Because we both lost someone."

"And what did she say?"

"How much she missed her son. We sat and talked about our loss. I know it sounds crazy, but we understood each other."

I can see the piece on the page and wonder how I can get a photograph of them together.

Annie stops and looks away. "She said that Nicky didn't kill Archie," she whispers.

"I suppose no mother wants to believe her child is a killer," I reply gently.

"I suppose not," Annie says, wadding her tissue into a tiny tight ball. "But she said he would never have lied to her. And that the police had misunderstood his suicide note. They took it as a confession. But it was about the wrong boy."

"Wrong boy?" I say, the hairs on my arms tickling under my jumper.

"Yes. I'm going to go back to the police," Annie says. "And show them the copy of the note."

"What? Have you got it?" I blurt. "Did Mrs. Donovan give it to you? What does it say? Can I see it?"

Annie suddenly stands, and I'm furious with myself for pushing her too hard.

"I think I've said all I want to," she announces. "More than I should, really."

"No, no, it's been very moving. And I'm sure it will help other families who are grieving," I try, but Annie has already moved to the door into the hall.

"Well, thank you for talking so openly," I say, putting my business card on the table. "Please call me if you think of anything you want to add."

I sit in my car for twenty minutes down the road from the Curtis house before realizing I am shivering and restarting the engine. I'm trying to get the story straight. Stories.

Karen's murder; the online dating brotherhood; and little Archie Curtis.

My rooting about online early this morning had given me the headlines about his killing, but I still can't seem to make any connections with the current investigation.

Yes, Archie Curtis was found dead in Knapton Wood, and so was Karen Simmons. But what else is there to link them, apart from location—she was an adult, he a child. Everything else is different, isn't it? Down to the time of day and season. But Karen's killing has clearly woken something in Annie Curtis. And brought her back to Ebbing. I'm shivering again. There's something here, I know it. I just need to keep digging.

I find an address for Mrs. Donovan and ring Miles to give him a heads-up about my exclusive interview.

"It happened sixteen years ago," my idiot news editor sighs. "Why would anyone be interested? I'm not. The bloke who did it is dead. The story's dead. Let's concentrate on the here and now, shall we?"

I swear loudly when the call ends and swerve away from the curb to drive to Mrs. Donovan's house anyway, but after a few meters I pull over again. I've got so much on already—Karen, the column, bloody Rob still pestering me. And Pip. Oh, God! I've promised to take her shopping and I'm already late. Have I really got time for a cold case rabbit hole? I decide I'll look at it later, when Pip's in bed.

I turn the car around and head for the shopping center.

FIFTY

ELISE

Saturday, February 22, 2020

NOEL CLAYTON AND his solicitor rolled up on the dot of ten a.m. Mr. Grimes, who operated above a charity shop in Ebbing High Street, was well known to Elise—they had sat on opposite sides of the table often enough for him to give her a discreet smile.

"Good morning, DI King," he said, taking his seat beside his red-faced client. Neither man took off his coat. They were clearly not planning on staying long.

"Right," Noel Clayton started in immediately, wagging a fat sausage of a finger in Elise's face. "This is outrageous. I know my rights." She wished she had a quid for every time she'd heard that. They never did, really. She usually had to tell them.

"Of course, Mr. Clayton. Thank you for coming in. I have some questions that I hope will help us discover what happened to Karen Simmons."

"Well, I have no idea. I just found her body. And I've told you everything I know," Clayton fumed. "This is a waste of my time, and my wife is waiting for me downstairs."

Mr. Grimes laid a hand on his client's arm and murmured some soothing words.

"Let's get on, then, shall we?" Elise continued as if he'd never spoken. "You told me yesterday evening that you were in the Neptune at the same time as the victim on February the fourteenth."

"But I didn't see her," Clayton said and rolled his eyes. "I was at the bar, talking to some bloke."

"Who?"

"I can't remember. I was only in there for one drink."

"Are you sure? A witness we spoke to last night said you drank a couple of glasses of whiskey."

Noel Clayton's face darkened to a shade an interior designer might call Imminent Coronary.

"Well, two, then. What does it matter how many drinks I had?"

"Yes, Inspector," Mr. Grimes chimed in. "What is this about?"

"I am interested in the accuracy of your client's recollection of events," Elise stated sharply. "We have spoken to twenty-six people who were in the Neptune that evening, and every single person remembers seeing Karen. Apart from Mr. Clayton here."

Grimes gave a small shrug. "He says he didn't. Shall we move on?"

"Where did you go after you left the pub?"

"Straight home. You can ask my wife."

"We will," Elise said, making a note. "Did you leave your house again that night?"

"No," Clayton said firmly, but his hands fidgeted, tapping a ragged rhythm on the table. "I didn't know Karen Simmons beyond seeing her in the street," he declared. "And I didn't recognize her when I found her body in the wood."

"I see. I asked you last night if you photographed the scene when you found her," Elise said.

"And I told you I didn't," he snapped.

"But I understand you have a special interest in taking pictures."

"Who says?" he spluttered.

"You did," Elise said. "The first time we met. You said you were in Knapton Wood to photograph the sunrise."

Clayton swallowed loudly.

"Have you brought your phone in with you?" Elise pushed on.

"My client's personal photographs have nothing of relevance to this investigation," Grimes interrupted smoothly, "but he has agreed to let you see them to draw this line of questioning to a close."

Elise stole a glance at Caro and allowed one of her eyebrows to twitch upward.

"Thank you," Elise said as Clayton pressed a finger to his phone to unlock it and handed it over. He then looked straight ahead, hands clasping and unclasping in his lap while Elise and Caro scrolled through. The photos appeared to be of Clayton's last stock-take: There were dozens of shots of kitchen tiles, rolls of insulation, tools of every sort. The only human was his wife, standing in front of a display. There were also the usual number of accidental photos—blurs, people's feet, and corners of ceilings.

"Have you deleted any images before coming in today?" Elise said, letting Caro finish the mind-numbing trawl.

"No," Clayton said, holding out his hand for the return of his phone.

"Hang on," Caro said quietly.

It was one of the accidentals, so murky it looked as if it could have been taken in someone's pocket. Or in the dark.

But Noel Clayton's feet started tap-dancing under the table when Elise leaned closer to the screen.

"Look there," Caro said, fiddling with the settings to lighten the image. "See, at the edge. It's a tree."

Elise followed the line of the trunk. Her head snapped up to look Clayton in the eye. "You can see a branch," she said, "sloping down. Like the one Karen was sitting under."

"I can't see any branch," he muttered.

"Was this taken at the spot where you found her?" Elise pressed, her pulse racing.

Clayton shook his head, but his face was telling a different story.

"Did you take pictures of Karen Simmons, Mr. Clayton? You should know that our forensic experts will be examining your phone for deleted images."

"Perhaps I could have a word with my client," Mr. Grimes said.

———

OUTSIDE THE INTERVIEW room, Caro grinned broadly. "He's dumped the ones showing Karen," she said. "He must have missed that last one."

"But did he kill her?" Elise murmured. "He says he was at home with his wife all night. And he'd have to have balls of steel to take Evelyn there for a walk a few hours later and 'discover' the body."

"Perhaps he wanted another look? To crow over what he'd done? And record it."

BACK IN THE interview room, Noel Clayton was shifting in his seat. *Those balls of steel giving you trouble?* Elise thought as she and Caro took their places.

"I did not take any photos in Knapton Wood," Clayton said, his voice flat. "My wife was carrying my phone. I believe she may have dropped it. The camera could have gone off accidentally."

"Your wife?" Elise said slowly. She couldn't believe he was throwing poor terrified Evelyn Clayton under the bus.

She turned to Caro and nodded. Her sergeant got up immediately and left the room.

"She's only downstairs, so we'll see what she has to say," Elise said, and Noel Clayton struggled to his feet. "Sit down, please. We'll talk to her on her own."

"This is outrageous," he exploded—but he didn't sound outraged anymore. Just scared.

EVELYN CLAYTON WAS silent when she was brought up to a separate interview room. Elise realized it was the first time she'd spoken to her without her husband being present, and she felt a stab of irritation that she hadn't done it earlier.

The woman looked like a rabbit in the headlights. She had no one to prompt her now. No matter how often her eyes darted around the room.

"Mrs. Clayton," Elise said gently. "I just have a few questions about the morning you and your husband found Karen Simmons's body."

Evelyn Clayton's head went down, and her hair fell like a curtain to hide her face.

"Did you take photographs of the victim?"

"Me?" Evelyn Clayton squeaked, and her head shot back up.

"Did anyone take photos of Karen?" Elise said quickly.

"No, no," she protested. "I was so shocked, I just did what Noel told me." Her eyes lost focus for a moment as she remembered. "What has he said?"

"Did you have a phone with you?"

"No, I'd left my bag at home—I don't like leaving it in the car up there," she said, tucking her hair behind her ear with a trembling hand.

"Did you use your husband's phone?"

"No, Noel won't let me. He doesn't like anyone touching it. Anyway, he used it to call the police while I ran back to the car. I was so scared I fell over."

They let the Claytons go while they examined Noel's phone, and Elise watched as he hustled his wife into their car outside the police station. Evelyn was cowering in the passenger seat as Clayton roared off.

"God, I hope she's okay," Caro said from behind her. "Maybe we should check on her later?"

"Okay—do that, but we need to get on," Elise said. But she didn't know what was next. She reached into her pocket for her notes—they weren't there. She'd left them on her desk. For a second, she felt the queasy terror of being exposed as an imposter. A woman pretending to be a senior detective. Sweat prickled in her armpits and palms.

"Boss?" Caro reached for her. "You've gone very pale—are you okay?"

Elise wanted to say, *No, I can't do this anymore. I'm drowning in this investigation. I'm going to let Karen down.* But she forced herself to cough up a laugh instead. "Missed breakfast. I'm fine."

Finding Karen's killer was down to her. There was no cavalry coming.

FIFTY-ONE

ELISE

Saturday, February 22, 2020

AT SEVEN FIFTY-EIGHT p.m., Elise stood by her front door, plucking at bobbled wool on the sleeves of her jacket. She was aware of every inch of her skin. She could feel the silicone insert against her scar in her post-op bra, the mascara spiking her lashes, the red polish on her nails that she'd smudged while putting on her little black dress and had to repaint. She felt so unlike herself that she had to look in the mirror to make sure she was still there.

The knock made her stomach lurch, and she needed to pee again.

"Come in—I won't be a minute," she squeaked as she opened the door and fled to the loo.

"You look nice," he called as she disappeared.

Mal had chosen a posh pub deep in the Downs, all wooden beams and a haze of fish and brown butter. He wanted to take Elise's jacket as they were shown their table next to an open fire, but she insisted on keeping it on. She should never have worn her black dress. What had she been thinking? It was sleeveless and clung to her—and, she'd remembered too late, was what she'd been wearing on the night her ex had dumped her. Elise tried to focus on the menu but started perspiring in the heat.

"Are you okay? You look hot," Mal said. And then laughed. "Sorry. That came out wrong. Although, of course, you are. Oh, God, I'm getting this all round my neck. Are you sure you don't want to take your jacket off?" Elise laughed, too, and pulled it off—quickly, like a sticking plaster.

"That's better," she said, trying to stop her hands reaching to cover her chest. Drawing attention to it.

"I'm having the garlic prawns. How about you?" Mal said, pretending not to notice.

Elise shook her head. "Sea bass for me, please."

It was all so easy after that. Mal insisted she have a glass of Chablis to go with her fish while he stuck to sparkling water. "Designated driver tonight. Don't want to get in trouble with the law!" He beamed and she grinned back and let go of the tension in her neck and shoulders.

"These are great. Try one," Mal said. Elise reached over and picked up the smallest prawn, peeled it carefully, and then licked her fingers. He was right; it was delicious.

They didn't say much on the drive home. He put on some chill-out music, and they sat in an easy silence. Elise hadn't felt so relaxed for a year.

"Thanks for this, Mal. It's been exactly what I needed."

"And me." He glanced across.

He had to park in a road around the corner from the cottages, and they walked slowly home, arms bumping. Elise couldn't speak as she wrestled with what next. They'd get to her door first. Two more streetlights, then home. She should ask him in. But she'd decided to slow it down . . . hadn't she? Her heart drummed against her ribs and her stomach churned with anticipation as she wondered if her breath smelled of garlic. She was halfway to the sofa with him in her head when the dread tripped her up. And she felt the sensation of someone else's hand on her missing flesh.

"Good night," she said hoarsely when they reached her doorstep. She gave him a small kiss on the cheek.

"Right," Mal said, looking disappointed. "I wondered if you fancied a nightcap? I've got some Calvados and choccy."

Elise's key hovered by the lock. *Go on! Do it! It's time!*

But her phone vibrated in her pocket. "Oh, I'm so sorry—it'll be work. I've got to take this," she muttered, trying to disguise her relief. She quickly pushed the key in.

"Yep. Next time, hey?" he said, smiling.

"Definitely."

SUNDAY:
DAY 9

FIFTY-TWO

ANNIE

Sunday, February 23, 2020

THERE WAS NOTHING on the Sussex Today website when Annie looked first thing. She'd been terrified an interview with her would be there—what would Henry say? And then bitterly disappointed when it wasn't. She kept scrolling, even though she knew it wasn't there. All that pushing for information, but the reporter hadn't written a word. She lay back down in bed and buried her head in her pillow. Henry was right. It was all in her mind. No one else wanted to know.

"I'm staying in bed for a bit," Annie called down to Henry. "I've got a bit of a headache."

He didn't reply. Perhaps he hadn't heard her. Or didn't want to.

"There's nothing in the fridge," he shouted up a bit later, and she cringed. She'd been busted. The neglectful partner. "We'll go to Sainsbury's to buy stuff for lunch on the way back from surf club," he added, but didn't wait for an answer before banging the front door behind him.

Annie stared at the ceiling for a bit, then hoisted herself onto her elbows. Perhaps she just hadn't told the right people. She sat on the edge of the bed and found the number for the police station at Southfold. She listened to herself ringing the switchboard and asking to speak to the officer in charge of the murder inquiry as if on autopilot.

She heard someone call out: "I've got an Annie Curtis on the phone asking for you, boss. Shall I take a message?"

Annie didn't hear the answer, but they took her number and said someone would call her back.

"Mrs. Curtis?" DI King said when Annie picked up the phone ten minutes later. She couldn't speak for a moment. She suddenly didn't know how to begin.

"Yes. I'm sorry to bother you," she stumbled on. "I know you're busy, but I need to talk to someone about what happened to my son."

"In Knapton Wood?" the detective said. She sounded sharp. Like one of those pointed instruments that dentists use. Probing. "What do you need to talk about, Mrs. Curtis?"

"I need to know why it happened. The whole truth," Annie said. And that was it. That was what she needed. "There are things I don't understand. I mean . . ." She struggled to finish her sentence.

"Take your time," DI King said, but Annie could hear the note of impatience. "Look, where are you living now?" she added. "Are you still in the area?"

"Southsea," Annie said.

"Right. Well, perhaps it would be easier if you come in to see me."

"I can come now."

"Well, okay," DI King said. "You can ask for me at the desk."

ELISE KING DIDN'T look like the policewoman they'd sent when Archie died. She looked like Annie. Tired. Winter skin. Two women struggling to keep everything going.

"Come this way, Mrs. Curtis," the inspector said, her voice echoing off the bare corridor walls. "Actually, I had you on my list to contact."

This caught Annie off guard, and all she could say was "Oh, right."

"Yes, I wanted to talk to you about Karen Simmons's vigil last week," DI King went on, hanging Annie's coat over a spare chair in the interview room. "I'm trying to identify some of the crowd. Particularly the males. You were there with two men, weren't you?"

Annie's heart thumped so hard against her chest she was sure the detective could hear it. She wished she was still in her kitchen with the smell of toast from Henry's breakfast instead of the airless interview room.

"So, who did you go with, Mrs. Curtis?" DI King persisted.

"Er, my sons, Xander and Gavin."

"Do they live with you?"

"Only Gavin—he's fourteen—nearly fifteen. Xander's in his twenties. He works up in London but he's staying at the moment."

"Right," the detective said, and wrote down Xander's address and mobile number. Then looked back up at her.

"Can I ask why you went?" she said.

"Lots of people went," Annie said quietly.

"Yes, but if I can be direct with you, Mrs. Curtis, they hadn't had a child killed in that wood. It must have been a very special friendship with Karen to bring you back, surely?"

"Um, well, I knew Karen from when I used to live in Ebbing years ago," Annie said. "She did my hair back then. Karen was such a kind girl—she used to give the kids a sticker and a lollipop after their haircut."

"That's nice." DI King gave her a tired smile.

But Annie couldn't smile back. Couldn't move her face too much in case it cracked and all her grief came flooding out. She was already struggling to hold back her tears.

"Yes," Annie gulped.

"I can see that revisiting that time is very painful for you," DI King said, "but that's exactly what you did last week."

Annie shrugged helplessly.

"And you say you want to get to the truth about what happened to Archie sixteen years after his death. That there are things you don't understand. Can you tell me what you mean?"

The effort of holding it all in was making Annie's head ache, so she started so she could finish.

"I don't understand why Archie was killed," she blurted. "I've never understood it. It makes no sense. Xander was in a different part of the wood to Archie. Why did Nicky Donovan go looking for him? And attack him?"

The inspector paused and wrote something on a piece of paper. "How far was Xander from the den when he encountered Donovan?" she probed.

Encountered. We're back to the meat of the police interview.

"Er, quite a bit away. I was shocked how far he'd wandered. He wasn't supposed to go farther than the big tree, but he said they'd needed some more bits of wood."

"So he was completely out of sight of Archie?"

Annie nodded gratefully. Someone was finally on the trail with her.

"So how did Donovan know that Archie was also in the wood?"

"That's it. I don't know. That's what I've always wondered."

And DI King nodded to herself and wrote some more. "It was a complicated crime scene," she said quietly.

"You've looked at the files!" Annie cried, almost bouncing in her seat. "Why? What did you find?"

The detective stirred uneasily in her chair. "The association with Knapton Wood made me look," she said. "And I remembered the boy in the tree house—your son. Look, I've only scanned through them quickly. Why didn't you ask the original team your questions at the time?"

Annie shook her head. "I couldn't string two words together at the start. And the drugs they gave me to dull the pain dulled everything. I should have made myself do it, but no one wanted me to. My husband Henry didn't want me to. He just wanted to focus on rebuilding our life—for Xander. And then I had Gavin less than a year after Archie died, so I buried my doubts. But Karen's death has brought it all back. And I can't bury them again."

DI King nodded slowly, and Annie saw her glance at her phone. "Please," Annie said softly.

"Let's go back to the day Archie was killed, then?" the detective said.

"I couldn't remember afterward when it had gone quiet," Annie murmured. "It was only when Xander stood in front of me that I realized something was very wrong. He was so pale and crying, and when I pulled him to me and cradled his head, my hand felt wet and it was smeared with blood when I looked. Xander's hair was matted with blood." Annie ground to a halt. She could see her son's silent tears making tracks down his grubby cheeks and those dark, oozing clots and feel the blinding panic all over again.

"He couldn't speak at first," she made herself go on. "Then he told me Archie had fallen, and I tore through the gate toward the trees. I was calling for Archie. And then I found him."

She had to stop. She'd run out of road.

DI King said: "Take a moment, Annie."

She gulped a breath, and crashed on into the danger zone. She could see the scene as if it was unfolding now, that minute. And the blood was rushing in her ears again.

"I must have known he was dead," Annie heard herself say. "I used to be a nurse and I knew what death looked like—but I picked him up and ran back to the house screaming for an ambulance. My husband, Henry, told me later the neighbors heard me and ran out of their gardens. There were suddenly lots of people and someone rang nine-nine-nine and I sat on the ground with Archie in my arms. I remember the lady next door was pressing a tea towel to Xander's bleeding head and trying to comfort him. But he wouldn't be held. He stood beside me, not speaking, his little fists clenched at his jawline. My poor boys."

The detective cleared her throat. "That must have been terribly traumatic," she muttered. "And when did Xander tell you about Nicky Donovan?"

"At the hospital. The police went immediately and arrested him at his mother's house."

"The team was convinced it had the right man," DI King said quietly, as if to herself.

Annie tried to concentrate on what she was saying, but her thoughts kept skittering off. She swallowed hard. "I know. The police said people can do terrible things when they're under extreme stress. But . . . I know this sounds completely mad, but in his photo Nicky Donovan didn't look like a monster."

"Okay," DI King said, and Annie could hear the creep of pity in her voice. "But, sadly, killers don't always look the part. And the investigators were right to say that severe pressure can make people act out of character—or lash out. And Donovan was about to be accused of sexually assaulting your eldest son. I believe the team were working on the theory that he may have been trying to silence Archie and, in his panic, used too much force."

"No!" Annie gasped. "No one said that at the time. But his mother said he didn't do it," she whispered. "He told her he ran away in the opposite direction and never saw Archie." She could immediately hear how ridiculous she sounded.

"The police have to deal with hard facts to get to the truth," the inspector said kindly. "And there were clear indications that Donovan had contact with both of your sons. I've looked at the forensic reports, and there was evidence discovered on Xander's and Archie's clothing."

Annie couldn't look at her, and the detective cleared her throat again. "It is hardly surprising Donovan's mum protested her son's innocence," she went on gently. "No mother wants to believe their child is capable of murder. But it is hardly unbiased opinion—or based on anything other than refusal to accept facts. Poor woman. I wonder what happened to her afterward?"

"She lives in the same house. I visited her last week," Annie said, and the officer's eyes narrowed. "I just wanted to talk to her. You won't tell my husband, will you? I don't want to upset him."

"Right. But what did you and Mrs. Donovan talk about?"

"The suicide note," Annie muttered. She was exhausted by it all, but she'd started this. She had to see it through. "She had a copy of it. The police told us at the time that it was a confession, but she and I think they got it wrong. The note's about the wrong boy."

"What on earth do you mean?" DI King said, and Annie reached to get the photocopy of the letter out of her handbag. The detective sat and read it in silence, her lips pressing together so hard they almost disappeared.

"Do you see?" Annie pleaded.

"I certainly can't say on one reading," DI King said firmly as she re-folded it, but she didn't hand it back. "I would like to examine it further and discuss it with my senior officers. Is that okay?"

Annie nodded and got out of her chair to leave. She reached for her coat and then stopped. "Do you know a man called Ash Woodward?" she asked. "He spoke to me the other day. He was saying all sorts of strange things."

DI King took her hand off the door handle. "What sort of things?"

"He said he was in Knapton Wood."

"What?" DI King said, her voice echoing round the room. "When? When did he say he was in the wood?"

"The day Archie died," Annie murmured nervously.

"Really?" DI King's voice came down an octave. "Look, come and sit down again"—she ushered Annie back to her chair—"and tell me every-thing he said."

XANDER WAS STANDING with shopping bags on the pavement when she pulled up.

"Are you okay, Mum?" he said, opening the car door. "Where have you been?"

She fumbled for a cover story, but couldn't think of one.

"Southfold police station," she said eventually. "Talking to a police officer. She rang and asked me to go. DI King is trying to identify men who were at the Karen Simmons vigil the other night. In case they can help the investigation. She'd got my name and she wanted to know who I was with. She was nice. She asked for your phone number, so you might hear from her."

"Mum! I don't want you handing out my number," Xander said, scowling at her. "Anyway, there's nothing any of us can tell her."

"Well, I told her about Ash Woodward," Annie said.

"Oh, Mum," Xander murmured and put his arm around her, pulling her close. She stayed there, head resting on his chest. Seeking refuge.

FIFTY-THREE

ELISE

Sunday, February 23, 2020

ELISE RANG DS Larry Agnew as soon as she closed the door to her office.

She'd tell Caro after she'd made her call. Elise knew it could be simply a case of this new killing unearthing the grief and denial of two mothers. *Those unanswered questions must keep surfacing like bones in a disturbed grave,* Elise told herself.

But. But. Was there something there?

Her stomach, a reliable indicator over the years, told her there might be.

"I've obtained a copy of the suicide note," she said as soon as he answered.

"Oh?" he muttered. Then silence.

"Donovan only ever mentioned one boy in that note, didn't he? And it reads as if it's Xander Curtis he was talking about, doesn't it?"

"But the forensics said Donovan did it," Agnew corrected her tersely.

"Happy to talk about that in a minute," Elise pushed on. She knew that was going to be a pointless exercise. It would take Semtex to remove Agnew from his deeply entrenched position. "But maybe you could help me with something else."

Agnew grunted.

"I've got a potential new witness. Can you tell me who else you looked at on day one?" She wouldn't give him the name yet. Let Agnew confirm it first.

"A new witness after all this time? Who? Someone's yanking your chain, love," Agnew sneered.

"Who apart from Nicky Donovan?" she insisted.

"We did our job," DS Agnew exploded. "And don't you dare suggest otherwise. We had dozens of officers out interviewing everyone in the vicinity that day—the neighbors who saw Annie Curtis run out of the wood with Archie, family, friends. People who used the wood—the joggers, the dog walkers, the bird nuts."

And there it was. Elise's heart picked up a beat. "Who were they? The bird nuts?"

"I can't remember that, for Christ's sake."

But Elise knew and searched for the name on her screen with her spare hand while Agnew made his excuses and ended the call.

It had been in the casework all the time. In one of the appendices. Ash Woodward had been visited on the day of Archie's killing. He was listed as a "local man / bird watcher."

But there'd been someone on the force who maybe hadn't forgotten the whole knicker-nicker episode. "Check him" had been added in pencil to the notes in the paper file. But Ash had had an alibi. His mother had said he'd been in the garden with her.

Had he changed his story for Annie just to be part of the tragedy? Or had he finally been telling the truth?

A sudden buzz of activity outside her door brought her back into the room, and Elise immediately checked her phone and swore under her breath. She'd missed his text message.

Hi, had a great evening, Mal had written twenty minutes earlier. Shall we do it again? How about a curry on Thursday?

Thursday felt like a year away—and she couldn't eat spicy food—but she typed, Yes, please, instantly. But stopped herself adding a kiss.

"Boss." Caro's head came round the door with a huge smile plastered across it. "Didn't you hear me? We've got Karen's phone and handbag!"

Elise jumped up, energy crackling through her. The phone could be the key to the whole investigation. They might finally find out why she'd gone to Knapton Wood. Who she'd gone with. Who she'd called that night.

"Where were they?" she barked at Caro, like an excited dog being offered a bone.

"They were in a recycling bin behind the shopping parade in Ebbing High Street. Whoever dumped them made the mistake of wrapping them in a black plastic bag. Schoolboy error. It probably would be in the council landfill by now if they'd put it in the general waste bin. But some do-gooder spotted it when they were throwing away their washed yogurt pots and pulled it out to throw it in the right bin and it split."

Elise put her head back and laughed. She loved that sort of sliding doors moment. Where a second's inattention could change the course of the investigation.

Her head snapped down again. "When are they emptied?" she asked.

"The bins? Thursdays," Caro said.

"So the killer didn't throw away Karen's things immediately," Elise murmured. "He came back. Or he's been in Ebbing all along."

The locals of interest formed an ill-assorted identity parade in Elise's head: self-proclaimed stud Barry Sherman, bullying Noel Clayton, and the watcher, Ash Woodward. Ash, who claimed to have been in the wood at the time of the first murder. Elise knew she should keep Caro abreast, but she wanted to face Ash first. Her oppo was already impatient with her interest in the Archie Curtis case, and it could turn out to be the fantasy of a lonely, unhappy man. She'd hold off telling her for the moment.

"The phone data may take us straight to him." Elise forced herself back into the current case. "How long do the digital team say it'll take to do their thing?"

"Ah—I've spoken to them, but they say the phone is in a poor state. It might take a while."

Elise groaned. This was the hardest part of the job. The nerve-shredding wait. While the name of their killer could be sitting in a tiny piece of plastic.

"I'm going for a walk to get some air and think things through," Elise said. She could feel the first prickles of panic—was she losing her grip on the investigation? She had too many lines of inquiry. She needed to focus.

As she walked the town's one-way system, eyes to the pavement, she went back to the heart of the case. Karen. Poor, loveless Karen.

FIFTY-FOUR

KIKI

Sunday, February 23, 2020

THERE'S NO ONE else home now. Pip has gone for a sleepover at Gemma's—she's a new friend. I was flustered when I dropped her off—she's back to school tomorrow, and I hadn't met the other mother before, so I couldn't march in and lay down my usual ground rules: no films with "15" certificates—unbelievable how many kids in Pip's class have seen *It* and *Pet Sematary*—phones off at eight, bed by nine thirty. But my girl begged, and I know I've been off-grid a lot lately where she's concerned. So I said yes, just to see her face light up. And dropped her off at a posh, double-fronted house on the seafront. The mother came to the door briefly, a distracted woman in Diesel jeans and genuine UGG boots. "She'll be fine," she sang as Pip disappeared up her curving staircase arm in arm with Gemma. And I pulled my coat closed to hide a washed-out Hello Kitty T-shirt and nodded. Too embarrassed to mention bedtimes.

I'm already regretting it, catastrophizing about what Pip will get up to. But my phone interrupts the horror story unspooling in my head.

"Hello," a voice chirps. "It's Ronnie. I just wondered if you'd written anything about the Safe Ebbing group yet? I want to tell the others when it is going to be on the website."

Christ, I'd completely forgotten about it.

"Er, no, sorry, I haven't had a chance," I mumble and reach for the reporter's default lie: "But it's on the news list for tomorrow. How are you, anyway? I was so grateful for your help the other day."

"What? Remembering Annie Curtis?" I can hear Ronnie's smile down the phone. "That's okay. Have you managed to track her down? Such a sad story."

"Yes, actually, I've spoken to her. Lovely woman."

"Have you? Where is she now? And why was she at the vigil?" she rattles off her questions, and I get an unwelcome glimpse of myself on a doorstep.

"She's over Portsmouth way," I mutter and seek a quick exit. "Anyway, I'd better give the police press office a call—see what's been happening today."

"Well, actually," Ronnie pipes up, and I can almost picture her tapping the side of her beaky nose.

"Okay, what have you heard?" I smile back down the line. She is unstoppable, but she may know something.

"I know someone who knows someone in the police station canteen," she starts, and my smile begins to fade. *Thirdhand gossip.* "You know, people chat while they queue for chips. Anyway, apparently, they've found Karen's phone and bag in a wheelie bin at the back of the Co-op."

"Wow! Top information, Ronnie," I say, genuinely impressed, and she laughs happily.

"Put me down for a tip payment, then," she says. "And I'll keep my ear to the ground for more."

THERE FOLLOWS A tetchy exchange with the duty police press officer who is determined to bury the story.

"We can confirm new evidence has been uncovered," he says reluctantly after much pushing.

"In a bin in Ebbing High Street, I understand," I press him. "Are you looking at cameras in the vicinity?" Of course they are, but I need someone to say it or I haven't got a usable quote.

"We are not discussing operational details," the duty man says.

"I thought you wanted the public to help. They might have seen someone putting the bag in the bin."

"I'll put your request to the Senior Investigating Officer and come back to you."

"Today?" I try my luck.

"I'll put your request—" I hang up while he's still speaking.

While I wait, I go back to my new column. It's a disaster. I jam my finger on the backspace button and watch the last sentences I've written disappear. It's no use; I can't do it. How can I write about my first and only Tinder date without revealing how I let myself down? "The Secret Dater" is anonymous, but some of my friends—*oh, God, and Ma*—know it's me. The whole point of the column is to take a clear-eyed look at the dating jungle and warn women about the risks of rushing into anything. Stop them becoming Karens.

But I've fallen at the first hurdle.

I am deep in self-flagellation when a message beeps on my phone and I'm jerked back into my other problem.

Rob is still out there. My polite brush-off and full-on ghosting haven't done anything to stop his texts. Come on—stop playing hard to get, the message reads. I'll pick you up tonight at 7:30. Perhaps I can meet your daughter? X

Fear pins me to my chair. Of course he knows where I live. Where Pip and I live. And the fury I have been kenneling in my lower gut erupts. *This stops now!* I shriek in my head, heart banging.

I text him back: I'll be at the same bar at 7:30. He won't know what's hit him when I've finished reading him the riot act.

HE'S WAITING OUTSIDE like the last time and walks toward me, smiling and arms open.

"Hi, gorgeous," he says, and goes to pull me into him, but I step back, keeping a polite smile glued on my face.

"Hello, Rob," I say. "How are you?" He's more solid than I remember, and my nerve wavers. *I mustn't antagonize him,* I tell myself, then straighten my shoulders. We're in a public place. And this won't take a minute to end.

"Good. I thought we could go for a drive." And he winks.

You are kidding! I want to shout. But I play it cool, saying: "No, you're fine. Let's sit out here. I can't stay long."

Rob's smile tightens at the corners, but he reaches for my hand. I tuck it in my coat pocket. "Well, let's see," he says. "Maybe I can persuade you. What do you want to drink?"

"Oh, nothing, thanks."

"Come on!" he murmurs. "One drink."

"Er, okay, then," I say. "Just one. I'll have a lime and soda, please."

He comes back with the glasses and sits across from me at a small tin table on the pavement. I've turned my phone to record in my handbag. *For the column I'm going to write,* I tell myself.

WHEN I WAKE up, it's dark.

It takes a moment to work out where I am. My head is pounding as I feel around me and bump my hand on the bedside lamp. I sit up and fumble for the switch, closing my eyes tight against the blinding light. When I open them slowly, everything looks like it normally does. Doesn't it? Then I see with a jolt of alarm that the clock is showing that it's five thirty a.m. I've been out for ten hours.

I lie back down and peel my tongue off the roof of my mouth as I strain to remember what happened. Why have I got the hangover of death? I was at the bar. But I can't remember drinking. There are yawning holes in the rest of the evening. How the hell did I get home? I push the duvet back and freeze. I'm naked. I never sleep naked. My clothes are draped over a chair. And I can smell the ghost of a man's aftershave on my skin. It's a scent I thought was attractive once. Now it's suffocating.

Rob! Oh, God, is he here? I fall out of bed and cower, trembling, on the floor, listening for him. Interpreting every creak and gurgle of my ancient plumbing as Rob creeping up the stairs. I don't know how long I've been crouching here, but the dull ache in my calves brings me back to myself. I need to phone someone. Where is my phone? My bag?

I pull the discarded dress over my head and tiptoe unsteadily onto the landing. The light is on in the hall, and I duck down to look through the banister. I can see my handbag on the table and my coat on the floor.

I walk down in bare feet, shivering violently against the cold. The phone battery is dead, but when I plug it in to charge, there's a photo waiting for me. A selfie of the two of us in a strange bed. His face isn't visible. Just his hand stroking my hair back against a gray-and-silver-striped duvet cover. My eyes are closed as if in ecstasy. Only I know I was drugged.

Hi, Sleeping Beauty, the accompanying message says. Thanks for a great night. I'll call you later.

I slide to the floor.

He spiked my drink. And took a photo as a souvenir. Or an insurance policy. He could put it on social media if I try to accuse him. I attempt to get up, but my juddering legs won't let me. I must report it to the police. That's what I'd tell anyone else this had happened to. *He cannot get away with this,* I hear myself say to some other woman, shaking with shock. But he's got a photo of us together. It will be my word against his. The photo. They'd have to see the photo. They might not believe me. I'm not sure I can go through with it.

My phone beeps again and I scream.

Another photo. I try not to look as I fumble to delete it, but my eyes stray to the tangle of pale flesh filling the screen.

When it disappears, I sit in a fog, staring at the screen. There are other messages—from Pip, about a book she forgot to pack. And a voice recording that runs for three hours.

I press play and hear the sound of passing cars and Rob talking loudly as we sat with our drinks. I keep fast-forwarding, wondering when my battery ran out, and then sit weeping as I hear my slurred voice telling Rob to stop.

MONDAY:
DAY 10

FIFTY-FIVE

ELISE

Monday, February 24, 2020

KAREN'S PHONE HAD given up its secrets overnight—a memory dump had produced pages of data. The forensic analyst had already started mining it by the time Elise arrived at the data forensic lab in Little-hampton at just gone six. She'd been awake on and off all night, unable—or unwilling—to stop her brain revisiting every second of her first date with Mal. Each word, every look. The missed opportunity. She'd tried to switch to work mode, racing after the hares they'd got running on the case. Local? Stranger? Abduction? A date? But at four she'd got up and stood in the shower to try to sluice the chaos off. There was no point in going back to bed after that.

"Luckily, our victim hadn't bothered to change the default password. Never understood people who don't—it's like leaving your front door open," the techie muttered. Another early riser, he was sitting in the glow of his screen and blinked like a small owl when Elise snapped the office lights on. His *Star Trek* T-shirt had ridden up over his belly, re-vealing the grubby waistband of his Calvin Klein boxers. He smelled like stale bread, and Elise wondered if he slept in his clothes.

"So, the last communication our victim received before her phone went dead was at twenty-three thirty-nine. There was an exchange of text messages first," the techie said slowly.

"Who from?" Elise tried to look over his shoulder without inhaling.

"Number was withheld on her handset," he said, "so the victim won't have seen who was calling. But I've matched the call times to the service provider data. The number ends seven-four-nine, but it's a pay-as-you-go. Not registered."

Shit!

"Well, what did it say?"

"I'll come to that," he said, and Elise resisted the impulse to shove him aside and get on with it herself.

"Come to it now," she commanded. "Please."

"All right, all right. Keep your hair on." Elise's hand went immediately to her chemo curls, and she stared the blushing techie down. "Um, sorry, ma'am. I didn't mean anything by it."

"Leave it," she said wearily. "What have you got?"

"Okay," he stuttered. "So, at twenty-three twenty-seven the victim got the first of three texts from this source. It reads: 'I see you like the outdoors? How about getting together?'"

"Okay, not much to go on, is it?" Elise said, and Captain Kirk tried a comradely grin.

"Anyway, the victim replied, 'When? Free tomorrow.' So Seven-Four-Nine sent a second text immediately: 'Tonight is good. I'm only twenty minutes from Ebbing. Call you when nearby.'"

Bingo!

"That puts the meeting around midnight," Elise said. "It must be the killer. Isn't there anything else? Had he called before?"

"There's a ten-second call from Seven-Four-Nine later—at twenty-three thirty-nine, the last time Karen's phone was used. But it sounds like a typical late-night hookup to me," the analyst said, and Elise suppressed a shudder at the thought of those boxers. "You know the victim was on an app?" he added. "It's on her phone. She'd set herself up as LaDiva. She swiped right on someone called Bear earlier that

Friday night. At nineteen thirty-six. That account was deleted the next morning."

"Could it be the same man?"

The techie gave a small nod. "Could be. I'll try to link the two digitally."

ELISE STARTED A new list in her head as she drove back to Southfold. She almost took the lift at the station but made herself walk up the stairs and then went for a pee while she had the time.

Caro was in the ladies, rubbing her top with a wet paper towel, when Elise walked past and into a cubicle.

"Found a bit of Jessie's porridge." Caro grinned. "How are you doing?"

"Er, good. Not sleeping great and having my occasional lapses—but you know that," Elise called through the loo door. "Do you think anyone else has spotted it? Has anyone said anything?"

"No," Caro said, a beat too slowly. Elise heard the lie and put her head in her hands for a moment.

"It's happening less, Caro," she called.

"Yep," her oppo muttered, the *if you say so* unspoken but clearly heard. "Probably a good idea to have another look at your lists and see if there's anything else I need to know about."

"I was just about to check through," Elise said, pulling screws of paper out of her top pocket. She used to color-code them for urgency, but she'd forgotten to do that lately. There was too much else to do. They were stuck together and crumpled. Like her thoughts.

"Look, you're doing great—everyone says so." Her sergeant sped up to bring the heart-to-heart to a safe close. "It's still early days."

Elise paused to compose her face before opening the cubicle door. The thing was, it wasn't. It was a year since she'd first been diagnosed. And suddenly she was back in the consultant's room, hearing and not hearing the news. She'd gone on her own—she couldn't think of anyone she could share it with. Hugh was long gone and, anyway, it'd be nothing. A cyst with a wicked sense of humor or something.

But it wasn't. It was bad news. She'd seen enough of it in her job, and it was there on the consultant's face as soon as he walked into the room. She'd stared at him, but she hadn't been able to take in his words. All she'd heard was a loud buzzing in her ears. The oncology nurse had led her to a quiet corner afterward to tell her all over again.

Elise was due to have her three-monthly blood tests that week. She'd booked a lunchtime appointment on Thursday so she could disappear and be back without having to tell anyone at work. Not even Caro. She couldn't bear the thought of anyone else waiting for the results. She'd endure it alone again. Best that way.

"Anyway," Elise said, resetting the conversation as she emerged to wash her hands, "we've got a result from Karen's phone. She arranged to meet someone in Ebbing at midnight. No name, unregistered phone, but no abduction off the street."

"Thank God. We need a break."

"Yep. Now, what else before we go in?"

"Well, some goodish news—we've retrieved the photo of Karen's body on Clayton's phone," Caro announced.

"But that's brilliant," Elise crowed and sprayed water all over her trousers. "Oh, shit!"

"Okay, don't get too excited." Caro passed her a wodge of paper towels. "There are ice crystals on Karen's eyelashes if you zoom in, and those would have taken time, postmortem, to form. So the picture was taken after death. Oh, and the bastard also took intimate pictures. There must be a special place in hell for someone who upskirts a corpse."

"Christ, he must have taken them when he found her," Elise said. "But why?"

"Well, Mr. Clayton has also deleted some fairly gruesome ones of Mrs. C posing in the wood. I wonder if he was sharing them? I've sent Chevening and Thomson to pick him up. I'll take him when he gets here."

"Okay, so Noel Clayton's our cyberflasher, but surely he didn't mean to send that photo to Kiki Nunn? Why would he? So who did he really want to show it to? Can you organize a search of his place this morning? There may be other trophies. Come on, I want to get the team moving on the new info."

"Behind you," Caro said, lobbing the paper towels into the bin.

The first signs of fatigue had infected the incident room when Elise and Caro walked in. A miasma of stale breath and last night's fast-food run lingered, and officers were slumped in their chairs. No one was talking.

"Morning!" Elise said sharply, opening a window to let the burger smell out, and the bodies stirred.

"Karen Simmons wasn't taken off the street or from a nightclub— she agreed to meet a man in Ebbing on Valentine's night around mid-night," she said, and watched spines straighten. "We have the messages sent to her from an unregistered number. Her date said he could be in town in twenty minutes. He was in the area already."

"Wow!" DC Chevening said. "He's local. She might even have known him—she wouldn't have gone to meet a complete stranger in the middle of the night, would she?"

"Actually, I hear that's part of the thrill for some people," Andy Thomson said. "Just saying."

"Right, well, Karen had made contact with someone calling himself Bear on a dating app earlier that evening," Elise continued. "He may be our man."

FIFTY-SIX

ANNIE

Monday, February 24, 2020

XANDER MUST HAVE told Henry as soon as he'd got back from the shops yesterday. Annie had dithered over asking him to keep her visit to the police station quiet, but she hadn't wanted to ask her son to keep secrets for her.

When nothing happened, she wondered if Xander had decided not to say anything anyway. Henry was quiet, but no more than he had been lately. And she thought she'd got away with it for now.

But she should have known.

Henry waited until Xander had caught the early train back to London and Gav had gone to school.

He was sitting on a chair in the garden, no coat. Annie went out with a mug of coffee and perched on an old stool. "What are you doing out here? You'll catch your death. We should have put the garden furniture away properly. It'll be ruined by the summer," she wittered, for something to say.

"Xander says you went to talk to the police." He looked at her, daring her to lie.

No more secrets, Annie whispered in her head.

"Yes. I rang them, but the inspector said she'd been about to get in touch with me. To ask why I went to the vigil."

"Why *did* you go?" Henry muttered into his coffee.

"For Archie," she whispered. "It was where he died, too. And I needed to go back. We should have done it before."

"Why?" Henry mumbled. "It was too painful. And what was the point? He wasn't there anymore."

"He was for me. And Karen Simmons dying like that. It brought everything back, like it was happening all over again. I did tell you, but you didn't want to hear."

Henry looked away. "What did you tell the inspector?" he muttered.

"About Archie's death."

"What about it?"

Anne took a deep breath as she stepped off the cliff edge.

"My doubts about the investigation. You know I had them. How the police stopped looking once Nicky Donovan was arrested. How we never knew why he did it. We never heard him say, did we? I'm not sure the inspector was that interested at first. But then I showed her a copy of Nicky Donovan's suicide note."

Henry rose from his chair as if he'd been stung. "His suicide note? How did you get that?"

"From his mum."

"Oh, my God, Annie, what have you done? Where is this note?"

She got her phone out of her pocket and found the photo she'd taken.

He read it out loud in a sneering voice—"'I can't help the way I am'"—until he got to the end. Then he finished it in silence, his lips twitching.

"He only talks about one boy, Henry."

"Yes: Archie," he croaked.

"No. It's Xander, isn't it? You must see that."

"No, I don't. He didn't tell the truth to the police when they picked him up. He was still deceiving them when he decided to kill himself. He was a liar."

"Like you," Annie snapped. "You lied to the police, too, didn't you?"

He wanted to shout—she could see it in his eyes—and scream his innocence in her face. But Henry knew she saw through him. He slumped back in his chair.

"I did it for you," he said so softly she had to lean down to hear. "To protect our family."

Annie wanted to hit him.

"To protect yourself, you mean," she hissed at him. "You didn't want anyone to know you were banging some secretary somewhere while your child was being killed."

"Annie," he gasped. "You cannot believe that."

"I do." And the madwoman escaped. Annie was screeching the words that had roiled inside her head for years and the whole street would be able to hear and she didn't care. "You blamed me for not watching them," she shrieked.

"I didn't . . ." He faltered. "I never said that."

"You didn't need to. I could see it in your eyes. Hear it in your silences. But you weren't even there. You were screwing around instead of looking out for your children!"

Henry tried to get hold of her, but she wrestled free and ran to the house. "Who was she, Henry?" Annie yelled from the door. "Was it worth losing your son for?"

"Shut up!" he yelled back as he caught up and shoved her through the door. She knew she had frightened him properly, and for a second Annie felt triumph surging through her. But then he started to sob and she was his wife again. The hardwired need to comfort him rang through her body, and she reached for him.

"Get off," Henry wept, pushing her back. "You don't know anything about it. You didn't want me—it was all about the kids. I didn't exist as far as you were concerned. And she wasn't some one-night stand. I loved her. I was going to leave you. We were going to leave Ebbing to make a new life."

Annie couldn't breathe, as if he'd punched her in the chest, but the adrenaline pumped her back up. "Ha!" she heard herself shriek. "I would've packed your bags for you. Thrown a bloody party! Why did you bother to stay?" But she knew. It was the same reason she had. Their dead child.

Henry was sobbing, bent double by the door. "Stop it, why don't you stop it?" he gulped.

And she did. Annie went and sat at the kitchen counter and tried not to look at him. The row was already replaying in her head. The "what if?" torture game thrumming in her head. What if she'd left him before Archie died? There'd been times—the debts, the sexting—when she'd allowed herself to think about it, but she'd told herself she loved Henry too much to give up on him. Now she knew he'd given up on her. What if he'd gone off? Where would she be now? Would Archie still be here? Would they all have started new lives? *We were going to leave Ebbing,* he'd said. And the truth lit up in her head. The other woman hadn't been at the office. She'd been from Ebbing, too.

"Who was she?" Annie asked again, and Henry stood up to walk out. "Don't you dare," she spat. "I knew her, didn't I?"

He put his hands to his face. "I didn't mean it to happen," he said. "Who was she?"

He started to cry again.

FIFTY-SEVEN

KIKI

Monday, February 24, 2020

Elise King ignores my first call. My name must have come up on her screen, and I'm probably the last person she wants to hear from. But I dial again. And again.

"Kiki!" Elise snaps, her irritation ringing in my ear. "Can we make this quick? I'm up to my neck, here."

"Um," I say and immediately choke to a standstill. I mustn't cry. I can't speak if I'm crying.

"Kiki? Are you there?" Elise barks. "Are you all right?"

"Er, no, not really," I croak. "I need some help. Some advice. Can I talk to you? Off the record?"

"Off the record? What is this about? Is it about my complaint to your news editor? I really can't talk about that."

"No," I say.

"Look, is it urgent?" Elise says, and I hear Caro Brennan talking beside her. "Sorry, Kiki." Elise cuts me short. "I've got to go—I'm in the middle of several things." And I cling on to the phone and fight to control my breath.

"Please," I say.

"Hang on, Caro," she hisses to her sergeant. "Okay, what's happened?" she demands.

"I've been raped," I sob. "By an online date." And close my eyes. It's out there now. I can never unsay it.

There's a beat of silence, and I hang there, wondering if she even heard me. "Where are you?" Elise speaks, professional and urgent. "Where is he?"

"I'm at home and I don't know where he is," I gulp. "But not in the house."

Her voice softens. "Okay. Hold tight. Don't answer the door or the phone to him. We're on our way. And, Kiki, don't shower or wash. It could be important."

AN HOUR LATER, I'm sitting with her in Southfold's teal-and-gray rape suite. The reporter in me notices that it's been rebranded as the Comfort Suite, but it is no less grim.

A doctor is on her way to examine me and take swabs, and I sit shivering, dreading the idea of anyone touching me. Like he must have done. The stickiness prickles my thighs. *Oh, God, I just want to sleep.*

But the specialist officer is wheeled in to ask her questions. Who? Where? When? I feel wrong-footed. Asking the questions is my job. Normally. But nothing is normal now.

I try to focus on my answers, but having Elise in the room distracts me. She is watching quietly from her matching sofa across the room. But she's taking in every word, and I wonder what she's thinking.

"Can I ask something?" Elise says when the interview pauses. The specialist officer and I nod. "Why did you meet him a second time? After he stalked you?"

It is what I would have asked. *What sort of idiot are you?*

I groan. My eyes are like slits and my throat aches from all the crying, but I need to explain myself.

"I just wanted it to stop," I croak. "And I thought it would if I told him, face-to-face, to leave me alone. Stupid, I know. But I really thought I could handle the situation."

"Okay, this is not your fault in any way," Elise says quietly and comes to sit beside me. "It sounds like you were drugged—the bloods may confirm what he used, but not everything hangs around in the system this long. We just need to find him—now. Let's go through the description again."

"Solid," I rasp. "Sort of light-colored hair. Good-looking, longish face. He said he worked in security. Freelance, like me. I've been trying to remember what he told me about himself, but he spent all his time asking me questions, talking about me. I was so flattered." I stop, straining not to cry before whispering: "But I suppose he didn't want me to know who he really was."

"No," Elise replies. "It looks like he went equipped with the drugs last night. He's done this before."

I shiver and wrap my arms around myself.

"Can you describe his vehicle?" Elise asks.

"Er, it was silver, I think. Quite small. It smelled of old cigarettes and a vanilla air freshener. Look, I'm sorry, I should have taken more notice on that first date, but it was dark and I was . . ."

"Distracted," Elise says. "I understand. Look, I'll come back after the doctor's seen you. But I need to arrange for officers to search your house—it looks like Rob took you home afterward. Your body is the crime scene, but he may well have left other evidence in the house. We could be lucky. This man may be on our system. And we've got the voice recording to nail him when we find him."

The police have downloaded the recording and the messages and photographs Rob sent, and I feel sick at the thought of strangers looking at them.

I start to cry again. It is all becoming too real.

"I haven't told my mum yet," I weep. "Let me ring her first, please. I don't want Pip upset."

"Make sure she gets a morning-after pill in case he didn't use a condom," I hear Elise murmur to the doctor as they cross paths in the doorway.

———

MUM GULPS ALONG with me when I phone from the police station and tell the tale.

"Oh, love," she whispers. And we both go.

"I don't want Pip to know anything about it," I say when we quieten. "Will you pick her up from school and take her to yours? Just tell her I've had to go on a job? This is my mess and I'll deal with it."

"You should never have gone on those dates," Ma says, as I knew she would. My stomach curdles, and I can taste vomit-stained regret at the back of my throat.

"Don't say that," I tell her. "This is down to the man who put roofies in my drink so he could rape me. This isn't my fault."

WHEN I FINALLY get home, the police have been and gone, but it feels like I'm being gaslighted. The kettle has been plugged into the wrong socket. The book I left on my bedside table is now on the dressing table, and my toothbrush is missing.

I flop down on the stripped bed and switch my phone back on. There are no new texts—none since I got in the police car—and I wonder if he knows I've reported him. If he's out there, watching me . . .

I jump up and peer around the curtain into the empty street below. No one there. I cry with relief and make myself walk downstairs. I wince as I place my feet—I'm still tender from the swabbing. And the embers of my earlier anger catch and flare. He has done this. He has turned me into this frightened, weeping wreck. And Elise said he'd done it before. There are other women just like me, jumping at every sound, trying to scrub him off their bodies.

I sit on the stairs, clinging to the banister. I just want to go to bed and sleep but I can't. I need to stoke my anger up to keep me afloat. I'm going to write my way through this. Use my voice. And find those other victims.

TUESDAY:
DAY 11

FIFTY-EIGHT

ANNIE

Tuesday, February 25, 2020

ANNIE HAD BEEN unable to breathe when he'd said the name. She'd made him repeat it three times. But each time, her brain had rejected it as impossible.

Karen Simmons. Dead Karen.

In the silent hours that followed, Annie had kept finding herself searching for the moment it had happened. Had their eyes met in the mirror as she trimmed his hair? Or in the Neptune on one of Henry's boys' nights out? Or had Henry sought her out? Karen had been pretty and bubbly. Shiny hair and makeup. Not weighed down by two rowdy boys who sucked the energy—and love—out of her. Henry must have basked in that kind of attention.

He'd said he hadn't existed in their house. That she'd failed him. That was how he'd squared it with himself.

And maybe he was right. Perhaps she had driven him into Karen's arms. *My fault.*

Annie was moving around the sitting room, straightening pictures and plumping cushions on autopilot. Sleety rain was hitting the window, and she'd had to put the main light on to see what she was doing.

There was no other sound in the house. Henry had gone off to work first thing without saying a word.

They hadn't spoken since Monday morning. Henry had moved into Xander's room. Snoring like he had a right to sleep while Annie fought her pillow in the early hours. He'd got it off his chest, she supposed, and probably felt cleansed somehow by his confession. But now it sat on her, crushing her, tormenting her with a slideshow of imagined encounters between Henry and the woman he'd planned to abandon her for.

She was pretending to read a book in the sitting room when he walked back in hours later, and she didn't look up. But Karen was immediately in the room with them. Annie suddenly wondered who else knew. She cast around her memories for knowing looks or sniggers from the people they'd lived among in Ebbing. Maybe he'd told his mates at work? She burned at the thought. It made her jump up and march into the kitchen and stand in front of him.

"Did everyone but me know?" she said.

His head jerked up. "No, of course not."

"Did you see her again?"

"No." Henry's breathing became ragged as his distress built, but she wouldn't let him off. "Archie dying changed everything. I had to be here for you and Xander."

"Had to?"

"Wanted to be. Needed to be. And then Gav came along, of course."

"In a way, I wish you had left," she gasped. "Our life's been a lie, hasn't it?"

Henry got up and came round the table. "What do you want me to do, Annie?" he said, taking hold of her shoulders. "I don't know what you want."

"I want to get rid of all the dishonesty," she said. But didn't know how. There were too many layers. And she was scared to dig too far down, in case there had never been anything there in the first place. No foundations. Just echoing emptiness.

"Okay," he murmured, and Annie could hear the relief in his voice. "We'll talk more. Do more things together as a couple. We'll go out tonight if you like. Look, I'll just pop out and get the car washed before my appointments tomorrow. Is that all right?"

Annie just looked at him. He clearly thought that was it. He'd drawn a line under it and was getting back to domestic chores, back to normal. How could he do that? Slice and dice his life so nothing mattered for longer than a day?

"No, Henry. Not all right," she snapped. "We should tell the police about your affair with Karen."

His arm dropped to his side and he stepped back. "What are you talking about? Why? It's ancient history. Do you really want the boys to know? Do you want to destroy our family all over again?"

What he meant was: What sort of a mother would she be if she wanted to do that? How could Annie argue against that? He knew her weakness. He was too clever for her.

Annie looked at the man she'd loved for what felt like forever. And had never really known.

FIFTY-NINE

KIKI

Tuesday, February 25, 2020

MILES WON'T TAKE his eyes off his screen, so I invade his personal space and start to hum annoyingly until he tuts and looks up.

"Have you read it?" I ask. He nods and looks back at his computer.

"Miles!" I croak. "Sorry, but it is so bloody rude. I'm talking to you."

My news editor pushes his chair backward and begins chewing at a thumbnail.

"I don't know what you expect me to say," he mutters, unable to meet my eye. "It's horrible. Why did you let it happen?"

"Er, I was drugged, Miles." I whirl his chair around to face me. "I didn't let anything happen. I was raped."

He blinks at the word and swallows hard, the muscles in his throat struggling against the emotion.

"No, no, I get that," he murmurs. "But why do you want everyone to know?"

"I don't. But I have to, because this isn't just happening to me. Don't you get it? Lots of other women—and men, actually—are having dangerous experiences with online dating. Bloody hell, Karen Simmons was murdered. People need to be warned."

"It's just it's a bit meta—and does that work for our demographic?"

Miles edges his chair backward away from me and seeks refuge in impenetrable exec-speak.

"Welcome to the real world," I say, hating the catch in my voice. "Look, you asked me to write about middle-aged dating to reach a new audience, do you remember? And now I have."

Miles blinks. "But, Kiki, I think you'll regret it," he says. And undoes me.

"Sod it, I'll put it out there myself," I sob as I walk out the door.

MILES RINGS A couple of hours later. I almost don't answer but pick up on the fifth ring.

"Are you okay?" he says, all gruff and out of his comfort zone. "I was a bit worried, that's all."

"No, of course I'm not," I growl. "But thank you for asking," I add grudgingly.

He clears his throat, and I imagine that throbbing Adam's apple. "I'm sorry if I came across as unsympathetic—I was just really shocked it had happened. I guess I'm finding it hard to deal with. Look, please will you change your mind and come back?" he says, his voice running through the register as if it is breaking all over again.

He's only twenty-four, I tell myself. The closest he's knowingly come to a rape victim is probably in a two-hundred-word news story.

"I need some time, Miles," I murmur. "But I will come back." I'm making it sound like a magnanimous gesture, but the truth is I'll have to—I need the monthly salary to pay the bills, never mind ski trips and branded trainers for Pip.

"That's great." He breathes out his relief. "Oh, so, probably not the moment, but just so you know, I've got some new intel for you on the BOBs in Ebbing."

"Have you?" I know I sound flat, but I just can't rouse myself. I'm losing power, and the last of my energy is focused on simply keeping myself upright. But my weakness lets Rob back in and I flash back to setting out to meet him like a lamb to the slaughter. I can see his face.

That tight smile. The moment when he must have decided and reached for the roofies or GHB to put me in my place. Remembering makes me feel as if I am being pushed, inescapably, toward the edge of a dark hole. And then I fall.

I jerk back into the room, and Miles is still burbling in my ear. "Yes, I think the Captain works in a bar. He's posted about creating cocktails with porno names."

I try to respond, but I'm suddenly too tired to even hold my phone up and have to lie down on the kitchen floor with it beside my ear.

"Okay, thank you, Miles," I murmur. "I'll call you in the morning."

I roll onto my back and force myself to think about the rest of the day. But it swamps me. Okay, just the next hour. I'm wondering if I can make it to the shower when I suddenly give a silent scream. The Captain is Barry Sherman, isn't he? The smirking Barry Sherman. He and the rest of the Band of Brothers are out there. Two of them still faceless. And Rob's tight smile suddenly looms back up to taunt me. Oh, God, is Rob one of them? Is he Deadpool or Bear? Was he lying in wait for me on the app? Hunting down the REPORTER BITCH to teach me a lesson. To stop me.

I kneel, then lever myself up as if in slow motion. *Up. Don't let this sink you. Keep going.* I sound as if I'm shouting from the coach's bench.

In the shower, I pretend to be rinsing Rob off for the last time and dress in my favorite jeans and jumper. I look like me in the mirror when I make myself stand there. "Chin up!" I mouth. It's a mistake. It's what my dad used to say when things went wrong, and tears burn my eyes. *No!* I command. *Find Rob!*

You should ask Barry, the reporter murmurs from somewhere deep within me. *He must know.*

I pick up my car keys and drive straight to the Lobster Shack. I find Sherman lounging in his office chair with a whitening gum-shield in.

"Hello, Captain," I say. And his eyes go dead.

"I've been reading your posts about having sex with Karen. Two out of five seems unnecessarily cruel. Even X-Man gave her a three."

"For Christ's sake," he splutters after yanking out the device in a shower of saliva and gel. "Okay, I had sex with Karen. So what? It was very occasionally."

"I see."

"There was no relationship," he hurries on. "It was just sex. And she was happy with that."

"Was she?"

Sherman stares at me defiantly and spreads his thighs. "Who are you, anyway? Some nobody reporter, poking your nose in everywhere. It's none of your bloody business. I don't have to tell you anything."

"Did you ask Karen to pose for Lenny? For one of his photo sessions?" I plunge on—nothing can stop me now—and Sherman blinks nervously.

"I don't know who you mean," he mutters and looks away.

"Sorry, should have used his real name. Noel Clayton."

Sherman's face sags. "Look, I hardly know the man," he blusters. "I buy the occasional tube of superglue from his place."

"Come on! You swap indecent photos with him. I've seen your posts online," I say, holding his eye. "The chats with Eamonn, Lenny, and X-Man. I know who you really are. But who are Bear and Deadpool?"

He flushes a deep red and clamps his legs back together. "No idea. It's just a bit of fun," he squeaks. "We're all consenting adults."

"Well, that's good. What about Karen? Did she consent?"

He rears up from his chair. "She wasn't interested. End of. I had nothing to do with her death—and you have no right to ask these questions."

"Perhaps the police will want to."

"Get out!" he bellows.

I do. I sit in my car where I know he can see me and phone Elise.

"Hello, how are you doing?" she says.

"I'm waiting for the tests to come back to make sure Rob hasn't given me an STD as a bonus," I say, fighting down the bubble of emotion rising out of my chest.

"That must be bloody hard," Elise says, and the sliver of kindness almost tips me over.

"I'm working and that's helping," I say too loudly.

"Are you? What sort of work?" I can picture her eyes narrowing.

"I've tracked down a group of six men who discussed Karen in intimate and degrading detail," I say quickly.

"Bloody hell," I hear her mutter under her breath. "Who are they?"

"They go by anonymous nicknames online—but I've been on dates with a couple of them and got a lucky break. I've identified four of them."

"Dates?" Elise sounds appalled. "Is Rob one of them?"

"I don't know," I say quietly. "But I think he might be. Look," I plead my case, "I needed to get into the group, and going undercover was the fastest way."

"The most dangerous way, given what happened to Karen." *And you* hangs in the air between us.

"Kiki, you need to step back from this," she rasps. "For your own good. This is way too close to what you have been through." Her exasperation rings through every word.

"I can't just lie on the floor and wait. I need to be doing something."

"I get that," she says quietly.

"Okay. So two of them live in Ebbing."

"Christ on a bicycle!" Elise explodes. "Who are they?"

"Noel Clayton and Barry Sherman," I say. And there is silence on the other end of the line.

"How long have you known this?" Elise eventually growls.

"Clayton—a few days ago. I was going to come to you earlier but then . . ." I trail off. "And I confirmed Sherman just now. Just before he threw me out of his bar."

"Right, I'll get the team to bring both of them in. What about five and six—the ones you haven't identified?"

"Deadpool and Bear," I say, and I hear the whoosh as she sucks in her breath.

"Bear?" she barks. "Are you sure? Have you got any information on him?"

"Er, yeah, I'm sure, and no, no info," I mutter. *She's already looking for him, isn't she?* "Why? Do you know who he is?"

"Not yet," she says.

"I'm on it," I say, adrenaline spiking.

"No, *we're* on it," Elise snaps.

"Of course," I say with my fingers crossed. She's right, but how can I? Finding Rob may save my sanity. I can't have him out there. Circling. Watching.

SIXTY

ELISE

Tuesday, February 25, 2020

ELISE'S HEADACHE THROBBED in her left temple. The team had been briefed, and cars were picking up Sherman and Clayton. She needed to digest the details of Kiki's information properly before they got there. But she couldn't settle to it.

Kiki's rape had affected her more than she'd expected. It had felt intensely personal for a second when she'd looked into Kiki's devastated eyes. Elise had quickly pulled back to professional concern, but inside, she was angrier than was healthy. She ought to let Caro take the lead on this. Give herself some space. She had Karen to think of.

Elise fished for paracetamol in her top drawer, dry-swallowed the tablets, and immediately regretted it. The taste made her gag, and she raced to the ladies.

She had her face down in the sink, scooping water into her mouth, when Caro came and found her.

"We haven't got much time before Noel Clayton and Barry Sherman get here, boss."

"Just getting ready. Have we got clear timelines for their known movements? We know they were both at the vigil on Wednesday."

"Yeah, Clayton with his photos of Karen," Caro said. "I'll print it all out."

Elise went back to her office, the bitter taste of the pills still coating her tongue.

She was looking for a mint in the bottom of her bag when her phone went.

"They're here," Caro said.

BARRY SHERMAN SLUMPED down in his chair and rubbed at his face as Elise dissected his sexual encounters with Karen.

"To clarify," she said crisply, "you admit you had sex with Karen on Thursday the thirteenth, twenty-four hours before she was murdered. When you told us you took back her scarf?"

He nodded.

"Was there a scarf?"

He shook his head wearily. "That must have been another time."

"Or you lied to us?"

"Look, I didn't want people to know I was seeing her. It wasn't good for my image."

"I don't think lying is particularly good for it, either," Elise snapped. She had him on the run, but she made herself pause. She mustn't get cocky. That was when mistakes were made. She needed to do it all by the book. She stood and leaned against the wall for a moment to settle herself.

"And on the Friday? Did you call again?"

"No, I've told you. I never spoke to her again," Sherman said, panic making his voice pitchy. "You must be able to check that on her phone records."

"Do you know who did?" Elise said quietly, taking her seat again and leaning into the question. "Was it one of your friends on the Band of Brothers forum?"

Sherman's face went blank. "I've no idea what you are talking about," he said in a monotone. "I want to talk to my lawyer before I answer any more questions."

SIXTY-ONE

KIKI

Tuesday, February 25, 2020

TELLING ELISE HOW far I got should have been exhilarating, but it isn't. I don't even feel outrage at being made out as a dangerous chancer and pushed to one side for the real investigators to do a "proper job." The truth is, I'm finding it hard to feel anything. It's like when I had Pip and they gave me an epidural to deaden the pain and half of me just disappeared. I remember lying there, looking at the lifeless legs at the bottom of the bed as if they belonged to someone else.

I pinch my arms hard just to experience something. Then wander around my house, straightening books and picking up Pip's shoes, pretending I know what I'm going to do next. But everything feels fake. Like I'm acting out being Kiki Nunn. I've tried to box it off, but it is there—a low hum of pain, like a terrifying tinnitus that blurs and disorientates me.

I'm distracting myself with sorting the mess on the kitchen table when I find Karen's photo albums. We used a couple of the pictures from them on day one of coverage, but I should really get them back to Mr. and Mrs. Simmons. I start flicking through the stiff pages, back to the beginning—the launch of Karen's own salon. They're just badly taken snaps, mainly: customers raising glasses, half in frame or caught with their eyes closed or walking out of the picture.

I suddenly stop. Annie Curtis is there, holding on to two laughing boys. I must have seen it before, but I didn't know who they were then. I look at their faces—blissfully unaware of what was to come. *Like me* rings in my head, and saliva fills my mouth. I swallow hard and force my eyes back to the album. When I get to the last page, the protective plastic over the photos is wrinkled, so it distorts the images, and I try to smooth it with my thumb, making it worse. I tut to myself, hearing my mother doing the same thing, and wish she was here with me. Soothing, caring. I peel the plastic back quickly, to sort it out on her behalf, but when I lift one of the photos to straighten it, there's another slipped in behind it. It's been taken at the salon, but there are no opening-day balloons and bunting in the background. And this one is pin-sharp. It's a man looking straight at the camera. It's such an intimate gaze that I feel I've walked in on . . . something.

Who are you? I haven't seen this face before. I turn the photograph over in case Karen wrote his name, but there's only a tiny heart drawn in ballpoint pen and a date: 9 August 2004. I shiver. This was taken the day Archie Curtis died.

Ronnie doesn't answer my text, and I cast around for someone else. Annie is there in the salon pictures. Maybe she knows who it is. I pull my boots on and am out of the house in minutes, grateful for the distraction.

HER CAR IS outside, and she answers quickly when I knock.

"Oh," she says, lips so tight she practically spits it. Annie is humming with tension, and I think she must be in the middle of an almighty row. But the house is silent behind her.

"Sorry to call unannounced," I burble. "But I just wondered if you had time for a quick chat? I need your help with a photo I've found."

Her mouth thins even further so her lips disappear. "Not really," she snaps. "It was a waste of time last time, wasn't it?"

I feel myself blush. She must hate me. Putting her through all that and not publishing a word.

"I'm really sorry, Annie," I say. "I tried, but Karen's murder has swept everything else out of my news editor's mind."

"Yeah, I get that," she mutters. "Anyway, the police were interested. I've been to talk to DI King at Southfold."

"Really? What did she say?"

Annie sighs. "That it was a complex crime scene. But she's taking it to her boss."

"She's looked at the case? Is she going to reinvestigate?" I need to know what she's told Annie before I approach Elise for comment.

Annie's phone rings and she looks at it. "Got to go," she mutters, and pushes at the door as she walks away. But it only half closes.

"Hello, Xander," she says inside the hall.

I edge into the gap to listen. She's talking about the police and the case being reopened, and I strain to hear. But Annie must suddenly remember I'm here and comes back to shut me out. I stand on the doorstep, steeling myself to knock again, but I've seen the expression on her face. She won't talk to me. I walk slowly back to the car, looking for another route. There's always another way into a story. And I realize I've just heard Annie tell her son. He now knows everything. I wait half an hour, then search for him online. He works in the city for a posh insurance firm. I ring the office number and ask for him.

"Hello, Mr. Curtis," I say when he answers. "I wondered if I could talk to you about the reopening of your brother's murder case."

There is empty air, and I wonder if the line has gone dead. But then he speaks. A soft voice. Younger than I'd expected. He must be about twenty-five, but he sounds more like late teens.

"You've been talking to my mother?" he asks. "Please, can you leave her alone? I don't want her upset."

"Then perhaps I should speak to you instead. I'm coming to London later this afternoon." Well, I am now. "Can we meet when you finish work?"

"And you won't bother my mum again?"

"I'm happy to put my questions through you," I say carefully.

A BITTER WIND is funneled up the narrow street outside Xander's City of London office when I arrive, and I pull my collar up as I wait to be buzzed into reception.

I sit among the trembling orchids and untouched magazines and watch the long escalator from the mezzanine for his arrival. I spot him looking for me. There's something familiar about his face—I've seen him somewhere before. *Probably the vigil,* I tell myself.

He doesn't shake my hand but stands awkwardly beyond reach as a flood of sharp suits eddies around him. Tall, guarded eyes, hint of curls where he needs a haircut.

"I thought we could get a drink in the bar down the street," he says. "But I can't stay long."

I'll have to work faster, then.

"Look, I should say straightaway that my mum may have got things a bit round her neck," he says when we both have a glass of expensive white wine in front of us.

"In what way?"

"The police are not really reinvestigating Archie's death. Mum just has a couple of questions."

"Yes, she told me. She doesn't think Nicky Donovan killed your brother, does she?"

Xander takes a gulp of the wine and puts his glass down carefully. "Mum is very upset about everything at the moment. With this new death."

Why does he keep calling them deaths? Why is he not using the word "murder"?

"Do you mind if I take notes?" I say and pull out my notebook. The picture from Karen's album falls out onto the floor, and we both reach to pick it up.

And I know where I've seen Xander's face before. It's the man in the photo. I can't speak for a moment as I struggle to make sense of a connection. But I don't need to.

"Why have you got a picture of my father?" Xander asks, blinking at the image.

"Your dad?" I look again. Of course it is. He's got his eyes and chin. Xander flips the picture over and sees what I already know. It was taken the day Xander found his brother murdered in Knapton Wood. The day his father lost his son. The worst day of both their lives. I shiver with anticipation for his reaction. But Xander simply places it down on the table and looks distractedly around the room as if searching for the exit.

"Goodness," I blurt to end the awkward silence. "You look just like him."

Xander's face darkens. "I am nothing like my dad," he hisses. And I wonder where that anger comes from.

"You're not close, then?"

"Not really," he mutters. "We're very different. He's a salesman— that's all about putting on a show."

"And you're the quieter sort?"

He half smiles and finishes his drink in one gulp. "My father likes to be the center of attention. That's not my spot."

"I've never met him," I say.

"Oh, you'd get the full treatment," he says. "He loves new people. Especially women. He's a man with weaknesses, my dad."

I take in his hard-edged stare. He's clearly not talking about a doughnut habit.

"What sort of weaknesses?" I smile, trying to keep my voice light.

"My father used to have a thing for young females who were impressed by a well-cut suit and salesman's patter. Made him feel big, I suppose. But it made Mum cry. She found out about a couple of them. But not all."

"But you did?" I urge him on.

"Dad used to forget I was in the back seat of the car sometimes on the way to school and would take a call. Then pretend it was a work colleague when he caught sight of me in the rearview mirror. And . . ."

Xander stops, clamping his lips together.

The hard eyes are a front, I realize. This is a man in pain.

"Things must have been very tense at home," I say. "Particularly after your brother was killed."

He closes his eyes, shutting me out completely.

"Why do you think Karen Simmons had a photo of your dad hidden in her album?" I try to lure him back.

"Why do you think?" he snaps and signals to the waiter to bring two more glasses. "I was only nine when he started taking me and Archie to get our hair cut," he says, so softly I have to lean closer to hear. "I loved it at first—I didn't do much with my dad, really. And this was a special boys' outing. But they kept looking at each other in the mirror over our heads. Him and Karen. And whispering when he paid the bill. And disappearing through that rattling curtain at the back, leaving us waiting out the front. Dad told me it was our secret. Something I couldn't tell anyone about. He said it was a special thing, just between us. But it made my stomach hurt. I wanted it to stop."

He rubs his eyes and I sit stunned.

"That must have been so distressing," I say quickly, keeping him on track. "Your mum said the other day that you pretended you'd been adopted when you were younger. I can understand why you might have wanted a different dad."

Xander looks up, startled.

"Well, kids imagine all sorts, don't they?" he says, his voice hoarse. "It was just a game I played. In my head, sometimes."

"Did your dad stay in touch with Karen after Archie died?" I press, the adrenaline making my voice rasp. *Could it be him who went to the wood with her?*

"I've no idea," he says. "I made my own little world—and left home as soon as I could. I couldn't bear the sadness in that house."

"You were there the night of Karen's murder, weren't you?"

"Er, yes. For dinner. I was introducing my fiancée, Emily, to them.

All a bit sticky, to be honest. And, actually, Dad was acting pretty weird when he took us to the station. He got all tense and even Emily couldn't get a word out of him." He looks at his phone for the millionth time. "Right, look, I've got to go. Emily's on her way. We're having dinner."

"Can I use this information?" I say, and he shrugs.

"Do what you want," he mutters as he pays the bill. "I'm sick of secrets."

I sit on after he leaves. *The sins of the father* pops unbidden into my head. Because, finally, there is a link between the two killings: Henry Curtis.

SIXTY-TWO

ELISE

Tuesday, February 25, 2020

WHEN ELISE UNLOCKED her front door hours later, she was ready to drop to her knees and sleep where she landed. But there was a note on the floor.

"Hi. You've been busy. Fancy another glass of wine?" It was signed "Mal." And the tension went out of her shoulders for the first time that day.

She was still standing with it in her hand, wondering if she had time to shower before she went, when Ronnie appeared at the door.

"Hello, you." Her neighbor grinned and waved a huge cling-filmed wedge of pasta. "I've brought some lasagna for you—I bet you're not eating properly while all this is going on."

"I don't need meals-on-wheels, thanks," Elise grumbled, but her empty stomach gurgled so loudly they both laughed. "Oh, come in, then," she said. She'd knock on Mal's door afterward.

"There's loads here—are you eating as well?" She guided Ronnie through to the kitchen.

"No, I had mine with Ted ages ago. He's taken to eating at pensioner o'clock. I'll stick this in the microwave."

"Good day?" Elise asked as she got a fork out of the drawer.

"Same old," Ronnie said. "What about you? You look a bit pale and interesting."

"Just a headache. It's all a bit full-on at work."

"Yes, I heard you've arrested Barry Sherman."

That explains the lasagna.

"This is delicious," Elise said, trying not to smile. "You've excelled yourself."

"Shut up." Ronnie laughed. "It's barely edible. Now, tell me what you know."

"Is that your interrogation technique, then? Bad food and kick the door down? You need to go on a course. Go on, then, what are people saying in town?"

"Well, some say they're shocked about Barry. But others are not surprised. You heard Doll and Mrs. Amos in the Neptune the other night. He's got a reputation as a lech. Never tried it on with me, obviously."

Elise looked at her neighbor, dressed tonight in saggy leggings and a maroon sweatshirt with *Retired. Not My Problem* on the front.

"No, well. His loss, I'm sure," Elise said as she shoved another wodge of pasta into her mouth. "Look, let's not jump the gun. There's a lot more work to do."

"Of course. Anyway, I heard you've found Karen's phone," Ronnie added.

"Who told you that?" Elise snapped.

"Friend of a friend who works in the police canteen."

"This town runs on gossip," Elise muttered.

"You can't blame them—one of our neighbors has been murdered and it's all anyone's talking about. They're desperate for information. Anyway, it's good, though, isn't it? Finding it. There'll be forensic evidence on it."

"I expect so," Elise said carefully. She didn't want Radio Ronnie informing all and sundry about her every move. "What else are they talking about, your informants?" Elise moved her on.

"Oh, I don't know . . ." Ronnie murmured.

"Go on, spit it out!" Elise laughed.

"Just that people are worried about Ash Woodward. He's gone very quiet and has been wandering about Creek End and down by the wood. He's always been a bit of an odd duck, but he's got a kind soul. He was so patient with his mum when she got dementia. And now he nurses his sick birds."

Birds. The word made Elise startle, and her hand went to her pocket of forgotten tasks. Ash and his birds were on a piece of neon-yellow paper. Scrawled after her last sparring match with Larry Agnew. She smoothed it and put him at the top of the pile.

WEDNESDAY:
DAY 12

SIXTY-THREE

KIKI

Wednesday, February 26, 2020

I ARRIVE AT Southfold police station early doors. I want to catch Elise as she walks in, not fight my way past the gatekeepers on reception.

I've left a message on her phone, but she hasn't rung back. I hang around in my car, fidgeting as I watch for her to drive up. I sat up late last night, torturing myself over Henry Curtis. I tried to write the story Xander had given me as soon as I got home, but it kept dissolving on the page. What did I have? One source—a child at the time—and an affair that may have happened sixteen years ago. Nothing to say there had been any recent contact. It was all too tenuous, and Henry Curtis could deny the whole thing. Annie had said Xander had a vivid imagination.

I had to find a better way in. A cold case review would be ideal. What I needed was Elise to confirm it.

She turns up on cue. Sees me waiting and waves me over.

"You're an early bird!" Elise says, and a ghost of a smile flickers across her lips. I wonder if she might be warming to me.

"I had an interesting conversation with Annie Curtis yesterday," I say lightly.

"Did you really?" The smile dies. "Goodness, Kiki, you have your fingers in everything. Did Annie ring you?"

I shake my head. "No, but I understand you're reviewing the original investigation into Archie's killing. That there are unanswered questions."

She pulls a face. "Come on, Kiki. I know you've got to try, but why would I comment on that?"

"Because I've got something to trade," I say quietly. "I also spoke to Xander Curtis. Do you fancy a coffee?" We walk in silence to the nearest café.

Elise's brow furrows as I show her the photo of Henry I found—"Did you have permission to take those albums?" she snaps—but the line deepens as I lay out Xander's story. There is a pause while the waiter slides our coffees onto the table. Then Elise tests my information line by line.

"An affair? But he doesn't know if there was any contact with Karen after Archie was killed?" Elise says half to herself. "Henry Curtis might have moved his family away, but Karen was only thirty minutes down the coast."

"The temptation could have been overwhelming," I say, urging her on.

"Okay, this is all speculation, so please hold off writing anything until we've had a chance to talk to Henry Curtis. I don't want him tipped off," Elise murmurs as we scrape the chairs back to leave.

She's going to put it to him. I need to keep her onside.

"Of course," I say.

"Okay, so, off the record, we are taking a look at aspects of the Archie Curtis case. It's at a very preliminary stage. Make sure it comes from an anonymous source—and don't over-egg it."

I write the story and file it straightaway. Miles says it is brilliant. I love that he is making the effort to sound interested but can't help bristling at his patronizing tone.

"Do you feel like coming into the office?" he asks uber-carefully, as if I'm made of glass and may shatter at any moment.

"Why? Have you got some mind-numbing press releases waiting for me?" I reach for sarky banter to stop him.

"Yeah, I have, as it goes." He plays his part, the relief that I'm not a sobbing mess making him sound a bit giddy. "Fancy it?"

"Well, if you put it like that. I'll be there shortly."

I try to sing along with the radio as I drive, like I always do, until I can safely bury myself in planning appeals and craft fairs. But the words keep dying on my tongue. I distract myself with Pip. She doesn't know any of it. Ma and I agreed she didn't need to. "She's so young," Ma had said. "Don't frighten her." And I went along with it.

But my girl looked at me this morning with a new wariness in her eyes. "Is something the matter, Mum?" she said quietly, pushing her Weetabix around the bowl.

"No, love," I murmured, and tried to pin a smile on. "Just a bit tired. Like that school shirt!"

Pip had looked down at her graying top—the victim of too many mixed washes—and grinned. "I'll pop into the shops at lunchtime and buy some new ones," I said fake brightly. It was a dead cert for moving her away from my horror.

I BLOODY HATE shopping centers; the synthetic spend-more music and the smell of bath bombs and popcorn make me headachy at the best of times. But I promised Pip.

I find the shirts, but it's lunchtime and the queue for the one open till defeats me. I sit to gather myself on one of those tired old lady chairs in the corner of the store and catch up on emails while the world of commerce continues around me.

There's an alert for the BOBs sitting in my inbox, and I feel the numbness creep back into my legs. My protective shield. My finger trembles as I watch it move to click on the link.

The poisonous BOBs seep into the store. They are back in full misogyny mode on the chat room today. X-Man has been on a five-star date—his post is studded with aubergine and sweat emojis—and Deadpool boasts he is close to hitting his target of sleeping with a woman every twelve hours. And I think of my girl, giggling over shoes and Harry Styles, and wonder how I'm ever going to protect her from men like this. *Maybe I can put her in a convent,* I'm thinking when a movement on the other side of a display catches my eye. A figure. Tall, dark jacket. It's only a glimpse before it disappears, but something inside me dies. *Is it Rob? Has he followed me?*

The fear pushes me out of my seat, and I look round wildly, my thoughts scattering. *What will he do? Shut up—it isn't him. But will he approach me? It isn't him. And spill out the sordid details of our encounter in front of all these people? Pretend I was part of it? Not the victim? I can't let him.*

Everything is too bright and shiny in the mall, and I have to screw up my eyes against the light as I scan for him.

There's no sign and I'm beating myself up for letting him get under my skin, when I suddenly see him. He's in a glass lift, rising above me. I don't think he's spotted me, but then he looks down. And waves.

SIXTY-FOUR

KIKI

Wednesday, February 26, 2020

I THINK I'M going to be sick as I run, hand over my mouth, to the nearest exit.

The crowd in the city center swallows me whole, and I feel safer, but I don't ring Elise until I'm sitting right at the back of a busy café.

"I've just seen Rob, my rapist," I whisper. "He's in the shopping center."

"Are you sure? Did you get a picture?" Elise says, and I groan.

"It was him. He waved. But I was so panicked I didn't get my phone out. And he was in one of those glass lifts, above me."

"I'll put out an alert. Sit tight."

I order a coffee for me to watch go cold. The waitress pushes me to have a muffin, but I'm so jangly that the thought of putting food in my mouth makes me want to throw up.

I startle when Elise finally rings back. "We're looking at the CCTV, but it's going to take time to find the right tapes. Why don't you go home and I'll call you when we're ready."

I'm making my way to the bus stop when someone suddenly says, "Hello, Kiki," close to me. I yelp and whirl round.

"Sorry, I didn't mean to startle you." Ash Woodward is standing in front of me, blinking into the low sunlight.

And I feel a hysterical sob of laughter rising up my throat because it's not Rob.

"Er, hello," I blather, stupidly grateful for a familiar face. "How are you doing?"

"I'm okay," he murmurs. "Trying to keep busy. I've been looking at places Karen used to go to," he says, his droopy eyes holding mine.

"The nightclubs?" I ask. He is the last person I'd imagine bopping under the strobes.

"I never went in. I just waited to make sure she was okay to get home," he murmurs. And I shiver, imagining him standing in the shadows, watching and obsessing.

Ash clears his throat.

"Oh, sorry, I've got a lot on my mind." I flounder for something to say. "Umm, you know they found her car in Brighton . . ." He must, but his eyes light up.

"I read that, but which car park was it? Do you know?" he says, more urgent now. "Where did he leave it?"

I stare at him uneasily. " 'He'?" I bleat, feeling the shoppers swish past us as if we don't exist.

"The man who killed Karen," Ash whispers, back to sad eyes.

"How do you know it was him driving the car?" I whisper back. "And not Karen?"

Ash looks away. He knows something I don't, and my whole body tenses. *How am I going to get him to tell me?* is all I can think about.

"I'm going to grab a coffee and a warm-up," I say gently. "You look like you could do with one, too. Come with me?"

"ARE YOU OKAY? You seem a bit on edge," I say when we are sitting knee to knee in a tiny seafront café.

Ash looks at me over the dusty plastic plant in the middle of the table. "A bit," he murmurs. "People have been banging on the side of my static. Shouting horrible things about me being a weirdo and a pervert. I don't know who has been saying these things."

I wonder if it's Barry Sherman and his band.

"And I haven't got Karen to tell now," he adds.

"No, you must really miss her," I say softly. And his lips tremble.

"Every day," he whispers.

"You can talk to me," I coax gently and quietly turn my phone to record. And he nods to himself.

"You were saying about Karen's car," I say, pushing a plate of biscuits his way. "How do you know it wasn't Karen driving the car?"

"She couldn't have," he sighs. "She was already dead."

I fight to keep calm, but my hands are shaking so hard I have to hide them in my lap. Ash doesn't seem to register the effect his words are having. He is deep inside himself. He automatically tears open a packet of sugar, tips it onto the table, and makes paths through the crystals with his finger as he thinks. Until I can bear the silence no more.

"How do you know, Ash?" I murmur.

His finger stops moving and he lifts his head. "I saw," he says. "Karen was dead when I found her in the wood."

"You found her?" My voice squeaks with the effort not to shout, and I look round to see who might have heard. "But why were you there? What were you doing in the wood at that time of night, Ash?"

"I saw her drive off from her flat," he mumbles. "I was just making sure she got home safely from the Neptune and I tried to follow her. She shouldn't have been driving and I was worried. But I lost her. I cycled around for a bit, and around midnight I thought I saw headlights up at the wood. I just went to see. She'd parked up."

"Was Karen alone?" I urge.

He shakes his head, eyes blank. "There was someone else in the car with her."

My stomach flips.

"Who was it, Ash?"

I can hear the saliva in his mouth rattling against his breath.

"Ash?"

"I think it was Barry Sherman," he says, and I can feel the flush racing up from my chest.

"Did you see Barry Sherman in the car?" *Have I got the final piece of the jigsaw?* My fingers are digging into my thighs so hard I can feel bruises beginning to bloom.

"She was having a secret affair with him—it must have been him."

"But did you see him? Did you follow them into the trees?"

He shakes his head wearily. "I should have done, but I told myself not to get involved and I went home. But I couldn't sleep. Couldn't stop thinking about her. I went back out about one o'clock—I couldn't help it. I just wanted to make sure she was home safely," he murmurs. "But her car wasn't parked outside the salon. And the windows of the flat were dark."

"So you went back to the wood?" I press him quietly.

"Just to check," he says, his voice flat. "Her car was gone. But she wasn't. She was just sitting there against a tree when I found her."

"Can you tell me what you saw?"

Ash closes his eyes for a moment and describes the scene in detail, mentioning the false nails and the bare legs. It's what I saw, too. He was definitely there. But was it as a guardian angel, or a killer?

"I didn't touch her," Ash blurts, as if I've said it out loud. "I just left."

"But why didn't you call the police?" I say, knowing that is what I should do as soon as I leave.

"Because I knew I'd be the main suspect if I did. Mum always told me not to put myself in the picture."

"Can I get you anything else?" a young waitress suddenly asks, breaking the spell, and Ash immediately shoves his chair backward, away from me and my questions.

"Ash," I say. But he shakes his head and ricochets through the café tables before I can stop him. I sit in stunned silence while the waitress removes the empty cups and tuts loudly at the mound of sugar.

SIXTY-FIVE

ELISE

Wednesday, February 26, 2020

ELISE HAD ANDY Thomson in the shopping center's security office, collecting the recordings from ten different cameras in the public areas, plus one from each exit.

"I'm going thirty minutes either side of Kiki Nunn's timeline to start with, but there is a ton of it," he phoned in to tell her. "And it was busy this lunchtime. So . . ."

"Okay," Elise sighed heavily. "Let's get it over here and sit Kiki Nunn in front of it for a couple of hours. See if we can find his face in the crowd."

She tried to rally her spirits. This man was hiding in plain sight in the dating community. Changing his name and small details as he moved between apps. But not his face. He would be out there.

And it wasn't as if she didn't have other things to do. Elise busied herself deleting the critical mass of emails cluttering her inbox. She checked daily but flicked over the dross—the memos sent to her and what appeared to be every officer on the force, for no discernible reason. She was binning them by the dozen, enjoying the quiet thrill of a deep clean, when she saw the name Ash Woodward on a vanishing mail. She had to dig around in the junk folder to hook it out. He'd sent it to Crimestoppers, and it had been forwarded to her by one of the team.

Dear DI King, I have spoken to Annie Curtis about this and I want you to know what I saw in Knapton Wood in 2004. It was a boy. And a man, he'd written. They were just standing with their arms around each other and I thought it was a boy and his dad.

She could hear Ash's whispery voice in every word. Elise moved forward onto the edge of her seat as she read, as if she could disappear inside the screen and enter Ash's world.

But the man put his hand on the boy's bottom and rubbed it slowly. Not like a dad. And the boy shouted something and they broke apart. The man crashed through the trees to the car park and I heard a motorcycle roar off. The boy disappeared the other way—in the direction of the houses. It was over so quickly and I wasn't sure what I'd seen. I was still watching the blue tits when I heard a woman screaming and I ran toward the sound. Mrs. Curtis was carrying a child, and the boy from earlier was beside her but I could see there were loads of people gathering and I never liked crowds. So I turned around and went and got my bike and cycled home.

I'm sorry I didn't tell the police when they came to the house. I didn't want to draw attention to myself. And I didn't see anything, really. Did I?

But he had. Elise shut her eyes and let out a low groan. Nicky Donovan had run away, just as he'd told his mother, and been on the other side of the wood, climbing onto his motorbike, when Archie Curtis was killed.

And Ash had seen and heard it all. He'd given Donovan an alibi, sixteen years too late.

The blood flow to her legs was being cut off by her sitting to attention, and Elise rubbed her thighs and shuffled back onto her chair. She frowned in concentration as she analyzed the text.

Of course, he's also placed himself within yards of the crime scene. Is that what he's really telling me? That he had something to do with little Archie Curtis's death?

SIXTY-SIX

KIKI

Wednesday, February 26, 2020

THE SALT IS eating Ash Woodward's caravan from the outside; the metal seams and window frames are rusting, and the windows are streaked with seagull shit. It is the most depressing door I've ever knocked on. In a film, it would have "ax murderer" written all over it.

I pull my coat collar up against the howling wind, mount the concrete-block steps to the door, and rap loudly. Nothing. Harder the second time. But the only sound is the wind battering the trees at the back. I've got to be quick—Pip has gone swim training for a couple of hours. But when I transcribed Ash's confession in my car, parts of the recording were too muffled to hear. I want to get it all straight before I ring Elise. And write my exclusive.

Maybe he's asleep? I go round the back and clamber onto a planter full of weeds to peer through a grimy window.

"Kiki?" a voice says sharply, making me startle and nearly lose my footing.

Elise King is standing only a few feet away, scowling up at me. "What are you doing?" she barks.

Bloody hell. I curse my luck. *Why is she here, anyway?*

"Just trying to see if Ash Woodward is in," I say, determined to stand my ground. I can knock on anyone's door I like.

"And is he?" Elise says, hoicking herself up beside me to have a quick look, too. She's on her own—no Caro Brennan today.

"Nope," I mutter, hoping she'll leave. Fat chance.

Elise goes round to the door and bangs hard. "It's DI King, Mr. Woodward. Please open the door."

In the end, she fetches Gordon, the owner of the caravan site. Gordon comes with his jailer's bunch of keys and lets us in. I hear his gasp from outside and rush up the steps behind Elise. The acid stink of vomit makes me gag, and I clamp my hand over my nose and mouth. Ash is lying face down on the floor under the table. Elise pushes Gordon back outside and scrambles to feel for a pulse in Ash's neck while I help turn him onto his side. It's freezing in here—the gas bottle in his heater must have run out—but he is colder. I can feel it, even through his clothes, and my eyes fill with tears.

"He's dead, isn't he?" I whisper, and Elise looks up, grim-faced, and nods. I fight it, but I have to stifle my sobs with my hands.

"He told me he was in Knapton Wood," I gulp.

"Yes, I know." Elise cuts me short, and I look at her crouching over the body. *Does she? Ash said he hadn't talked to the police.*

I start to ask how she knows, but I've become invisible. Elise is all business now, phoning for an ambulance and shouting to Gordon to get up to the entrance to direct the paramedics. I watch her pick up a bottle of pills from the tabletop.

"Oh, God, did he kill himself?" I blurt. "Did he do it because he had let out his secret?"

Elise quietens me with a warning look.

"We won't know until we get the toxicology report," she says firmly. "No point speculating."

When I get up off the floor, I stagger and have to catch hold of the counter where Ash kept his feathered patients. I look in the boxes, but all the birds are lying motionless. "Are you okay?" Elise says, voice full of concern. "It's probably the shock." But I notice she is wobbly on her legs, too.

"Let's get some air," she mutters, guiding me outside. "I need to make some more calls."

I hear the ambulance siren echoing against the open sky miles before it screeches up to the static. I'm waiting for my moment to tell her the full story about Ash's confession when a strong gust of wind blows me against the caravan and something hits me in the chest, making me yelp.

Elise whirls round, mid-dial. "What?" she snaps. I pull a soggy green rag off me between one finger and thumb.

"Sorry, but, God, look at this! This campsite is a tip," I say. And that's when I notice another rag sticking out of an external air vent near my knees. "Why's he done that?" I murmur.

"Done what?" Elise murmurs back as she returns to dialing.

"Bunged up the vents," I say, and we look at each other, eyes wide.

SIXTY-SEVEN

ELISE

Wednesday, February 26, 2020

Kɪᴋɪ Nᴜɴɴ ᴡᴀs shivering in a tatty purple camping chair on the cinder path when Elise got to her.

"Have they checked you over yet?" Elise asked crisply. "I've been given the all clear, but the paramedics say it was a good job we got out of the caravan so quickly. The levels of carbon monoxide inside were still high enough to poison us."

Kiki didn't speak. The reporter was horribly pale.

"How are you doing?" Elise said, softening her voice. "I need you to come and look at the CCTV from the shopping center. Do you think you're up to it?"

"I've been better," Kiki murmured. "And I'll review the tapes, but we need to talk. Urgently."

Elise tried not to groan. Everyone needed her urgently. Was Kiki a priority? Probably not. Lucy Chevening could take her witness statement.

"Ash told me earlier he was in the wood," Kiki started.

"Yes, as I said, we know. He told Annie Curtis and sent me an email detailing what he saw."

"Did he? Really? That he saw Karen's body?"

Elise steadied herself on the back of Kiki's seat as she fumbled to snag on to what the reporter was telling her.

"Karen's body?" she repeated slowly, weighing each word as she sank onto another folding chair.

"Yes. He went looking for her when she drove off from home that night," Kiki gabbled, not meeting her eye. "He said he was trying to keep her safe. But when he saw her car up at the wood, there was someone in it with her. And when Ash went back later, Karen was dead."

"When did he tell you this?" Elise exploded.

"At lunchtime today," Kiki whispered. "I was going to tell you. Of course I was. I wanted to transcribe my recording of the conversation before I did, but there were bits I couldn't quite make out, so I came to talk to him again. To clarify. But . . ."

Kiki closed her eyes as if in submission for what was to come.

"What are you talking about? You should have reported this immediately!" Elise ranted in disbelief. "What were you thinking of? Your stupid exclusive story? We are trying to find a man who brutally murdered Karen Simmons, who may kill again. And we've just lost a crucial witness."

The reporter's eyes opened again.

"Or the killer?" she murmured, voicing Elise's exact thoughts.

Caro Brennan appeared at Elise's side.

"All right, boss?" she murmured. "Everything okay?"

"Make sure we get Ash Woodward's prints and DNA swabs on the system, pronto," Elise hissed. "Wait until you hear this." Caro's eyes bulged as Elise recounted Kiki's admission.

"Where's this recording?" Caro snapped at the silent reporter. "And the transcript. Send them to me immediately." Kiki fumbled with her phone for a moment, and the DS stalked off to review the evidence.

"And you . . ." Elise blinked rapidly, fighting to get her fury under control. "You do not leave until we have taken a full statement."

"But I've got to fetch my daughter from swimming," Kiki stammered. "Can't I come back later?"

"No," Elise snapped, standing over her. "You'll have to make other arrangements for her. You are needed here."

But as soon as Kiki had walked to a quiet spot to make her calls, Elise slumped back down. The showdown had sapped all her energy, and the effort of standing was suddenly too much. She sat on in her chair, reading the transcript on her phone and struggling to make sense of the new scenario.

Unbelievably, Ash had been in Knapton Wood on both occasions. Is that what he'd come to tell her six days ago? All that nonsense about Barry Sherman calling at Karen's flat? Ash had been there to confess, hadn't he? But she hadn't let him. Elise reran the interview in her head and stopped on Ash's startled face when she'd asked him what he'd seen. Why the hell hadn't she coaxed him further? She cursed herself for rushing it and missing that chance. Her own sliding doors moment, maybe. Elise looked over at Kiki's huddled figure and swore under her breath. *The bloody reporter had known how to handle him.*

She glanced at the SOCOs photographing the vents. It was the same green material in both. But could Ash's death have been an accident? She knew people did reckless things like block up air vents to stop their heat escaping. Without realizing the lethal consequences. But had Ash?

Elise picked away at the evidence for suicide. He'd put himself in the vicinity of two murders. Was it a guilty conscience? But there was no confession in the caravan. Nor in the email she'd received. And engineering suicide by carbon monoxide poisoning wasn't a simple matter. Elise watched as the officers carried the small cardboard boxes of his former patients down the step. Would someone who loved animals as much as Ash choose a method that would kill his precious birds as well as himself?

She staggered upright when Caro approached. "Have you listened to it?" she croaked.

Caro nodded. "We've got to pick Barry Sherman up immediately, boss," she said. "Ash Woodward said he thought he was in Karen's car."

"Thought?" Elise murmured. "Or wished? He may have made the whole thing up—we can't test his story now, can we? Let's not forget that Ash had been stalking Karen all evening, by his own admission. He could have lured her to the wood and killed her. And blamed Barry. She'd rejected him as a lover. It's a powerful motive for revenge."

Elise knew the line between love and hate was as fragile as a spider's web. And as complex.

She'd been there. Lying awake at night, planning how to punish her ex, Hugh, for leaving her for someone else. She'd burned with the humiliation and injustice of it. She'd wanted him to suffer as she had. Thought seriously about sending anonymous texts and intimate photos of Hugh to the new woman, accusing him of further infidelities. To drive a stake into the relationship. Her fantasies had gathered speed and detail until the final scene where Hugh was begging Elise to take him back. And she was laughing in his face. It had given her an incredible high at first. But the furred-tongue taste of self-loathing was always close behind.

In the end, the only retribution she'd taken was breaking Hugh's beloved Crystal Palace FC mug. Ash Woodward might have gone down a very different route.

"Maybe," Caro said. "Let's find out."

ELISE PLUNGED STRAIGHT in when Sherman was brought into the interview room. "We have a witness who says you were in Karen Simmons's car with her the night she was killed."

Sherman rocked back in his seat. "I wasn't. I absolutely wasn't there. I had nothing to do with it." He paused and rubbed his face ruefully. "Look, I was with a woman that Friday night. She came over after the bar closed. I wanted to tell you at the beginning, but she begged me not to say."

"How convenient. Who is she? We'll need to talk to her, to check your alibi," Elise said.

Sherman ran the tip of his tongue along his veneers.

"Mina Ryan," he muttered. "She made me promise not to say anything. Because she'd get in trouble."

"Mina? Why? She's single, isn't she?"

Sherman sighed. Elise watched him take a smug sip of water. Like a quiz show contestant when they give the right answer. "She'd left her kid on his own at home," he said. "She was terrified you'd find out."

Elise wrote, "Ash was lying," on her pad and underlined it so hard her pen went through the paper.

"I see," she said crisply. "And what time did Mina Ryan leave?"

"I'm not sure. About one a.m.? We did the deed, had a drink, and she took herself home."

Elise gritted her teeth at his brutishness. "You didn't drive her, then?"

"No. Like I said, I'd had a couple of drinks. Couldn't risk losing my license. Anyway, she said she didn't mind walking."

"On her own, at one in the morning? It's a good thirty minutes from your pub."

He shrugged. "Not if you go the back way. Look, I offered to call a cab, but Mina said she didn't want to be recognized by one of the drivers. Anyway, the point is, she can tell you exactly where I was and what I was doing while Karen Simmons was getting herself killed."

A PHONE CALL later, they were all round the interview table again.

"Mina Ryan said she didn't know what we were talking about, Mr. Sherman," Elise said sharply, drilling straight down to the heart of the matter. "That she was never there in your pub flat."

Sherman gaped. "But it's the truth," he hissed. "I was trying to protect her and she does this to me?" His mouth hardened. "Okay. You need to talk to Noel. He'll tell you."

"Tell me what?" Elise said. But her stomach was telling her. Mr. Clayton and his photos. "Was he there? Why didn't you mention him before?"

"Mina didn't know," Sherman muttered. "It was just a bit of fun. And the photos were unusable."

The evidence was there when they looked again, in the hundreds of deleted pictures recovered by the techies. Two blurred, badly lit images that only made sense when they looked at them with knowing eyes.

MINA COVERED HER cried-out eyes to blot out the evidence when Elise showed her. "How could they? What sort of filthy perverts are they?"

Elise pushed the tissues toward her.

"I shouldn't have gone, but I was so fed up after the evening I'd had with Karen," Mina finally continued, voice flat and exhausted.

"Did she know you were seeing Barry?"

"No. But I didn't know she was seeing him, either. He played us both, didn't he? Getting us to keep it secret. I bet he enjoyed that power trip."

"Did he ring you?"

"No, I rang Barry and he said to come over. But the babysitter had gone."

"Why didn't Barry come to you?"

"The neighbors," Mina muttered. "One of them is still friendly with my ex. Word gets back very quickly. Look, it was only for an hour and my son sleeps like the dead."

"Your ten-year-old son."

Mina pulled her hair over her face. "Zac hadn't even moved when I got home," she whispered.

"What time was that?"

"One twenty-five. I walked as fast as I could—I hate those alleyways—and looked at the clock when I came in. I'm so sorry I didn't say before," she added quietly. "I was so frightened I'd get in serious trouble, and I didn't want my ex finding out. We've got a custody thing going on."

"Bloody woman. She's let us run around after Barry Sherman, wasting police time," Caro muttered when she and Elise stood in the corridor. "We should charge her with withholding evidence."

"Not now, Caro. Let's focus on the fact that her testimony has knocked our main murder suspect out of the inquiry. And Clayton. They were otherwise engaged during the period Karen was meeting and being killed by her date. Neither of them was in the car. So the only person we've got in the wood now is Ash. And he's dead," Elise snapped and strode off.

THURSDAY: DAY 13

SIXTY-EIGHT

ELISE

Thursday, February 27, 2020

ELISE'S PHONE PINGED as she was putting on her coat to leave. An alert. And her flesh crept. Her hospital appointment was today. She must have sent herself a reminder. Elise looked to check what time she had to be there and saw the other entry on her calendar. *Mal?*

It was second date night. How had she forgotten? How had it come round so quickly? She should cancel. How could she go out on a date when there was so much happening on the case? She scribbled on a blue Post-it to ring him later and make her excuses. But she couldn't stop thinking about him all the way to work.

"Are you okay?" Caro asked when Elise walked into the room. "Bit pale this morning."

"I'm fine," she muttered, and busied herself with email. There was a message from the lab on Kiki Nunn's rape. No matches for the assailant's DNA on the database. She went to dial the reporter but stopped. She'd remembered she had to do something first.

"We need to go to see the Curtises," she told Caro.

"We haven't got time for that, boss."

Elise took a breath and let it all out.

"Henry was having an affair with Karen when Archie Curtis was killed," she said, watching Caro's mouth fall open. "He was planning a new life with her but stayed when his son was murdered. He has been living half an hour from her ever since."

"Bloody hell, where did you get that from?" Caro rasped, eyes wide.

"Kiki Nunn. Xander Curtis told her about it the day before yesterday."

Caro scowled. "She's got her nose in everywhere. And I suppose she's going to broadcast it all over the net?"

"She says not. But we need to go straight after the briefing in case she changes her mind."

"Ash Woodward may be dead, but he is still a suspect," Elise said, noting the weary cast of some of the faces in the incident room. "He was in the wood that night, and he told us he followed Karen after she left the Neptune. He was obsessed with her—called himself her 'guardian angel.' And he knew she was in a sexual relationship with Barry Sherman. He had motive and opportunity."

"Easy, boss," Caro muttered. "I think we need to tread carefully here. At the moment, we have only his unconfirmed testimony that he was in the wood. There is zero forensic evidence to link him to Karen's death," she warned. "Nothing to show that he had any physical contact with her."

"But the lab is still working on samples from the scene," Elise said irritably. Why was Caro pissing on their main line of inquiry?

"And I've checked the CCTV at Sunny Sands—it shows him coming and going on his bike at the times he gave Kiki Nunn," Chevening piped up from the back of the room.

"He would still have had time to kill her," Elise countered, trying to close her down.

"And it's very unlikely that he drove Karen's car to Brighton," the young DC persisted.

Elise whipped round to face her. "Why?"

"He can't drive," Lucy said. "He's never had a license—or a passport, actually. I checked after he produced his library card as an identity document downstairs."

"Bloody hell," Andy Thomson said. "But he might still know how to. Some of the kids who nick cars round here haven't passed their test."

Seriously! Elise wanted to shout. "Look, let's check and double-check our information on Ash," she said instead, struggling to hide her disappointment in front of the team and looking down at her latest list. *Cancel date* jumped out at her. Christ, she'd forgotten to ring him. Was it too late to call it off?

"Hi," she told Mal's voicemail. "I'm really sorry but I've got to work tonight. Can we—"

Her phone beeped in her ear. Incoming call. It was him. She went to stand in the corridor to take it.

"Elise? Hello. Just missed picking up. What time am I calling for you tonight? We can walk to the curry house if you fancy stretching your legs."

"Er, I was just leaving you a message. Work is absolutely manic."

"Then you are definitely going to need some decompression time—and food," he laughed. "Shall I knock at eight?"

She felt herself nodding and said yes. She deserved this. And her appointment dread slipped down a notch.

Elise was buzzing when she went back into the incident room.

"Right," she told Caro. "Let's go and see what Henry Curtis has to say."

SIXTY-NINE

ANNIE

Thursday, February 27, 2020

ANNIE ALMOST CRIED with relief when she saw DI King and another police officer walking up her path. She didn't know how she had summoned her, but she didn't care. She was there.

"Thank you for coming," she said to DI King as she opened the door and ushered them through.

DI King nodded and opened her mouth to speak, but they were already in the kitchen, with Henry sitting there. Annie avoided his eye while DI King introduced herself and DS Brennan to her husband.

"Ah! Hello," he said, all easy charm, and put out his hand to shake Elise's as if she were a new client. "Look," he carried on, smiling his slow smile. "I'm not sure what we can help you with, but please have a seat."

"I'd like to talk to you about your relationship with Karen Simmons," DI King replied quietly.

Oh, God! She already knows. Annie clasped her hands together as though in a prayer of gratitude. She didn't need to break her promise now. Henry couldn't accuse her of sneaking around behind his back. Like he had. They had come to him.

Henry started coughing, choking on his shock, and Annie risked a glance at him. He looked terrible. His blue shirt was sticking to his chest and darkening under the arms as he burbled about how it had been nothing. And so long ago. Trying to make it disappear.

But when DI King asked, "Where were you on the evening of Valentine's Day?" his eyes and her heart fluttered.

"At home having a family dinner—wasn't I, Annie?" She couldn't speak so he did it for her. "Yes, our son Xander and his girlfriend came down from London to announce their engagement," he said, eyes wide open now.

"Did they stay overnight?"

"No, I took them into town to catch their trains."

"What time was that?"

"Er, ten thirty-ish. Emily was catching the last one to London—that was leaving first—then Xander was getting a Brighton train to meet his mates. It was a bit tight so I just dropped them off at the station entrance."

"What about afterward? Did you come straight home?"

Annie could feel dread clutching at her stomach.

Will he lie? Will I let him?

"Yes, of course," he said smoothly.

She cleared her throat quietly, and he glanced across at her.

"Can you confirm that?" DI King asked.

"Well—" Annie rasped.

"Oh, that's right," he said quickly. "I had a problem with the car."

"What sort of problem?" DI King said.

"A warning light flashed up. I had to look up what it was online and my phone battery had run out, so I had to wait until it charged with the motor running. I fell asleep. It'd been a long day. And then I had to fiddle with the settings on the car computer. They're all electronic now."

He was talking too much. Too many excuses, but DI King clearly wasn't being distracted by all his noise.

"What time did you get home, Mr. Curtis?" she asked again.

"Midnight? Or just after? I'm not sure now. I just wanted to get to bed."

"Do you know?" The inspector turned to Annie. "Did you wake up when your husband came in?"

"No," she said, but he interrupted before she could say anything else.

"I didn't get into our bed." He was stumbling over his words to get there first. "Annie had work the next day, so I slept in Xander's old room."

"I see. So no one can confirm what time you returned? Did you speak to Karen that night?" DI King asked, and a single droplet of sweat ran down the side of Henry's face and dripped into his coffee. Annie wondered if Elise King had noticed. Of course she had.

"No. This is ridiculous." His voice rose. "Why would I speak to her after all this time?"

He looked to Annie for reassurance. But she wouldn't give it to him. How could she? Now that she didn't know what sort of man he really was.

"We'll need to talk to you again, Mr. Curtis," DI King was saying. "After we've carried out further inquiries. We'll need to examine the clothes you were wearing that night. Have they been washed?"

Annie got up without a word, went into the utility room, and pulled Henry's flowery shirt and jeans out of the overflowing washing basket—another neglected domestic duty. DS Brennan took them off her and put them in plastic bags while Henry watched, his face blank.

"What about a coat?" the officer added. "Did you put one on to go out?"

"Er, I don't think so," Henry said, his face dazed. "We were in a hurry. No—I remember it was cold and I had to put the heater on full."

"Which is your coat?" DS Brennan said, looking at the rack in the hall.

"This one," he muttered, and unhooked his waxed jacket for her.

"Thank you. What about this?" And she pulled an overcoat from under one of Annie's.

He frowned. "I don't know what that one's doing in here. I usually keep it in the car for client visits."

"You've got dirt on the cuff," DS Brennan said, lifting a sleeve. "Do you know how it got there?"

Henry shook his head.

After the police left, Annie and Henry didn't speak. They went and sat on different floors of the house. He in the sitting room to ring round for a solicitor. She in the bedroom to figure out how the hell she was going to tell Xander and Gavin.

In the end, she snatched up her phone and dialed her eldest son. He'd know it was urgent if she was calling in work hours.

"Mum?" he answered.

"They're questioning your dad about Karen Simmons," she said quickly.

All she could hear was Xander breathing. What was he thinking, her quiet boy?

"The police came this morning and took away his clothes," Annie blurted, unable to bear the suffocating silence.

"I'll call you back in a minute," Xander whispered. And was gone. Annie sat and waited, rerunning the detectives' visit in close-up in her mind. The bead of sweat rolling down Henry's face. The flicker in Elise King's eyes. DS Brennan lifting the sleeve of her husband's best coat. She clutched the duvet to her face like a child's comforter and inhaled her husband's sleep smell. And buried her nose farther in. This was the man she'd chosen to spend the rest of her life with. The medical rep with all the chat she'd fallen in love with at the hospital Christmas party. Annie had spent too much of her nurse's pay on a dress—midnight blue and strapless—that made her feel like a different girl, and he'd danced with her all night. Her dad had loved him, too. He'd finally had another bloke in the house to talk football with. And they'd been so happy, hadn't they? Even when the children came and life got grown-up and serious, he'd known how to make her laugh. And when Archie died . . .

She should have been screaming Henry's innocence. But she didn't know what to believe anymore. He'd hidden so much from her. Could he be hiding more?

Could he have killed Karen? Was her husband capable of that?

The trill of the phone jerked her back into the room.

"Mum?" Xander said. "Tell me what's happened. Where is Dad now?"

"Downstairs," she muttered. "Looking for a solicitor. I have to tell you something, Xander. Your dad had an affair with Karen years ago."

There was a beat and Xander sighed. "I know," he murmured. "I've always known."

Annie felt heat shiver up her neck. "But how could you?" she cried. "I didn't know, and you were a child when it was going on."

"I suppose Dad thought that, too," her son muttered. "Thought it was safe to flirt and carry on in front of a kid."

"Oh, darling, I am so sorry. Why didn't you tell me?"

"Because he said it was our secret. A boys' secret, to make me feel special." Xander's voice caught on the word "special." "But it gave me a stomachache."

"Oh, my lovely boy!" Annie broke down. Why hadn't she known? She should have protected him. She was his mother. But she'd failed him. And Archie.

"I'll come, Mum. Does Gav know?"

"No, he's at school." She tried to control her ragged breath. "Are you going to ring your dad?"

"I don't think so," he grunted. "I'll text you when I'm on the train."

When she went downstairs, she found Henry sitting with his tablet on his knee, his head tipped back on the sofa cushion, staring at the ceiling.

He lurched upright when Annie came in. "I've got a woman in Portsmouth who can take my case on. If there is a case. I've told her it is a stupid misunderstanding. All circumstantial. I'm seeing her in an hour to talk it through before the police call me in for an interview."

"Okay," Annie said, picking up his empty mug from the little side table she'd found in a charity shop when they were first married. Going through the motions of normal life.

"Will you come with me?" he murmured. Her first test of loyalty.

"Er, no," she said. "Well, you might be ages, and I think I should be here in case Gav gets home before you, don't you?"

Henry nodded, but he didn't take his eyes off her.

"You know this whole thing is nonsense?" he said. "Don't you, Annie? You know me better than anyone. I couldn't kill someone—it's ridiculous."

But she didn't know anything anymore.

"Put Gavin's old puffa jacket on," she said instead. "It's cold out."

SEVENTY

KIKI

Thursday, February 27, 2020

I KNOW THE #MeToo support for my date rape column should have
buoyed me up a bit, but I feel swamped by it. By the sheer scale of the
misery that is pouring into the "Secret Dater" site and Twitter and Tik-
Tok accounts. And it's feeding into my own.

It's my fault—I've been completely open about the vulnerability of
being a quietly lonely woman and the power a bit of flattery and attention has to breach your defenses. And it has chimed. God, it has been a
full peal for some of the women who've contacted me. They've been
there, too. There are hundreds of them.

I thought finding other survivors like me would make me feel stron-
ger. But I am struggling under the weight of it. This isn't a self-help
group in a church hall, holding hands and nibbling comfort biscuits. It
is a roar of pain. A chorus of insistent voices, pecking at me, demanding
my attention.

Miles rang earlier this morning. "Hi," he said, voice tight, as if he
could hardly bear to speak. "Look, I've totally screwed up," he muttered. "I've had a kicking from on high for not running your piece as a
'Secret Dater' column. Any chance I can do that now? Please."

"Okay," I said, unable to add his agony to my misery burden.

"You are a total legend." He signed off.

I sit reading on through the messages, groaning in sympathy. Until Stef G. stops me dead.

I think Rob raped me, too, her message reads.

I swallow hard and type: I am so sorry. Please DM me.

Stef G. isn't her real name. And she doesn't want to meet in person. Too exposing. I get that—I did the same, didn't I? Ducked down behind anonymity. But men and women hiding who they really are may be what is allowing this to happen.

Stef rings me with her number withheld. She's a divorced mother of two with a stressful job who just wanted to have some nights out.

"I wanted to be me occasionally," she says. "Not someone's mum or boss."

"I totally get that," I reply. "But why do you think it was Rob?"

"Your description. And the texts he sent afterward."

"Did he drug you?"

"Yes." Stef gulps. "The last time. And sent me a photo of us. I couldn't go to the police. Why would they believe me? I'd been on four dates with him. He was charming and he made me laugh—well, you know that." There's a beat of silence. "I'm so ashamed I've let him get away with it," Stef says softly, "but I couldn't face the humiliation."

"Do not blame yourself." I enunciate each word deliberately. "Why do we do that? Tell ourselves that it's our fault for wearing the wrong clothes, smiling too much, giving unintended signals?"

"I know you're right—it's what I tell my daughters, for God's sake— but when it happens to you . . ." Stef murmurs.

"Okay, so let's hunt him down. Where did you go on your dates? Perhaps you found out more about him than I did."

"Bars in and around Hove—never the same place twice. Actually, the third one was at a pub a bit farther down the coast. He said he had a dodgy tire. Anyway, I drove over to meet him in Ebbing."

Ebbing?

"Can you remember the name of the pub?" I say, heart in mouth.

"Er, the Lobster something, I think—on the seafront, anyway."

Barry Sherman's bar. Of course.

"Go on," I urge her.

"We sat at the outside tables in the dark, under the heaters. He didn't want to go indoors. He wanted to go for a drive, really. But I didn't want to. I told myself that I didn't know him well enough to drive off with him."

"No. I wish I'd been that smart." I choke on the memory, then make myself push on. "Did you get any more information about him? Job? Marriage? Anything?"

"No. It's unbelievable, isn't it? But he didn't talk about himself. It was all about me. And I fell for it. But I decided to call it a day that last time—we were in Hove, and he was putting on the pressure to have sex, but it wasn't what I was looking for. That's when he drugged me."

There is silence on both ends of the line. Both of us struggling to contain our emotions.

"I am so sorry," we both say at the same time.

"We have got to stop him," I urge. "Or there'll be other women like us."

"There already are," Stef whispers. "Two women have contacted me through another forum. He was using a different name when he attacked them, but it's him."

"I'VE SPOKEN TO another victim of my rapist," I say when I call Elise. And stumble to a halt. *My rapist.* I hate that it sounds as if he is part of me.

"Who is she?" Elise says, cutting to the chase. She's not about to indulge in small talk after what I've screwed up with the murder investigation. But she can't ignore me. I'm a victim of crime, and we are nose to the trail together.

"No full name, but she was taken to the Lobster by Rob."

"He's definitely one of the brotherhood, then, isn't he? With Messrs Sherman and Clayton," Elise says, and her voice seems to echo. She sounds like she's in a public building. I can hear people's names being called. "But which one is he?" she muses to herself.

"Elise," I interrupt. "Look, I've heard about at least three other women raped by 'Rob'—through my latest column."

"Christ! Have you spoken to them, too?"

"Not yet. I'm sending you a transcript of my conversation with Stef," I say. "Can we talk when you've read it? And then you can push Sherman on his association with sexual predators—and their connection to Karen. It is all getting very close to him. He may give you names."

"Ah!" Elise says softly. "You haven't heard. We've released him. Barry Sherman has an alibi from two people."

"No way!" I yelp.

"Afraid so. Our inquiries continue."

I hear "Elise King to Room Eight" being called.

"Are you at the hospital?" I start, but she cuts me off.

"Sorry, got to go."

I might have to wait hours if she's having tests and sitting in a waiting room. My energy slips down several notches, but I hoist it back up. *I don't need to wait,* I tell myself.

I PM Stef online. "Have you heard anything from the other survivors? Will they talk to me? I just need one piece of solid information to start the process. I don't even know what car he drives."

"Oh, I do," Stef writes back. "It's a Toyota Yaris. I used to have one. And it's in a photo I took of a sunset in Hove. I didn't know it was his car until he drove off."

She sends the picture over. The number plate is obscured by other vehicles, but there is a sticker in the back window. My clammy fingers slip and stick to my screen as I enlarge the photo. *Paddle boarders do it standing up.* And the name of a shop. *Breaking Waves.*

The surge of emotion makes my chin tremble, but I push back against it. "I'm coming for you, you bastard," I hiss.

BREAKING WAVES IS closed for lunch when I get there. But I sit in my car and wait until a tanned woman with her hair in bleached locs saunters up.

"Hi," I call as the woman unlocks the door.

"Hi—come on in," she calls back. "I'll just get the lights on. Feel free to have a look around."

I push through a rack of board shorts until the shop spotlights illuminate an alcove papered with photos of people surfing, drinking, and partying.

"Ah!" The woman laughs. "You've found our wall of shame. Don't look too closely—there are some real shockers in there. So, what are you after?"

I take a breath. "It's who, really. One of your customers, I think."

The woman stops smiling. "Why? Are you police?"

"I'm a reporter," I say. "I'm writing about a man who is preying on women online."

"And you think he comes in here? Look, I know most of my customers pretty well, and none of them are creeps."

"No, well, he doesn't show out as one. He comes across as funny, charming, and caring. That's how he reels victims in. And then . . . Well, he's accused of serious sexual assaults."

"No way! God, I've just been reading an amazing online piece about this—you should download it. It's called 'The Secret Dater.'"

"That's me," I say, my voice cracking, and she comes out from behind the counter and puts her arms around me.

"What's his name?" she asks.

"Um, he told me and another victim he was called Rob, but that's probably not his real name. He said he was in his late forties. A fit guy. And he's got a sticker for this shop in the back window of his car. One of those." I point at the display.

"Okay. They're quite new stock. They came in in January. But I've given away loads. The thing is, a lot of the blokes who come in here are fit. You'd need to narrow it down a bit?"

"Drives a silver Yaris."

"Sorry, don't do cars. Does he have a tattoo? That's more my thing."

"Er, I don't know."

"Well, there are a couple of older paddle boarders who come in now and then. They're on the wall, actually."

She crosses to the patchwork of pictures, searching for faces. "That's one of them." She points and I lean closer. It's not Rob. The shop owner moves to one side. And I can't breathe. Or speak. He's there. Standing in a group of men with their wet suits unzipped and pulling silly faces for the camera.

SEVENTY-ONE

ELISE

Thursday, February 27, 2020

ELISE HAD IT all planned: straight back to work after her bloods were taken. She spent the half hour she sat among the anxious faces in the waiting room sorting her afternoon into twenty-minute slots. But everything went to hell when she got all weepy as soon as she entered the cubicle. The nurse, a young man with full sleeve tattoos on both arms, quietly ushered her into a side room.

"I'm sorry—this is ridiculous," Elise said, but he shook his head.

"Course it isn't," he said. "This is tough, and you can't be brave all the time. No one can."

He was bang on, and Elise cried harder into her tissue.

"Let it out," the nurse said gently. "I'll come back and check on you in a moment."

And she sat there, half enjoying the release, half beating herself up for her weakness. When she was running or managing to work at full power, she could almost forget that she had cancer. Even if it was just for a couple of minutes. But losing that bone-aching awareness meant that coming back to the reality—when her spine twinged in a new place or her skin felt hot to the touch—was shattering. Elise breathed slowly through her mouth. Her tissue had disintegrated, so she wiped her nose with the back of her hand, like a child. She suddenly wanted her mum to walk through the door and tell her things were going to be all right. And she made herself laugh and then cry again at the absurdity of a detective inspector running a murder investigation with her mother in tow.

WHEN SHE WALKED through her door, Elise lay on her sofa—just for ten minutes, she told herself—with a wet tea towel on her face, trying to reduce the puffiness before she went back to the office. She'd told Caro she was at the optician's—she could blame any redness on drops being put in or something.

When someone rang her bell, she struggled to sitting and called, "Who is it?" at the closed door.

"It's Mal—I saw you come home. Have you got a day off? Looking forward to tonight—but I've got warm pasties for lunch if you're interested."

Oh, God, he can't see me like this. Elise scrubbed at her face with the tea towel as if she could just wipe the misery off.

"Sorry, I'm . . . I'm a bit tied up," she said. But the treacherous catch in her voice betrayed her.

"Elise? Are you okay?" Mal called softly through the door. "Can I help?"

Elise pulled the door open with the tea towel still clutched in her hand.

"Oh!" he said. "What's happened? Have you hurt yourself?"

"No. It's just I've had a difficult morning." Elise's lips trembled. All she really wanted to do was bury her face in his old jumper, in his wonderful salty sea smell, and feel his warmth. But it would mean letting it all out in front of him. And that was too scary to contemplate.

"Have you eaten?" he asked gently, and stroked her arm. She could feel every inch of skin he touched. "I've got these pasties from the bakery," he said, holding up the grease-stained bag, and she could smell their safe, peppery aroma. "You'll be saving me from myself by having one." He grinned.

"I'll get some plates," she mumbled, and led the way. Elise's appointment card was lying on the sofa—too late to snatch it up. But maybe it was best he saw it—she wouldn't have to explain.

They ate in companionable silence, exchanging smiles and sighs of approval as they savored their food. It all felt so wonderfully right.

"Thank you for coming to the rescue today," she said, reaching across the table to stroke his hand.

"Very welcome." He smiled back.

"I need to get ready for work now," she murmured.

"Why don't you take your cup of tea upstairs and have a shower—it always makes me feel better," Mal said, stacking her plate on his. He kissed her lightly on the cheek as she stood.

"I'll let myself out," he called after her. And she heard the front door close from upstairs.

SEVENTY-TWO

KIKI

Thursday, February 27, 2020

THE LOBSTER SHACK is locked up, but I knock anyway. I can hear someone moving around inside and bang harder.

"We're closed," a woman shouts through the door. "I'm still sorting things out—the manager is . . . well, he's not here. Come back this evening."

"I don't want a drink," I shout back. "I'm a journalist—I'm writing about the Karen Simmons case. I promise it won't take a minute."

The bolt is drawn back, and the woman swings open the door.

"Thanks. Look, I need some help identifying someone who's been in your pub."

"Is it someone to do with the murder?" she says, fishing for her glasses in her pocket.

"I don't know yet," I say, handing over the print from the surf shop wall. The barmaid looks hard. "Well, I know him," she says, pointing at one of the younger men in the image. "He's my little brother. And this one's Barry, of course," she adds.

Sherman's smudgy face is at the back of the group.

"Barry's done a bit of paddle boarding. He likes the social side, apparently. For that, read 'surfer girls.'"

"What about him?" I ask, moving my finger along the line.

"Oh, Bob? Or is it Bill? Sorry, but he's not in here every night or anything," the woman says. "Nice bloke—always chats to the staff."

"What does he do for work?"

The woman shrugs. "Actually, it's funny. He told one girl he was a lifeguard. But he let slip to someone else he used to be a police officer."

"A police officer?" I croak. "And he lives locally?"

"Not sure. But he's renting. He was moaning about the cost of holiday lets."

"Okay. Is it Bob or Bill? Have you got his full name?" I know I'm being too pushy, but I need something concrete to go on.

The barmaid gives me a wary look. "No," she says, the friendliness ebbing away. "It's a pub, not a job center."

"I don't suppose he ever used a debit card in here?"

"Er, I expect so. Everyone does now. Why?"

"His full name would be on that, wouldn't it?" *You don't win the raffle unless you buy a ticket,* my old editor used to say. But the barmaid isn't having it.

She frowns. "It would. But I can't go ferreting through customer records for personal stuff. I'd get the sack. Now, I need to get on."

I leave my business card as I exit, just in case she has a change of heart. I'll chase down his address another way. If I have to, I'll just drive the streets, looking for a silver Yaris with the surf shop sticker.

First I go to stand and scan Ebbing High Street, trying to get my head back on track. If I'm honest, I don't really know what I would do if I came face-to-face with Rob. I've played a game of confronting the rapist in my head, where I'm the avenging Fury in full Technicolor, screaming his guilt into his face, seeing the terror in his eyes. But in this gray, depressed street where shopkeepers are already turning lights on against the gloom of winter and people are walking with eyes to the pavement, all I feel is fear.

I shiver and pull up the hood on my coat as I walk on. A light flickers in a window ahead. Ebbing Property and Rentals. I walk faster and push open the door.

Mina Ryan glances up from her screen. She looks terrible. Hollowed out.

"Hi, Mina," I say. "Are you okay?"

Mina shakes her head. "Can we not talk about it?" she murmurs. "It'll only set me off, and I can't keep crying all over the place. The bosses have been so good about giving me time off, but I've got to try to get back to some kind of normal."

I nod in sympathy. I wonder what Mina's normal looks like. Other people's lives.

"What about you?" Mina says, straining to appear interested. "You must be busy."

"Yes. That's right. What with Barry Sherman being arrested. He'd been seeing Karen in secret, apparently."

Mina flushes. "That was all a mistake. The police got it wrong. He's been released."

How does she know? "Have you spoken to him, then?" I say and sit down.

"No. Well, look, I've got to get on," Mina says nervously.

"Right," I say. "Actually, the reason I came in was to ask you to have a look at a photo for me—I'm trying to trace this bloke. The one stood next to Barry."

Mina sighs heavily and takes it.

"Oh," she says, "I've sorted out a couple of short lets for him over the winter. Why are you looking for him?"

"For a story I'm doing," I say quickly. "Have you got a full name?"

Mina writes it down, and the address. "He's got it on a shorter lease than they were looking for, to be honest," she says, safely back in professional mode. "But Ebbing in February is a hard sell. And he doesn't like to be tied down, he says. Anyway, what's the story you're doing?"

But I'm already halfway out the door.

SEVENTY-THREE

KIKI

Thursday, February 27, 2020

I GO STRAIGHT to his address and bang on the door. I don't know what I'm going to say, but I just want to see his face when he realizes he's been exposed as a rapist. I'm shaking, knees threatening to buckle under me as I wait for the sound of footsteps, for the light in the dimpled glass of the door to change as he approaches. But no one is coming.

I go and cup my face against the front window. There are no lights on inside. Has he seen me? Is he hiding? Well, I won't let him.

I walk fast to the end of the terrace and find the alley that leads to the back of the properties. I hold my breath as I tread softly past uneven fences, ducking my head down to stay out of sight. And count the gardens, trying to match the numbers. But in the end I don't need to. There's a silver-and-gray duvet cover hanging stiff with cold on a washing line. It's the one in the photos on my phone.

I squat down for a moment and force myself not to cry. Then I struggle to my feet to look straight into his kitchen. But there's no one there. I breathe, taking great gulps of air. *It's okay*, I recite in my head. *I know where you live. I'll come back.*

But as I turn to leave, I catch a movement out of the corner of my eye. It's in the window next door. I almost scream. I must have miscounted. Rob is standing, bare-chested, looking at his phone. I wonder if he's lining up his next victim. And then he moves, and I gasp. He is completely naked. I can't move. He will see me if I do. And I don't know what he'll do. I'm not a reporter here. I'm a victim. Just feet from my attacker.

I tell myself I'll count to five and then run, but when I get to three, another face appears. At an upstairs window. A woman. *Oh, my God!* And I stop counting and just run, stumbling over my terrified feet so I ricochet off fence panels.

I only stop when I get back to my car and can lock all my doors.

I dial the Southfold incident room with trembling fingers, and DS Brennan answers the phone.

"You need to speak to the press office," she snaps when she hears my voice.

"I've just seen the man who raped me," I blurt down the phone.

"The man in the shopping center? Where?" DS Brennan blurts back. I've got her attention now.

"He's inside a house with Elise King," I squeak, choking on the thought of what might be happening behind that front door.

"What?" DS Brennan shouts.

"He's there in the house with her. Naked. He's downstairs, and I saw her at an upstairs window."

"But she's at an optician's appointment. She left to go just before lunchtime."

I want to scream. *Why doesn't she believe me?*

"I think she is inside number seven Mariner's Cottages," I say slowly, spelling it out so there's no room for doubt.

"Number seven? But she lives at number five."

"Next door?" I bleat, and try counting the backyards again in my head. "Okay. The man I know as Rob rented number seven under the name Mal Coles."

"Mal," DS Brennan yelps. "Bloody hell!"

"He's drugged and raped at least four women," I add breathlessly.

"Shit," DS Brennan says and puts me on hold. Thirty seconds later she's back. "Elise isn't answering. Can you see the front of her house from where you are?"

"Yes. I'm parked just down the High Street."

"Stay there. Ring me if there's any movement. We're coming."

"This is his picture," I say when Caro Brennan and a second police car pull up behind me.

"Are you sure it's him?"

I nod. "He was here all the time. Calling himself something different."

"Does he know you've been looking for him?"

"No. I knocked as soon as Mina gave me the address—but there was no one in."

"What were you thinking? What if he'd become violent?" Caro hisses.

"I wasn't thinking," I admit. "I just wanted to see him frightened. Like he frightened me—and the other women."

"Look, sit tight while the team get into position. I'll knock as soon as everyone's ready at the rear of the properties."

"I can't see her," Lucy Chevening radios in from the back. "Just the male suspect at number five."

Thirty seconds later, I walk behind four officers to Elise's front door.

Bam, bam. Caro bangs so hard the glass shivers. And we wait.

I suddenly hear someone move inside.

"Elise! It's Caro," the sergeant calls, mouth to the door.

The glass in the door darkens, then goes light again as the person retreats.

"Elise is busy at the moment," a man's voice says faintly, and I shudder. It's him. "Can you come back later?"

"No. I need to speak to her now," Caro calls back. And there is silence.

The radio crackles into life. "Suspect is out the back door, pulling on his trousers and letting himself into the next-door garden. Now inside number seven," Lucy reports.

"Do the door," Caro barks at her team. And they steam into number five.

"Oh, God," I shriek, and point at a half-empty glass on the table. "Has he drugged her drink, too?"

Then Elise appears on the stairs in a dressing gown, face all blotchy. "What the hell is going on?" she shouts.

"Elise, are you all right?" Caro squeaks. "Didn't you hear me knocking and shouting?"

"I'm fine. I was just having a shower and thought it was Ronnie and Ted having one of their rows next door. What are you doing here?"

"We are arresting Mal Coles," Caro says quietly.

"Mal? What for?" And Elise notices me at the back of the group. "Oh, shit," she says and sits down hard on the stairs.

"He was in your house, Elise," Caro says, sitting down next to her. "Did you let him in?"

"Well, yes, earlier. He came in to make sure I was okay," Elise says, her voice flat. "He brought lunch. And he let himself out while I went upstairs to shower."

"He didn't leave, Elise," Caro murmurs. "Kiki saw him standing at your kitchen window. He'd taken his clothes off."

Elise automatically pulls her dressing gown tighter around her. She is so pale.

"Is it him? Is he Rob?" Elise asks me, and I nod.

There is suddenly shouting in the street, and Caro and Elise rush out, ordering me to stay where I am. But I wait and creep after everyone else. I need to see this.

"Elise!" Mal calls out to her. "Thank God! Tell them they've made a terrible mistake."

But she just looks at him.

"I'm arresting you on suspicion of an offense of rape, committed on February the twenty-third," DS Brennan says and cautions him.

I wonder if he's trying to remember who it was on the twenty-third. Running through his sexual conquests. Perhaps he doesn't even think of us as individuals.

Mal shakes his head in anger. "Rape? Are you serious? I don't need to rape anyone. I'm beating women away with a stick."

"What a lovely image that is," Caro mutters. "Let's get in the car, shall we?"

"You know that this is ridiculous, don't you?" Mal makes one last appeal to Elise, eyes pleading. But I won't let him pretend to be that man. I step forward from behind the officers on shaking legs.

"Hello, Rob," I say loudly, and his head jerks round. When he catches sight of me, his eyes go dead. He ducks his head down and gets in the car, but he can't resist a last glance back. I look him in the eye, hold him there for a microsecond, and then wave. He grimaces and turns away.

But I keep my hand hoisted in victory as the car drives off.

SEVENTY-FOUR

ELISE

Thursday, February 27, 2020

ELISE STOOD IN her office, too agitated to sit, while Mal was being processed. She'd spent her career keeping home and job separate. But here they were, colliding and shattering. How had she not seen who he really was?

Mal Coles had known who she was. Had spotted her loneliness immediately. It must shine out of her. But what sort of madness was it for him to groom a police officer? Was it part of his game? She knew some men got off on almost getting caught—the dirty thrill of brinkmanship. Or was she a "Get Out of Prison Free" card? If she'd slept with him, she'd have been compromised.

Elise swallowed hard. *Stop! You didn't. End of. And you were vulnerable. Especially today.*

She banged her fist against the window in frustration.

"Careful, boss," Caro said, hurrying in. "You'll break it. I'm asking an officer from Southfold to take your statement. Okay?"

"Yes, of course," Elise muttered. "But I haven't been assaulted. Nothing happened."

"No. You were lucky—others haven't been. We've got four potential rape victims so far, and there could be more."

Elise closed her eyes. He'd been standing, naked and unseen, in her house. Elise's stomach lurched, and vomit burned in her throat. What would have happened if Kiki hadn't turned up? What would he have done next? She could hear his footsteps coming up her stairs as if in some low-budget horror movie. And see his face, transfigured. Would she have been one of his video trophies?

Her eyes snapped open again. "Okay, I'll do the statement in a minute. But I need to focus on him as a suspect in Karen's killing," Elise said, reasserting herself as SIO. "He's got to be one of Kiki's toxic brotherhood. Is he Bear? Did he contact Karen the night she died?"

"Possible. Although his MO seems to be more of a long game. Building trust—and anticipation, probably—and getting the victim where he wants them," Caro murmured.

Elise gulped. She'd been there. "True, but maybe he had done that with Karen? We don't know, do we? Do we even know who he really is?"

"He's got credit cards in three different names in his wallet," Caro said. "We're running all of them through the database."

"He told me he worked in IT after leaving the military and applied to join the police."

"Did he tell you that today?" Caro asked.

"Er, no. Last week," Elise muttered. "He came round to mine for a drink. To be neighborly."

"Okay."

"And I had dinner with him last Saturday," Elise added, feeling her face heat up.

"You never mentioned having a date! Did he try anything then?"

"No," Elise snapped. "Do you think I'd have let him in my house if he had? We were due to go out for a curry tonight, actually."

"Right. Be sure to mention that in the interview—because he will."

Elise's stomach clenched. Of course he would. He'd try to make out there was some sort of big romance. "Look, I'll leave you and Lucy to interview him." Elise tried to keep the panic out of her voice. "I've got lots to catch up on."

But she couldn't escape him. A photo of Mal Coles, aka Rob or Bob, was on the board in the incident room. One of the officers was running his face through TinEye and Google Images for matches. "I think this is him," he called out. "Timothy Malcolm Colman. He was serving with the army in Cyprus in 1999."

CARO CAME BACK up after the interview and sat in Elise's office. "He says Kiki had had a bit to drink but was more than willing. He took her home and put her to bed afterward. He actually said: 'What kind of rapist does that?'"

"Dear God! And the photographs and texts?"

"He said she got off on them. Part of their game, apparently."

Did he mention me? was on her lips, but Caro cut in.

"You should know that he said you were coming on to him. That's why he stripped off. Said he must have misread the signals."

Elise breathed out slowly. "Bastard," she allowed herself, and moved on. "Okay, did he know Karen?"

"Says no, but he's a cool customer, boss. Been in a few tight spots, I imagine. And got away with it."

"But not this time. Does he know there's a recording of him attacking Kiki?"

"Not yet. He's in with the lawyer at the moment. Cooking up his story."

Elise watched online as Caro told Mal about the recording, searching his impassive face for the charming man who had made her want to be kissed. And gritted her teeth against the memory.

After he was charged with rape, he was led away. "She's making this up," he sneered—his parting shot. "That's what they do, women like her."

ELISE LOOKED AT the timeline they had assembled for Timothy Malcolm Colman in the incident room. He'd married an older woman within a year of coming out of the forces.

She turned to face the team, catching their expressions changing. Was she still the boss? Or a victim they'd just rescued?

"Where's his wife?" the boss barked at the team.

"She died a year ago. From cancer, according to the death certificate. Oh, sorry," Chevening said, blushing.

"For goodness' sake, Lucy, don't apologize. It's fine," Elise muttered. "I can cope with you mentioning cancer." But her stomach had tightened. When were the results of the blood tests due? "Actually, he told me it was his mum who had it," Elise barreled on. "Can't help lying, can he?"

"We've established Timothy Colman did swipe Karen," Lucy added. "But to be fair, he swiped anyone and everyone—including some blokes. The digital boys are chasing down the phone numbers, but he was operating under several names: Rob, Bob, Bill, and, randomly, Deadpool."

Not Bear. Elise took a breath and swallowed her disappointment, telling herself that at least he was confirmed as the fifth man in the Band of Brothers.

"Get back in and ask him about the last member of their group. Have we pinned down where he was on February the fourteenth? And have we heard from Kiki Nunn?"

Elise dialed her rather than wait. "Hi, how are you doing? I know I told you to stand down before, but thank you for ignoring me."

Kiki gave a snort of laughter. "I'm going to remind you of that later," she said. "Are you okay?"

"Er, yes, yes." Elise hurried on, determined to stay in detective mode. "Look, have you got anywhere with the women on the forum? We need to place Mal Coles—Rob—on the night Karen was murdered."

She heard the groan and tightened her grip on the phone.

"I am so sorry, Elise," Kiki said. "I was about to call. He was with a woman he met on Tinder. She recognized him from my column and she is sure about the date—Valentine's Day. She said he picked her up in Littlehampton around eleven thirty, miles away from Ebbing, and his clothes stank of curry."

"Shit! We'll need a statement. Thanks for chasing it. By the way, he uses the name Deadpool."

"Of course he does," Kiki muttered. "Only Bear out there now."

FRIDAY:
DAY 14

SEVENTY-FIVE

KIKI

Friday, February 28, 2020

I CAN'T EVEN be bothered to get dressed this morning. I sit at the table in a grubby T-shirt, knickers, and socks while Pip whirls around the room, talking about school and a missing book.

"Mum!" She is suddenly standing in front of me, her sweet face pale and tense. "What's wrong?" she murmurs. "You don't look well. I'm going to ring Grandma."

"No, no," I say, my voice still growly from lack of sleep. "I'm fine. Just tired." She doesn't look convinced, but I force myself to get busy. I wash my face. Put on clean clothes and makeup. Brush my hair. And drive her to school. I'm shattered by the effort when I get back, but I make myself reread the piece I've written about the Archie Curtis case review and push it through to Miles to upload. But I'm too tired to resist the riptide of my memories and am pulled under into the teal-and-gray nightmare of the rape suite, worrying about Rob talking his way out of it. Telling the police how I wanted it. How I loved it.

I'm not sure how long I've been sitting here. Five minutes? But when I look at the kitchen clock, half an hour has passed. Ma says I should go and get some help. Talking therapy, she means. But, Christ, it's all I do. Talk to strangers.

I scroll through my notes from my interview with Xander. And park therapy. I need to get back into it. Find Bear. Could it be Henry Curtis? There's been no word from Elise on him since I gave her the information. I don't even know if she's read my memo, let alone acted on it. She could have stuck it at the bottom of her to-do pile and forgotten.

Or maybe the police have been there, at the house, combing through the story. I slam the lid on my laptop and haul myself out. *Keep going,* I tell myself. Annie Curtis might talk to me this time, now I've written about the case being reopened.

There's no sign of police activity at the house. No sign of anyone. I'll wait in case Annie's just at the shops, but I get restless in the car. I take a stroll down their road—guessing the householders from the ornaments in the front windows. There's a horror five doors up—dusty artificial flowers and a big Darth Vader figure. *A goth and his gran?*

A baby suddenly starts howling and I look around. A red-faced man holding a matching infant is trying to wrestle it into a pushchair.

"For God's sake, Jasper," the man groans, and looks over at me with desperate eyes.

"You've got your hands full," I say, crossing the road to him. "My daughter had colic and screamed for a month. But it gets better. There's a magic way to hold them."

The man stops jiggling his roaring son and says: "Show me."

When I follow him into the house, I see his living room looks like a ram-raided Mamas & Papas: toys, formula packs, discarded nappies, and soiled clothes everywhere. "Sorry about the mess," he murmurs. "My partner's at a spa."

I sit him down, lay his son on his forearm, hand under his tummy, and get him to sway gently. And the baby burps loudly and his eyes close.

"Oh, my God," he says, genuinely awestruck. "You are a baby whisperer."

"Well, that's not my real job," I laugh. "I'm a reporter."

"Really? What are you doing in our road?"

"Waiting for someone. I'm writing about a cold case. The murder of a little boy—Archie Curtis. I don't know if you remember it." I doubt it. This bloke would have been a child himself.

"Actually, yes—my mum was terribly upset about it. I remember her reading bits out of the paper to my dad. So, who lives in our road?"

"Archie's family. At number fifty-nine. Do you know them?"

"Really? God! I've talked to her—it's Annie, isn't it? She always stops to ask about Jasper if she sees us pushing him up and down the street. But the husband's just in and out of his car. I've never spoken to him. I nearly did the other night, though. Banging his car door like that in the early hours. He woke the baby just when I'd got him settled."

"Oh? When was that?" I say, edging forward. What was Henry Curtis doing out in the middle of the night?

"Dunno. All our days and nights have run into each other."

"Right," I sigh.

"Actually," the dazed parent mutters under his breath and levers himself up with Jasper clinging to his arm like a monkey. He lifts a pile of disposables and pulls out a notebook with cartoon cherubs on the front.

"We're keeping a feeding chart," he says, turning the pages. "Here we are. Jasper had fed at one forty a.m. but wouldn't settle. I remember I was walking up and down in here, trying to get him to sleep, when the husband reversed into a space right outside. He slammed the driver's door really hard, and the baby started crying again. My partner had to give him another feed. At two twenty-eight."

"You must have been really peed off," I say, trying not to sound too excited. "So what day was that?"

"Er, Friday the fourteenth. Actually, it was the fifteenth by the time he parked."

"Are you sure it was him?" I push, and take a photo of the page.

"Oh, yes. I was going to have a word with him but by the time I opened the front door, he was inside and a light went on upstairs."

"Brilliant, thank you," I say and clench my fists to stop myself pumping the air.

According to Xander Curtis, his dad had dropped him and his fiancée off at ten thirty. And now I know he had not returned until four hours later. On the night his ex-lover Karen Simmons was murdered in a wood he knew all too well.

SEVENTY-SIX

ELISE

Friday, February 28, 2020

ELISE'S PHONE WENT and she answered on the first ring.

"I've just spoken to a man who saw Henry Curtis come home at just before two twenty-eight a.m. on February the fifteenth," Kiki Nunn said. "You're welcome."

Elise briefed Caro to get the neighbor witness reinterviewed, then took herself off to stand beside the technician examining Henry Curtis's clothing. The minutes ticked past, and she knew Caro would be shouldering the day's tasks alone, but she couldn't tear herself away.

"I'm looking at traces of saliva detected on the right lapel," the techie said. "My colleague is analyzing the soil found on the cuff."

"Great," Elise said. "You don't mind if I watch?"

"No," the techie said slowly. She clearly did, but she'd have to get over it.

The markers filled the screen, and the technician breathed noisily as she read them.

"It's a match to Karen Simmons's DNA." She smiled at Elise. "I'll get this typed up and sent over, shall I?"

Elise skipped down the stairs.

"Match?" Caro mouthed at her.

"Yep. We're off to the races!"

"I'll go and get him myself."

"Hang on," Elise said. "Catch me up. Noel Clayton?"

"A count of voyeurism. I bet he'll argue that Sherman told him Mina Ryan consented, but let's see."

"Right, is Henry Curtis's number in Karen's phone records?" Elise ticked it off on her fingers. "Have we looked?"

"Yes, of course—and no. Not his registered mobile, anyway. We'll search the house for other handsets."

HENRY CURTIS WAS talking animatedly to his solicitor when Elise peered through the glass in the door an hour later. He looked up for the challenge today. A lot better than she did, probably. He shut up immediately when the handle turned.

"When was the last time you wore your black overcoat?" Elise dived in as soon as Caro had finished pressing buttons and recording those present.

"February the twelfth. I visited a new factory site near Southampton," he said, his answer delivered with full salesman eye contact.

"What were the conditions on-site?"

"Muddy. I was with a group of investors being walked around a field. Five of them," he said, and Elise wondered if he'd prepared a PowerPoint presentation overnight. "They were being shown where their money was going. I must have got dirt on my coat during that visit."

Caro wrote down the details. They'd have to get samples to compare, Elise thought.

"Have you had the coat long?"

"No. I got it in the sales last year. It was sixty percent off—quite a buy, actually," Henry Curtis said, his confidence at full strength now. He looked like he was about to close a deal.

"I see," Elise said, relief flooding through her, and sat back. They'd got him. "The thing is, Mr. Curtis," she said evenly, "we have evidence that Karen Simmons had contact with your bargain overcoat."

"That's impossible," he cried, presentation trashed. "She couldn't have. I've already told you, I haven't spoken to or seen Karen since I ended our relationship in 2004."

"But you bought it last year—fifteen years after you say you last saw her. So that can't be true, can it? We have a witness who saw you return home on the morning of the fifteenth just before two thirty a.m."

There was a pause while he took that in. "I told you," he eventually muttered. "I fell asleep in my car. Must have been for longer than I thought."

"Four hours unaccounted for, Mr. Curtis, with your phone off. Were you meeting Karen Simmons that night? The night she was killed?"

"No." Curtis rocked in his chair, face in hands. "No, no."

SEVENTY-SEVEN

ELISE

Friday, February 28, 2020

THE CURTIS HOUSE was being searched and Lucy Chevening had been hunting down Henry Curtis, his movements on the night Karen died, tracking his car along with the ANPR and the world-weary expert upstairs.

"Time of drop-off matches his story," she told Elise during a break in the interview. "We've got him parking outside Portsmouth and Southsea station in the taxi rank and leaving four minutes later."

"Show me," Elise said.

The station CCTV had caught the car pulling up under the lights of the main entrance at ten twenty-eight. They watched as the images unspooled and the occupants of the car got out and did their Scottish reel round the vehicle. Henry first, in shirtsleeves. He went round to let Emily out of the back seat while Xander got a bag out of the boot. Henry slipped back into the driver's seat as the young couple walked off.

"Look," Chevening said. "He doesn't drive off straightaway. His phone lights up in his hand—he's checking messages. Ninety seconds later he sets off."

"It's too early for the texts Karen received," Elise muttered.

"I know, but he could have done it later. Anyway," Chevening went on, "one of the local officers has done the drive from the station to the Curtis house this morning. He clocked it as a sixteen-minute journey, but it would probably have been quicker at that time of night. Curtis said he noticed a problem with the car in one of the rat-run streets he uses as a shortcut. Doesn't know the name of it and nothing on any cameras yet."

"How convenient," Caro said. "He told his wife the next morning he was taking the vehicle into the garage to get it checked out. Can you follow that up?"

Lucy nodded, the task logged. Elise felt a twinge of envy. That was how she used to do things. No need for endless bits of paper and notes to self. It would get better. The consultant had promised.

"The garage Henry Curtis uses hasn't had the car in for repair," DC Chevening reported back five minutes later. "But he had it cleaned inside and out, three days ago."

Caro had been busy, too. "He messaged a colleague from work that night," she said. "I've finally managed to speak to him. Henry owed him money—a lot of money—and the colleague admits he threatened to tell their boss. Henry could have lost his job over it. He spent until eleven thirty online on a work phone, setting up two new credit cards and transferring balances. Then he switched both phones off."

"Last known position?" Elise said.

"At a service station off the A27, four miles from Ebbing."

"Twenty minutes from Knapton Wood," Elise murmured.

An hour later, they had more to bury their suspect. The dirt on the right cuff of his coat matched soil samples from Knapton Wood.

"Henry Curtis must have used that hand to force Karen's head into the ground," Elise said. "Poor woman. He was only living half an hour away from her. And she'd never left Ebbing. It must have been tantalizing to have her so close. He was the man Ash Woodward saw in Karen's car, wasn't he?"

Elise stood, took a breath, and bounced on her toes to get her circulation going. "Ash told Annie he was in Knapton Wood. She might have mentioned it to Henry. Maybe he panicked and stuffed rags into the vents at Ash's caravan to make sure Ash never repeated what he knew? We need to get back in and up the pressure on Henry."

But Henry Curtis did not oblige. He doggedly persisted with his denials, his answers shrinking to single syllables. "No," he said to everything by the end, exhaustion dragging his voice down to a growl.

They put him in the cells while the Crown Prosecution Service looked at their evidence and assessed the likelihood of conviction.

The team kept going through the motions, but Elise knew they were holding a collective breath for the outcome.

When the phone rang, she felt the shiver go through the room.

"We can charge him," she announced into the silence.

"Fuck yeah!" Caro said.

SATURDAY: DAY 15

SEVENTY-EIGHT

KIKI

Saturday, February 29, 2020

I GO STRAIGHT to the Curtises' house this morning. I've got to keep Annie onside to be in pole position for the first interview if they charge Henry. I've bought biscuits and flowers from the service station on the way to sweeten my approach and am getting my head together when I turn into their street. *Shit!* The TV cameras are here already, and I spot a small huddle of reporters sitting on a low wall.

"They've gone," my mate on *South Coast News* mutters as he grinds out his cigarette underfoot. "Must have been last night."

"Bloody hell!"

"Don't worry, there's a presser at Southfold at eleven. Word is they're charging him."

"But where have they taken the family?" I mutter, opening the biscuits and offering them to the cameraman.

He munches appreciatively on two custard creams, sparks up another ciggie, and lets out a smug plume of smoke. "Actually, I heard one of the cops mention the Travel Inn at Portsmouth docks," he whispers.

———

I AVOID THE eye of the constable standing under the forgotten remnants of Christmas decorations in the hotel foyer as I push the button for the lift. I can hear the constant roar of traffic on the nearby motorway and wonder if Annie has managed to sleep.

Gavin Curtis is sitting on the end of his unmade bed watching TV when Annie opens the door to their room.

"What the hell are you doing here?" she groans. "Have you heard anything?"

"No—I just wanted to see how you're doing," I say, hoping to pre-empt any protest.

"How do you think?" Annie says. She leaves the door open and goes and stands at the window, looking out at the car park as I put my pathetic offerings on the other bed.

The sound of a flushing toilet fills the silence, and the bathroom door flies open. Xander appears and stops in the doorway when he sees me.

"This is Xander," Annie says, and I realize he hasn't told her about our meeting. "He's come down to look after us."

"I'm trying," Xander mutters, but I notice he doesn't go over to his mother.

"I'm sure it's a big help for your family," I say as Annie disappears into the bathroom. "Can we have a quick word?" I whisper, and Xander nods and follows me out into the corridor.

"God, this is dire," I say, and he grimaces. "Look, I don't want to cause trouble between you and your mum. Have you told her we've talked? About your dad?"

"No. I'm not sure that would be helpful at the moment. Was it you who told the police about the affair?"

"I had to, Xander. You do see that."

"Yep." But he won't look me in the eye. "I'm still shocked about what my dad has done," Xander goes on. He thinks Henry is guilty. I wonder if Annie knows that. If she thinks it, too.

"He's made such a mess," Xander adds to himself.

"Right," I say. So many secrets in that house. Like a network of badly dug tunnels too close to the surface. Making the crust shiver with tension. People living with the ever-present risk of the whole thing collapsing in on itself. And burying them.

"I've asked Mum to come and stay with me in London." He shrugs. "But she wants to stay locally so Gav can carry on going to school. And she says she wants to go and see my father—God knows why. After the way he's treated her. And now this . . ."

"Do you think your dad killed Karen?" I ask him point-blank.

Xander appears to close down in front of me. Eyes expressionless. But he doesn't say no.

"Oh, I think Mum's calling me," he suddenly says. She isn't, but I let him go back in. Annie is standing, looking at her phone, and Gavin is lying with his back to the room, curled round his tablet and eating the rest of the biscuits.

"Can I use your loo before I go?" I say, and then go and sit quietly on the edge of the bathtub for five minutes to catch my breath before I tackle Annie. I hear raised voices in the next room, and when I open the bathroom door I discover that Elise King and Caro Brennan have turned up to talk to Annie. I take a panicky step back out of sight.

"What's happened?" Annie squeaks, fear rising and spilling into the room.

"Come and sit down, Annie. I have news," Elise says. "We have forensic evidence that Henry had recent physical contact with Karen—and a witness who saw Henry get home at two thirty a.m. on the night Karen died."

Annie staggers to her feet. "What are you saying?" she cries, her voice all high and wild.

"Henry has been formally charged with the murder of Karen Simmons this morning," Elise says quietly, and Gavin howls and throws his arms around his mother. "That's why I'm here. I wanted to tell you and your sons before we announce it later today."

"Thank you for coming," Xander says, moving to stand between the detective and his family. "But I think we need to be on our own now."

Elise and Caro Brennan file out, and there is a suffocating silence in the room.

"I should have left him a long time ago," Annie suddenly says. "I knew things weren't right, but I pretended to myself that they were. It was easier to stay. I am so sorry. I should have taken you boys and started again. But then Archie died. And I couldn't."

"Stop it, Mum. It's not your fault. It's him," Xander says. "I'll get you a glass of water." And he walks straight into me.

SEVENTY-NINE

ANNIE

Saturday, February 29, 2020

XANDER REFUSED TO come with her after the police left. Gav begged to be allowed, but he was too young and tender for the horror of police cells. She knew it would destroy him to see his father like that. So she stood with him, their foreheads touching, as she reassured him before he pulled away, weeping.

"We need to go to him. He needs us there," she said, making one last plea to Xander. But he wouldn't even look at her.

"Are you serious?" he told the window. Just like his father. "I'm not going. I don't even want to hear his name after what he's done. After what he's put me through. Us through. How could he have been so stupid? So self-obsessed. Hooking up with bloody Karen again, and killing her to stop her telling anyone. Christ!"

"Stop it! We don't know that. And . . . and . . . it could have been an accident." She grasped desperately at straws. "We don't know what happened!" she shouted. "And he's your father."

"I'll take you," Kiki said, suddenly appearing out of the bathroom, and Annie jerked round.

"What the hell are you still doing here?" Annie yelled.

"I'm sorry. I was about to leave when the police arrived," Kiki murmured. "Why don't you get your coat and I'll drive you to the police station? You don't have to talk to me if you don't want to."

Annie slumped down on the nearest bed. Did it even matter that this reporter was witnessing her family's free fall? Everyone was about to find out anyway. "Okay, thank you," she muttered as she stood and let, the reporter drape her coat around her.

"Xander," Annie whispered. But he didn't even turn around as Annie and Kiki left.

"You look so tired," Kiki said as she started her car. "Did you get any sleep last night?"

"No—it was a nightmare," Annie muttered. "I could hear Gavin groaning and thrashing his legs." She didn't say she dreaded what he was dreaming about. What Henry in his police cell was dreaming about.

"Poor Gavin," Kiki said. "So hard for a kid his age. My daughter is only a couple of years younger."

Annie looked at Kiki. She was a mother, too. "He cried when his dad left for the police station yesterday," Annie confided. Her youngest had gone quiet while she'd packed a bag, dry-eyed. "We need to let the police get on with their work," she'd said. "Remember to bring your charger."

Annie hadn't said, "Everything's going to be all right." She knew Gav had been waiting for it. But it wasn't, was it? Nothing was going to be all right.

She'd made the mistake of thinking that the worst thing that could ever happen to her had happened. But no. There'd been more. She was no longer simply the mother of a murdered child. She was the wife of a potential murderer. Sitting in a traveling salesman's hotel on an industrial estate off the motorway—a waiting room for what was to come.

"I just hope I don't have to uproot Gavin from school and his mates and find another town to disappear into," she blurted, and Kiki looked over in sympathy. "I'll have to get a job that will pay a middle-aged woman enough to support a family. Sell another tainted house." Annie felt like she was disappearing under the weight of it all, but she couldn't cry anymore. There was nothing left.

AT THE POLICE station, the heating was making the handful of people in the waiting room melt into their plastic chairs. Annie picked a row in the corner away from everyone else after making her request at the desk. She sat, not speaking, as Kiki stared at her phone. Annie was deep in her catastrophe when she was called back to the desk.

"They won't let me see him," she said when she returned to her seat. "He's still being processed. They told me to talk to his solicitor."

"Okay, but we need to move now," Kiki said urgently as she gathered their things. "The reporters are beginning to arrive for the press conference. I've just seen the TV news van drive round the back."

Annie grabbed her bag and pulled Kiki's hat down over her hair as instructed. "Just walk normally," her new best friend murmured. "Not too fast or you'll draw attention to yourself."

But nothing felt normal—Annie felt as though she was on fire, every nerve in her body screaming at her to run, but Kiki kept a firm grip on her arm as the two women strolled through a side entrance and away from the media circus. After ten minutes and constant checking behind them, Kiki parked Annie on a bench on a scrubby piece of grass, telling her not to make eye contact with anyone while she went and fetched her car.

Annie sat, her shoulders aching from the tension. She should just walk away. Ring Xander to come and collect her. But she couldn't face his doubts. Or being imprisoned in that awful hotel room.

Kiki drew up and she got in.

"DO YOU BELIEVE Henry?" Kiki said after they'd parked up and the silence had gone on too long.

Annie wanted to say, *Of course I do*, but it stuck in her craw.

"I don't know what to think," she croaked. "But I'm scared that

Xander has made up his mind. He was talking about what his father has done back at the hotel. As if it's an open-and-shut case."

Perhaps it is and I'm just fooling myself. Annie tortured herself with the thought and looked across at the reporter.

Kiki spread her hands as if she had no idea, but her eyes said different.

"He has gone through so much already," Annie said, racing to protect her child. "Archie died, but Xander was a victim, too."

"He told me," Kiki murmured.

"When? When did he tell you that?" Annie squeaked.

"When I went to see him last Tuesday," Kiki said quietly, not meeting her eye. "He agreed to meet me to talk about the police reexamining Archie's murder. And, well, he talked about his childhood. And how Henry made him keep his affair with Karen secret. Maybe that's why he is lashing out at his dad. He's still angry, Annie."

"It's possible. But he didn't tell me about talking to you," Annie said. "Why didn't he?"

"I don't know," Kiki replied, shifting to face Annie. "But he is very protective of you. He's a good son."

Annie sat in silence after asking the reporter to drive her back to Yew Tree Lane, then ducked under the tattered police tape and sat alone under the trees. All new questions dancing in her head.

EIGHTY

ELISE

Saturday, February 29, 2020

"We've got some results, boss, on the Archie Curtis case. Not great news," her sergeant said, head round the door that afternoon. "But I did warn you." Elise clasped her hands to her chest defensively and waited.

"They've looked at the profiles from Archie's clothing, but there's no evidence of Ash Woodward having contact," Caro went on.

"Right. So," Elise muttered, scrolling through the files on her computer to buy a bit of time to pull herself together, "what have we got?"

"Er, fuck all, if you ask me," Caro groaned.

"We have got Donovan's hair on Archie's T-shirt," Elise plowed on, refusing to give in to complete despair. "But if Ash Woodward was telling the truth, Donovan couldn't have had contact, could he? He was driving away at the time of death."

"The only other DNA identified was Xander's, of course—the brothers had been playing together all day," Caro said, pulling up a chair.

"And it was Xander who found Archie," Elise said, piecing it all back together.

"Xander had Donovan's hairs on his clothing, didn't he?" She flipped back to a previous page. "From their encounter. One could have been transferred onto his brother's clothes when Xander found him."

Caro nodded.

"Nicky Donovan wasn't there with Archie, was he?" Elise said. "He was at his mum's having a ham salad."

"But who was?" Caro said. "We've got nothing to put Ash Woodward there. All we've got is Archie and Xander."

SUNDAY: DAY 16

EIGHTY-ONE

KIKI

Sunday, March 1, 2020

Annie Curtis won't answer her phone this morning, and I force myself out of bed to drive over to her hotel. I know that if I don't, other reporters will find her and I risk losing my advantage.

I go straight up and tap softly. I can hear movement and I'm calling, "Annie . . ." when Xander opens the door. He looks as if he's just come out of a deep sleep, his eyes unfocused as he rubs his face.

"Mum's not here," he says.

"Oh, that's a shame. Will she be back soon?"

His eyes narrow. "No. She's taken Gav home. To the house. I'm staying here. I keep telling her we need to leave the area, but she won't listen."

I need to get straight over there but something about him makes me hesitate. I nod sympathetically. "How are you doing?" I say softly. "You look a bit out of it. How are you coping?"

"I'm okay," he croaks. A door opens across the hallway, and an inquisitive face appears.

Xander stands back out of sight and then waves me in so he can shut the door.

"Do you want a coffee?" he mutters.

"Er, I can't really stay," I say, but he's already tearing open packets of instant.

"Is Emily coming down to be with you?" I say, taking the only chair.

"No." Xander squares his shoulders and pretends to be busy with the drinks.

"I'm sorry," I say. "It must be hard for her to take it in. Hard for everyone."

"What did you want Mum for, anyway? The lawyer has said she mustn't talk to anyone," he says, moving me on and perching on the corner of a bed.

"To tell her some news about a man called Ash Woodward."

"Not that sad little fantasist who killed himself?" Xander mutters.

"Er, I don't think they're saying it was suicide," I correct him.

"Oh, right," he says.

"He told your mum he was in Knapton Wood the day Archie died," I go on.

Xander's mouth hardens and he does a half-hearted shrug. "Yes, she said. But I told her he was probably just a nutter who wanted to get himself noticed," he says.

"You don't remember him? From back then? Did you ever see him in the wood?"

Xander's head jerks up, and he slops some of his coffee on the duvet. "No," he snaps.

"So it was just you and Nicky Donovan?"

He nods. I can smell his distress, the sharp scent of sweat.

"I'm sorry to bring all this back up, Xander, but your mother wants it to be revisited—by me and the police. She has questions. Did you know that Nicky Donovan's mother told your mum he'd chatted to you the week before in the wood? That you'd got on well. Had a connection. That was why he went back."

"I'd never seen him before," Xander gasps. "He was lying to save his skin. That's what the police said."

"What did he say to you that day?"

"I can't remember. I try not to think about it. For fuck's sake, I was a child. I've spent years trying to put it behind me."

"I'm sorry, but the thing that really puzzles me—and your mum—is how Nicky Donovan knew Archie was in the wood, too."

"Mum? When did she say that?" Xander stammers. "I—I don't know. He must have heard him."

"Could you hear Archie?"

"I can't remember."

"Can you remember which direction Nicky Donovan ran when you pushed him away?"

"I don't know," he mutters, fists clenched at his jawline. He doesn't sound sure anymore. His composure is starting to fray at the edges as we stray deeper into the wood. "I didn't see. I was too frightened to look back."

"It must have been terrifying," I soothe. "And where was Archie?"

When Xander finally speaks, he enunciates each word as if it's in a foreign language. Like he's making the words last to delay the next question.

"I left Archie under the big tree. I told him to clear a space for another bit of the camp," he continues. "And I went to get sticks and stuff to make the walls. He wanted to come, too, but I made him stay."

"Tell me again about Nicky Donovan," I press.

"He tricked me," Xander says quietly. "He had this lovely smile and gave me one of his sweets."

"But why did you trust him?" I ask. "Weren't you afraid of talking to strangers?"

Surely his parents had warned him? Mine did. Hinting and nudging at the unspoken horrors lurking behind such an encounter. I should have listened, shouldn't I?

"He called me 'son,'" Xander whispers under his breath. And I'm not sure I've heard him right.

" 'Son'?"

Xander looks up at me, eyes unfocused, still in that moment. "He said, 'Hello, son,' when he saw me. And he smiled his lovely smile. And I just wanted him to be my dad for a moment. I let myself believe it. It wasn't real, but when he said he could come back to the same place, same time, I couldn't stop thinking about him."

"So you did meet him before?"

Xander nods reluctantly.

"And you went back?" I edge him on.

"But it wasn't like the first time," Xander says softly, as if to himself. "He still smiled. But he got hold of me and touched me and I knew it wasn't right, what he was doing. And he wanted me to keep it a secret. He was just like my real dad, wanting me to keep secrets."

A tear trickles out of one eye.

"What happened then, Xander? Did you push Nicky away?"

"Yes. I ran off and I banged my head on a branch and it hurt so much. I was bleeding and crying when I got back to Archie."

I realize I'm holding my breath. *Wait, just wait.*

"And he tried to comfort me . . ."

"Archie was alive when you got back to him," I leap in. Of course he was. There'd never been anyone else there.

Xander puts his hands over his face and wipes his eyes slowly before speaking.

"It was an accident. Archie made me tell him what had happened. About Nicky. And then he jumped up and was shouting that he was going to tell Mum. And I couldn't let him. It would make Mum cry and I couldn't bear it. I got hold of the back of his shirt and we were fighting and I lay on him like we sometimes did in play fights. To stop the noise. But then Archie stopped squirming."

There it is. Finally. Annie's answer.

I pass him a tissue, our fingers accidentally touching for a split second, making him jerk back.

"What happened then?" I say quietly.

He looks at me, shadows beginning to bloom under his exhausted eyes.

"It was like a terrible dream," Xander goes on. "When I turned him over, he wouldn't talk to me. And I knew it was bad and I was going to be in trouble. I tried to sit him up—so he looked like nothing had happened—but he kept toppling over. And his face was all dirty, so I wiped it with his T-shirt. Then I walked out of the wood."

EIGHTY-TWO

KIKI

Sunday, March 1, 2020

ELISE SOUNDS LOOSER than I've ever heard her when I ring. They've got their man for Karen's murder. And the buzz behind her is at jubilation pitch.

"Many congratulations," I say, joining in before I spoil her day. "You've done a great job. But, look, I need to tell you about something else."

"Go on, then." I can hear someone laughing close to her. "What is it now?"

"Elise," I say, my voice beginning to shake. "I've just had the most extraordinary conversation with Xander Curtis. He told me he accidentally killed his little brother."

"Stay where you are," Elise says, voice tight. The confetti guns are clearly going to have to wait a bit.

I meet her in the foyer of the hotel, and she takes my arm and marches me over to a pair of stiff purple armchairs that were never meant for human buttocks. I repeat the bones of the interview, and she sits in silence. She doesn't look as though she can trust herself to speak for a moment. But she finally blurts: "It makes sense, doesn't it? It's what Caro said. All we've ever had at the scene was Archie and Xander."

I just nod.

"Where is he now?" she asks, and I give her the room number. Elise rings Caro. "We're arresting Xander Curtis for Archie's killing," she tells her quietly.

"What do you think Annie will say?" I ask Elise as we wait, and she groans. The next horror show.

"I honestly don't know," Elise mutters, the strain showing on her face.

"She told me she wanted answers when she started this," I say. "But not this one. Never this one." Elise shakes her head in sorrow. "He said he had to stop Archie telling her—so she wouldn't cry again," I add. "How will she live with that?"

"I don't know," Elise croaks, and looks at me. "And I'll have to go and see Nicky Donovan's mum as well. God, what a shit show."

EIGHTY-THREE

ELISE

Sunday, March 1, 2020

"I'LL RING THE Crown Prosecution Service when I've had this and see
what they want to do," Elise said, dunking a sustaining chocolate finger
in her sergeant's tea when she finally got back to her office.

Xander Curtis had just repeated to them exactly the same story he'd
told Kiki Nunn. A tale of two children caught up in a tragic accident.
And a lie that took root and grew.

"They won't want to prosecute him for this, surely," Caro said, moving her tea to safety. "He was only just ten. His birthday was in July—
he was just a couple of weeks inside the age of criminal responsibility.
God, I could weep for him."

"And the defense psychologists would have a field day," Elise murmured. "A distraught child who'd been assaulted by a stranger and
didn't want his mum to know."

Still didn't. "Are you going to tell Mum?" he'd whispered to Elise as
he was driven to the police station.

She'd have to know now.

ANNIE CURTIS OPENED the door of her house before Elise had time to
knock. She must have seen her in the car, watched as Elise sat staring

out the windscreen as the minutes ticked by, wondering and dreading what was about to arrive at her doorstep.

"I've got your answer, Annie. I know why Archie was killed," Elise said, standing in the hall.

Annie flushed, hands to hot face. "Oh, God!"

"And who really killed him."

"Who?" she whispered, and her knees buckled beneath her. Elise grabbed her arm to support her. She steered Annie into the living room and sat her down on the sofa. She looked so small, shrunken by shock and disappearing into the cushions.

"Annie," Elise said slowly and simply. "I am so sorry, but Xander has told us this morning that he killed Archie."

"No!" Annie screamed, her hands flying up as if they could stop the information reaching her, then falling back to her sides. "It's not true. Why are you saying that?"

"Xander says it was an accident," Elise carried on, trying to keep her voice calm.

"An accident?" Annie Curtis wept, clinging to the only safe word. "What happened to my boys?"

"Xander went back to Archie after Nicky Donovan assaulted him. Archie wanted to tell you about it, but Xander didn't want you to know. He tried to stop Archie and there was a tussle. And Archie stopped breathing."

"Oh, God, no," Annie wailed as the image of that terrible moment played in her head.

"This is my fault, isn't it?" she sobbed, and looked up at Elise. "I never should have asked you to investigate, should I? Henry said no good was ever going to come of reawakening our ghosts."

"You simply wanted to know the truth," Elise said.

Annie looked away, eyes dead now.

"Not this truth," she whispered. "My poor boys."

MONDAY:
DAY 17

EIGHTY-FOUR

KIKI

Monday, March 2, 2020

Mrs. Donovan takes a bit of persuasion to open the door. Elise King has already been here first thing this morning, but she's given me a couple of hours' head start on the rest of the media. "You're welcome," she said down the phone.

She's releasing a statement at midday, announcing a review of the original investigation by the Independent Office for Police Conduct.

"Who are you?" Sylvie Donovan asks nervously. "What do you want?"

"It's about Nicky," I say. "I want to write about what really happened in Knapton Wood."

Nicky's mother sits wordlessly at first, then weeps for her dead boy and the years of loss she's endured. And I take it all down.

"Annie Curtis rang me earlier," Mrs. Donovan says when her cat settles on her lap. "Have you spoken to her? Poor woman. She didn't know it, but she lost both her boys that day. It must have scarred Xander's life. Knowing he'd done something so terrible. Even if it was an accident."

"That is very generous of you, Sylvie," I say.

"He was just a child," she says. "And my son has his own sins to answer for."

The fury I'd been expecting comes only when Nicky's older sister arrives, eyes flashing, firing her accusations of police brutality into the air.

"Why wouldn't they listen to him? They killed him," she shrieks while her mother looks on in silence.

Afterward, I sit in my car outside for five minutes, letting my head calm. I know the attack on me has left me vulnerable—my skin thinner and emotions too close to the surface—but this case has shaken me more than any other I've covered. I can deal with uncontrollable, spitting anger—I've had to, a few times over the years—but this has hit me hard. I squeeze my eyes tight shut for a moment, then force them open and start the car, I've got to get going—Henry Curtis is due to make his first court appearance in an hour. But my hand trembles as I do up my seat belt.

EIGHTY-FIVE

KIKI

Monday, March 2, 2020

XANDER IS STANDING outside the court building with his mother and little brother when I turn the corner. Elise has released him on bail while the CPS make a decision. I walk slower so I can look at him—at the smooth face, the old eyes. Annie is beside him. She calls him her boy, but he's a twenty-five-year-old man. Old enough to have his own boys.

"How are you doing?" I ask him on the court steps.

"He's okay," Annie says, voice brittle, not letting him answer. "Go in, Xander, and take Gav. It's freezing out here."

When the boys are out of earshot, she leans in to me and hisses: "We've had dog mess smeared on our front door, you know. We'll have to look for somewhere out of the area to rent."

"I'm sorry," I say.

"This is all *his* fault." Annie can't even bring herself to say her husband's name. "If he hadn't chased after that woman, Xander wouldn't have had his life ruined. His father screwed up his head with his vile secrets. He wouldn't have gone looking for comfort from strangers. Archie . . . well, he would still be alive. And my boy would be getting ready for his wedding—you know his fiancée has dumped him? His father and that woman brought this down on us."

She has squared her circle—Henry and Karen are the villains. Xander, the victim. I look at her bitter, thin face lit up by hate. It never fails to astonish me how people can reshape realities to suit.

Annie disappears inside as Cliff and Mary Simmons arrive, arm in arm, holding each other up.

"Go on in," I say to them. "You don't want to wait in the cold."

"Our family liaison officer, Jenny, is just parking the car. We don't want to go in without her," Mrs. Simmons says. "And I don't want to be anywhere near that family."

"This is going to be very hard for you," I say. "Coming face-to-face with your daughter's killer."

Mrs. Simmons nods, misery etched on her face. "But we need to. We need him to know that he is seen. That we are here. For Karen."

Inside, I strip off my coat and take my seat in the press bench, to the side of the prosecuting team. There's a moment of calm before proceedings kick off when barristers and instructing solicitors whisper strategy and the public gallery fills. Just in front of me, Annie Curtis is bracketed by Xander and Gavin, dwarfed by her protectors. Gavin is sitting too close to his mother, gnawing at his fingernails. And not looking at his big brother. His eyes go straight to his dad as Henry is brought up from the cells.

Henry John Curtis stands in the dock, looking wretched and old in a gray prison tracksuit. Annie Curtis doesn't even look at him. She and Xander sit with hands entwined.

There's a sudden shuffling of feet as everyone stands for the magistrates. I sit sideways to watch Xander Curtis as the charge is read to his father and his barrister makes applications. Xander isn't even in the room. His eyes wandering. His mind elsewhere. I wonder where he is. What life will be like now.

He must feel my stare because he glances over at me, then lets his gaze drift to his loved ones and accepts his mother's kiss on the cheek with a ghost of a smile.

EPILOGUE

XANDER

Mum's put the house on the market at last, and the van's coming this afternoon to take our stuff to a rented place near Grandma's. I should be helping, but I had to come back here. For the last time.

The smell of the wood—that rich stench of rotting vegetation—fills my senses as I walk farther in and I take deep lungfuls of it.

I felt like shit when I woke up this morning. I'm not sleeping right. The doctor has given me something to help, but I still dream about Archie. His scabby knees and how he used to push his hair out of his eyes when he concentrated. And his face that day. It's the first time in years I've had night terrors. I used to wake from them screaming, but they gradually faded away, slipping between my clammy fingers, losing their detail, then their outline.

But they are back.

And I can taste the panic and anger again, coating my tongue, as I push through broken branches and saplings. And then feel the calm. When it all stopped. And I sat him up and wiped his face clean. Like I did Karen's.

My heart is pounding now, as it had when I walked out of the darkened station, the only passenger to get off at Ebbing. And the headlights flashed. My date had come as arranged, and my pulse was racing in anticipation—this moment often more exciting than the actual sex in my experience.

It'd been a last-minute decision—I'd been noodling on the dating app on the train down from London while Emily was in the toilet. And spotted LaDiva. Some of the boys on the forum had mentioned her— local and worth a go, according to X-Man. I'd swiped and she'd swiped me back.

But I didn't text her until later. When I was sitting on the train to Brighton, stewing in the aftermath of that difficult evening with my family. A Brighton hookup would have been handier, really, but the evening had been all about the past. And the past was Ebbing.

Anyway, LaDiva looked fun. And I needed some fun. And she'd agreed to pick me up off the train and look for somewhere still open for a drink.

But then she wound down her window and shouted, "Oh, my God, it's you!" like she knew me.

And I thought I must have the wrong car. But there weren't any others.

"It's me," she was babbling as she untangled her seat belt. "Oh, God, I can't believe this."

"Er, hi," I said, and caught my first proper look as she stepped into the headlights. She was wearing some cheap sparkly dress, had clearly had a drink already, and was a lot older than she'd said. I should have walked away. But there was something about her face.

And I was trying to remember, when she said: "Oh, Henry!" And I felt the old stomachache start low in my gut and spread to my chest so I couldn't breathe for a minute.

"No," I said. "I told you. It's Bear."

Karen's face crumpled and then her legs. "I'm sorry," she croaked, clinging to me. "It's just I thought it was him."

She let me drive when I insisted and said something about late opening for Valentine's Day at a local bar. I wasn't really listening. I'd already decided where we were going. She prattled on about the terrible evening she'd had, and I sped up as she got louder, and I veered dangerously close to the curb a couple of times before I got a grip on myself. I was going to be pulled over by the police if I didn't slow down. I'd have to give my name, and everyone would know. Emily. Mum. Karen Simmons was going to ruin my life all over again.

By the time I turned into the car park at Knapton Wood and switched off the engine, she was half-asleep. I walked round and shook her, and she got out and slipped her arm through mine as I guided her into the darkness beyond the tree line.

"Where are we going?" she said.

"Just for a little walk to get you some air," I muttered. She went quiet but she clung on to me.

"I think we should go back now," she said suddenly and let go of my arm. "I'll ruin my shoes." She tried to laugh, but I could hear the scratch of anxiety in her voice.

"You do know me," I said quietly, hearing my words being sucked into the blackness as I pulled on the gloves I'd found in the coat pockets. "You used to cut my hair. When my dad brought me to your salon."

Karen pivoted and lost her balance, sitting down heavily on the ground.

"Oh, my God! You're one of his boys," she rasped, and turned her phone on so she could see me properly.

I crouched down beside her, my face lit up by the screen. I wanted her to see me. To know. "Yes," I said.

"No, no, this is a horrible mistake," she whispered, trying to get up. "I didn't know it was you. Of course I didn't. Xander, you must believe me." She was crying and falling over her words. "Oh, God! I was going to be your other mummy," she wept. "Me and your dad were going to have you for weekends when we got a house. With a garden. We were going to have so much fun. You, me, and Archie. Lollies every day."

She had got to her knees. I could smell sugar on her breath, like the sweets she gave me for being a good little boy. And I just stared at her, the years of hate bubbling up and bursting in my head.

"I want to go home now," she said, gulping her words. "I won't tell anyone."

"No," I growled, not recognizing the sound that came from my mouth. Frightening myself in the dark. I pushed her to the ground, keeping my hand on the back of her head, as I had with Archie, making her shut up as the memories flooded my brain. The sticky perfume of hair spray and the intense looks between Dad and this woman in the mirror. Their disappearance behind the bead curtain to the back room, the rattle and movement of the colored spheres of glass as they did whatever they did. And me and Archie sitting there in the chairs, licking our lollies. Red and yellow like the beads. I knew something bad was happening. Very bad. Knew I mustn't say anything to Mum. Mustn't make her cry any more. My father did this to me. It is his fault that I killed Archie.

Karen had stopped moving, face down in the leaf litter. I used the torch on my mobile, flicking it on and off so I didn't have to look for too long, and then put it on the ground to cast a faint light as I grasped her shoulders and sat her up. I'd wiped the dirt from her cheeks with my gloved hands. And tiptoed away.

I felt Karen watching me with her dead eyes, and I walked faster and then ran out of the wood, her gaze burning into my back. I took her car and drove the back roads to Brighton, parked in the multistory, and went searching for my mates, screaming the wrong words to rock anthems with them in our Elvis wigs until the nightclubs closed.

I'd expected the police to come knocking the next morning. But as I sat in my hotel room in Brighton, I realized I had a way out. The coat. It'd been a snap decision to steal dad's coat from the car boot at the station. I'd slipped it out with my bag to punish him. He was so fucking proud of it, and I was going to dump it in a bin. But it'd been so cold when I got off the train that I'd put it on and worn his gloves. Someone must have been looking out for me that night.

Because LaDiva had clung on to it, slobbered over it. The police only had to find it to connect him to the killing. I took it home a few days later. Simply hung it up on the hooks by the door and pulled one of Mum's coats over it. Hidden in plain sight.

And then I told the reporter about my dad's affair with Karen. Her face when I told her. She ate it up and spewed it out to the police. Of course, they came sniffing around him. It'd been so easy.

I lie back on the leaf litter and stare at the canopy. Almost perfect.

Of course, the truth about Archie was something I never thought would come out. Sixteen years had embedded the lie in our lives. No one was ever going to question it. But that pathetic Ash Woodward was going to tell. Unearth it again all these years later. I had to do something, didn't I? And it, too, was so easy in the end. I read about it on the internet and shoved a few rags into his air vents while he was out. Gone.

He was my third, then. Or fourth, if I include Nicky Donovan. Okay, I know it was suicide, but it was me who named him. He deserved it. Filthy pervert—the world's better off without him. Anyway, it's going to be okay. Emily will come back. She'll forgive me, just like Mum has. Both of them cried when they found out, but they know it was a terrible accident. Not my fault. A series of unfortunate events. God, I loved those books as a kid. They know I'm not a monster.

I roll over to look at the tree where I propped Karen up, and remember her face. And Dad's face in the dock. Haggard and done.

And it is.